Tangible
press

Stirring Tales of the
Henchmen
The Definitive Crime Trilogy

By
N.K. Hart

Stirring Tales of the Henchmen:
The Definitive Crime Trilogy

Copyright © 2021 N. K. Hart
Published by Tangible Press
www.tangiblepress.net

Up the Crime Ladder originally published 2014 by Tangible Press.
The Future of Crime originally published 2017 by Tangible Press.
Misadventures in Crime originally published 2020 by Tangible Press.

ISBN: 1-7375810-1-9
ISBN-13: 978-1-7375810-1-7

Library of Congress Control Number: 2014933960

Cover design by N. K. Hart

Printed in the United States of America

THE
THRASHER™

Preface

This series of books came to life when after watching a James Bond film, which by the way was a very compelling and wonderful movie, I found myself a bit stymied by the main villain's henchmen. They, without question, swarmed out after the famous and dashing MI6 Agent James Bond, guns blazing (or in at least one instance, spearguns loaded and ready to fire), in deadly hand-to-hand combat to confront him. Without saying, many of them where trounced into death by our British number one Good Guy…James Bond. All the main villain had to do was order up James Bond's demise and the henchmen, right down to the man, jumped into deadly action.

I was amazed. What could compel these men to run full force into the face of death? It couldn't be that every one of them are psychotic murderers troubled by schizophrenia and bent on killing. That many in one organization? Was it the wage? What did the job-wanted ad look like? "Flexible hours and a penchant for murder. Must obey without question."

And the job interview. Where would it be held? In a man-made mountain in the middle of a forgotten sea? And what would the HR Manager ask? "What kind of weapon do you prefer, an Uzi or a Bowie knife?" What would the perspective employee ask of HR? "Do you have a 401k plan? Dental?"

Again, what compels a man to become a henchman? What could he be offered by way of employment compensation that would make joining and staying with a crime organization so tempting that he would just accept the one clearly understood hazard of the job, an untimely death, in order to be employed by a very accomplished Bad Guy?

My conclusion was that the answers to these questions needed to be found and needed to be made public if not for my own curiosity then for posterity.

So, I give you The Henchmen Series, for the first time collected into a single edition. I fervently trust that you will enjoy the reading of these books as much as I enjoyed the writing of them. – NK

BOOK ONE

UP THE CRIME LADDER

N. K. HART

Indeed, history is nothing more than a tableau of crimes and misfortunes.
--Voltaire

Chapter One

A New Week Begins

It had been at least two weeks since Argyle had been on a really good caper. Two weeks, and nothing more than run-of-the-mill capers, but maybe this week would be different. Argyle Stevens (yes, like the sock) arrived at the office -- early, as usual. It's a seedy old four-story warehouse squatting in a derelict part of the city located, appropriately enough, next to a slow-moving section of the stinkiest river in North America. Sometimes the jetsam that had been pitched into this stinky river by upstream activities can be seen floating serenely past, buoyed by a thick layer of sludge.

The building is made of red brick and mismatched windows that wear a coat of grime and soot that probably dates back to the 1800's when this part of the city was vibrant with industrial businesses and big deals and the river didn't stink.

The lower part of the squatty red brick building is covered in urban graffiti, none of it resembling anything intelligent. The spray paint that had been used to draw crude pictures and to spread lies about rivals is faded now. And most of the old posters that had been glued up in their typically random patterns have all peeled and chipped away only to reveal more of the same underneath.

Most of the other warehouses in this section of the city are abandoned, their windows broken, their doors caved in. Yet, as inviting as all of this would seem to the inevitable druggies and gangs who would in a moments notice take advantage of the free rent, there are no squatters. Over the past several years there have been incidences of violence throughout the warehouse district that have left a few dead bodies strewn about, but the police aren't in much of a hurry to respond to calls from this area. They have found that, for the most part, this area of empty warehouses stays relatively crime free as it seems that the criminals are taking care of the crime. The police are not readily inclined to interfere with the balance of nature.

However, there is one building that defies the description of its neighbors… the seedy old four-story red brick warehouse.

On any given day, such as this one, the alleyway is busy with cars and vans driving up to one of the four steel roll-up garage doors, where they wait for clearance before driving through to the parking lot that takes up the entire first floor. If needed, there is additional overflow parking up on the second. The spaces closest to the elevators are numbered and saved for the more elite employees with the number one space reserved for The Thrasher's armored jet-black cruiser, the one with all the cool weapons on-board. Don't park in that one! Ever!!

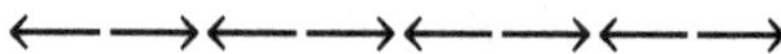

Today is Monday. The noise in the parking garage is almost deafening and the air is laden with exhaust. Some months ago, the employees formed an antique car club and if what was meant by an antique car is any car that's paint is faded and is full of dents, the upholstery ripped and patched with duct tape, then what they had was an antique auto. Mostly the club was an excuse not to repair any damage or fix anything mechanical, like a busted muffler, because it was common knowledge that if anything has been fixed, the antique value of the auto would be ruined. Who knows? Someday a real collector may want an original antique auto.

Argyle found a parking spot in the eighth row and eased his 1958 VW Beetle into it between a faded blue Nissan and a recently washed white KIA. He put the bug's gear in park and gently pulled the hand brake lever up. It was then that he let out a breath and sat back in the driver seat and took a moment to relax the muscles along his neck and shoulders.

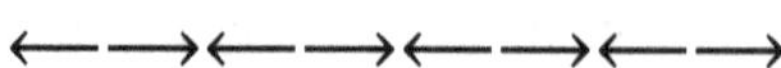

Argyle is a good-looking, thirty-five-year-old single guy who stands 6'1'' tall. He's managed to keep his physique trim and well-buffed, a habit he learned during his stint in the military. During his relatively young life, he had several brushes with the law, but none were worse than a week or two in county, to Argyle's great surprise, none too severe as to stop his credit card applications from being approved.

While serving time… ahem, for his country… Argyle found that he really enjoyed those times when the bullets were flying and the noise levels went up. Something would happen to him. It was as though he were in a trance. He would get caught up in the moment and find that he was laughing maniacally and firing wildly. Most of the men in his squad would try to avoid him thinking that he would be the one to get them all killed, but Argyle didn't seem to mind that at all. It was as if he hadn't noticed their fear and general mistrust of him. He would just shoot his gun. Ahh. Good times.

After he was asked to leave the military, Argyle spent many hours wondering what kind of a profession existed that would allow him to shoot big guns and like it… a lot. One slow summer morning, as he sipped a frothy, hot double espresso nano creamed mocha sunrise brew at his favorite coffee bar, La Nerdza, down on 87th and Peel, he absent-mindedly picked up a local paper to glance through the headlines.

There it was. On page three. Argyle's dream job. The headline read "The Thrasher Takes All In Bloody Heist." Argyle skimmed the article twice, each time catching a new piece of information before he stopped himself, plopped the paper down on the table and thought, *If I read slower, I may get it faster.* At which point he picked up the paper and started again, this time reading each line slower… The Thrasher had struck again. This time it was the heist of the Gobal Ruby, a fourteen-pound chunk of aluminum oxide worth… a bunch. Two guards had been shot as he was leaving the scene. Witnesses reported hearing The Thrasher loudly scream, "Merry Christmas to me! And to all a good night!"

Argyle set his double espresso nano creamed mocha sunrise brew down, stood up and declared to the entire coffee bar, that by that time was almost empty of patrons, "I know where I'll be working, do you?" and left.

The next week, Argyle was hired into The Thrasher's crime organization as a junior henchman. That was five years ago, and he's been climbing the crime ladder ever since.

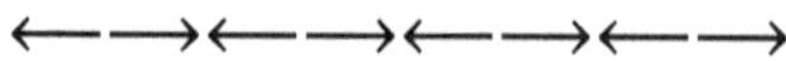

Taking a deep breath in and slowly letting it out steadied Argyle enough that he felt he could then start his day. Pulling his keys from the ignition and popping his door lock, Argyle pulled himself out of the drivers seat and up onto his feet. He carefully locked his Beetle and looked around the parking garage.

"Well, well. You look like something the hag dragged in!"

Argyle gave a small start at the overly-loud and seemingly sharp-toned words and turned to look over his shoulder. It was his best friend Ben.

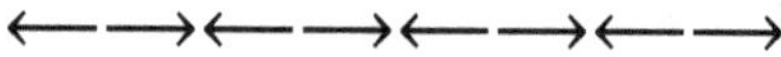

Ben Watson is almost twenty-seven years old, 5'7" tall, with dark hair and dark eyes. He fancied himself "cute", although that seemed to Argyle to be a bit of a subjective statement. Ben was an ex-military guy who, after his four years of service as a supply depot grunt, banged around the country for a year, drinking way too much beer. When he noticed he was drinking his money and losing his friends, Ben decided that it was time for a steady job.

Months before finding steady employment with The Thrasher, Ben would spend hours studying the local Want Ads and even applied to several job openings. He was hired by the downtown "Suds and Sack" as a bagger but was fired after one day because he could not get the hang of placing the chip bags *on top* of the six-packs. Customers were complaining of crushed chips before they had left the store!

Eventually, Ben was employed by a landscape maintenance company, The Trusty Rake, as a leaf blower guy. He worked on this for eight and one-half months and when he thought he had mastered leaf blowing, asked for a promotion to lawn mower guy. When the owner told him he wasn't ready to move up, Ben quit.

Finding himself unemployed yet again, and still flopping on a friend's couch, Ben took matters into his own hands and used his friend's computer to search job postings on FredsList. This turned out to be a challenge for Ben because he didn't really know how to use a computer. His friend suggested that he start with the tutorial "How to

Find a Job on FredsList – A Job Searching Experience Made Easy."

It wasn't easy at all. Ben was constantly hitting the wrong buttons, changing pages, and getting sidetracked on YouTube. He found the funniest kitten videos! Ben tried to upload his own videos but, again, he managed to press the wrong buttons and in the end only succeeded in crashing his friend's computer.

One month later, Ben stumbled onto this job posting…

> **Wanted:** Man with the ability to stick to the plan. The successful candidate must be loyal, friendly, brave, and above all, obedient. Some college is helpful but not necessary. Whiteboard skills… *a must!* Candidate should be able to handle a gun, but owner will consider other firepower experience as relevant.

Ben applied and was accepted into the Thrasher Organization as a Junior Henchman. With his first paycheck, he bought a dilapidated tugboat and spent three weekends getting it to run. Well, sputter. The boat sputtered. It wasn't much of a boat, it looked more like a tugboat but Ben liked to think of it as a Small Displacement Camp Cruiser. Sounded better than tugboat and at twenty-one feet long, Ben could sleep inside out of the weather.

In order to trim his expenses and save up the dough for an upscale chick-magnet apartment, Ben had been living on his boat… for almost five years. Ben named it The Party-Oh Boat. And on breezy nights, when the stinky river didn't stink too much, he would sit on a sun-cracked white plastic chair on the back deck and watch the jetsam slowly floating by and think… about girls.

To say that Ben eventually worked his way up to Henchman would be a bit of a stretch. Ben made it to Henchman job level by attrition. He simply waited until he was next in line to fill a vacancy. Argyle thought Ben to be a nice enough guy even though he was a bit of a slacker. Still, they ended up being friends. Eventually, they started talking about more than just sports; they talked about girls, too.

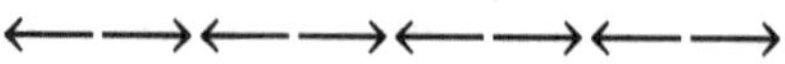

Argyle said, "Hey! And, it's *the cat.* The saying is, you look like something *the cat* dragged in."

Ben, smiling ear to ear, said, "So, you look like a bedraggled old dead-thing with dirty matted hair?" Ben caught up to Argyle and in a brotherly fashion, lightly punched him in the arm and danced away a foot or two, laughing.

Argyle slapped his thigh and did a fake laugh at Ben's lame joke and when Ben stepped close enough, grabbed him in a headlock and gave him a noogie.

Ben, struggling but not getting loose, had his face pressed into Argyle's side. He managed a few muffled apologies before Argyle released his grip.

After letting go of Ben's head, Argyle held his noogie hand up at eye level with his palm facing out and looked at it closely. "What the hell kind of hair gel are you using?" Then he brought his hand a bit closer to his nose in order to sniff at it. With his face twisted up into a painful sneer, Argyle sniffed out hard, making a loud sound as he forced all the air out of his lungs and whipped his hand straight out as far from his nose as he could get it and said, "Yikes! You smell like the stinky river!"

"I know," said Ben. "I think I may have crossed the water line with the bilge line when I changed tanks this weekend." Totally embarrassed, Ben scuffed at the parking garage floor with his shoe until Argyle spoke.

"Better shower before going in. And shampoo twice."

Elevator #2 had been filling up fast and just as the doors started to slide shut, Argyle made a quick leap, smashing himself in behind the door tracks. Smiling at Ben he said, "Sorry buddy. See you downstairs." The doors clicked shut and the elevator groaned and lurched as it started its descent, leaving Ben standing with a growing group of newly arriving henchmen queuing up for the next available elevator car. And as Ben pressed the call button, he slowly glanced around behind him and noticed that each of the persons grouped around him were holding their noses and leaning away.

Down on Subfloor One, the activity levels were high. The locker room was crowded and filling with steam from the dozens of showerheads that had been running almost non-stop for the past hour as the nightshift henchmen were getting ready to leave and the dayshift henchmen were arriving to start their day.

Argyle was just pulling on his steel-toed boots when Ben walked through the entry doors and said, "Man, no one would let me on the elevator. I had to wait 'till it was empty and ride by myself."

Argyle said, "I hope there's enough soap left, you're going to need it." He stood ready to jump away if Ben came any closer. Warily eying Ben and looking like a tensed-up cat, Argyle continued, "If you hurry, I'll wait. We have ten minutes 'til check-in. It's green jumpsuit and boots today. Hurry up!"

Ben glanced up at the over-sized garishly lighted marquee sign over the doors and read: Today! Misty Hedge-Foam Green Tailored Jumpsuit With Matching Tri-Toned Socks, Paired With Buff-Black 12-eyed Steel Toed Work Boots (boots on sale today for only $156.99). This week's caperware include: #13, #2, #6, #18, #4, and #37 (Small cleaning deposit required).

Turning back to Argyle, he said, "Oh great. Today's a work day." Ben opened his locker and kicked off his shoes, all the while grumbling under his breath.

Argyle said, "I'll wait outside," and stepped out into the foyer to idly watch as the nightshift henchmen piled into the elevators that would take them up to the parking garage and out into the sunlight.

Eight and one-half minutes later, Ben stepped out into the foyer wearing his green jumpsuit but Argyle noticed that Ben was pulling at the crotch and wriggling around in an agitated fashion as he walked. Raising an eyebrow, Argyle said, "What's up with you?"

Ben replied, "I think my suit shrunk in the laundry. It's giving me a wedgie."

Shaking his head in amusement, Argyle said, "Don't let Barry see you doing that. You know how he gets when he thinks someone's unhappy." And with that, Argyle made a slow slicing motion across his neck with his hand while making loud gagging noises. When he had finished the ghoulish pantomime, Argyle stood grinning, defying Ben to keep pulling at the back of his jumpsuit.

Ben's eyes opened real wide and he said, "That's right! I almost forgot." He took his hand away from his crotch and tried to walk straight but the result was sort of an awkward chicken strut that made Argyle snort with mirth.

The two buddies lined up with the others who had finished changing into the wardrobe-of-the-day and were waiting to deposit their seventy-five cents into the turnstiles that allowed them to continue on to the elevators.

Barry… ahem, The Thrasher, had the turnstiles installed to offset the rising costs of doing business and to recover the cost of a recently replaced hot water heater after some wise guy thought he could fix its water leak, but hosed up the gas line with the water line causing a small explosion.

It was pandemonium ten-fold when all of the showerheads blew off and flames shot out! The showers were down for a week as Thrasher thought to teach everyone the importance of good piping.

Argyle and Ben stepped off the elevator at Sublevel Two and made their way through the maze of desks and tangles of loose cables to their workspaces. The office area was a large open area dotted with small desks and wobbly chairs. Along the walls were mounted antique torture devices from medieval times with a few, here and there, that Barry invented. Some of these devices looked very painful while others just looked confusing. Mounted up in the corners and along the walls of the office space were several surveillance cameras that were constantly sweeping back and forth. Occasionally one would stop to zoom in on an unsuspecting victim, pausing momentarily to 'stare' before moving on. Next to the cameras and situated along the walls at measured intervals, were large speakers that had been hooked up to a Public Address system that Barry used quite often to broadcast his ideas and friendly advice to his overly large staff of henchmen.

As if on cue, Barry's voice now boomed out of the P.A. system. Henchmen stopped in their tracks to listen…

Attention. Attention! All henchmen! (tap, tap, tap…is this thing on?) *This is your wellness tip for today:*

Hypervelocity should be avoided unless you have eaten a hearty wheat-based breakfast. Don't make me show you what would happen if you didn't. You might look like a smashed tomato, one my dear old mom used to burst over a flame just to feed me a hot meal when it was cold and rainy and I was hungry. (his voice rising…) *But not anymore! I do not need burst tomatoes and you do not need hypervelocity without whole wheat.* (Barry's voice now congenial…) *Thank you.*

When Barry's voice faded and the static crackling of the P.A. system fell silent, everyone resumed what they were doing.

Argyle plopped down in his chair and leaned back, stretching the chair's back and making it squeak. The chair regained its original position by popping forward, but Argyle repeated the motion again, apparently amused by the noise it was making.

Ben sat down opposite him and fixed a slight grin on his face every time one of the cameras swept by, losing it when he was out of the camera's line of vision and squirming in his seat as he tried unsuccessfully to loosen the grip that his jumpsuit had on him. This action started to resemble an odd facial exercise accompanied by a bit of butt wiggling because the cameras swept by every three seconds.

Argyle, rocking and squeaking in his chair, curiously watched Ben for several minutes while Ben twitched his face in time to the cameras. When he became bored with that, he drew his finger across a column of his desk calendar until it hovered over the entry marked: Monday. It reminded him that the week was just beginning, and he smiled with the possibility that there could be a shoot-out this week. *Just think positive, Argyle, old man*, he thought.

Argyle's mental revelry was interrupted by a low-ranking henchman, Alexey, as he stepped up and dropped a scrap of paper on Argyle's desk and said in a thick Russian accent, "The boss wants to see you in Jeffery Dahmer meeting room." Alexey turned to leave but his foot got tangled in all the loose cables and he tripped into the next desk, cussing under his breath as he worked to free himself.

Ben watched Alexey for a minute then said, "Did you know he," thumbing at Alexey, "was ex-KGB?"

Argyle, ignoring Ben's comment, read through the note, twice, and said to Ben, "Hey! Barry wants to see us. Maybe he's got a good caper for us. Maybe he needs us to shoot something. Let's go!"

Both men got up from their desks and stepped around Alexey, who was now hissing in frustration and still trying to unwrap the cables from his ankle.

Argyle and Ben stepped into the back hallway that separated the office pit from the meeting rooms and were almost bowled over by an onrush of over a dozen scurrying henchmen. Flattened against the wall, so the fleeing henchmen could get out, Argyle, watched the flow of bodies and said, to no one in particular, "Wonder if the cappuccino machine has been fixed?"

After the mad rush of henchmen ended, Argyle and Ben started toward the Dahmer meeting room (all of the conference rooms are named after famous mass-murderers and serial killers. There was the Ted Bundy, Joel Rifkin, Charles Ng, and the Leonard Lake… all very nice rooms). The guys slowed their pace when they noted that the door was closed. Suddenly a gunshot rang out and both men froze in their steps like statues. The next thing they heard was scuffling sounds coming from inside the meeting room and both leaned in closer trying to determine what the hell had just happened. The door suddenly jerked open to barely a foot wide and Barry's secretary, Miss Q squeezed out into the hallway.

After adjusting her glasses back up on her nose, Miss Q straightened up, smoothed her skirt down and smiled at Argyle and Ben before saying, "It'll be just a minute. The Thrasher's ten o'clock meeting has just ended."

Miss Q planted her feet and stood in front of the door smiling nervously, trying to pet her cheek that was now twitching a bit out of control. The small group stood quietly looking at each other, no one saying a word when they were jolted by the sounds of more curious muffled noises that started to filter through the door. Just as quickly as it all started, it stopped and became eerily quiet.

Suddenly, a raspy baritone voice announced, "Now."

Miss Q smiled and nodded to Argyle and Ben and opened the door, while saying to them, "The Thrasher will see you now."

Argyle and Ben stepped inside and stood motionless at the end of the meeting table. With slight apprehension both men listened as Miss Q quietly closed the door behind them.

The meeting room had a long table running down the middle with chairs enough for twenty. Well, at the moment, only nineteen because one of the chairs had a dead body in it. One that had been hastily covered with a wrinkled old sheet, but still, an obviously dead body. Argyle and Ben stood frozen waiting for something to happen.

The Thrasher was seated at the head of the table facing away from the room. After a minute of dead silence… no pun intended… The Thrasher started to rotate his chair slowly around to face the meeting. The chair was making a horrible squeaking noise that seemed to go on and on and that succeeded in making the hairs on the back of Ben's neck frizz up. Eventually, The Thrasher stopped turning his chair and mercifully the rusted ear-piercing squeaks of the chair stopped. The Thrasher leaned forward in the chair with his elbows on the armrests and his fingers intertwined under his chin and held his head at an incline to glare menacingly at Argyle and Ben. After a minute of this, but only when the two henchmen were thoroughly unnerved, The Thrasher spoke, "Ah, misty hedge-foam green. One of my favorite colors."

Argyle and Ben smiled nervously and glanced at themselves and each other, stammering out short insipid remarks like "Does look good" and "I agree, Boss, nice color" but when they looked back at The Thrasher, he was staring at them again which made them instantly fall silent.

The Thrasher unwound his six-foot-three-inch frame from the chair and stood up. It was then that Argyle noticed that The Thrasher was wearing his favorite jet-black Victorian cape with matching skin-tight black leather pants. Argyle was about to offer a compliment on his choice of wardrobe when The Thrasher spoke up, "Henchmen! I have a job for you."

Argyle excitedly said, "That's great Thrasher! Are we going on a new and exciting caper? Did you think up a good one? When do we leave?"

The Thrasher had slowly taken six steps toward the men while Argyle was babbling his excited questions. Suddenly he halted Argyle's stammering with a quick jerk of his hand as he held it, palm outward, in Argyle's face. The quick movement made both Argyle and Ben flinch and caused The Thrasher to chuckle. Lowering his hand, The Thrasher said, "The job I have for you is this… you two will conduct on-site interviews to fill an opening that has just come up."

The Thrasher, Argyle and Ben all turned slowly around to look at the sheet-wrapped body when The Thrasher suddenly whipped his cape up and around and strode toward the door saying over his shoulder, "Larry Edwards has just resigned."

Chapter Two

Really? A Crossbow?

"Donuts in the break room!"

Every time these words are spoken, it means that another henchman has left the employ of The Thrasher. Donuts are Barry's idea of boosting morale, but no one is really sure if it does the trick or not. On the one hand, it's slightly disturbing to know that one of your fellow henchmen has met an untimely end, although it was most certainly deserved; on the other hand, donuts are very tasty!

As Argyle and Ben entered the break room, they began thinking about their assignment: finding a replacement for Edwards. They can thank Edwards for the donuts, but no one really knows for sure what he did to make Barry so angry. "To Edwards!" Ben said as he lifted his donut as if to make a toast. "To Edwards!" responded Argyle. They both took big bites out of their donuts, which caused the sprinkles to scatter to the floor.

"Sprinkles again? I hate sprinkles," Argyle frowned.

"You know what I like?" said Ben. "Those little powdered donuts. Why can't Barry give us some of those?"

Just then the camera swept by and Ben and Argyle stopped talking long enough to freeze their faces into a smile. As soon as the camera spun in another direction, they resumed their conversation; only this time it had nothing to do with donuts.

"So, where are we going to find someone to replace Edwards?"

"How about FredsList?" Ben said helpfully. "That's how I got this job."

"I don't know. Trying to find a good candidate on FredsList is like playing Russian roulette." Argyle then looked at Alexey and said, "Or in your case, Alexey, roulette."

Alexey just frowned and said, "In Russia we don't play games."

Obviously, he didn't get the joke.

"I have a better idea," said Argyle. "Let's give it to Miss Q. After all, this falls more into her line of work. We're all about the danger and excitement, and this doesn't seem like a very exciting assignment."

Ben thought for a moment and said, "Maybe we should put together a list of things we're looking for in a candidate."

"You mean things like 'self starter', 'at least five years experience with a major crime syndicate'?"

"That's the idea," said Ben. "'Must have a proven criminal record', 'Experience with explosives and grappling hooks a plus'."

"'Must be able to work under intense pressure', 'Loyalty an absolute must'."

"Of course, we'll need good references."

"Absolutely. This is The Thrasher's organization we're talking about, not just any old outfit."

After Argyle and Ben had finished putting together a list of qualifications for the job, and after fumbling around a bit on the Internet looking for likely candidates, they gave up and set out down the hall in search of Miss Q. They found her sitting in her office in front of her laptop and proceeded to explain their dilemma and gave her the list of qualifications they were looking for. With a slightly sour look on her face, she agreed to set up some interviews for the next morning.

When Argyle and Ben returned to their desks, they found their chairs missing.

"What? Not again!" said Ben. Both Ben and Argyle looked around to see if someone had absconded with their chairs. "Just when I got it adjusted the way I like it," Argyle said in exasperation. Back to Miss Q they went, to see if there was anything she could do about this missing chair situation.

"Boys, let me see what The Thrasher has to say about this."

A look of dread came over Ben's face, because anytime Barry was brought into a problem situation, it never went well. Miss Q got on the phone and gave Barry a call.

"Hello, Thrasher?" she said in a very small polite voice. "This is Miss Q. I'm fine, how are you? That's good. The reason I'm calling is because we seem to be having a problem with our chairs again." Suddenly she jerked the phone away from her ear and Argyle and Ben could distinctly hear yelling coming from the earpiece.

Slowly, Miss Q returned the phone to her ear. Argyle and Ben noticed a slight twitch on Miss Q's lip, and Argyle said, "Maybe this isn't a good time…," but Miss Q just sort of shook her head and proceeded to listen to Barry's angry rant until the yelling seemed to stop and she gently put the phone down and turned to face the two henchmen.

Then she smiled with her twitching mouth and said, "The Thrasher says he would like you to go down to the wardrobe room and check out two caperware #7 outfits for the both of you and then proceed to the nearest Better Buy to obtain some new chairs. He apologizes for any inconvenience this may be causing you."

"Hot damn! A caper!" Argyle exclaimed. "Better get my gun ready."

The wardrobe seamstress could be heard rummaging through the storage racks, "#5, #6, ah here it is: #7." She returned to the checkout counter and handed two bundles to Argyle.

Argyle pulled the uniform out of its storage box and gave it a quick look. It was a two-piece costume, with the top being a blue polo shirt with a Thrasher logo in the upper left front, and a pair of beige khaki pants. "What the hell is this? There doesn't seem to be any place to put my gun. How are we supposed to pull a caper with this nerdy uniform and no firearms?"

"Looks like we'll have to improvise," said Ben.

After checking out a crime van through the supply henchman up on Sublevel One, Argyle and Ben grabbed an elevator up to the second level parking.

Argyle said, "Oh man! Look at this Piece-Of-Crap. All dented and dirty. We're gonna have to run it through a car wash before the caper."

"Yeah, this kind of stuff really burns me up," said Ben. "Probably gonna need gas, too."

"Well, let's hope it starts."

After getting the van gassed, making sure they got the ten cents per gallon discount for including a car wash, off they went to the nearest Better Buy in search of deluxe office chairs.

When they arrived at the store, they initially managed to blend in as if they were salesmen, but once they started to roll the chairs that they chose toward the front door, one of the security guards approached them and asked, "What are you doing?"

"We're just taking these chairs, if that's alright with you," said Ben.

The security guard looked them up and down with a menacing look until his sight fell upon The Thrasher logos emblazoned on their polo shirts. Suddenly, his eyes got real wide and he took two steps back and said, "Take what you want. We don't want any trouble."

Argyle smiled at Ben and the two proceeded to exit out the front door with their prize chairs and no one made a move to stop them.

"Heh," said Ben, "these Thrasher logos sure go a long way, don't they?"

Argyle frowned and said, "Yeah, but I sure wish I could have used my gun. I never get to use my gun."

"Cheer up, Arg. There's always next time."

When they returned from their caper, both Ben and Argyle were in possession of two very nice office chairs that they proudly rolled into their office space. "No one better take THESE chairs, damn it!" was the only thing Ben could think of to say as the other henchmen watched them with their prizes. They were still wearing their #7 uniforms.

"What the hell are you guys wearing, anyway?" said Joe.

"What, this? This is our 'caperware.' Duh," Ben said with slight disgust.

"Looks more like 'geek-ware' to me," said Joe.

"Just ignore him," Argyle said to Ben. "They're just jealous."

"Yeah, that's it, jealous," smirked Joe.

With that, both Ben and Argyle headed to the wardrobe room to return their #7s. Another fine day's work done!

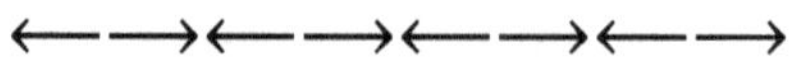

Tuesday morning: The first thing Argyle did when arriving to work that morning was to visit Miss Q to see how the job search was going. Miss Q handed Argyle a single resume and he said, with a puzzled look, "That's it? Just one?"

"It's hard to find good candidates these days. This was the only one that looked appropriate. None of the others were a match."

Argyle looked it over and shrugged.

"Your candidate is in the Manson Room down the hall." Miss Q then returned to her work, effectively dismissing Argyle.

Argyle knocked on the door of the conference room and entered, which was the polite thing to do before entering a room. The person sitting at the table got up and offered his hand. Argyle shook his hand politely; noticing that it was soft and slightly clammy, which he figured was because the person opposite him was nervous. Who wouldn't be? Job interviews are nerve wracking!

"Good morning. My name is Argyle," he said, as he consulted the resume in his hand, the one that had just been handed to him not fifteen minutes before he was told to run this new candidate through the paces.

"Argyle, like the sock?"

Argyle just stared at the young man and said, "You're Gilbert, right?"

"Yes, Gilbert Alan Martin the Third," he said not as pompously as the name might imply.

"So, how did you find out about us?"

Gilbert looked puzzled. "You answered my ad on FredsList, didn't you?"

Argyle flipped through the resume quickly and responded, "Oh yeah. Well, what do you know about what we do here?"

"Not much, really. All I know is that I'm interviewing for the position of 'Junior Henchman', and the organization is run by 'The Thrasher'. Right so far?"

"That's right. So, let me ask you, what makes you want to be a henchman?"

"Well, my last job was in the accounting department for Professor Meglamon. You may have heard of him? He's pretty big in crime. Although lately he's hit on hard times and had to downsize when he had trouble finding new recruits. I figured this was a good time to move out of Accounting and into the field. I really think I'm ready for that, and I didn't think there was any room for advancement in Professor Meglamon's organization. Plus, the uniforms were getting very silly."

"Yeah, I heard that Professor Meglamon was having trouble. I heard that he was killing too many of his henchmen and the ones that were still there were starting to lose trust in him. Well, I can assure you that that isn't a problem here with Barry."

"Barry?"

"Oh yeah, sorry. That's The Thrasher's real name. But we never call him that to his face. Just so you know! If anyone did, they would end up like Edwards."

"Who's Edwards?"

"He's the guy you're going to replace, if you get this job. Long story, but it's not important now."

Argyle rustled through the papers, most of them blank, in front of him while an awkward silence fell over the room.

"Was he fired?"

"Something like that."

Looking at the one and only page of Gilbert's resume, Argyle was starting to run out of questions. Finally, he said, "I see you have a degree in Chemistry from the U of A. That might come in handy here when we need to make explosives."

"Explosives are my specialty," said Gilbert with great enthusiasm.

"Nice!" said Argyle. "Have you ever been on a caper?"

"No, but I really want to! Can I ask you this, what sort of capers have you planned? If you can tell me, that is."

"Did you sign our non-disclosure agreement?"

"I signed something. I think that's what it was. 'Under pain of death not to reveal any secrets,' etc. The usual."

"Okay, well I can tell you that we have some big projects coming up. One of the reasons we're bringing in more henchmen is because some of our upcoming projects are going to be very profitable – and very dangerous, I might add, and we're going to need a larger crew. Are you okay with danger? How are you with pain?"

"I think I can handle myself with the best. I played some basketball in school and was good at track and field."

"That will come in handy, I suppose." Argyle continued shuffling through his notes and said, "I have a few exercises I'd like to put you through, if you don't mind. We here at The Thrasher Organization value loyalty above all else. Here's a hypothetical situation: suppose you're out on a caper with about a dozen other henchmen and Barry turns to you and tells you to shoot henchman #3. What do you do?"

"What did #3 do to deserve that?"

"Doesn't matter. It's hypothetical. Do you shoot him? Yes or no."

"Absolutely, I shoot him. The boss said so. It's done."

"Here's another scenario, and remember, there are no right or wrong answers. I just want to see what your reaction would be. The boss sees Professor Meglamon on the ledge of the building coming our way. The boss sends one of the henchmen out onto the ledge to do battle. The henchman does his best, but he winds up falling 30 stories to his death. He sends out another one, and they do battle but Meglamon is just too good. Henchman #2 falls to his death. He then sends you out to do the same. What do you do?"

"I do it, of course. Just because the first couple of guys didn't beat Meglamon doesn't mean I won't. I think I can take him! But I was wondering, why not everybody just rush him all at once instead of one at a time?"

Argyle thought for a second and said, "That's not the way we do things around here." Then Argyle continued, "Do you think there might be a conflict of interest there? After all, you used to work for him."

"No, no. If I'm working for Barry – I mean The Thrasher – then I have no loyalty to any of my past employers."

Argyle smiled and nodded his head. "Good. Good. Another thing we value is the ability to accept punishment gracefully. Let's say you're asked to go after Barry's nemesis and somehow you fail to kill him. When you return to the lair to report your failure, what would you expect Barry's reaction to be?"

Gilbert thought for a moment and said, "Well, I suppose he would be pretty pissed off. I suppose I could expect a stern lecture or, worst case, I guess I'd get fired."

Argyle slowly shook his head and made some notes. Gilbert noticed and said, "Wrong?"

Argyle responded, "Not that it would ever really come to that, but I imagine the punishment would be much harsher. Are you prepared for that?"

"I guess failure is not an option," Gilbert smiled.

"No, it's not. That's what comes with being a henchman."

"As I say, I'm ready to move up. Whatever it takes."

Argyle liked what he was hearing and was starting to think this Gilbert character had some good henchman potential. He stood up and walked toward the whiteboard. "How about we try a few exercises on the whiteboard? Are you good with that?"

Gilbert thought to himself, *Ugh, I'm never any good at this sort of thing, I never know what to say until later,* but he heard himself saying, "Sure, no problem."

"Okay. Let's see how you are at planning a caper. Draw me a simple diagram for how you would go about robbing a jewelry store."

Gilbert went to the whiteboard and chose a black marker. After testing it with a few squiggles, just to make sure it was full of ink, he drew a round circle.

"What sort of jewels are we talking about?"

"I don't think it matters. Make something up."

"Okay. Diamonds," said Gilbert as he drew the word "diamonds" into the circle he had just drawn. Then he drew another circle and connected both with a straight line. Argyle couldn't figure out where Gilbert was going with this, but he let him continue. Inside the other circle he drew a bunch of stick men. *This is going nowhere*, Argyle thought.

"Wait a minute, aren't you going to need some caperware?"

"Caperware?"

"You know, capes, masks, vests, whatever."

"Oh yeah, capes," and then Gilbert proceeded to draw little tiny capes on each of his stick figures. Then he drew a truck on the line that connected the two circles and said, "I figure we all pile into this truck with our explosive devices…"

"Explosive devices?"

"Yeah, we would all be equipped with our own personal bombs…"

"Who has the detonator?" said Argyle.

"Well, The Thrasher, I suppose."

"Go on."

"We all pile out of the truck when we get to the jewelry store," he said as he drew another line between the truck and the circle representing the jewelry store, "and we rush into the store with our bombs in hand screaming, 'Freeze, motherhumpers! Hand over your jewels!'"

Argyle frowned and looked down at his papers on the desk and made a few notes. Gilbert didn't look too pleased but continued anyway. "I know it's not much of a caper, but it's simple and effective. There's nothing more terrifying than a man with a bomb and a crazy unknown person holding the trigger."

Argyle was thinking that Gilbert wouldn't be called upon to plan a caper, and anyway he's been on worse – and recently.

"How do you feel about The Thrasher holding the detonator? Doesn't that make you a little uncomfortable knowing that he might, at any moment, press the trigger and blow you all to hell?"

"Not at all," said Gilbert. "He's the boss. He knows best."

Ah, blind loyalty. Nothing better, thought Argyle.

"So, what can you tell me about Professor Meglamon? Other than the fact that he's been downsizing – with extreme prejudice – why are you looking to leave his organization?"

"It was starting to get boring around there. No exciting capers, just mostly highjacking trucks and that sort of stuff. You know, Meglamon's a real 'old school' crime boss type, and that's sort of passé. I think The Thrasher is the future of crime. Also, Meglamon had a real top-heavy management structure and the debt-to-income ratio was way off. And he wears bow ties."

Argyle nodded his head and thought *I think this could work out having an ex-Meglamon guy on staff. Wait until Barry hears about this.*

"So, tell me. Where do you see yourself in five years?" Argyle asked.

Gilbert thought for a moment or two. *Damn, the old "where do you see yourself in five years question".* He hated that question, but he tried desperately to think of an answer that wouldn't make him appear too arrogant. There's nothing an interviewer hates more than to think that the person he's interviewing is out to get his job.

"I'll be happy to be your right-hand man. Just the best henchman that money can buy!"

So lame, thought Gilbert.

"What do you think your biggest weakness is?" asked Argyle.

Oh God, not the "what's your biggest weakness" question. "Well, if I had to come up with something, I think my biggest weakness is that I don't give myself enough downtime to just relax and enjoy life. I'm always on the move."

The typical dodge, thought Argyle. *Turn a weakness into strength.*

He decided to let it pass because it was, after all, a really stupid question.

"And your biggest strength?"

"The same," replied Gilbert with a smile, hoping it would amuse enough to get by. It worked, because Argyle let out a laugh and said "Good one!"

"Well, I think it's time to turn you over to the next person. Wait here and I'll be right back."

Argyle left the room and went to get Ben, who was sitting at his desk throwing a wadded-up piece of paper in the air and catching it. It was just something to pass the time.

"Your turn," said Argyle. They both went to the Manson Room and Argyle introduced Ben to Gilbert and left them alone.

Two minutes later, Ben came out with Gilbert in tow and headed to the front room where Gilbert would, presumably, wait for the next interviewer, but there was to be no other interviewers. It was just going to be the two of them. Argyle was puzzled at the short interview time; after all, he had spent nearly an hour with Gilbert. What could Ben have asked Gilbert that cut the interview so short?

Ben asked Gilbert to wait a few minutes and returned to the office.

When Argyle met up with Ben, he asked him, "What happened in there?"

"What?" said Ben. "Oh yeah, I think he'll do fine. I'm going to recommend him for the job."

"Yeah, but that was so short. What did you ask him?"

"Just one question: What do you like better, Star Trek or Star Wars?"

"What was his answer?"

"Star Gate."

"So, what do you think?" Argyle asked Ben.

"Yeah, I think we should hire him. He's a Star Gate fan. That goes a long way."

Well, you have a point there," said Argyle, "but even more important is the fact that he used to work for Meglamon."

"Really? I didn't know that."

"Well, you didn't bother to ask him any questions, did you?" said Argyle with some frustration.

"Sure I did. I asked him the Star Trek/Star Wars question. That was the first time anyone answered with a completely different movie. That shows thinking outside the box."

"Anyway, I think his knowledge of Meglamon's organization could come in handy. Let's go talk to Barry about this."

Ben suddenly stiffened and tried to suppress a look of panic. As the camera swept his way, he worked up a sickening smile and said, "Are you sure that's a good idea? We shouldn't bother him with trivial things like this."

Argyle smiled directly into the camera and waited for it to continue its sweep through the office. When the camera had swung out of view, both Argyle and Ben resumed their previous expressions.

"What are we waiting for? Let's go talk to Barry."

Both Ben and Argyle walked off to see Miss Q in Sublevel One, but Ben was still not sure it was a good idea to risk getting into Barry's field of vision.

"Is The Thrasher around?" asked Argyle when they walked into Miss Q's office.

"The Thrasher is busy at the moment. Could you leave a message?"

"This is about the new hire. We would like to schedule an appointment with him as soon as possible. He might be interested in knowing that the guy we're considering hiring once worked for Professor Meglamon…" Before Argyle could finish his sentence, he heard the booming voice of The Thrasher coming through the speaker in the ceiling… "Wait right there!"

Within minutes, Barry had calmly walked through a hidden door to the left of Miss Q's desk. Then he just stood there and stared at Ben and Argyle, waiting for one of the two to begin talking. No way was Ben going to start, so Argyle waved the resume he was holding in his hand and said, "This guy," then he looked at the paper in his hand to find the name of the person he had just been interviewing, "Gilbert

Alan Martin the Third…"

"We just call him 'Third'," Ben piped in, immediately regretting it. Barry turned his stare toward Ben and continued to focus on him while Argyle kept talking and Ben began to get noticeably uncomfortable.

"The interesting thing about him is that he used to work for Professor Meglamon."

"Professor! Professor of what?" snorted Barry. "Where did he get his credentials, out of a cereal box? I will *destroy* him." Barry clenched his fist and turned his steely gaze toward Argyle.

"I think we may be able to use his past experience with Meglamon to good advantage, and besides he has a decent background in explosives," said Argyle.

Barry pondered this for a few moments and said, "Yes. Let's hire him. You," he was referring directly to Argyle, "and *you*," pointing at Ben, "will train him and gain as much knowledge as you can regarding this so-called 'Professor Meglamon'."

Argyle nodded his head and said, "Will do." Ben said nothing. Barry stood there and stared at each of them in turn, saying nothing. After what seemed like an interminable silence, Barry turned on his heels and headed toward his secret passage, his cape fluttering behind him.

"Well," said Ben, "let's go tell Third the good news."

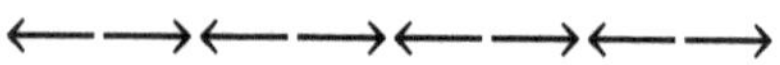

"So, Third, you're hired. Can you start today?"

Gilbert was so excited he could hardly let out a garbled, "Yes."

"Great! We're going to lunch. Want to come along? We can discuss the job a little more."

"Sure!" said Gilbert. "Where are we going?"

"Well, it's Tuesday," said Ben, "so that could only mean one thing. Taco Barn!"

The three of them proceeded to the parking garage and got into Argyle's 1958 VW Beetle. Gilbert was confused. He had been expecting a Camaro or a Stingray or some other muscle car rather than an old VW bug.

"So, how much money does a henchman make anyway?" Gilbert asked.

Argyle could see where Gilbert was coming from. "You're thinking about this car? Hey, this is a *classic*. Cost me a lot of money to restore it. Don't worry about the money. One or two good capers and you'll be lining your underwear with gold!"

"Yeah!" Ben added, "and more donuts than you can handle!"

When they arrived at the Taco Barn, the three of them went up to the counter as one. "So, Third, let me do the ordering," Ben said as he reached in his jacket for his gun. He kept his hand on the gun while he ordered. After the three had placed their orders and the little zitty-faced kid behind the counter rang up the charges, Ben took out his gun and said, "To go."

Argyle stopped by Miss Q's office to obtain all the permission and contract forms that every newly-hired henchman must sign before their employment is official.

Argyle and Ben, with Gilbert in tow, returned to the Manson meeting room and quickly settled Gilbert down to a quiet afternoon of New Employee paperwork.

After pointing Gilbert to a chair, Argyle said, "Here ya go," as he dropped the sixty-two-page pile of paper in front of him, making a weighty thud.

"Read these carefully and sign where indicated," pointing at a signature block. "And initial each page."

Gilbert quickly flipped through the first handful of pages and stopped to scan page thirty-two. His face scrunched up into a question and said, "Hey! There's an organ donor card here. What's up with that?"

Argyle said, "That's standard stuff, Third."

Smiling, Ben said, "Don't worry… they won't take any parts you're still using!"

Gilbert went back to flipping pages but now looked at them much more closely.

Ben said, "I need a cup of coffee, those tacos are wreaking havoc in my guts. Want anything, Third?"

Gilbert nodded and answered, "Yes please. A chocolate yoohoo. If you have it."

Argyle said, "I'll come with you." And both men went to the break room.

"Oh, look! Donuts!"

With a mouthful of donut Ben said, "Third is going to be busy signing papers for an hour. Let's go work out."

"Yea." Argyle said as he flicked some sprinkles off his shirt. *Man, I hate sprinkles.* Then added, "I'll get Alexey to take Gilbert and his papers up to Miss Q when he's finished."

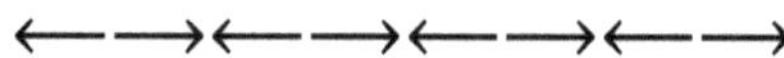

After having his photo taken for his badge, and a GPS chip inserted into his neck, which was the norm for all henchmen (The Thrasher liked to know where his employees were at all time) and his locker assignment, Alexey guided Gilbert to the office work area. This afternoon would be orientation and basic training, and Gilbert was really looking forward to it.

Ben greeted Gilbert, "Hey Third!" waving an arm in the air, "Welcome to The Thrasher Lair. Let's get started."

Argyle just sort of nodded at Gilbert and went back to updating his Facecram page.

"First thing you're going to need to know about is the wardrobe room on Sublevel Five," Ben said as he led Gilbert down toward the elevators that would take them to Sublevel Five.

"Each henchman is expected to check out the jumpsuits that have been designated for the week."

The ride down was short. When they disembarked on Sublevel Five, Ben continued.

"Here you will see a fine assortment of capes, jumpsuits, belts, pants, boots, and just about everything you would need for any caper."

Gilbert noticed that the vast array of clothes was catalogued with numbers and neatly stacked behind the counter in boxes and on hangers. He also noticed that practically every piece of clothing was complete with a Thrasher logo.

Ben continued, "For instance, the marquee in the locker room always lists what you will be wearing for every day of the current week." After eying Gilbert up and down, he asked the seamstress at the counter for a junior size eighteen, number eight jumpsuit and when it had been delivered, handed it to Gilbert. It was bright red with a blazing yellow Thrasher logo on the upper right chest.

Gilbert gently took it and folded it over his arm as they continued with the tour of the facilities.

Back up on Sublevel Two, Ben pointed out various offices and conference rooms, walking right past rooms labeled "Jeffrey Dahmer", "Jack the Ripper", "Caligula", "O.J. Simpson", and so forth. They briefly stopped at Miss Q's office and Ben said, "You already know Miss Q". She nodded with a smile and they moved on.

When they got back to Gilbert's work area, they found that his chair was missing. "That happens a lot," Argyle said. "You'll just have to grab one from one of the conference rooms. I don't think the Hitler room is currently being used. Take one of those."

On the way to the Hitler room for his chair, Gilbert couldn't help but notice all the really neat torture devices that decorated the walls. Some were familiar and some not so familiar. He made a mental note to ask about them later.

When he got back to his work area with his new-found chair, Argyle said, "Hey Third, after you put on your jumpsuit, here's what you're gonna do. On your way back from the locker room, stop by the break room and steal three chocolate bars from the candy machine. Do it without being seen or damaging the machine. You've got fifteen minutes, so get going."

Ben watched Gilbert leave the area then turned to Argyle and asked, "What 'cha doing?"

Argyle shrugged, "I've got the munchies."

"Hey!" Ben shouted after Gilbert. "Get the ones with the peanuts!" but Gilbert didn't hear.

Twenty minutes, then thirty minutes passed.

Argyle, his face scrunched up in annoyance said, "Third must have gotten lost. I'll check the break room."

From the hallway, Argyle heard muffled whimpers coming from the break room and when he reached the doorway, he saw that Gilbert had reached up into the vending machine through the delivery bin, got his arm stuck, and was now struggling to free himself.

"Well, well, well Third. Your first caper and you're not doing so good."

Gilbert looked crestfallen. He had so wanted to snatch the candy and show the guys he was a henchman at heart.

Argyle banged the machine on the left and kicked it in the lower right and behold, five chocolate bars dropped past Gilbert's arm into the delivery bin.

As Argyle collected them he said, "Better get your arm out of there before Barry sees you," and strode away.

When Gilbert had freed himself and returned to his desk, Argyle said, "Let's take a trip down to the Obstacle Course to begin your training."

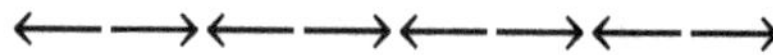

The Obstacle Course on Sublevel Four was in use by only one henchman at the moment, but Argyle still used his badge to gain entry. He held the door open for Gilbert and followed him in. The large gym-like area contained rope ladders, faux skyscraper ledges, tunnels, spike-filled pits, and various climbing areas – everything a good henchman would need for training. Gilbert looked at everything in awe and couldn't wait to start learning the ropes, as it were.

"What I'd like you to do," Argyle said, "is grab a gun – any gun, a knife, and a crossbow. Once you've secured those weapons, I want you to go to that area over there with the rope hanging from the top of that roof, see it? Then I would like you to climb the rope to the roof of the structure, without dropping any of your weapons, and then rappel down the other side of the structure. But here's what I want you to do: while rappelling down the side, pull out your gun and shoot it at that target over there, and when you get to the bottom, I want you to take your knife, throw it at that other target over there, and then finally take your crossbow and hit that target way over there. I'll time you."

Gilbert sized up the situation and went over to the weapons area and selected an Uzi, a large combat knife, and a crossbow. He made sure everything was loaded and ready to use. *I've never fired a crossbow before. I hope I can do this,* he thought to himself. Then, when he was ready, he went over to the rope ladder area to begin.

"Now!" Argyle said as he stared at his watch. Climbing up was a little bit of a struggle, but Gilbert was in okay shape, being only 26 years old and fresh out of college, and in spite of a bit of flab around his waist, he managed to get to the roof rather quickly. Then he moved to the other side of the building where the other rope was and, before starting to rappel down, got his gun ready. As he was descending, he fired the Uzi at the first target. A burst of bullets sprayed out with one round striking the other henchman in the thigh. He yelped and fell to the floor in pain. A second burst of rounds managed to fire through Gilbert's rope and he fell to the floor with a thud.

"Ow, that wasn't how I wanted that to go," said Gilbert.

"Okay, try it again," Argyle responded.

So, Gilbert went through it from the beginning, but this time he managed to avoid shooting through the new rope that he had rigged. When Gilbert got to the bottom, he very quickly threw his knife, somewhat inaccurately, and then fumbled with the crossbow and completely missed the target.

"Move it, maggot!" Argyle yelled, but he was smiling broadly when he said it. "Climb that wall with your bare hands!"

Argyle was referring to the rock-climbing wall at the end of the course. Gilbert, being not quite in the shape that the other henchmen were in, struggled mightily to climb to the top of the wall, but somehow, he managed. When he got to the top, he threw up his hands and screamed "I am a freaking HENCHMAN!"

"Well… not yet…" said Argyle.

When Argyle and Gilbert returned to their office space, Ben greeted them with, "So, how did it go? Was Third all you could hope he would be?"

"He didn't do too bad, considering," said Argyle.

"Considering what?" said Ben.

"Considering that he's never fired a crossbow before."

"Ha ha! The crossbow? You had him fire the crossbow? No one

ever does well with the crossbow," laughed Ben.

Gilbert was of two minds upon hearing this. On the one hand, he was glad that no one else has mastered the crossbow, but on the other hand he was a little miffed that he was forced to fire the crossbow, thinking it was going to be a major part of the job.

"You mean, I won't be able to use the crossbow?" asked Gilbert.

"Oh you can use it, alright, just not very well. Let's hope it doesn't come up as a major part of any future caper. Speaking of which," said Ben, "we have a new one. Just came in straight from Barry. Well, straight from Barry by way of Miss Q, that is."

"Great! What is it?" said Gilbert. "Am I a part of it?"

"Oh yeah," said Ben, "a *big* part of it alright."

"Will there be any shooting?" asked Argyle. "Guess I need to load up."

"Wouldn't hurt to bring your guns, but I don't think you're going to need them. Barry wants us to restock our power bar supplies. Oh yeah, also we're out of toilet paper."

Gilbert and Argyle both looked crestfallen. "Goddamit! When are we going to get a caper I can really sink my teeth into? I never get to shoot anyone."

Argyle was very upset, but Gilbert was intrigued. "What do we do?" he asked.

"We need to go down to the wardrobe department and pick up caperware #27. We're going to raid Cashco!" Ben was shouting with his fist pumping the air.

"Number 27?" asked Gilbert. "What's that? Armor plated vests? Gladiator outfit? A Ninja costume?"

Argyle answered, "Number 27 is nothing more than Levis and Metallica T-shirts. What the hell's up with that?"

"It's a low-key operation, from what I understand. We need to get pictures taken and pick up our forged Cashco membership cards. The rest should be easy. We get in and get out – nobody gets hurt."

"Great." said Argyle.

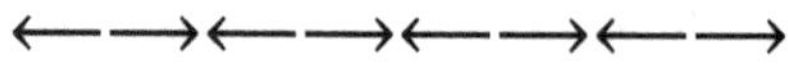

The henchmen returned from their caper carrying dozens of boxes of power bars and about three dozen packages of toilet paper. When the rest of the henchmen saw the goodies they were bringing, they let out a whoop and rushed to see what brands and flavors of power bars were obtained. There was some grumbling as some of the henchmen failed to see their favorite choices represented, but for the most part they were happy and grabbed some snacks after scanning their Thrasher cards for payment. The Thrasher liked to make sure that the cost of any drinks or snacks was properly deducted from the henchmen's payroll. After all, he wasn't running a charity organization.

Chapter Three

It's Been Barry from the Start

Barry Teasdale was born in a small rural town up state. One night when Barry was about four years old, his father went out to buy a pack of cigarettes and never returned. His mother didn't seem to mind too much and even made a comment about finally having a bit of peace for once.

Barry's mom worked hard, sometimes at two jobs at once, but always had a smile for Barry. She would tell him he was the only man in her life and let him eat pancakes any time he wanted. She assured him, constantly, that everything he did, be it mud pies or gluing a spring to a doorknob was a sure sign of genius. She petted his hair and hugged him a lot.

Barry responded by showing her everything he did and asking for her approval which she readily gave. He even went so far as to get her opinions on future projects being careful to omit the parts involving guns or bombs. He didn't want his mother to worry about him… too much.

Years later, rumors would circulate that one of Barry's school-mates had been teasing him and it had escalated into a fight with the schoolmate calling Barry a "Mommy's Boy". This enraged Barry so much, he shouted, "Don't you ever talk about my mother!" then pulled a gun and shot the kid. Right there! On the school ground! The rest of the rumor gets vague and over the years it has evolved into a story that has several possible endings: He shot the kid right between the eyes, the kid died but disappeared so nothing could be proven, the kid was shot in the kneecap and was crippled for life, the kid ended up working for Barry. And on and on it goes.

Barry couldn't really remember his father and when he asked his mom about him, she would only say that his father had to leave one day never to return. He didn't have any brothers or sisters, but this didn't upset him at all. He liked being number one. His mother took in laundry to support them and their small two-bedroom dump of a hovel that always smelled of bleach and lye soap. It was a run-down house with a detached garage and lots of clotheslines zigging and zagging around the back yard.

Barry grew up hating people that owned things and swore that before he was a man he would own things. Good things. More than anyone else. This thought was never very far from Barry's mind and seemed to motivate him throughout his young life.

Barry was always in trouble. Sometimes it was serious enough to get the cops involved, but he was very proud that he got away with many of his crimes, just like a super villain would.

Barry wasn't the nicest of children. When he was a young child, Barry would pull the wings off of flies, kick dogs, spit on sidewalks, and steal apples. He would present those apples to his mother for her approval, which she always gave to him, and then she would dice up the apples and put the little chunks into pancake batter for him. He would lie and would steal mostly useless items like glue solvent and staples. One time he stole dozens of boxes of shoelaces. He didn't know why. But none of these things sustained Barry's interest for very long.

When he was a teenaged boy, he stayed in his room more often reading crime novels and comic books. He was always very annoyed that crime villains got caught. This led him to develop a sort of problem-solving technique where he tried to figure out how the endless stream of comic book criminals *wouldn't* get caught. He worked these thoughts in his mind until he figured out how to escape from all the good guys that populated the comic pages. Slowly, he discovered that he had a talent for psychological crime and started to pattern himself after the comic super villains. Developing his best deviant behavior, Barry scoffed at all social norms. He cut school, threw rocks through store windows to sound the burglar alarms, stole coins from vending machines, and scratched the paint of very expensive cars.

Barry fancied his life as a super evil genius with great mental capacities and inventive abilities far beyond that of mere villains. He planned capers and thought about what his super villain costume would look like. It was then that Barry came up with his cool super villain name: The Thrasher.

Barry transformed himself into The Thrasher because of his deep and passionate love of crime. He thought long and hard about what his super villain name would be before he picked The Thrasher. Thrasher. He loved that name. It meant to beat and to flog and to defeat overwhelmingly. It was the best. And it was fairly easy to become The Thrasher because he liked thrashing things. You name it, Barry would thrash it. With a smile.

As a young man still living with his mother, Barry tried to make a nuclear bomb but failed when a mail-order shipment of plutonium didn't show up. He then turned to making mechanical torture devices, some of which were really inventive, even though they were unusable. He carried out small one-man capers where he would break into hardware stores and steal tools and spare parts. It was in this way he managed to transform the dilapidated garage into a very functional workshop.

As a man in his fifties, Barry, now known as The Thrasher, had expanded his business into the seedy old four-story red brick warehouse with all its sublevels, ran a henchman crew of one hundred and pulled lots of capers. He's living the dream.

Realizing that he had a payroll to meet, Barry had to rethink the whole shoelace thing and begin to steal items of more value, such as gold and diamonds. But Barry was resourceful and also stole things of a more utilitarian nature such as showerheads and copper pipe-fittings and office chairs.

Now, Barry runs one of the biggest crime organizations in the world. Imagine that. The whole world! Fame didn't come without a price. Barry is now sinister, he rants and he kills henchmen for hardly any reason. However, there is an up side. Barry also uses his evil genius mind as a creative force. He works on caperware design and, every once in a while, produces another torture device to adorn the office walls.

Chapter Four

It's All About the Sharks

The alarm clock came awake with a horrible clang that sent Argyle (yes, like the sock), into a stiff jointed contorted jerk, scrambling out of his comfy warm bed onto the cold bare floor – standing alert for danger and ready to fight. Once Argyle was awake, he gazed around, his face held in a look of confusion, until the realization that he was alone and in his own bedroom sank in. And talking to himself, Argyle said, "Yeah. I do that every time. Maybe I should replace the alarm clock."

Today is Wednesday.

Argyle went through the motions of getting dressed for work and grabbed a toasted bagel and his keys before stepping out into the hallway and locking his apartment.

Argyle lives on the fifth floor of a cold-water walk-up. The rent is cheap and the neighborhood is just kind of so-so, well really it is borderline mediocre, but the apartment is located a mere thirty minutes from the seedy red brick warehouse where he works. Taking surface streets. Especially if the lights were mostly green.

The apartment building stairwell was fairly busy at this time with a lot of the other renters leaving for their daily commutes and Argyle tried to be friendly, smiling at this one, saying "hi" to that one but he was really uncomfortable with this daily ritual. To save himself from the stress of it, he thought of the stairwell as a tactical par course and had turned his leaving and returning into a strange social game, one where he would hurry through to the end, and then award himself points for making it without running into anyone. It was the only way he would survive the social niceties of the awkward situation.

Once inside his beautifully restored classic 1958 VW Beetle,

Argyle could slough off the stress of the stairwell with the definitive click of the door lock.

Argyle finished changing and was admiring himself in the locker room mirror. He thought he looked pretty nice in his Wednesday jumpsuit. It was a nicely tailored white one with a very large and flashy Thrasher logo on the back. Argyle counted at least ten cargo-pant type pockets on the pant legs, each one billowing out and held closed by a series of snaps. He could probably carry a lot of ammunition in those pockets! There was a nice black belt, not too wide, with a silver buckle that held an artistic interpretation of Thrasher's logo stamped on it. A nice touch. The pant leg was hemmed just a hair short so the purple plum-colored socks with a small logo on either side could be seen. A pair of pale powder blue ballet style flats completed the ensemble and as Argyle took in the front and side views of himself in the full-length mirror, he smiled and nodded to his reflection and thought to himself, *I hope there's a good caper today. I haven't shot my gun in three days!*

Argyle made the walk through the turnstiles and the ride down in the elevator in a very short amount of time. In the back hallway connecting the break room and the office space, Argyle ran into Davis and five other henchmen from the nightshift. It appeared that they were returning from a caper and noting this, Argyle couldn't contain his curiosity as he reached out and lightly touched Davis' arm in an attempt to hold him up for a minute of conversation.

"Hey Davis! Long time no see. Been on a caper?"

Davis and his five henchmen cohorts all stopped their chatter and stood in a loose group with Argyle.

Davis and his band were dressed in tight pink leotards with huge stiff pink tutus fixed around their waists. A grouping of three red silk roses had been pinned at waist level close to the right hip with a matching red rose adorning an elastic band that all the henchmen wore as headbands – with the rose placed over the right ear. Their faces had been plied with heavy pale-pink makeup and powder and gobs of dark purple eye shadow ringed their eyes giving them an almost raccoon-like appearance. And as Argyle gazed at them, taking it all in, he noticed that each henchman's caper costume had been completed with glittery red ballet slippers.

As Argyle stood with his mouth agape, Davis said, "Yea, hey Stevens. Long time." Davis nervously shifted his weight from one leg to the other and started plucking at the tutu at his waist. "We're just coming back from a good caper. Thrasher needed a lot more material for caper costumes, ya know, like capes and masks and glittery things. He said that he was out of pink thread, too."

The group sort of snuffled and smiled to each other in camaraderie over doing a caper together and here and there were high-fives and knuckle bumps. Davis continued, "We made a good haul and managed to boost a lot of jewelry and cash from the last seating of the Swan Lake crowd before they knew we weren't part of the show. You should have seen Carter doing allegros in the aisles! Hey Carter! Show 'em what you did!"

The small group made an opening and Carter stepped into it, making to balance himself with his feet sorta splayed out and his knees bent. From this stance, he leapt three times from his right foot to his left and then back, at which point he pulled a Beretta 9mm from inside his tutu and menaced one of the other henchmen and demanded that he turn over his wallet. The group busted up laughing!

Davis turned to Argyle and said, "Well, it's been a long night and we're not getting overtime pay for this. Goodnight Stevens." And the small group smiled and waved goodnight and continued on down the hallway goofing around and bumping each other as they went.

Argyle stood watching the band of henchmen, with their overly muscled buttocks stuffed into those tight pink leotards and noted how the tutu around Carter's waist barely covered his expanding beer gut. Giving his own flat belly a little pat, Argyle thought, *I bet I'd look great in a tutu. Wonder if they got to shoot their guns?*

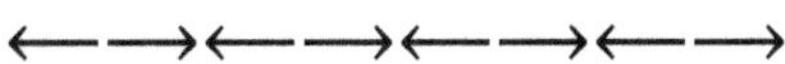

Argyle, cup of steamy hot peppermint latte chocolate chip frothy in hand, sauntered out into the office area and nodded hello to one or two henchmen already at their desks and who were trying to look busy by flipping papers and moving stuff around the desktops.

As Argyle gingerly made his way to his own desk, through the tangle of cables and cords strewn about the floor, he noticed that Ben was already sitting at his desk waiting for him.

As he approached, Argyle also noted that Gilbert was sitting down, which was different because yesterday he did not have a chair and had to stand next to his desk after he read and signed all the new guy paperwork.

Argyle looked from Ben to Gilbert and asked, "Where'd ya get the chair?" At which point Ben raised his eyebrows and jerked his thumb over his shoulder indicating that Argyle should look in that general direction. What Argyle saw was one of the other dayshift henchmen just standing by his desk looking feebly around wondering where his chair might be. Gilbert just sat, slightly smiling, waiting for Argyle to say something.

Argyle made a little harrumph noise in the back of his throat and sat down, sipping his espresso and relaxing into his new squeaky-backed chair. The trio sat in silence for a minute. Ben twitching a smile as the camera swept by, Argyle sipping his drink and Gilbert, glancing expectantly from Argyle to Ben, eager to start the day.

Argyle had taken a pencil from the holder perched on the top edge of his desk and had been drumming a complicated version of Iron Butterfly's "In-A-Gadda-Da-Vida" with the eraser end, when he noticed a slip of yellowed paper laced with crooked handwriting had been placed on his desk, probably sometime after he had left at the end of his shift yesterday.

He picked it up and read it, twice, before saying to Ben and Gilbert, "Hey. We're to clean the shark tank this morning. Before lunch." Argyle took a gulp of his espresso and said, "Third! Your training continues."

Gilbert had been sitting on the edge of his seat, anxious with expectation and when Argyle had said the word "training" he couldn't contain himself any longer and jumped up with joy, clapped his hands one time and shouted, "Alright!" and stood bouncing on his toes like an excited puppy.

The boys had to go up the elevator to the locker room so Gilbert could change into his work suit. That meant back through the turnstile on the way up… 75 cents… and again… another 75 cents… on their way down to Sublevel Three.

Argyle and Ben were waiting by the turnstiles for Gilbert to change into the designated shark tank-cleaning suit. Ben was passing the time by picking at his fingernails and Argyle was leaning on a turnstile wondering if he started using slugs, just how long could he get away with it, when Gilbert appeared.

Both henchmen looked up and froze for a moment staring and gape-mouthed at what they saw.

Gilbert waddled out of the locker room. There was no other way to describe his quick-stepped gait and the listing back and forth. Gilbert was waddling his way forward with a thoroughly distressed look on what could be seen of his face. He was suited up in what only could be described as a giant sponge.

From head to foot and everywhere in between, Gilbert was a sponge. His head was encased in sponge with only a small circle around his eyes, nose and mouth left open, presumably so he could still navigate. Both his hands stuck out at the ends of huge sponge sleeves and he clutched two more sponges between tightened fingers. His feet, poking out of huge sponge leggings were encased in two large square hunks of… you guessed it… sponge.

Everyone in the area had stopped in their tracks and looked at Gilbert, who was standing still looking like he was about to cry. Most of the onlookers were sniggering behind their hands while others guffawed out loud and moved on. Argyle and Ben, with wide toothy smiles spreading across their faces, overcame their silent stares and stepped toward Gilbert.

Argyle said, "Third, you look ready to work!"

Ben added, "Yeah buddy, we'll be right there with you."

Gilbert, sniffing back tears said, "Okay. But how am I gonna get through the turnstile?"

At this, Argyle waved two other henchmen over and between them and himself and Ben, lifted Gilbert up and tossed him over the turnstiles. Padded by the sponges, Gilbert bounced once and rolled a short distance to stop up against the doors of elevator #2 that just then slid open. Gilbert was wriggling in an effort to get up but only succeeded in rolling his way on to the elevator just before the doors slid shut and started its clunky decent.

Argyle and Ben fumbled with the turnstile and missed elevator #2 so hit the call buttons for all the elevators and waited for another elevator car to arrive. Argyle stood motionless, watching the lighted floor indicator of elevator #2 for a clue as to where they might eventually find Gilbert.

As they stepped off of elevator #4 onto Sublevel Three, Argyle spotted Gilbert about ten feet away from the doors. He was propped up against the wall on his side with his feet sticking out to the right and his head to the left, waiting quietly.

Sublevel Three was one of the largest levels in The Thrasher's secret lair. There were at least six sublevels but no one was really sure of that. Only Barry knew the exact number of sublevels there really were.

Sublevel Three housed most of the henchmen training areas where everything from the many uses of duct tape to the wide variety of pocketknives available were meticulously explained.

There was a par course, too. Many of the henchmen scheduled time here for practice as Barry expected his henchmen to stay in shape and caper-ready. The par course was also used as a testing area for newly hired henchmen and as a punishment area for when a henchman displayed poor performance while out on a caper. And sometimes, Barry used it if he just felt like punishing someone.

There were various anti-rooms, all connected by dank hallways sporting more of Barry's bizarre collection of torture devices. Most of these rooms were unused but stood waiting to be developed into something sinister.

The par course was set up around the perimeter of a very large open space, presumably in the middle of the sublevel. It occupied two levels of height. The bottom level was a course of obstructions, both man-made and natural that one had to navigate in a specific amount of time. There were spikes that shot up from the floor, there were hidden barbed-wire tangles designed to trip you up and nets that would encase a man, carrying him upward to dangle helpless thirty feet in the air above a raft of sharpened spikes.

Argyle had always been light on his feet, he thought of the bottom level of the par course as an extension of his cable-strewn office.

The top level looked like an indoor track with difficulties to be avoided, the worst of which were trap doors that would suddenly open underfoot, plummeting the unsuspecting henchman into a series of chutes, delivering him into the inescapable depths of the premier showcase of Sublevel Three… the Shark Tank.

Barry loved his shark tank with all the dead men's bones that littered the sandy bottom interspersed with piles of rocks and bits of seaweed.

The tank itself was huge. It stood almost forty-five feet tall, was sixty-five feet long, thirty-three feet wide and held a nifty 396,000 gallons of sea water. It took up all of the space of Sublevel Three's huge great room that wasn't occupied by the par course that ran around it. As henchmen made their way through the course, they had unobstructed views of the six enormous Great White Sharks that constantly circled the thick plexiglass walls of their domain. Barry had an observation bubble installed in the middle of the floor and could raise himself up by way of a hydraulic lift plate so that it seemed as if he were standing in the tank among his sharks.

The first time that Argyle had seen Barry "standing" in the tank, it really freaked him out. He had been running the bottom par course and had been making good time when a shark, moving slowly past the plexiglass wall, had suddenly flipped its tail. This startled Argyle into looking into the tank, where he saw Barry "standing", a hideous grin on his pale drawn face and waving his arms around in what appeared to be delight. Argyle stood motionless with weird gaping noises emanating from his throat until another henchman slapped him on the back, forcing a normal breath and, as Argyle sat sputtering, explained about the lift plate.

Now Argyle is so used to the sharks and the occasional "Barry sighting" that he barely notices either anymore. Today, however, will be different. Today he has a new guy, Gilbert the Third, to train.

Ben had propelled Gilbert forward, steering him toward the tank. Gilbert's eyes were as wide as saucers and as he started losing his nerve he also started to drag his feet. The closer he stepped, the more it seemed that his feet were sticking to tar.

Ben said, "We've all done this before. See," holding up his hands, "I still have all my fingers!"

Gilbert stuttered as he tried to speak but all he could manage was a high-pitched squeak, followed by loud uncontrollable hiccups, all the while following the sharks with dilated pupils.

Argyle strode over holding a snorkel and a heavy supply of three-strand nylon rope he had just retrieved from a supply room. "Here, Third, put this on." Thrusting the snorkel at him.

Gilbert reached for it but couldn't do much other than stand there holding it out at the end of the stiff sponge sleeve.

Argyle tossed Ben a look and said, "Better help him with that."

Ben tried to fit the snorkel onto Gilbert's head but found that the large sponge helmet prevented an easy fit. Ben said, "I know." And disappeared down the hallway. He was back within seconds, holding a roll of duct tape and then got busy fitting the snorkel to Gilbert's sponge-head.

Meanwhile, Argyle was tying the nylon rope around Gilbert's bulbous sponge body – under his arms, across his back, down around his stiff sponge legs, all the while giving Gilbert instructions.

"First, you use the snorkel to gulp down a bunch of air, be quick 'cuz those sponges are gonna soak up a lot of water and you'll begin to sink."

Gilbert mumbled, "Uh-huh," through the snorkel's mouthpiece.

Ben had gotten the mouthpiece fitted into Gilbert's mouth but the goggles sat sideways and the air tube poked straight out instead of up, making Gilbert look like a manatee sucking on a giant lolly pop.

Both he and Argyle started laughing and Ben said, "I can fix this." And got busy with more duct tape.

Argyle continued, "We'll lower you down using this." And held the rope in front of Gilbert's eyes.

Gilbert mumbled, "Uh-Huh."

Argyle then said, "Ben and I will pull you back up and you take another breath of air before we move you to the next spot where you'll sink… like a wet sponge."

Ben, positioning himself in front of Gilbert and looking through the goggles at him said, "And don't forget to wave those sponges around. Remember, you're in there to clean the glass, not have a nice time!"

"Okay, let's do this!" Ben stood in front of Gilbert and motioned him forward until Gilbert was next to a sturdy lift table. He almost toppled over when Argyle and Ben maneuvered him onto the table and started to crank it upward, all the time calling out encouragement to Gilbert.

"You can do it!"

"Thrasher likes the tank walls nice and clean."

"Steady now."

"Almost there."

"The sharks are tame as puppies!"

Argyle poked Ben in the arm and said, "What'd ya tell him that for? It's not true."

Ben shrugged and looked embarrassed and said, "I don't know. It seemed like a good thing to say and then it just came out."

They finally got Gilbert into the tank and managed to clean one whole side before Gilbert seemed to stop panicking and settle into a rough routine of gulping air and whipping his arms and legs around at random.

Argyle and Ben spent the time raising Gilbert up, letting him sink and talking about work-related things until the routine of the task lulled them into a sense of dullness and they failed to notice that the sharks seemed to be taking an interest in the giant flailing sponge and had started circling closer and closer.

Gilbert's only view was through the plexiglass looking at Ben and Argyle flex their biceps and triceps as they worked the rope up and down. This went on and on and on until it seemed to Gilbert that it would never end, when all of a sudden he noticed that he had come to a stop halfway up to his next gulp of air.

Argyle and Ben had stopped pulling on the rope and were staring dumbly into the tank. Gilbert was straining to see through the distortion of his goggles and the dull thickness of the plexiglass tank walls and his heart almost stopped at what he saw came into view. It was a reflection of a shark that had come very close to him. The shark had slowed down its glide and had one of its beady black eyes locked onto Gilbert's sponge covered bottom.

Panic and fear gripped Gilbert and he screamed through his air tube. What bubbled out to the water's surface was one garbled word… "HELP!"

This spurred Argyle to yell, "Pull!" and Ben to snap out of his stare and help Argyle yank the struggling Gilbert to the top of the tank, just a split second after the shark lunged at Gilbert's behind and tore off a chunk of sponge that it then began to whip around in a frenzy.

Gilbert was hauled, gulping air and coughing up seawater, out of the tank and onto the lift table. Argyle was looking closely at the area that the shark had ripped out and at the sight of it, raised his eyebrows and said, with an accusatory tone, "Better hope that The Thrasher doesn't find out you wrecked his best tank cleaning suit."

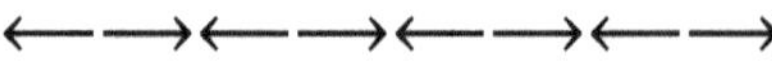

After patching the sponge suit with a spare mop head and some duct tape, Gilbert was lowered back into the tank to continue until all the plexiglass had been cleaned. Just the way Barry likes it.

With Gilbert standing over a metal grate, draining his sponges, Argyle glanced at his watch and announced that it was time for lunch.

"Ben. You go ahead. I'll help Third and we'll meet up in the office."

Ben gave a little salute and said, "Right. See you in fifteen," and hopped onto the next elevator up to the break room.

Argyle stood with his arms akimbo in front of Gilbert, who was trying to squeeze out the sponges by flexing his arms and doing squats and said, "Looks like you're about done, let's get you up to the locker room and changed. When you're finished, you can meet me and Ben in the office."

Fifteen minutes later, Gilbert, who was now dry and dressed in his jumpsuit, joined Argyle in the office. Gilbert asked, as he approached his desk, "Where's Ben?"

At that moment, as if in answer to Gilbert's question, Ben stepped through the doorway from the hall. "Here I am."

Argyle and Gilbert turned and saw Ben walking toward them. He was wearing a tight bright red body suit that had a Thrasher logo on the chest and a long bright yellow satin cape that billowed out behind him as he walked. He was wearing red high-top crime boots tied with black laces and as he strode across the office, the sound of small jingle bells could be heard. He was carrying a mask with fake lenses that made his eyes appear gigantic.

Argyle was so jealous! Ben was dressed for a caper! It was all he could do to sputter out, "Where you going?"

Ben started to catch Argyle up on what had happened. "I got back to the office and found a note," and waved his arm at his desk. "Hey! Where's my chair?"

Gilbert had been sitting quietly listening to Ben and when Ben looked at him with a questioning look, eying the chair Gilbert was sitting in, Gilbert responded with a little shrug and an innocent I-don't-know look as he shook his head back and forth.

Ben continued, "Well. I found a note from Barry on my desk. I guess Alexey put it there while we were downstairs cleaning the tank. I'm just on my way out. Barry needs me to get him some lunch. He wants an Asian noodle bowl from that roach coach that's always parked over on 2nd street."

Ben had taken a couple of steps around his desk looking for his chair, which set the bells tinkling.

Argyle wrinkled up his face and said, "Nice touch… they'll track your every step."

Ben, resigned to the addition of the bells to his crime boots, said, "Yea. Barry thinks it'll help me run faster and get his lunch back here still hot."

The three of them just looked from one to the other for a second and just as Ben turned to leave, the P.A. system crackled to life and all henchmen froze with rapt attention…

⚡ ⚡ Attention. Attention! (Pause) *Is this thing on? Dreams. Dreams can be all wavy and out of focus. Sometimes mushrooms run faster than chickens. It only goes to show that racing chickens, well, you could end up a capon that won't go through the sieve! That way is only heartbreak. And it's been my dream, since my childhood, to win the Nobel Prize for Crime because I do it so well. Better than that stuffy old crime lord* (Barry's voice is rising) *Professor Meglamon... who thinks he's so clever! He's a fraud!* (Calmer now...) *I'm the super evil genius. Me. Since I was a child I have also dreamed of trophies; big shiny ones with little statues of me...* (Barry's yelling now but enunciating very clearly) *...on top ...looking down at all those who laughed at me! They will be sorry. As sorry as a capon in a sieve! NOW GET BACK TO WORK!! ⚡ ⚡*

The three had been quite still, listening to The Thrasher's insightful litany, and when it was over, the P.A. system crackled itself into silence. Ben shrugged and turned to leave, and Argyle waved Gilbert to follow him to the break room vending machines for lunch.

Chapter Five

Back to Sublevel Three

Argyle (yes, still like the sock) had eaten his vending machine egg salad sandwich in complete silence as he had been deep in thought about missing out on two capers so far this week. *I could have gotten Barry's lunch for him. Wonder why he didn't send me? Maybe he's saving me for something big. That's it! I'll be going out on a really big caper and the boss wants me to be fully charged and ready. Better eat a power bar just in case.*

Argyle pushed his chair away from his desk and wadded up the used wrapper from his sandwich. As he stood up, he glanced in Gilbert's direction and noted that he was hard-gulping a bite of his vending machine bologna and Swiss sandwich and was making to jump up. Argyle waved him down and said, "I'll be right back," and slowly picked his footing around the floor cables and headed to the break room.

Argyle found himself standing in front of the long line of vending machines that populated the break room. He appeared to be mesmerized by the bright fluorescent lights backing the products and blinking their "buy me" messages. His mind was not on power bars. His mind was busy trying to think of how to impress Barry enough so that he, Argyle, would be sent on capers.

He had no idea how long he had been standing there blankly staring at power bars when a sudden voice made him jump.

"Hey buddy. Having trouble deciding between the Carob Celery bar and the Malted Broccoli Surprise bar?"

It was Ben back from the caper and now dressed in his white jumpsuit.

Argyle said, "Nah, gonna pass on the power bars. How 'bout you?

Have you had lunch yet?"

Ben had been peering into one of the vending machines and turned to Argyle and answered, "Yea. I grabbed a dozen pork pot stickers along with Barry's soup and munched 'em down on the way back. I'm good."

Argyle nodded and said, "Okay, then let's get back to work," and stepped into the hallway back to the office.

Gilbert was just finishing up his box of chocolate milk and was making air rushing sucking sounds through his straw as Ben and Argyle reached their desks. Ben noticed that his chair was still missing and waved Gilbert out of his chair and took it, rolling it over to his desk leaving Gilbert to stand.

Addressing Argyle, Gilbert said, "One of the guys was here and said to tell you that you should call Miss Q."

Argyle asked, "Which guy?" He could feel the excitement starting to build. Was this a caper?

Gilbert looked around the large office area and pointed to a hench-man, who had tripped over a twist of cables and was currently trying to yank his leg free. Argyle looked and noticed that it was only Alexey. He never brought caper news. Argyle also noticed that one of the cam-eras had stopped, no doubt attracted to Alexey's futile struggle, clicked down through three zoom positions and seemed to be "watching" with interest.

Argyle flipped the handset off the desk phone and pressed the num-bers for Miss Q's extension. After a brief one-sided conversation, Ar-gyle hung up and announced to Ben and Gilbert that they had a job and it would be a perfect opportunity for more new guy training. Their as-signment is… assembling the new Torture Table.

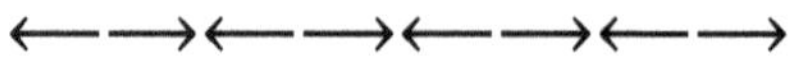

There were fifteen cardboard boxes, some long, some tall, some wide, and some small. They had been delivered under cover of darkness and were stacked up in the hallway in front of one of the larger rooms in Sublevel Three.

Gilbert followed Argyle and Ben off of the elevator and into the great room that housed the par course and the shark tank. As Argyle led the group around to the left, headed to the back hallway, Gilbert, against his will, glanced at the shark tank and gave an involuntary shudder at the sight of a Great White gliding along the glass. Was that shark looking at him? Could it be possible it recognized him? Gilbert looked quickly away and picked up his pace, putting Ben between himself and the tank.

Argyle had taken a few steps down the dimly lit hallway but had stopped to look at a new torture device displayed on the wall. Gilbert, scooting along too closely behind, bumped straight into Argyle's side almost knocking him over.

"Oh. Sorry. I was thinking about sharks."

Laughing at Gilbert's clumsiness, Ben said, "And I'm sure they're thinking about you, too!"

Argyle pointed to the device that was on display and asked Gilbert if he could identify it.

Gilbert leaned in closer to it and after a moment or two said, "Nope. Don't have a clue. What is it?"

Argyle, continuing down the hallway said, "We don't know what it is. We were hoping you could tell us."

Halfway down the hallway, Argyle stopped in front of a double wide heavy looking set of metal doors. He pulled a large key ring out of one of the cargo pockets on his jumpsuit pant legs and fumbled through the assortment of keys that crowded the ring. After unsuccessfully trying several of the keys, he finally heard the heavy lock snap open. Then he put his shoulder against the door and pushed.

Gilbert stood transfixed as the door's rusty hinges ground open. The room beyond was dark and a musty odor wafted out through the widening crack in the doorway.

Ben nudged Gilbert by poking him in the back, meaning to get his attention, but it startled Gilbert and he let out a stifled little screech. He jumped around looking at Ben, his eyes huge and dilated.

Ben gave Gilbert a wide toothy smile and said, "Grab some boxes, and let's go."

Argyle disappeared into the darkness and after banging his shin on something and kicking something else, stumbled to the breaker panel and flipped the light switches on.

Huge halogen ceiling lights blazed to life illuminating the

cavernous room.

Gilbert blinked his eyes to adjust them to the sudden brightness and as he started to focus, he slowly became more amazed and a bit afraid of what he saw.

The room was about one third the size of the great room but had the same tall ceiling. The room itself appeared to be hewn out of rock even though the floor and most of the wall height was smooth and even. Everything smelled of mold and algae and Gilbert was sure he heard the sound of water dripping, somewhere off in the distance.

The room was divided into sections of a sort, by the installation of various devices and the space that each one needed for operation. There was a rack down at the far end. Gilbert knew what it was, he had seen one in an old movie he had watched on late night TV about a year ago. The screams from the racked man frightened him so badly he snapped the TV off and pulled the covers over his head.

Next to the rack stood a large… thing… made of planks of wood and metal straps. It was bolted together and slightly rusted and here and there it had been repaired with duct tape. It wasn't too obvious as to what it would be used for, but just looking at it made Gilbert's skin crawl.

Many curious looking devices stood here and there around the room. Some were familiar, like the Iron Maiden that was also patched with duct tape. Other not so familiar devices crowded the remaining space. There was an overstuffed chair that had red and blue wires dangling out of it and was plugged into a 220v outlet. Gilbert let his mind ponder its use but decided that maybe he didn't want to really know how it worked.

Argyle was standing, looking at one sizable space off to the right in a back corner and contemplating the area. "I believe that this spot will do fine. Third!" Gilbert jumped at the sharp sound of his name. "Clear all these rags and hand tools into a pile against the wall, then help bring more boxes in."

Thirty minutes later, the space had been cleared. Gilbert found an old broom lying on the floor next to a torture device a few feet away and swept their work area clear of cobwebs and bits of dusty rags that appeared to be caked with dried blood.

All fifteen of the boxes had been brought in and unpacked, their gleaming shiny metal contents and plastic bags of bolts, screws and finishing nails laid out in nice even rows.

Ben had the assembly instructions and was squinting at the small print and making faces at the diagrams trying to make sense of it. If it weren't for the picture of the completed unit on page one, he might never have been able to guess what it was.

Argyle turned to Gilbert and slapping his hand down to rest on Gilbert's shoulder, said, "So, Third. You mentioned on your résumé that you've had a bit of technical experience. In fact, you're a bit of a nerd, right?" Argyle gave one of his big smiles and nodded encouragement, waiting for Gilbert to answer.

Gilbert, thinking to brag a bit about his experience and to maybe make himself out to be more worthy in the eyes of Argyle and Ben, said, "Yes. I have extensive experience with computers. I used to rebuild them in my bedroom after everyone else was asleep. Once, I made my voice come out of a tiny speaker I hid in my little brother's pillow, it scared him pretty good. I laughed about that for days." Gilbert looked from Argyle to Ben and back and noticed that both men were grinning at him. It made him terribly uncomfortable, so he quickly added, "But I shot a gun once!" At which, Argyle busted out laughing.

"Well, Third, old buddy. Here's what's gonna happen. You are going to assemble this torture table and we're going to time you with this stopwatch." Argyle had retrieved a nice looking stopwatch from one of the billowy cargo pants pockets of his jumpsuit and was holding it in Gilbert's face and making it spin in circles by twisting its chain between his fingers.

Continuing, Argyle said, "Barry likes his henchmen to be fast. When he says 'go', he expects everyone to go… fast. Really fast."

With his hand still resting on Gilbert's shoulder, Argyle dug his thumb into Gilbert's soft flesh, just a bit, smiled, arched his eyebrows up into a look of joy and shouted, "NOW!"

When Argyle shouted, Gilbert had jumped as if electricity shot through his body momentarily freezing him to the spot where he stood. A split-second later, his own mind shouted one word: move! In an adrenalin-fueled panic, Gilbert looked about him at all the parts and stepped this way and that way among the displays of shiny pieces and bags of bolts as if he were stepping through a minefield.

Suddenly it occurred to him, R. T. F. M. Read The Freaking Manual. Gilbert, his fear already to the point of tears, his eyes wide and darting all over the piles of parts, lit on the sheaf of papers in Ben's hand and made a mad grab for them. Gilbert was barely aware of Ben's laughter as he snatched at the papers, tearing the front two pages with the effort.

Gilbert thought, *Oh no. The picture of the table is torn. I hope that's okay.* But his eyes and his mind had both raced on to page one, an inventory of the parts and the tools needed. He looked up at Argyle, his face falling into a downcast shadow and noticed that Argyle was smiling and pointing at something. Following the direction of Argyle's finger, Gilbert saw what he needed: a pile of tools tossed against the wall. In spite of the fact that some were rusty and some were chipped, Gilbert was elated and eagerly threw himself into the pile. It took precious minutes to sift through the tools and produce at least some of what he needed to start work.

Barry wants his henchmen fast.

The words almost burned as they came back to haunt Gilbert over the next hour.

Meanwhile, Argyle and Ben had made themselves comfortable and were lounging on various pieces of equipment. Argyle was sitting in a torture chair with one leg slung over the chair arm and his back wedged up against a metal plate that was designed to carry an electrical charge and that was bolted across the chair's back. He was examining his stopwatch and wiping some smutz off the chain.

Ben found a bench and had wiped it off so that it was clean enough to sit on. He was lounged against the wall with his legs splayed out in front of him, picking at his fingernails.

The two men were talking.

"I heard that there's a big caper on for graveyard tonight."

Argyle furrowed his brow and said, "Oh yea. Where'd ya hear that?"

Ben stopped chewing on a hangnail long enough to say, "Heard it from Anderson in the break room, this morning. It's hush-hush but it might be a big one."

Argyle had slipped his index finger through a ring at the end of the stopwatch chain and was twirling the watch around in a half arc and catching it in flight. Deep in thought, Argyle repeated the action four more times before he said, "Wonder if there'll be any shooting."

Ben said, "Better yet, wonder what caperware they'll have."

The two men fell silent, each to their own thoughts.

Gilbert had been working steadily for an hour, if you can call moving parts and tools around, working. Although he had worked up a good sweat, Gilbert had only managed to sort the pieces and parts into loose groups and was now clearing a space where the eventual table would stand. He had been sputtering and making winded sounds as he lifted heavy sheets of stainless steel and dragged rolls of thick cable to this place or that.

Argyle caught the stopwatch on one of its flying arcs and checked its face. "One hour, Third. You've been at this for one hour."

Gilbert jumped at the sound of Argyle's voice and immediately went into panic mode, accelerating his actions into an almost comical dance-like movement.

Argyle and Ben looked on in almost a trance; Gilbert's actions were fast and furious, punctuated with grunts and puffs that were periodically interrupted by furtive glances at the instruction manual.

Ben was the first to shake it off. "I'm gonna go get a juice box. Want anything?"

"Yea. Maybe a water. Better bring one for Third, too."

Two more hours passed and Gilbert was feeling pretty good about what he had accomplished. There were several tasks left to do but the table was up on its legs and some of the apparatus had been added. It was starting to look pretty darn good.

Gilbert relaxed enough to let his mind wander. As he looked at his work, he wondered what the space helmet looking thing did and took special note of the metal wristbands with the optional 120v sockets, thinking that they would probably hurt… a lot.

Argyle called out, "Third! It's 4PM. Step it up!"

Gilbert looked up from his work, smiled with a confident ease and gave Argyle the thumbs up. Changing out the drill he had just finished using for a pair of pliers, Gilbert went back to work.

Ben was sitting on his bench watching the activities, which at first had intrigued him. Now, however, since the work had gone from Gilbert struggling to Gilbert thinking, Ben had lost interest. He had tried fighting the drowsiness that was upon him but after a minute gave up and stretched out on the bench. Within moments Ben was asleep and emitting hushed little snoring noises.

By 5PM Gilbert had all the major components of the torture table assembled and was finishing up work on the master control board. This part was a bit tricky. Gilbert had to make sure that the wiring for the unit was correctly routed through their circuits into the wireless control pad. Otherwise, it wouldn't work and that would probably make Barry angry. And no one wanted that!

Argyle was playing with a spider he had caught as it dropped down from the ceiling. He was teasing it by letting it touch down on two of its eight legs then lifting it up by its web so that it had to spin more to drop down again. He wondered how much web was actually in a spider and would the little critter eventually run out of it.

Just then, Ben's leg muscle twitched, sending him sprawling onto the floor and waking him in a shock. "Wha… wha… where am I?"

Gilbert had just plugged the torture table into a nearby outlet and stood back with pride and in wonderment as the gleaming apparatus sprang to life with beeps and brightly blinking lights.

The state-of-the-art torture table and most of its components were made of high-test stainless steel. The bed was six inches thick and housed a complicated network of circuits, wires, and switches. Along the sides there were metal straps that would clamp down to secure wrists and ankles and at the head of the table hung a helmet that could be strapped onto someone's head. The helmet would send data to a magnificent array of displays on the control pad. It could show electrical activity along the scalp, voltage fluctuations, neuron disruptions and a bunch of other things. All very handy when several of the table's functions are operating at the same time. Don't want brain death to occur before the victim talks!

A weird globe sort of device was mounted at the foot of the table. It looked like a little disco ball light, although when activated it did not give off soft colored lights. To the contrary, it shot out laser beams in any of six preprogrammed patterns, slicing the victim like a big pastrami.

After these two features, all the other standard apparatus that included electrodes and pulse generators were secondary.

Gilbert clapped his hands in delight and said, "It works!" More in surprise than by a declaration of fact.

Argyle stepped up and clapped Gilbert on the back. "Nice work, Third. It only took four- and one-half hours but there's one more thing."

Gilbert turned to look at Argyle. The look on Gilbert's face was slowly changing from pride to confusion.

"We've got to test it."

Ben, standing on Gilbert's right, grasped his arm and said, "Come on, buddy. Up you go!"

Gilbert immediately started struggling and mewing, "Come on guys. You're kidding, right?" as Argyle and Ben lifted him up and wrestled him onto the table. Argyle pushed one hand against Gilbert's chest, holding him down.

Gilbert was flailing his arms and legs in a futile attempt to free himself and jump off the tabletop. His main thought was to flee but he was unsure of where to go. Maybe he could hide in the locker room.

Ben started laughing and said, "He looks like a big ol' bug on its back!" And after Argyle agreed, Ben strapped Gilbert's right arm and leg to the table.

Argyle let up on his grip and strapped Gilbert's other arm and leg and then stood back to gaze down at Gilbert's unsettled face.

"It's a joke, right?" Gilbert whimpered, looking pleadingly from Argyle to Ben and back.

Argyle said, "It won't be a joke if the table doesn't work when Barry wants it to."

Ben started poking Gilbert under his arms and in his ribs tickling him and making him laugh. "Stop that! HAHA! Stop! Ahhh!!"

After another poke or two, Ben said, "See. This could be fun. Relax!"

Argyle picked up the control pad and was admiring the design.

"Wireless." Tipping it so Ben could get a look.

In their fascination with the gadget, the two guys lost themselves in discovery.

"What's this button do?" Ben reached across and touched the screen and a coiled red cable attached to a headband that Argyle had hastily slipped onto Gilbert's brow, flashed a red light and sent a zap of electricity into Gilbert.

Gilbert gritted his teeth and when the zap was over, cried out, "Hey! That hurt!"

The guys had fun for another five minutes, pushing buttons and watching Gilbert jump and twitch.

Argyle nodded with satisfaction and smiled and said, "What about this one labeled Laser?" And touched the screen button that immediately activated the bizarre array of lights that swished this way and arced that way.

Gilbert was beside himself with fear. He was crying and struggling against his restraints. When the lasers danced close to him, he shrieked, "AAHHH! That's not funny! I'm not kidding! Get me outta this!"

One of the laser beams started to cut through Gilbert's jumpsuit just above his ankle, sending a stream of smoke that smelled of a burnt cotton polyester blend upward. Argyle touched the stop button, and the laser unit terminated its deadly track. Smiling like a proud parent, Argyle said, "The Thrasher is gonna love this!"

It took about thirty minutes to clean up the torture table area, leaving it ready for Barry's inspection and for the trio to make their way back to their desks.

Argyle dialed Miss Q's extension and on the fifth ring, she picked it up.

"The Thrasher's office. How may I help you?"

Argyle, using his sweet voice tone said, "This is Argyle Stevens… S…T…E…V…E…N…S. I'd like to speak to Thrasher, please."

Miss Q replied, "I'm sorry but The Thrasher isn't taking calls right now. May I take a message?"

A bit dejected at the news that he wouldn't be able to personally speak with The Thrasher, Argyle said, "Please tell Thrasher that his brand-new torture table is ready for his immediate use."

Argyle could faintly hear Miss Q scribbling a note, and then she spoke, "Oh! The Thrasher will be so pleased. He's been looking forward to this all day. Is there anything else, Mr. Stevens?"

Having replied "no", Argyle said "goodbye" and hung up. He sat for a minute, looking at Ben and Gilbert, who were both looking back at him with expressions of expectation, although Gilbert's look was mixed with guarded mistrust.

Suddenly the P.A. system came alive with a hiss and a loud static crackle that made everyone jump, but all that could be heard was static and the mumblings of The Thrasher who was really angry at the technician responsible for making sure the P.A. system worked as expected. Suddenly two shots rang out and there was silence for a moment. A short time later, the P.A. sounded, much clearer this time…

Attention. Attention! All henchmen! (tap, tap, tap… this thing better be on*!) I've called you all together today to talk about the future of Thrasher Enterprises. Now, many of you have come to appreciate my abilities as a master of mechanics as I have steadfastly brought forth many wonderful torture devices, some of which are on display around the lair.* (Two of the cameras started zooming in on henchmen faces and in turn, the spotlit henchmen immediately looked at the wall-mounted torture device closest to them and smiled and nodded approvingly.) *Some, close to me, have a deep and abiding respect for my business acumen as over the years I have continually honed my skills in crime management.* (Clapping can be heard in the background…) *Thank you Miss Q, as usual your timing is impeccable! To continue. This leads me to my point. I believe the future of Thrasher Enterprises lays in the creation and use of a robot army of super henchmen! I can see it now… an unstoppable army of robots to do my bidding,* (Barry's voice rose in intensity and volume…) *…to cater to my every whim. I can see them swarming over the city, squashing Professor Meglamon right out of business… forever!* (Calmer now…) *I ask you: what could be better than that? Thank* *you. You're dismissed.*

When Barry's voice faded and the static crackling of the P.A. system fell silent, everyone sat in shocked silence for a minute then resumed what they were doing.

Smacking his palms down on his desktop, Argyle said, "We're on unpaid overtime now. Let's say we go get a drink?"

Chapter Six

Boys Night Out

It was shortly after seven that evening when the boys entered McClusky's Eight Ball, a dark little dive bar that was tucked into a short dark alley over on 9th street. The only thing marking the entrance was a flashing neon sign of an 8-ball dropping onto a rat… squishing it over and over again. The place was a favorite with Thrasher's crowd, so it was like Old Home Week when Argyle (again, like the sock), Ben and Gilbert piled in through the heavy wooden front door.

Finding three seats at the bar, with Argyle taking the seat in the middle, they ordered up.

The bartender on duty tonight, Max, a grizzled old man with a plastic hip and a patch over his left eye, nodded a greeting to Argyle and said, "A vodka martini, right?"

"That's right, thanks," said Argyle as he reached for the small bowl of complimentary pretzels.

"What'll you have this time, Ben?"

Ben thought for a second and then answered, "I've always wanted to try a Long Island Ice Tea. I've heard there's no tea in it."

Max said, "There's no tea on my watch!" Then, leaning forward on his elbow, Max stared at Gilbert with his beady right eye and said, "What are you drinkin' tonight?"

Gilbert was transfixed by the staring eye and had to shake himself out of it before he answered, "A Shirley Temple. Heavy on the Temple… two cherries."

Max continued to stare for another ten seconds and completely unnerved Gilbert. Max, his lips parting into a wide, rotten-toothed smile said, "Is that so." Pausing. "Comin' right up!"

After Max set their drinks in front of them and moved down the bar to other patrons, Argyle, Ben and Gilbert sat quietly for a minute. Argyle spoke first.

"What a day. I didn't get to go on one caper. You're lucky, Ben. You saw some lunchtime action."

Ben said, "Yea. It was a real eat-and-run kind of thing."

Argyle asked, "And what about the big caper that's on for tonight? What do you know about it?"

"Heard it from Anderson as he was leaving this morning. He said he had to get a lot of sleep cuz night shift was going to be out on… a big one… as he called it. Don't know anything else though," Ben answered.

After another moment of silence, Ben asked Argyle, "Are we going to get dental coverage this year? I have a molar that's starting to bug me."

Argyle said, "No one's talking about dental but there's a rumor that everyone might get a Christmas bonus. Geeze, I hope it's not another coupon for dry cleaning."

"Yea, me too," Ben added. "I tried to cash the last one in, but the dry cleaner said the coupon was only worth .01 cents… of credit!"

"So, what do you think about Barry's announcement?" said Argyle.

"The robot army?" said Ben. "I don't know. What do you think, Third?"

Gilbert tried to put a positive spin on things and said, "It could be a good thing. All those robots doing our bidding. Plus, you can't kill a robot. Nothing can kill those suckers!"

"Yeah," Ben added, "while they're shooting at the robots, we're out there getting the loot, safe as anything."

"Don't you see what's happening here?" Argyle interjected. "Those robots are gonna *take our jobs!*"

"You mean, like, outsourced? Barry would never do that. He needs us."

"What for? With a robot army, you don't have to pay them or feed them or provide health care or a 401K," said Argyle.

"Hell, we don't get those things now anyway!" Ben responded.

"It's coming. It's coming," said Argyle, shaking his head in a mixture of disgust and doubt.

Gilbert thought about it for a moment and said, "But still,

somebody is going to have to maintain the robots, right? That could be us."

"I don't want to be a freaking IT guy. I want to fire my guns!" Argyle was starting to get a little depressed, but he snapped out of it very quickly. What choice did he have? His future with the Thrasher Organization was assured, he thought, and besides, it would be a long time before Barry could assemble a robot army. That could be years into the future, and by that time Argyle would surely be the number two man in the organization.

The trio sank back into a subdued quiet. After a time, Argyle caught Max's one good eye and hand signaled that they were ready for another round.

"You're paying for this one, Ben. Gilbert gets the next one," said Argyle.

Ben leaned forward to look past Argyle at Gilbert and said, "Third! You missed a good caper two months ago. Thrasher robbed an armored car right near here on 15th Street, comin' out of the Big East Bank. Remember that one, Argyle?"

Argyle, smiling at the memory, said, "Yea. That was a good one. I almost got to shoot my gun." He took a sip of his fresh martini and smiled again at the thought of shooting guns, then said, "Thrasher wasn't too happy, though. The armored car had just dropped off the loot and was empty. He pitched a fit and then robbed the driver, who only had $21 in his wallet and 15 cents in his pocket."

Ben, snickering, said to Gilbert, "You should have been there, it was funny!" Then continued, "How 'bout that time we hit that warehouse and made off with five hundred gallons of methylantiracine? You got to shoot your gun that time, Argyle."

Argyle stared at the bloated stuffed green olive settled at the bottom of a few sips of vodka, put his glass down and said, "Well, sort of. A rat came flying out from behind the barrel, spooked me and I had an automatic reaction. I shot it. I shot a rat. Doesn't count."

"Oh yes it does!"

Gilbert asked both the guys, "What's methyl-anti-racing?"

Ben looked pensive and Argyle shrugged his shoulders and said, "We don't know." Then snapped his fingers and addressing Ben, asked, "Remember that really big caper last year, the one where we raided

Meglamon's hideout, except it wasn't?"

Ben looked off into the distance and smiled in recollection of the event. "I remember the caperware. We were all dressed in black, like ninjas and each wore a huge Thrasher logo on our chest. The eyes lit up. Man, it was neat."

Argyle smiled, sipped his martini and said, "Thrasher thought Meglamon would cry like a little girl when he saw dozens of Thrashers comin' at him. And it would have been something to see had we gone to the right address."

Gilbert followed the story with rapt attention but couldn't help blurting out, "I remember that! I was watching the news when it came on that The Thrasher had struck again!" But quickly added, "Then what happened?"

Argyle, resignation reflected on his face said, "Well… Thrasher was pretty pissed off. He thought he would be getting rid of Meglamon once and for all. He was shouting and stomping his feet and then shot the three guys who were standing closest to him."

"Donuts in the break room!" Ben raised his empty glass and started laughing. "Anyone else got the munchies?" And sliding off his bar stool, made his way to the loo.

Gilbert waved the bartender over and politely asked for another round and more pretzels. Max, just for fun, glared at Gilbert with his beady eye until Gilbert squirmed, then said, "Ok. Comin' right up!"

Argyle got up and made his way to the jukebox, dropped a bunch of coins in the slot and punched a series of buttons. The jukebox sprang to life. The rack of 45s spun slowly around, and the mechanical arm plucked one out of its slot and placed it on the spinning turntable. By the time Argyle sat back down, Blue Moon by The Marcels had started up.

Ben returned to his seat and tipped his glass to his lips, emptying the last few drops but causing the ice cubes to crash against his face. Setting the glass down, he casually looked around the bar and spotted Milford sitting with a babe in the back booth. When Milford raised his own glass in salute, Ben smiled and did the same in return.

The babe sitting with her back to Ben, turned to see what Milford was looking at. Ben noticed that it was Ruthie, a girl he had dated once. His face lit up with a smile.

Recognition came to Ruthie, who scrunched up her face and pinched her nose with two fingers, then mimed the words, "Pee Yew" and turned her back to Ben. She whispered something to Milford and they both laughed.

Ben turned back to his glass of ice cubes to brood.

Gilbert spoke to Argyle, "When will I get to go on a caper?"

Argyle snorted air out through his nose and said, "Eventually. After your training and probation period."

Ben leaned forward and looked at Gilbert, "Hey, Third. What do you do for fun? Got a girlfriend?"

Max, his plastic hip aching, limped over with the next round of drinks. "That's three Long Islands, Ben. You're officially cut off. Argyle, you've got another four and you're done. And you, new guy, the sky's the limit for you and Shirley! HA HA HA!"

Gilbert was a little embarrassed but smiled as he tried to look in control. He lifted the maraschino cherry out of the drink and snapped it off the stem in one decisive movement. As he savored the syrupy cherry taste, he started to answer Ben, "I don't have a girlfriend." Then quickly added, "Yet!" He chewed the cherry until it was paste then swallowed it with an audible gulp. "How 'bout you, Ben. Have a steady girl?"

Argyle answered before Ben could, "Nope. Just a long line of first dates!"

Ben shrugged, "What can I say? They take one look at my boat and start making excuses." Ben was definitely getting high from three Long Island Ice Teas and slurred the word "excuses" into something sounding like "eek-shoe-sis".

Max had heard the slurring and turned to look at Ben. Pointing one finger at his good eye then turning his hand toward Ben, pointing two fingers, gave Ben the clear signal that he was being watched.

Ben just smiled and nodded. He turned to Gilbert and said, "Maybe we can double date sometime." Tapping Argyle's arm, Ben said, "No, wait! We should triple date with you and Audrey. Right?"

"Wrong!" Argyle continued, "Audrey doesn't like couples dating. She thinks it makes everyone fake it like they're having fun when they're not. So, that's out."

Another song came on the jukebox. This one was The Lion Sleeps

Tonight by The Tokens and at least half the bar crowd was singing along. Most of them off key.

Gilbert was bopping his head, enjoying himself. He turned to Argyle and said, "I love this tune. It's so retro." Then made sucking sounds through his straw.

Argyle, his brows furrowed, just looked at Gilbert and wondered if he would ever make a good henchman or if he was only good for… more donuts.

Over the loud, out of tune singing, Ben asked Gilbert what he did for fun since he didn't have any girls to mess around with.

Gilbert, trying to be heard over the din, yelled, "I collect vintage explosive devices. I'm really into WWII land mines right now!"

Both Ben and Argyle, taken aback by Gilbert's statement, stared at him in disbelief.

Argyle settled his racing mind then said, "I wouldn't have thought you had it in you, Third." He clapped Gilbert on the back and gave a hearty laugh then sat back and slapped Ben on the back with his other hand. "There's hope for our little trainee, yet!"

Ben nearly toppled forward. He was holding his drink and the force of Argyle's slap spilled a few drops of it onto the bar. Ben occupied himself with trying to recover it and was, for the most part too loaded to add anything of substance to the conversation.

Gilbert was beside himself with joy. There was hope for him!

It was now a few minutes to eleven. The Jukebox was silent and the crowd had thinned down to four hardened alcoholics and one floozy. The alcoholics were grouped at the other end of the bar discussing some non-event and the floozy was asking a passed out drunk in the back booth for a ride home.

Argyle finished off his fourth martini, popped the last green olive into his mouth and said, "Time to go home. Tomorrow's another day with another dollar… or another donut."

Chapter Seven

A Professor Is Made

The Professor's claim to contemporary fame is legendary. He planned and executed a most brilliant caper: he robbed a government train carrying 75.5 million in gold bullion, 3.2 million in securities, and 15.0 million in newly printed five-dollar bills. For the most part, he did it without the government knowing and was far, far away before it was noticed. The only reason the Professor's name has been linked to the crime is that he, himself, brags about it. He's so enthralled with himself, he can't help talking about it with whomever will listen.

It wasn't always so. He was born Meglamon Bizarro and when he was a small child, he lived in the shadow of his famous crime father, Doctor Bizarro.

As a child, Meglamon loved to play in his father's crime lair. He liked the guns and ammo room well enough, but his favorite place was the chemical stockpile room. There he would dip his plastic army men into vats of corrosive alkalis to watch them melt and twist into weird deformities. He would then pit his troop of disfigured solders against a set of perfect little privates to see which side would win the war. It was always his brigade of melted deformed guys that won. Corrosives were good.

Doctor Bizarro was a tough crime villain and as such, young Meglamon found it very hard to measure up to his father's strict standards. He tried to live up to dad's expectations but always fell short. Nothing he did was ever good enough and he found himself the victim of frequent beratings in public.

In spite of this, Meglamon inherited his father's crime business and he immediately did two things: he hung a portrait of his father behind his desk in his new crime office (to remind him of what a piece of crap his dad was) and took the moniker of Professor (for respect from his newly inherited crime employees).

Basically, Professor Meglamon has been in the crime business his entire life. Now, at 70 years old, with his 5'8" frame stooping over and his white hair stuffed into a ball cap that sports his logo, he resembles more a broken man than a vicious captain of crime. He claims to be a perfectionist, but he always buttons his signature lab coat wrong.

In Professor Meglamon's heyday, the lair was always jumping with henchmen and support teams coming and going and busy with the current caper.

Now, however, crime is down since the rise of other crime syndicates in the city. This has caused the Professor to do company layoffs, cut henchmen perks, and frequently display unbridled anger at the smallest of things. And who is to blame for all of this? The Thrasher, that's who. This upstart is the current threat and Professor Meglamon's biggest nemesis! Damn him!

As the economic depression wears on, the lair gets shabbier. Burnt out light bulbs aren't so quickly replaced. The computers are old... Windows 95 is the current operating system. And if a henchman needs wireless, well, he has to go the coffee shop on the corner. Sometimes the lair has no heat.

If crime doesn't start paying, Professor Meglamon may face foreclosure on his lair. That would mean downsizing... again. It may even mean moving into a trailer parked somewhere in the warehouse district.

How embarrassing.

Chapter Eight

Stealth Mode Is Best

Gilbert was ten minutes late… and on his third day at work! Finally, he got changed into Thursday's right half dark forest green - left half lemon-yellow jumpsuit with shiny hi-top brown boots (two sizes too big). He got all hung up trying to get the wide brown belt to stay adjusted. The overly large Thrasher logo buckle flopped when Gilbert took each step and he had to keep stopping to hitch it back up.

When he finally reached the office, he thought he saw Argyle roll his eyes and whisper something to Ben, who glanced at Gilbert and smirked.

Argyle and Ben had been munching donuts. They found a veritable mountain of 'em in the break room when they went for coffee that morning. Apparently, last night's caper hadn't gone too well.

It took Gilbert another five minutes of struggling to get a chair moved to his desk but after he managed it, he sat quietly smiling at Argyle.

After a bit of cold shoulder, Argyle spoke. "You're late, Third. That's not good."

"I know. I think I had too many Shirley Temple's last night… I must have gotten too high on grenadine… it made me miss the alarm." When Gilbert saw the look of doubt on Argyle's face, he quickly added, "It won't happen again… I swear it!"

Argyle, rocking in his chair said, "Okay. I believe you."

Sitting up and turning to face Ben and Gilbert, Argyle said, "It's time to continue your training, Third. I think you'll like what Ben and I have come up with. Very interesting stuff."

Ben got up and waved Gilbert to follow. "We're going down to the Training Center on SL3… past your fish buddy."

Oh, Gilbert knew what that meant. He would have to walk past that bad shark, again. It made him shudder with the thought of it.

The Training Center on Sublevel Three had been modeled after army and marine boot camps but with a Thrasher twist.

All henchmen were required to climb rope netting and shimmy under barbed wire. One never knew when these skills would be needed so one had to stay sharp, and besides, it was pretty standard stuff.

The guys made their way past the shark tank to the Training Center room. Gilbert scuttled quickly past, holding his breath and trying not to make eye contact.

Ben used his badge to open the door and reached inside and snapped on the overhead lights. Argyle stepped through and started flipping big switches at a large panel. Within seconds, sounds and motions started up throughout the Center.

The room flooded with bright halogen stadium lighting that made Gilbert pinch his eyes closed for a couple of seconds. When he finally opened them, he was overwhelmed with what he saw.

To Gilbert's right was a bunch of moving machines. One had a heavy ten-foot-long bar with huge padded ends that was slowly rotating in a circle. Just below it was a rocky course complete with random pits big enough for someone's foot to become wedged in. Another machine was punching up into the air with a thud then resetting back into the floor to start again.

To the left, way down at the other end of the room, where the lights were very dim, popping sounds and showers of sparks would flare up in random spots every few seconds.

In the middle of the space was a large swamp enclosed by an iron fence. It contained live alligators and was belching an acrid fog that crept out over rocks and mud and dead trees covered in Spanish Moss.

It made Gilbert's heart skip a beat, but he tried to look brave.

"Today your training will continue. We'll start with the basic Night Infiltration Course," said Argyle, sweeping his arm in the direction of the darkened part of the room.

"The object of this training is to sneak around the course for up to ten minutes and grab all the booty you can. The more, the better." Argyle pointed to a weird looking goggle thing and said, "Grab that pair of night vision glasses and begin."

Gilbert took the glasses and started toward the infiltration course. His thoughts were running wild. *Wonder what kind of booty is in there. Will I be able to keep it? I've got ten minutes… better grab it all!* And with that, Gilbert stepped into the darkness.

Right away something bit him, and he let out a shriek as he hobbled up and down rubbing his ankle. Looking down he saw that he had stepped on a rusty bit of metal and maybe wasn't bitten at all. "That was lucky!"

"Eight minutes, Third!" It was Argyle's voice.

Gilbert bent over and focused the glasses on the path through the course and stepped along the best he could. As he walked, he picked up anything that might be booty, including the bent metal he tripped on.

When he finished the course and had rejoined Argyle and Ben, Gilbert's arms were full of all kinds of objects that he proudly displayed.

"Look, I have a tennis ball, a crushed soda can *and* a used plastic water bottle… that's five cents right there!" Gilbert was smiling as he continued to dump his booty into a pile on the floor.

"Hmmmm," murmured Argyle as he wrote a few lines on his little note pad.

Ben said, "You've got thirty seconds to return all this junk and get back here… Go!"

Gilbert jumped and collected all the bits of cracked plastic and rusted metal and made a mad dash for the night infiltration course. He threw everything in all cattywampus and raced back.

Out of breath, Gilbert huffed, "How'd I do?"

Ben answered, "Too bad, that was thirty-one seconds."

"The next bit of training will help you track down the booty if it's being carried off by the bad guys," said Argyle. "You're to use your extra senses to navigate the obstacles over there." Argyle pointed to the area of moving machines and little pit falls.

"I think I can do that, it looks easy!" Gilbert smiled.

Argyle shrugged and said, "Well, you're going to do it in stealth mode.”

Ben stepped up and dropped a soft canvas bag over Gilbert’s head and as he gently secured it said, “No peeking!”

The guys led him to the starting point and gave him a soft shove forward.

“Remember to use your hearing and your finger tips to make sense of the course. You’ve got fifteen minutes to finish,” said Argyle.

“Use your spider senses little Jedi,” called Ben.

Gilbert thrust his hands out in front of him, fingers splayed wide in an effort to protect his head. His eyes were wide open but he couldn’t see anything but the inside of the bag. Then… WHAP! He was smacked in the ribs and tumbled over. It nearly knocked the wind out of him.

Ben winced and said, “Yeow… *that* hurt!”

Gilbert got up and stumbled forward a few more feet. This time he heard a swish and ducked. He was pretty sure something had just whizzed past his head.

“Hah! Missed me!”

“Seven minutes, Third!”

Gilbert stayed low and worked his way forward, picking up a little speed as he went. He was five feet from the end point and heard Ben cheering him on. With a bit of confidence, Gilbert thought the worst was over. But as he carelessly went ahead, he stepped on a plate in the floor, triggering it to pop up three feet, and knocking him off balance. It just so happened that the panel tossed Gilbert across the finish line to land sprawled out on his face at Argyle’s feet.

Ben gave a whoop, “Atta boy, Gilbert, you made it!”

Gilbert had the wind knocked out of him and lay like a broken toy right where he landed.

Argyle bent down, pulled the Velcro strap loose, and tugged the bag off of Gilbert’s head and said, “Good job, you did it in fifteen.” And made a note on his pad.

“We’ve got one more before we shoot guns! My favorite part of training,” said Argyle. “You ready for this, Third?”

Gilbert rolled over and sat up rubbing and blinking his eyes. “I think so. What have I got to do?”

“You’re going to find the warrior within you,” smiled Argyle. “If

Thrasher decides to do a caper that is, let's say, a bit unconventional, all henchmen must be ready to go. You agree?"

Gilbert stood up and faced Argyle. "Just say the word and I'm ready to go!"

"Well, the word is 'speed'," said Argyle.

Gilbert followed Argyle's gaze to the Swamp Assault Course that appeared to take up most of the Training Center's floor space. His mind shouted: *Holy Crap! What kind of caper is that! Wish I had a hand grenade...*

"Just go as fast as you can. Avoid the 'gators and come out the other end alive *and* with all your parts. Simple."

Gilbert nodded slowly and took a furtive step to the small gate in the iron fence surrounding the swamp pit. He took a deep breath, unlatched the gate, inched it open and stepped inside.

Ben offered a bit of advice. "Remember, stay alive!"

And Gilbert was off and running as fast as his slightly chubby and now muscle cramped legs could move.

Argyle was astonished! He never figured Gilbert could move so fast.

Gilbert, his adrenalin pumping, was barely aware of his feet. He kept his eyes on the gate at the other end of the swamp and just moved. He was pretty sure his life depended upon it!

As his legs pumped, Gilbert became aware that he was stepping on rocks and in the muck as he moved along. He glanced down long enough to see two stepstones in the thick, sticky mud and made for them taking the first one with ease. Pushing off hard, Gilbert splayed his legs wide and came down hard on the second stone thinking to launch himself onto the solid dirt on the other side, but the stone started to sink into the muck.

A loud roaring and very nasty hissing sound sliced through the air. Gilbert had a split second of recognition: the second step stone had actually been the head of an alligator! Shit! He just stepped on an alligator! Gilbert dove with all his might straight for the dirt landing and lunged for the gate. Holding his breath and focusing on the gate latch, Gilbert got through the fence and slammed the gate shut before collapsing into an exhausted heap.

Ben laughed out loud and said, "Gilbert! You're alive!!"

Argyle, standing over the prostrate heaving Gilbert, said, "Good job. Let's go shoot some guns!"

After Gilbert caught his breath and Ben had put the courses back in order, which included tossing bloody chunks of meat to the alligators, the guys made their way to Sublevel Four where all of The Thrasher's guns, ammo, and laser gear were stored. Sublevel Four held lots of explosives and housed a nice shooting range.

Standing at the counter looking up at the gun and laser menu on the wall, Argyle said to Gilbert, "Check out any gun you want."

Ben asked the gun clerk for a rifle/grenade launcher thinking to have a bit of fun with it.

Gilbert studied the menu then said, "I'll take the Cobra, please."

Argyle said, "Good choice. It's a machine pistol worth its weight."

"Oh," said Gilbert, "I just like the name."

Entering the shooting range, Ben spotted three booths near the end and led the small group down the line past other henchmen shooting guns.

"We've got forty-five minutes," Argyle said. "Shoot at will!"

It was late morning by the time Argyle, Ben, and Gilbert returned to the office. After they found chairs and had been sitting for a few minutes, Argyle addressed Gilbert.

"You did okay with your gun training although you're gonna want to hit the target more often."

Gilbert blushed with embarrassment. "Sorry about dropping it that one time."

Ben stopped spinning in his chair long enough to say, "One of the most important parts of shooting a gun is not to drop it."

"Yeah. Thanks," said Gilbert.

Argyle rocked back in his chair and was concentrating on his eraser-tapping version of "In-A-Gadda-Da-Vida" when a thought occured to him.

"Third! You have one more task today before we break for lunch."

Gilbert sat at attention. He was determined to do the best he could at anything they asked him to do and become a full-fledged henchman.

"Anything!"

"Load up my laptop with games. Especially Spy-vs-Robot. I like that one. They fire guns a lot."

Chapter Nine

The Silent Nod

Argyle and Ben walked into the break room and saw what was left of the two-dozen donuts lying on the table.

"Hey Third! Get in here," said Ben. Gilbert entered the break room and said, "Hot damn! Donuts again! What's the occasion?"

"Anybody know?" asked Ben. One of the other henchmen, Al, said, "Didn't you hear about Cartwright?"

"No, what happened?"

"Oh man, wait until you hear this!"

Argyle bit into a donut and frowned as some of the sprinkles fell off and made a mess. "What happened to all the glazed?" he said.

"Oh, those were gone long ago. You have to get here early. Anyway," Al continued, "we were out on a caper last night and..."

"Wait a minute," interjected Argyle, "you guys were on a caper and you didn't bother telling me?"

"Barry didn't think you were needed. Anyway, as I was saying, we were on a caper..."

"What kind of caper? What did you guys do?" Argyle was obviously very upset at being left out of the action.

"It was another jewel heist. What difference does it make? Will you let me finish?"

"Let him finish, Arg," said Ben.

"Yeah, I wanna hear this too," said Gilbert. Everyone turned to look at Gilbert as if he had overstepped his bounds, but he didn't seem to mind.

"So, we got this guy tied up, I think he was the manager of the jewelry store or something, because we were trying to get the combination of the safe and he wasn't talking. Thrasher gives Cartwright the silent nod, you know slight tilt of the head and quick downward nod, right?”

“Sure, that’s the signal to break the guy’s arm,” said Ben with confidence.

“Yeah, well apparently Cartwright didn’t know that because instead of breaking the guy’s arm, he slit his throat!”

Gilbert’s eyes got real wide and Ben turned to him and said, “Are you listening to this, Third? This is what happens when you don’t study.”

Argyle rolled his eyes and said, “Sheesh! What a dope. Everybody knows the silent nod means break an arm, not kill the guy. So, I guess you guys never did get the combination.”

“Right. And Thrasher was livid! He shot Cartwright dead right then and there, and now,” he looked down at the table, “we have donuts,” he said as he reached for a powdered sugar donut.

Argyle thought for a second and said, “Well you can’t really blame Cartwright too much. After all, those signals are pretty complicated. Just one slight variation of the head nod off and you can easily misinterpret the signal. For instance, a nod to the left means break a leg; a nod to the right means break an arm; a double nod with a wink means strap him to the torture table; and a steady glare with no head movement whatsoever means throw him in the shark tank.”

“Uh, I think you have that wrong, Arg.” said Ben. “The nod to the left isn’t break a leg, it’s shoot him in the kneecap.”

“Are you sure?”

“Yeah, let’s look at the guide. Oh, I don’t have mine with me. Can I see yours, Third?”

Gilbert was momentarily startled and responded, “I don’t have a guide. No one ever gave me a guide. Where’s this guide? I’m going to need the freakin’ guide!”

Ben laughed and said, “Calm down, Third. I’ll get you one. And you better study, unless you want to wind up like Cartwright.” Then Ben reached for another donut and said, “Sprinkles? That’s all we have?”

“You should have come earlier,” said Al. “There were plenty of choices. One thing about Barry, he knows his donuts.”

Ben and Gilbert were sitting at their desks when Argyle came back from the supply room with the rulebook that Gilbert had requested. Ben was busily spinning in his chair and Gilbert was studiously studying the Thrasher internal web site to get a better feel for the organizational structure. The structure was diagrammed in a pyramid with a picture of Barry Teasdale at the very top and at the bottom a single long line of dashes that were meant to represent the minions, of which Gilbert was one of many. He was happy to see Ben and Argyle pictured quite a ways above the minion level, but still several layers below Barry and Miss Q and a few others whom he did not recognize.

Argyle was waving the book in his hand and was getting ready to hand it over to Gilbert when suddenly the P.A. system came alive with a familiar voice…

Attention. Attention! All henchmen! (tap, tap, tap…is this thing on?) *Image and marketing. What do these things mean to you? Well. Here's what they should mean to you because it's what they mean to… me! I'm more than a volatile image. But don't get me wrong, I love explosives!* (haha!) *However, I'm striving to be that mental image that will stick in the minds of everyone. This must be cultivated, like a spear of asparagus. Lovingly attended to until the time of harvest… and harvest I will! I'll haunt the dreams of millions before I'm done.* (Cough, cough, Miss Q, get me some water.) *Where was I? Oh yes, Marketing. It's all in the communication. I have a value that must be communicated. My organization is good for the economy. Local businesses love me! They know my business and it helps to make them better. You, my henchmen, are to market The Thrasher, promote our business and in the long run you will promote the health of our organization. Thank you.*

Gilbert looked at both Ben and Argyle for some sort of explanation as to what he had just heard, but neither one acknowledged anything out of the ordinary.

"Here's that rulebook we were talking about earlier. I think you need to study this carefully, unless you want to wind up like Cartwright. Or Wilson. Or, what's the name of that other guy that left us recently?" he asked Ben.

"Which one?"

"You know, the one that talked back to The Thrasher while we were on a caper." Argyle scratched his head in thought.

"I wouldn't exactly call it 'talking back'. He just asked him a question." Ben replied.

"It was more in the *way* he asked the question, as if he were questioning The Thrasher's authority. You just don't do that here. What was his name?"

"Hell if I know," said Ben.

Argyle shrugged and turned back to Gilbert, who was busily scanning through the rulebook pages.

Gilbert was intently studying this page…

THRASHER'S GOLDEN RULES:
1. Don't bore The Thrasher.
2. Don't piss-off The Thrasher.
3. Don't annoy The Thrasher.
4. Refer to Rule #1.
5. Don't try to help by making suggestions or enhancing the action. In other words, DO NOT IMPROVISE.
6. All Thrasher questions are rhetorical.

The list ended, however there were a lot of secondary rules listed on page after page, and Gilbert was starting to get the feeling that he would never be able to memorize all of the details of the rulebook. He thought, *no wonder the attrition rate for henchmen was so high in this organization.* Then he came to a page that read:

SILENT SIGNALS:
1 nod = break a couple of fingers
2 nods = break a kneecap
Scratch the nose = throw in vat of acid

Sideways nod to the right, no wink = break an arm
Sideways nod to the left, one wink = roundhouse punch
 to the jaw
Double nod, one wink = strap him to the torture table

…and so forth. There was a lot to learn, and the complex system of nods, double nods, and even triple nods made the whole enterprise very daunting. Still, Gilbert was determined to persevere.

"Quick!" said Ben. "What does *this* mean?" Ben then shook his shoulders very fast like some sort of monkey. Gilbert was startled and started leafing through the book to find the answer. "I… I… I don't know…" he said, feeling quite alarmed.

"It means it's time to knock off for the day and go get a few drinks. You coming, Argyle?"

"Sorry guys, but I've got a big date with Audrey tonight. This is our first anniversary."

Gilbert asked, "You're married?"

"No, it's the first-year anniversary of our first date. One year ago today. But you guys go and have a good time. Some other time, though. So, Third, you be sure to read through that book and memorize all the details. Your life will probably depend on it."

With that, they all filed out to the elevators, Gilbert tightly gripping the rulebook so that it wouldn't get lost. Ben saw the camera spin by his way and he put on his biggest smile. Argyle looked down at his phone to see if there was a message from Audrey.

"Hey Third," Ben said as they were going up in the elevator. "What'cha doing tonight? Anything special?"

"No," said Gilbert. "I'm just going to study this rulebook. I don't want to make any mistakes."

"Tell you what. Why don't you come down to my boat and I'll help you study."

"Wow! That would be great!"

"Okay, then just follow me." And with that they were off.

Ben's boat was just a short distance from The Thrasher headquarters, so they both walked. Gilbert couldn't wait to see Ben's boat. He figured that it had to be something monumental, considering that Ben's a henchman working for The Thrasher, so he was expecting a luxury sailing yacht, or maybe a really cool sailboat. Gilbert could picture himself at the helm of Ben's massive sailboat, the wind whipping through his hair, his arm around a beautiful babe, reliving his latest caper with Argyle and Ben. Maybe he'd make enough money to buy his own boat someday. He couldn't wait to see what the future had in store for him.

Chapter Ten

But It Floats

"Here we are at the 'Party-Oh-Boat'!" said Ben.

Gilbert looked at the exterior of the boat and was not impressed. It was just a small boat that appeared to be only suitable for fishing; plus the stink of the river was a little off-putting, but he put on a brave smile and said, "Nice boat." And his dreams were dashed.

"Yeah," beamed Ben as he boarded the boat. "Many a good time has been had here." Gilbert followed in after. The interior was as he expected: rough and unkempt, pretty much like Ben himself, so in that way it was a perfect match for Ben's personality.

"What'cha drinkin'?" asked Ben.

"Do you have an ice tea?"

"Better than that. How about a Long Island Ice Tea?"

Gilbert thought about that a second and said, "Isn't that what you were drinking the other night? Those are pretty strong, right? I don't think so. I don't drink."

"I was just kidding. I don't know how to make one of those. But anyway, if you want to be a henchman, you're going to have to learn how to drink. It's in the rulebook. Look it up."

Gilbert started thumbing through the book in an effort to locate the exact rule Ben was referring to. Meanwhile, Ben went to the refrigerator and took out two bottles of beer. "Here, try one of these for starters."

Gilbert reluctantly took the bottle and sniffed the opening. He never did like the smell of beer, and this one was no different from any other. But *what the hell*, he thought. He took a drink and made a slight face. *I guess now is as good as any time to start drinking*, he thought. After all, it's in the rulebook.

"Speaking of the rulebook, can we sort of go over these rules one by one? Starting with this one," Gilbert said, indicating rule #1. *"Don't bore The Thrasher.* What does that mean?"

Ben shrugged and said, "What do you think it means? Basically, it means keep your words to a minimum when you're talking to him. In fact, it's best not to talk to him at all, unless he asks you a question, and even then you should think very carefully about what you say, unless you want to wind up like Carpenter."

"What happened to him?"

"Long story. Let's just say that he was a little too long-winded for Barry's liking. He no longer works for us. Actually, Carpenter was a huge bore, so I can't blame Barry. Just don't go into any long stories when you're trying to explain what happened on a caper, for instance. If he asks you how it went, just say something like 'it went well' and be done with it. Trust me on this."

Gilbert took out his pen and started making notes next to rule #1. "Got it. Now how about rule #2? *Don't piss-off The Thrasher.* That sounds pretty self-explanatory to me, but do you have any examples?"

"Well, let's see. I think the prime example is Professor Meglamon. Nothing pisses off Barry more than an arch-enemy, so unless you have plans on confronting The Thrasher or going behind his back to team up with Meglamon, I think you're pretty safe there. Just try to avoid eye contact as much as possible."

"Rule #3: *Don't annoy The Thrasher.* Now on first reading, that just appears to be a variation of rule #2. What do you think of that?" Gilbert took another pull on his beer and found he was starting to get used to the taste. Also, he found he was getting slightly warm and feeling a little more relaxed in the company of Ben.

Ben smiled and said, "That one's a little mysterious and open-ended. It's hard to tell what will annoy The Thrasher from one minute to the next. Best to avert your eyes. Ready for another beer?"

Gilbert looked down at his bottle and realized he had been steadily draining the contents without even knowing it. "Sure," he replied. "Now what the hell is this? *Refer to rule #1.* Huh?"

"Just one of Barry's little jokes, I think. He probably just wants to emphasize that he does not, under any circumstances, want to be bored by any of his henchmen. That's all." Ben then went to the refrigerator and grabbed two more bottles of beer. He opened both and handed Gilbert a fresh bottle. "What's next?"

"Well, looking at this list of rules I have to wonder who came up with these. Was this really written by Barry… I mean The Thrasher? I mean, check this out: *Chinese food shall never be eaten out of the carton with chopsticks. Chinese food is to be eaten in a civilized manner, with a knife and fork on a regular plate.*"

Ben nodded. "Nothing bothers Barry more than to see someone eat Chinese to-go food out of the carton with chopsticks. It annoys him no end. Ah, that's a good example of rule #3."

"Well, the thing is, the rule doesn't specify whether the plate should be ceramic or paper. What do you think?"

"If I were you, I would avoid eating Chinese food altogether. By the way, in China they don't call it 'Chinese Food'. They just call it 'food'."

Gilbert thought about that for a moment and made a note in the book: *no Chinese food.*

"Here's another one: *ALWAYS RUN UP!* He strongly emphasizes that. What does he mean by this?"

"Barry believes that when you're on a caper and you're trying to escape, the higher up you go, the safer you will be. Any good escape plan should involve going up the stairs to the roof, if possible. You can't lose."

"That makes sense," Gilbert said as he made another note. "Here's another: *When driving, always keep your eyes on the road.* I guess The Thrasher doesn't like his drivers to be distracted. I guess he had a bad experience with a driver?"

"Oh yeah. Did you notice that scar on his cheek? No, of course not, you haven't met him yet. Anyway, that happened during a fender bender when one of his drivers wouldn't stop turning his head to talk to the guy in the seat beside him. He smashed into a car parked at a stoplight and Barry scraped his face on the GPS unit mounted on the seat in front of him. He immediately shot the driver, and just for good measure got out and shot the driver of the car in front of him."

"Wow, that's pretty harsh. Guess he had it coming, though. Here's another: *All Thrasher questions are rhetorical.* What does that mean?"

"Well, this goes back to the best advice I can give you if you want to advance your career with The Thrasher. Try to stay out of his eye-sight. But if you do come into his view, and he asks you a question, never answer it directly. Chances are he's just trying to bait you."

"But how will I know when he really wants an answer?"

"Refer to rule #6: *All Thrasher questions are rhetorical.* It's a real grey area, but you'll know when to give an actual answer. Usually, you'll know it when he points a gun at your head."

"Great," said Gilbert, with a frown.

"How are you doing on that beer?"

Gilbert was surprised that he finished off a second beer. He was getting a little woozy. "I don't drink I can think another beer," he said with a strong slur to his speech. "What the hell… Gimme another one."

"That's my man!" said Ben as he went to get another beer.

"I don't think I can go through any more of these rules tonight," said Gilbert, "but I really want to thank you for helping me out… you're the best!"

"I think that's the beer talking, but alright." Ben and Gilbert clinked bottles together and drank in silence for a minute or two. Then Gilbert felt bold enough to start asking some personal questions.

"Hey Ben, is it true you spent some time in Iraq?"

"Yep. Two tours of duty."

"Wow! What was that like?"

"It was hell, man! The weather inside that tent was stifling, to say the least, and with bullets flying every which way… I thought I was never going to make it."

"What were you, Infantry? Tactical? Bomb Squad or something like that?"

"No, I was a supply clerk."

"So… you didn't really see any action?"

"No… no… no… I saw *action.* I came *this close* to being shot at a couple of times."

"So, is that how you and Argyle met? Over in Iraq?"

"No. We met here on the job."

"What's your best caper?" Gilbert said as he drank some more of his beer. He found himself suddenly becoming very sleepy and thought he might pass out at any moment. The room seemed to be spinning and as he looked at Ben, he saw two of him sitting there. He could barely follow a word Ben was saying any more, but still he tried to appear interested. He thought he heard Ben say something about kidnapping Donald Trump, but he couldn't be sure.

"Ah, well," Ben said as he looked at the nodding-out Gilbert in front of him. "Looks like you're staying the night." Then Ben went to the fridge to get another beer before turning on the TV to watch a little Cinemax before heading for bed himself.

Chapter Eleven

Love Is in the Air

It was the one-year anniversary of the first date for Argyle and Audrey. To celebrate, Argyle took Audrey out to their favorite restaurant – a very expensive affair for which Argyle had to make a reservation months in advance.

Argyle's girlfriend, Audrey Eckhart, is a beautiful woman with dark hair and jade green eyes. At 5'10" tall, she looked really good standing next to Argyle.

Audrey's career is in Investment Strategies and just now is working for a large bank in downtown where she helps develop cutting-edge strategies for new advertising campaigns. She's very stylish, always buying the latest trends, and loves jewelry, not overly garish items but tasteful… and expensive.

Argyle and Audrey had just ordered a bottle of champagne and were studying the menu when Argyle's phone rang. "I have to take this," Argyle said. He smiled at Audrey, but she did not smile back. She continued to study the menu and tried not to think too much about the phone call Argyle was listening to.

After a few minutes passed with Argyle not saying anything and just listening to the voice on the other end of the line, Audrey said, "Is that Barry?"

Argyle just nodded. Audrey quickly grabbed the phone away from him and put it to her ear. She listened for a bit to Barry's rant and rolled her eyes. Then she opened her mouth to speak, but before she could get a word out Argyle quickly snatched the phone back from her.

Argyle continued to listen to Barry's rant, but Audrey grabbed it again and listened with some slight amusement. She put her hand over the mouthpiece and said to Argyle, "Mice running around with rabbits? What the hell?"

Argyle just shrugged and gestured for Audrey to return the phone. Instead, she said, "What's all this about turnstiles?" Finally, Argyle took the phone away from Audrey and continued to listen intently. Eventually it ended, and suddenly there was silence on the other end of the phone. Argyle just shrugged and put his phone away.

"What looks good?" he said.

Audrey just stared at him. "What was that all about?" she said.

"Well, you know Barry. He likes to call every now and then, just to keep in touch."

"The guy's a friggin' lunatic. You do know that, don't you?"

"Hey, I'll have you know he's a true crime genius. There's not many like him."

"What are you doing still hanging with that creep? You can do better, you know. I keep hoping you'll quit that job and find something with a future. Have you thought about taking some night classes?"

Argyle just snorted and said, "This is what I want to do. I was *born* for this type of work. It suits me. Besides, Barry isn't going to last forever. Someday he's either going to get caught or wind up dead, and then the organization is going to need someone to take over. That's where I come in."

"Seriously? Your goal in life is to become the next crime lord for the Thrasher Organization? Why won't you consider working at my Father's company? It pays well and you won't have to wear any silly costumes or risk your life for a maniac."

"Can we change the subject? We're supposed to be celebrating our one-year anniversary, not talking shop."

Audrey fell silent for a few moments and said, "I'm sorry Argyle. I just hate to see you wasting your potential when you could be doing so much more."

"Hey, remember the day we first met?" said Argyle.

"I'll never forget it," said Audrey with a smile. "You looked so cute in your caperware. And the way you said 'freeze motherfü@¥ers!' made me fall for you in a big way."

"When I came into that bank with the rest of the guys and I saw you sitting behind your desk, I just knew I had to ask you out."

"I'm glad you did, but I remember that when you came in the next day, I didn't recognize you at all without your mask."

"I almost didn't tell you it was me, because I thought you wouldn't want to go out with a henchman."

"Well, I wouldn't normally date a henchman, but there was something about you. I think it was your honesty that attracted me to you. You didn't try to hide the fact that you were with the gang who robbed the bank. It didn't bother me, though."

They held hands and looked at each other for a few moments until the waiter arrived and interrupted their reverie.

"Can I take your order?"

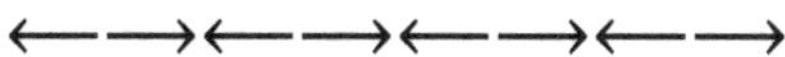

Argyle thought the dinner went great, right down to the chocolate cupcake with the sparkler on it. He was sorry that it caught the tablecloth on fire but he didn't think that was his fault. And the waiter need not have given him a dirty look… he had left a hefty eight percent tip!

The ride back to Audrey's was non-eventful and as they pulled up in front of her apartment, Argyle thought that making six green lights, running two yellow ones, and having to only stop at two red lights was pretty good.

Settling down on the couch for a bit of lip-locking Audrey interrupted his thoughts.

"Argyle, where are we going with this?"

"With what?" Argyle said as he held her in his arms and kissed her.

"With our relationship. Where do you see it going?"

"Right now, I see it going into the bedroom."

"Be serious for a second," said Audrey as she pulled away from him and moved down the couch with her arms folded. "What kind of a future do you see for us? Do you see us someday getting married, or what?"

"Would it bother you that much to be the wife of a henchman? You know, we could probably find a place for you in the organization. Maybe you could be our new wardrobe lady. I hear that Miss Wolf is probably going to leave us. That would be great! We could commute together and meet for lunch and all sorts of things." Argyle was getting very excited by the idea of them working together, but Audrey was not so enthusiastic.

"Are you insane? You want me to work for Barry? No friggin' way! I don't even like the idea of you working for him."

"Well, it's my life. It's my career. I'm not going to just throw it away and work in a factory. No way."

"Then I guess we have nothing much to talk about," Audrey said with a pout. Argyle was silent for a moment and then went into the kitchen and opened the refrigerator and pulled out a bottle of Dom Perignon.

"Audrey, let's not fight. This is our first-year anniversary. We should celebrate. Let's drink this fine bottle of champagne and think of the good times yet to come. What do you say?" Argyle was already opening the bottle as Audrey spoke.

"Argyle, would you at least please just *think* about getting a new job? That's all I'm going to say for now, but you should really take a look at what's out there that doesn't involve a grappling hook and an orange and black jumpsuit with a Thrasher logo on the front. That's all I'm saying."

With that, Argyle popped the champagne cork and poured two glasses and presented one to Audrey. They raised their glasses and Argyle said, "Here's to another wonderful year together, and I truly do love you."

Audrey smiled at Argyle and said, "And I truly love you too. I know we can work this out."

They clinked their glasses and started to drink when suddenly Argyle's phone rang.

"Oh crap!" said Audrey, and she put down her glass while Argyle took out his phone to answer it.

"It's The Thrasher," said Argyle with a serious look.

"Of course, who else would it be?" Audrey said with some exasperation. Then she sat down on the couch while Argyle listened in silence to what Audrey assumed was yet another Barry rant.

After a few minutes, Argyle hung up the phone without a word and said to Audrey, "I'm sorry honey, but I have to go. The Thrasher needs me for an emergency caper!"

Argyle was quite excited by this news. It probably meant he would get the chance to fire his weapons, and any opportunity to fire his weapons was a GOOD thing. Argyle put down his glass of Dom Perignon without drinking it and said, "Keep this on ice for me. I'll try to be back as soon as I can."

"Don't bother," said Audrey. "If you walk out that door, don't even think about coming back."

"Aw, come on, I have to do this. This is my *career!*" Argyle was visibly upset, but there was no doubt in his mind he would have to leave and try to patch things up later.

"I'm dead serious," Audrey said. "It's either The Thrasher or me. Which will it be?"

"I have to go. I'll be back later," said Argyle as he headed for the door. As he was leaving, he heard Audrey say to his back, "Call me?"

Four hours later Audrey's phone rang. It was Argyle.

"Did I wake you?"

"Yes, Argyle, it's 4:30AM. Of course I was sleeping."

"Sorry it's so late but I thought I'd call to tell you that I'm alright. Tonight's emergency caper went okay."

When Audrey didn't answer, Argyle continued, "We spray painted Thrasher logos all over the place. On walls, on garage doors, even on a railroad overpass!"

Unimpressed, Audrey yawned and said, "Um huh."

Argyle wanted so much for Audrey to admire his career choice and his skills, so plowed forward, "There's real excitement and danger in that!"

"Um huh."

"Good night Audrey. I'll call you tomorrow about our weekend plans."

"Um huh."

Chapter Twelve

Barry Says "Jump"

How exciting! The massive marquee sign above the locker room doors read: Dayshift henchmen are to dress in caperware #6. Be ready to depart at 9:30AM. All others: pale papery blue jumpsuit shorts with orange stitching at pockets and hem. White socks (rolled down, please!) with dark gray slip-on nylon sandals.

Argyle (still like the sock) was almost out of his mind with joy. After this whole long week… who would have thought that today, Friday, he may be able to at last shoot his gun!

A few of the dayshift henchmen had already made their way to Sublevel Five to check out their caperware. Argyle queued up at the turnstiles with a growing number of other henchmen excitedly waiting for the next available elevators to arrive.

The conversations among the group were animated and exuberant as the excitement of a dayshift caper grew.

Argyle was joking around with Davis and Carter when he spotted Ben winding his way through the crowd to join him.

"Hey Bennie! Buddy! There's a caper today!"

Ben joined the small circle of henchmen friends and said, "Yeah! This is totally awesome, isn't it?"

"I am sooo glad I cleaned and oiled my gun last night. How lucky was that?"

"Haven't cleaned mine since I dropped it in the mud last week, but I think it'll be okay," said Ben.

Argyle glanced around and asked, "Where's Third?"

Ben thumbed it toward the lockers and said, "He's at the sinks trying to clean his shirt. He spilled his Frappe Dingleberry Froth down the front and is running it under the cold water."

"Well, he'd better hurry or he'll miss the ride down to Wardrobe," said Argyle, just a bit agitated.

Ben stretched up to look over the heads of the crowd and after a couple of seconds of scanning the area said, "Here he comes."

Gilbert was politely making his way through the chattering mass of people that crowded the turnstile area. At first glance, he looked flustered. His cheeks were a bit flushed and his eyes seemed to be darting all about. Generally, he resembled a person on the verge of panic. Finally, he reached the guys.

Looking him up and down Argyle said, "Geeze Third, you're all wet. What happened? Ya fall in?"

The small group of henchmen were looking at Gilbert and chuckling at him. He was totally embarrassed and could feel his face getting hotter as it grew redder.

"I spilled a little coffee and tried to rinse it out before the stain set. The faucet handle flew off in my hand and water blasted out like a fire hose. It took me forever to find the water shutoff under the sink. Then I had to mop the floor." Gilbert realized that his little tale of woe wasn't playing with these guys so fell silent and looked down at his shoes.

Ben jostled him with an elbow and said, "Ha ha! Looks like you're still in training!"

Just then all four elevators arrived, and the group pushed forward as the cars filled to capacity. Argyle, Ben, and Gilbert crowded onto car one and as the elevator lurched into motion Gilbert overheard someone ask if anyone knew what the caper was. Someone else answered that usually no one knew until the last minute.

Gilbert looked up at Argyle and said, "Is that true? We don't know the caper until it's time?"

Argyle considered for a moment then dryly replied, "Yes."

Gilbert looked pensive then asked, "So how will we know how to prepare?"

Ben noticed that a couple of the henchmen in the front of the car had turned around to see who was asking the lame questions and he also noticed their looks of annoyance. Ben waved them off and said, "Don't pay any attention to him. He's new."

Argyle clapped Gilbert on the back and said, "When you're a

henchman you're prepared for anything at anytime. When Barry says 'jump', what do you do?"

Gilbert, his voice self-consciously lowered to hide his discomfort, said, "Jump."

"That's right, Third. You jump. And that's about all there is to it," said Argyle.

It seemed to Gilbert that the rest of the elevator ride crawled as if time stood still. Just as he was checking his watch, the elevator jerked to a stop and the doors flew open to reveal the foyer of Sublevel Five where all the caperware was kept and where several seamstresses were busy at work.

The Thrasher took pride in the caperware he designed. And this pride extended to the care and storage of his precious creations, too.

Sublevel Five was created to house, care for, catalogue, mend, and manage caperware. It was organized like a Hollywood wardrobe operation and was run by a wardrobe manager by the name of Feartha Wolf. Feartha runs her department like a boot camp.

During her job interview, Barry took a liking to her right away. She stood 5'1" tall, had a pincushion worked into her hair, and glared at him with hard dark eyes as he asked her questions.

When she produced a portfolio of her work, Barry hired her. He loved her creative use of sequins.

Feartha Wolf proved to be an asset to Barry's creative talents and together they came up with the most visual caperware ever. Barry envisioned it and Feartha sewed it. Every piece was a real statement of Barry's position and power.

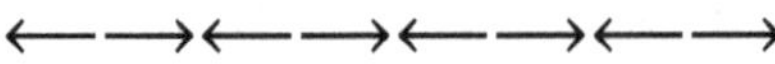

The lines of henchmen were long and the wait was estimated to be about ten minutes. Most of the men had been issued their caperware and were carrying the hanging garment bags through the crowd and gathering at the elevators for the ride back up to the locker room to change.

Argyle nudged Gilbert into line in front of him so he could help with his first fitting.

When Gilbert was at last standing in front of the counter, he smiled blankly at the assistant and said, "Good morning."

The assistant stared at Gilbert and knitted her brows together to reflect her growing impatience.

Argyle leaned forward and said, "He's new here. Gonna need a fitting."

The assistant nodded in understanding and quickly looked around before turning back to Gilbert and saying, "Go over there to station number three." Pointing off to the left and adding, "A seamstress will be right with you."

Shooing Gilbert away from the counter the assistant called out, "Next!"

Gilbert stood patiently at station three watching the bustle of the crowd. Assistants ran up and down the aisles of storage, seamstresses measured and called out sizes, and henchmen moved through the lines and back into the elevators with military precision. He was smiling to himself when Feartha appeared in front of him. It startled him so much that he flinched.

"What's so funny?" demanded Feartha. She stood in front of Gilbert with her hands balled into fists at her waist waiting for him to respond.

"I was smiling at the efficiency of the workers. I like it."

Feartha held her gaze steady as she retrieved a measuring tape from around her neck and wagged a finger at Gilbert indicating that he was to put his arms out.

Ten minutes later, Gilbert had been sized and was standing, holding his garment bag, at the elevators with Argyle and Ben who had waited for him to join them.

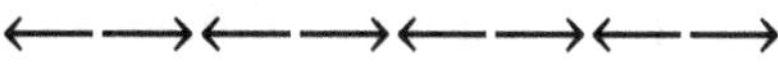

One by one the boys emerged from the locker room dressed in their newly issued caperware #6.

Everyone wore a shiny black bodysuit with heavily padded shoulders designed to make them look muscled and tough. Black holsters hung from a bright chartreuse belt and there was a long red cape that sported little Thrasher logos all around the bottom hem. The crime boots were also a delicious color of red and laced up to about eight inches above the ankle. The ensemble was topped by black leather headgear that fit close to the skull and strapped under the chin. But the crowning gem was a brightly colored Thrasher logo on a six-inch disk that had been affixed to a bouncy spring and glued to the top of the headgear.

The Thrasher thought it to be stylish yet would distract his foes enough to give him a crime advantage.

The usual caper plan was to group up in the office area and wait for further instruction, so the dayshift henchmen were going through the turnstiles and down to Sublevel One.

Argyle was grinning from ear to ear and sneaking glances at his reflection in the shiny stainless steel elevator doors. Turning this way and that way to see from all angles, he was clearly pleased with the fit of his caperware.

Ben was standing with the others. Every once in a while, he would make a quick move to mime that he was drawing his gun. The movement would make the Thrasher logo disk bounce around and if Ben moved fast enough, he could make the disk pop him in the head. Then he would laugh and do it again.

Gilbert was pretty excited about going on a caper. He was looking forward to some real crime action and was smiling and looking expectantly around the group. His caperware didn't quite fit him. It was a little tight around the middle and pulled his tummy into four thick rolls that together with the padded shoulders made him look like a little muscled sausage. His cape was too long and the spring on his Thrasher disk was bent so when he walked, it bounced to the right, banging into his head with every step. Very annoying, but he was determined to make the best of it.

Catching up with Argyle and Ben, Gilbert asked, "Does this make me look fat?" Argyle just rolled his eyes, saying nothing.

As the boys entered the office area, they were greeted with the deafening noise of broken and rusty chairs being furiously moved about. In reaction, Gilbert plugged his ears with his fingers and stood gaped-mouthed at the sight of dozens of henchmen, dressed in caperware, scrambling to grab a chair.

Two henchmen, with their Thrasher logos bouncing wildly, were in a tug-of-war over a chair that in the shuffle had become hopelessly tangled up in the loose cables and cords that festooned the floor. The two henchmen were starting to shout at one another and seemed on the verge of real violence, when the back of the chair broke off in one guy's hands. He stood motionless for a second while the reality of it sunk in, then dropped the chair piece and said, "It's all yours."

Argyle and Ben had ignored the melee and were sitting at their desks. Eventually Gilbert made the distance, tripping only once, and stood by his desk, waiting.

Ben was playing with his cape, holding it up across his face, Bela Lugosi style and jabbing the air with his free hand, held like a claw, menacing Argyle, who ignored him.

Eventually, the henchmen settled into a sort of restless calm, which for them more resembled a bunch of nervous kids who had been pumped up on sugar then told to be quiet.

The surveillance cameras that had been sweeping back and forth and zooming in and out finally calmed down. A few minutes later the P.A. system came alive with a harsh wave of static and the loud ear-splitting sound of feedback. The office fell silent. Then Barry's voice…

⚡ ⚡ *Attention, attention!* (Pause) *Is this thing on?* (A camera zoomed in on a henchman. He smiled nervously and eagerly nodded his head up and down.) *Good. I'll continue.*

Today's caper is going to be a good one. And by the way, you all look positively threatening in your caperware! (Many of the henchmen were looking around and smiling in agreement. Barry's voice was loud and harsh…) *I'm very pleased!* (His voice returning to normal…) *As I was saying, today's caper is vitally important to the ongoing notoriety of my reputation as the greatest,* (voice rising…) *most accomplished,* (voice growing…) *world famous,* (voice in crescendo…) *true mastermind of all time!* (Muffled sounds of Barry coughing can be heard, and then he continued more calmly…) *Today we are going to procure over $6 million in gold coins from* *the high strength class 3 concrete and steel vault of the Frangilic Brothers Exchange. The one uptown, not that dump they operate over on 62nd street. Grab your ropes, men... we're going to grapple today!*

The P.A. system fell silent.

Argyle pulled out the bottom drawer of his desk and brought out a heavy nylon rope that had to be at least seventy-five feet long and sported knots along its length. From another drawer he produced a grappling iron that appeared to have four distinctly hooked anchors welded to a heavy center shaft. This he dropped onto his desk with a heavy thump.

Gilbert followed suit but did not find anything except the inside of an empty drawer. Looking dejected, he asked Argyle, "Where's my rope and giant fish hook?"

"No. You don't get one. You're still in training," said Argyle.

Ben added, "Today you're just going to watch the masters at work."

"Well, okay. If you say so, but I could shoot a gun!"

Argyle leaned toward Gilbert and, looking at him very seriously, said, "Not today, Third."

Gilbert bristled at the idea that he wouldn't have a rope *or* a gun. In his agitation, he stuffed his ham sandwich lunch into the holster hanging, empty, from his caper-belt.

Just then a loud buzzer sounded, and all the henchmen got up, grabbed their gear and headed to the elevators that would take them up to the parking garage. They were to group up in the overflow parking area on the second floor where the caper vans were kept.

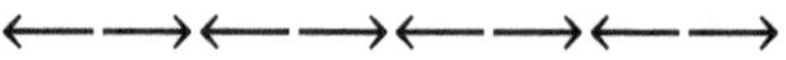

The ride over to the Frangilic Brothers Security Exchange was uneventful, although more than a few people stopped to stare at the caravan of black twelve-seat vans that drove through the downtown.

Gilbert was awe-struck with the whole process of a caper and in his excitement, he started to chatter. He talked, to no one in particular, about how excited he was to be a part of something so great and how proud everyone must be to be a part of such a wonderful organization as the Thrasher's. At one point Gilbert turned to Argyle and asked a question.

"Argyle. Is this the greatest caper ever, or what?"

Argyle smiled and nodded his head with the fond memory of another caper.

"It's right up there but I gotta tell you, nothing has yet to top the Liberty Bell Caper of '04." Argyle fell into a sweet revelry as he reminisced about the '04 caper.

"Barry had seen a public broadcast special listing the five most valuable things in America. They talked about national parks and craters and things like that, but Barry knew that he wouldn't be able to steal those things. However, when the show mentioned the Liberty Bell and its incalculable value to the American people, well, Barry just had to have it."

Ben popped up, "That was such a good broadcast, too!"

Argyle continued, "Barry worked out the details for days. He thought that he could extort about twenty million bucks out of the US government. When he was ready, we went to work."

Gilbert had been hanging on Argyle's every word. With barely disguised anticipation, asked, "Did you get to shoot your gun?"

Argyle smiled so wide that Gilbert thought he might be on the brink of euphoria.

"Yes... I... did! What a good caper. By the way... we got the bell, but had to give it back."

Gilbert asked, "Give it back! But why?"

Ben continued the story, "Cuz Barry forgot to plan the part about how to move something that weighed over two thousand pounds!"

"Yea. We managed to roll it out into the parking lot but couldn't lift it into the van. We were standing around brainstorming what to do when cop sirens were heard comin' our way." Argyle was slowly shaking his head. Then he continued.

"We left the bell, on its side, in the parking lot and got the hell outta there."

Argyle thought for a moment then said, "Barry was thinking about stealing the Statue of Liberty." He let a small puff of air out of his lungs then added, "But the Canadians didn't want to buy it from him and the French, well they told him to go..."

Just then, the driver banged the van horn to warn a kid on a skateboard to get out of the street, covering the rest of Argyle's statement.

Many of the henchmen in the van had been on that caper and listened to the story in silence. By the time Argyle had finished, the van was quiet and the rest of the ride became very solemn.

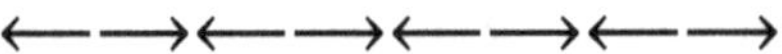

Today's caper plan was to park in the Exchange building's underground parking and for everyone to go up the stairwell to the roof. They would take up positions above the Frangilic Brothers offices, attach the grappling irons to the metal railings and on The Thrasher's signal, all henchmen were to grapple down and break through the windows into the offices. From there, it was a no-brainer. Secure that area and wait for Barry's entrance.

After everyone was assembled on the roof, Argyle took it upon himself to show Gilbert how to secure a grappling iron.

"You see. You find something to hook on to and then twist the rope around in a constrictor knot." And fiddling around with the rope, added, "I love constrictor knots. They really constrict."

Gilbert was watching intently and had absentmindedly pulled his ham sandwich out of his holster and had taken a bite. Through his now full mouth, Gilbert mumbled, "Ah huh. That looks nice."

Argyle looked up from his work and said, "Put that away! No one eats on a caper!"

Then in his really pissed-off voice added, "Didn't you read the rule book? That's rule #28!"

Gilbert stuffed one last bite into his mouth before reluctantly putting the sandwich back into his holster.

With all the grappling irons secured the activity levels among the group of henchmen dropped to a nervous shuffling.

Lewis had been assigned as the signalman and was at the roof's edge keeping his eyes glued to the second hand of his watch. He called out, "Ten seconds everyone. Ten seconds."

The henchmen formed loose lines of five each along the grappling ropes. They would take turns grappling. As soon as one was halfway down, another would start.

Lewis called out, "Five seconds." Then, "First line, go!"

The first wave of henchmen went over the side and the second wave stepped up and peered over the edge watching as they waited their turn.

Lewis checked his watch and glanced at the henchmen on the ropes and called, "Second line, go!"

And over they went.

Suddenly an ear-piercing scream filled the air and everyone rushed to the rooftop railing to look over the edge.

Argyle, Ben, and Gilbert, grouped together, peered down the side of the building and saw, to their horror, Henchman Hall, splattered on the sidewalk below.

Looking very concerned, Argyle was trying to calm the men by making settle down motions with his hands.

Ben said, looking at no one in particular, "Oh damnit. You know what this means, don't ya?" Argyle looked at Ben as he continued, "Now we have to take up another collection for a card and flowers for his family. Who's going to do this? Who's going to buy the card and get everyone to sign it?"

Then both he and Ben looked at each other as the same thought popped into both their minds. They slowly turned, smiles wide on their faces, and said in perfect unison… "Gilbert!"

Chapter Thirteen

Let's Review

The dust had finally settled. Upon returning to the lair, all caper henchmen had changed into the designated working jumpsuit, returned their caperware to Wardrobe, and had gone back to the office and break room area for lunch.

When Gilbert had completed his post-caper work and had joined Argyle and Ben at their desks, Argyle addressed him.

"Don't bother looking for a chair, Third. You have one more task to do before you can sit down. And since you've already eaten your sandwich…"

Ben shook his head and intoned, "Tsk, tsk, tsk."

"…you're spending the rest of the lunch period getting a sympathy card for Henchman Hall and getting everyone to sign it."

Staring at Gilbert and getting a degree of satisfaction at seeing him squirm, Argyle continued.

"And stop by the corner park to pick a bunch of fresh flowers."

Gilbert kicked at some cords by his desk and looked to Ben to help him out but got nothing. He stood for a second then said, "Okay. I'll be back real soon." And left.

An hour later Gilbert returned with a fully signed card and presented it to Argyle for approval. Argyle looked at it, and then stuffed it into the center drawer of his desk.

"Third. It's time to conduct your henchman training review – we're going to evaluate your first week on the job. Let's meet in the Bundy Room."

Ben said, "Follow me." And headed for the back hallway that led to the meeting rooms. Turning to Gilbert, who looked worried, added, "It's been quite a week, eh?"

As they made their way past the break room, Ben noticed that a couple of dozen donuts had been hastily piled up in the center of a table and made a fast detour to snag a bunch of the little powdered ones before they disappeared.

After filling his pockets, Ben said, "Gilbert, grab some of the chocolate topped ones for Argyle. He likes them best."

When the guys had settled into their chairs and munched all the donuts, Argyle started the meeting.

"Third. We've been watching you closely this week as you completed some of your henchman training. As you may have come to understand, The Thrasher has very high standards for his henchmen and as such, he expects each of them to be, well, to be all they can be."

Argyle made hacking sounds as he tried to clear donut from his throat. Eventually, he got up and reached down the table for a pitcher of water that had been left over from a previous meeting. After a good sniff to make sure that it *was* plain water, poured a glass then sat back down.

Ben and Gilbert glanced furtively at each other then back at Argyle, who continued.

"As I was saying: all they can be. Let's take a look at your performance for the week, shall we?"

Shuffling through the pages of a note pad, Argyle read to himself and mumbled "Right," and "Hmmmmm," and "Oh yeah," a couple of times while he organized. Then began.

"I'll just list the activities and we can talk about them. Ben, you add comments any time you want. Okay. Are we ready?"

Ben said, "Yhup. Fire away!" And pointed a finger at Gilbert, miming that he was firing a gun.

In a low voice, Gilbert said, "I can explain everything!"

And Argyle said, "Yes. So can I," and cleared his throat again.

"You may have noticed that we don't have enough office chairs. And while Ben and I are proficient at getting ours, we've noticed that you're not so good at it. Why is that?"

Gilbert looked from Argyle to Ben and back before blurting out,

"I like to stand!"

Argyle murmured, "Hmmm," and jotted down a note. Looking up he asked the next question, "During the Training Course, you had a difficult time climbing the rope, then you shot an innocent henchman in the leg. Can you tell me how that happened?"

Gilbert's mind raced over the event and his palms became clammy when he recalled falling off the rope after the gun blast. He steeled himself and answered.

"I was pretending to be on a caper. I know how The Thrasher likes it when his henchmen are tough guys. I was being a tough guy. I thought it was what you wanted." Gilbert fell silent and looked pleadingly at Ben.

Ben felt a little sorry for Gilbert. He kinda liked him and it was fun having him around this week. Someone new to pick on. After a moments thought, Ben spoke up, "I don't think it was all Gilbert's fault. That henchman could have picked some other rope to climb on."

Argyle bit on the eraser end of his pencil as he considered what he had just heard, then said, "Okay. I'll give you that. But, Third! You'll have to work on that some more."

Argyle flipped more pages then said, with a sort of smile, "You did very well in the shark tank. I think you got about seventy percent of it done before Flipper nipped you!"

Ben started laughing and almost couldn't stop. When Argyle joined in, it was almost too much for Gilbert and he started laughing, too, although he self-consciously touched his still sore rear.

"Oh geeze that was so funny! The look on your face, Gilbert, I almost wet my pants!"

Argyle said, "Okay. Let's settle down and continue the review. Although the whole shark tank thing *was* funny!" And at this, all three started laughing again.

"Let's talk about Barry's torture table. Most of the time you seemed to be in a panic. You've got to watch that in future. You ran a little late but in the end you built a good table. However…" flipping another page in the note pad, Argyle added, "…you didn't bear up during the testing."

"Yeah," Ben added, "You screamed like a little girl!"

"That's right," commented Argyle. "You did get a little high-pitched there for a second."

Hoping to sound like he knew what he was doing, Gilbert quickly added, "Yes, but I think the electrical current flowing from the black wires to the inline circuit and out through the red wires caused my vocal cords to squeak up a bit. It could happen to anyone. Yes, I'm sure that was it." Then he looked down at his fingernails feeling demoralized and thinking that the review wasn't going too well.

Argyle continued, "There's one last activity we need to talk about and that is Barry's Silent Signals. You're not very good at these, are you?"

Gilbert eagerly said, "I know a bunch of them, I've studied the rule book!"

Ben said, "Okay, then what does this mean?" Ben looked steadily at Gilbert and gave one nod.

"I know that one! Wait! Wait! I've got it… break a kneecap! Right?"

Argyle shook his head, "No. That's not right. One nod means break a couple of fingers. Two nods is break a kneecap. See the difference?" Argyle rustled more pages and took more notes.

All this made Gilbert very nervous and he started biting at a hangnail.

Ben sat quietly, looking at Gilbert and flexing his eyebrows up and down.

Finally, Argyle spoke. "Third. I think you've squeaked by this week with a C+."

At this, Gilbert jumped up, hollered, "Yippee," and made to give high fives to Argyle and Ben, who sat calmly looking at him. Barely containing his zeal, he sat back down but nervously twitched about in his chair.

When the grin on his face calmed down, he said, "I'm a henchman!"

"Whoa, whoa, whoa. Slow down cowboy. No one's a henchman just yet," said Argyle. "You're not a henchman until I say you're a henchman and I didn't say you were a henchman."

Ben left the room for a moment and returned with three more donuts. "Let's celebrate!" And passed them around, handing the one with the sprinkles on it to Gilbert.

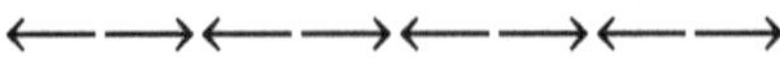

The guys returned to their desks but this time, Gilbert made sure Argyle was watching as he made a show of getting a chair for himself. Gilbert only tripped over cables once before managing to maneuver the lopsided chair into place.

They sat in silence for about an hour before Ben said, "I think I'm going to work on my boat this weekend. The roof could use a patch or two and I think the steering column needs fluid. The last time I tried to steer her, it made a lot of grinding noises."

Ben then pulled out the middle drawer of his desk and started moving the contents around. "How 'bout you, Argyle? What are you up to?"

Argyle was leaning way back in his chair with one foot propped on the desktop. He looked over at Ben and said, "Audrey and I may see a movie. Or we may stay in and watch TV. Or I may clean my gun. Or I may do all of these things. Or a combination."

Argyle took two pencils out of the holder and started tapping out "In-A-Gadda-Da-Vida" on his dark, gray nylon work sandal. After three minutes, he said, "I think I want a steak and baked potato for dinner tonight."

Lazily turning to look at Gilbert, Argyle said, "Third. You have homework this weekend. You're going to study Silent Signals. Ben's going to test you on Monday."

Ben smiled at Gilbert and said, "Yeah. Like, what's this one?" And went into a spasm of movements resembling a really jerky dance.

Gilbert stared at him with wide eyes and mouth ajar then said, "Poke out an eye with my thumb?"

At which Ben busted out laughing and said, "Wrong!" And laughed all the harder.

Clearly annoyed with Ben, Gilbert addressed himself to Argyle. "I'm going to work on my show-and-tell project. I'm building a bomb out of ordinary household items. I have an egg timer, parts from my digital alarm clock, baking soda, and a bunch of red and yellow wires that I pulled out of my thermostat. I'll bring it in when it's finished."

Argyle, barely listening, said, "That's nice."

The guys fell silent again but were yanked from their thoughts when the P.A. system crackled to life. It was Barry's voice…

⚡ ⚡ Attention, attention! (Pause) Good afternoon. There is a question that I would like everyone to consider. What is the future of crime? Philosophically speaking, crime is necessary to the balance of the universe. Without crime, there would be nothing but boredom. Eventually everyone would just sit and stare at a wall. Crime keeps life interesting. The current state of crime seems to have become static, not changing much in the last fifty years. My task for you, my henchmen, is to think outside the box – crime suggestions should be submitted by way of the comment cards found in the break room. ⚡ ⚡

The guys sat looking at each other for a minute, then Argyle slapped his hands down on his desk, stood up, and said, "Well, I'm outta here! See you Monday morning!"

UP THE CRIME LADDER

N. K. Hart

A Reader's Guide

Questions for Discussion Among Your Reader's Club Buddies.

1.) In your opinion, who was the cutest, Argyle or Ben? Why do you think that?

2.) When a movie is made of this book, who should play Argyle?
   A. Bruce Willis
   B. Jerry Seinfeld
   C. Brad Pitt
   D. Liam Neeson
   E. (fill in…) _______________________

3.) What color is the sponge suit that Gilbert wears in Chapter Four. Does the suit compliment his eye color? Divide into three study-groups and white board your evaluation.

4.) Who's leading this Reader's Club anyhow? Are you self-appointed or did you have to wrestle leadership away from a lesser

intellect?
Name them: _______________________

5.) Are you a 'Thrasher' type? What makes you think so? Really, tell it all.

6.) Have you known a Henchman? No, you haven't. Really?

7.) How many Henchmen does it take to steal the Liberty Bell?

8.) In your opinion who has the better office chairs… Cashco, Stiples, or Office Despot? Are you getting paid to say that? Are you getting any kind of endorsement from them?

BOOK TWO
THE FUTURE OF CRIME
TALES OF THE HENCHMEN
N. K. HART

"Obviously crime pays, or there'd be no crime."
--G. Gordon Liddy

"Behind every great fortune there is a crime."
--Honore de Balzac

Prologue

A year has passed and crime has moved on. The seedy warehouse, with its six sublevels is still standing, a little worse for wear, and still occupied by The Thrasher's organization. About six months ago a real estate tycoon toured the old district with the intention of turning several of the old warehouses into high-end, very expensive lofts for the rich jet-set crowd. His plans were marvelous. Marble, travertine, pewter, and crystal. However, one sniff of the stinky river and the industrialist, along with his entourage, fled as fast as their limo could take them.

And the stinky river flows on, a bit stinkier, but on it continues.

The seedy warehouse hasn't changed much in a year. The Thrasher's operations haven't changed either, there are basic capers that occur on a schedule, those are for maintenance of common consumables like toilet tissue and printer paper, and spur-of-the-moment capers made necessary by small emergencies such as when the main water pipe to the showers broke wide open last summer. But it's the big capers that send excitement through the ranks. These can happen at any time and this year Feartha Wolf's wardrobe team created the most spectacular caperware yet. Her use of sequins has been over the top brilliant!

The turnstiles on Sublevel One still fund the soda, sandwich, and candy machines in the henchmen's break room as well as the periodic appearance of massive piles of donuts, Thrasher's way of boosting morale when a henchman is "lost" in the line of duty.

The boys seem to be doing well.

Argyle Stevens and Audrey Eckhart are still together. They haven't planned any wedding bells yet but are happy in each other's company and spend most weekends together watching old movies on TV.

Ben Watson is still in residence on his tugboat, oh, please excuse the error… his camp cruiser, the "Party-Oh!" moored to the shore of the stinky river, exactly where it has been since he bought it. Ben thinks of himself as a playboy and probably always will. When he's not whooping it up in McClusky's Eight Ball, he's at home on the "Party-Oh!" with a six-pack and his cable watching his favorite old TV shows from the '50s.

Gilbert Alan Martin III struggled through more training in his quest to become a henchman and actually did make the Junior Henchman level but not because he excelled in his study of the company rules or had mastered the par course. No. It was due to timing. An opening came up, one that provided a pile of donuts to the break room, and Gilbert was "mostly trained" so received the promotion to Junior Henchman, Class One. There was no ceremony connected with it, just a two-minute meeting with Miss Q as she patiently explained that there was no pay raise associated with the new title.

Barry Teasdale, aka The Thrasher, is about the only one in his crime organization that has changed. He's become more reclusive, often absent for days at a time. His temper, while having always been short, is shorter. When he surfaces from one of his absences, everyone has learned that it's best not to engage him until his mood has been established.

Barry's been very busy in his private Sublevel, determined to dominate crime in the city (and a few towns to the north), then move ever outward to prove to the world that he is "the" super evil genius. Barry's ego has declared that he is talented, awe inspiring, and also a highly creative individual. His superego is off the charts and to prove it, he's stepped up his game. He's planted spies in his rival Meglamon's employ, although it hasn't rewarded him with any insider information as of yet. He's ramped up on capers that have delighted his top henchmen. Thrasher has masterminded some of the best capers to date, especially the daytime robbery of that BMW transport truck. The stakes are high and the cost is, well, costly. Six henchmen were "lost", either to jail or Boot Hill, over a three-month time period.

The heists are bigger in order to finance Barry's more costly experiments. But more on that later.

Right now, however, it's time to join The Thrasher and his crime organization in progress. Pay attention! There's a test.

Chapter One

Scarier Words Were Never Heard

"The Thrasher will see you now."

Ben Watson heard these words from The Thrasher's secretary, Miss Q, and shuddered. It's always a concern when holding a meeting with The Thrasher because you never know what's going to happen. Ben's buddy, Argyle Stevens, stood next to him and seemed to have a calmer demeanor. Argyle and Ben had been good friends since Ben started working in The Thrasher's crime organization, just about five and a half years ago. And even as Ben was very, very nervous, Argyle was collected and composed. Argyle didn't have a problem with a Thrasher meeting because he was convinced that he had a special bond with his boss, but Ben was not quite as sure of his own position.

Barry Teasdale, AKA The Thrasher, was the most feared Crime Boss in the city – or so he fancied himself, if it wasn't for his arch-nemesis Professor Meglamon he would rule the city! When Ben and Argyle walked into the semi-private meeting room, The Lizzie Borden on Sublevel Four, Thrasher was sitting at the head of the table cleaning his gun. He had all the bullets laid out and was swabbing the cylinders with a Q-tip when Argyle said, "You wanted to see us boss?"

Barry momentarily stopped what he was doing and stared at Argyle with what he thought was a menacing glare, and indeed it was very effective on Ben who gulped and darted his eyes about the room furiously trying to formulate an escape plan.

Barry spoke up, "Henchmen, I called you here today to talk about your progress in training your new recruit," he looked down at a piece of paper sitting in front of him and read from it, "Gilbert Alan Martin III, especially any and all information related to his former boss, the detested Professor Meglamon -- whom I will *crush*!"

Barry underscored his contempt for the Professor by slamming the palms of his hands on the table causing three of the bullets to tumble over and roll around in little circles. Ben gulped and felt that his eyes were huge open staring disks and struggled to look more composed. Argyle stood facing The Thrasher, nodding and smiling in agreement.

Barry continued, "What have you found out?"

Ben realized that they actually never got around to talking about Gilbert's time working for Meglamon, which was one of the reasons Barry agreed to hire him in the first place. Argyle also realized that that part of the mission had been completely neglected. After all the time they had spent training Gilbert, after teaching him how to clean the shark tank, after teaching him how to assemble the new torture device, and after going over and over the silent nods and other signals in the corporate rulebook so that he could become a valuable hench-man, they had completely forgotten to ask him about Meglamon. Now some fast thinking was required.

Ben looked at Argyle and said, "You want to go first, Arg?"

Argyle glared at Ben for a quick moment and said, "No, I think you've spent more time with him. You should go first."

You bastard, thought Ben. "We're still training Third," he spoke, hoping it would buy a little more time.

Barry picked up one of the bullets lying on the table and inserted it into one of his gun's chambers and calmly asked, "Third?"

"That's what we call him. His name is Gilbert Martin III, so we just call him 'Third'."

Barry frowned and shook his head and said, "Around here we don't use nicknames and we treat each other with respect."

Ben wanted to say something but bit his tongue. He was thinking that "The Thrasher" is a nickname in itself, and as for treating workers with dignity, tell that to the three guys he threw to the sharks a couple of weeks ago just because they didn't wash his armored cruiser to his satisfaction.

Barry slowly leaned back in his chair, making it squeak and grind in the most hideous way. He could tell by the look on Ben's face that it was deliciously unnerving. Glaring, he said, "And… "

Ben sputtered, "And, and, and," then caught a thought, "Junior Henchman Martin has been a little evasive about his employment with

Meglamon. We've been taking it a bit slow, gaining his trust. Isn't that right, Argyle?"

Argyle responded, "Yes, that's it." A little stunned with Ben's pronouncement.

Barry finished up glaring at Ben and slowly turned his gaze onto Argyle saying, "What else?"

Argyle had taken up Ben's explanation and said, "We think he's hiding something, maybe something big, but don't want to scare him off. We need more time." *Oh geeze, this isn't going very well. I'm going to kill that Ben if we ever get outta here.*

Barry pondered what Argyle had just said and as he silently deliberated what he had heard, picked up another bullet from the table, inserted it into an empty chamber, slammed the cylinder home and spun it around. When it stopped, Barry took aim at a portrait of Benito Mussolini hanging on the wall just behind Ben, the merest of inches to his left.

Ben felt his body go stiff with fright. It was all he could do to not move or say anything that would upset The Thrasher.

Barry closed one eye and looked down the gun's barrel over the sight and pulled the trigger. The gun made a loud clicking sound as it attempted to fire an empty chamber.

Ben's heart almost stopped beating but Argyle smiled broadly as he thought, *I can't wait to run this company. I'm going to have so much fun!*

Barry returned the revolver to the table and resumed swabbing the remaining bullets.

Ben nudged Argyle and when Argyle looked over at him, Ben jerked his eyes over to Barry, indicating that Argyle ought to say something. Argyle shook his head "No" and waved Ben off.

They stood in silence for two long minutes and jumped when Barry finally spoke, "You've got one week to extract information from Junior Henchman Gilbert Alan Martin III." And tapping a bullet on the table, to convey his annoyance, added, "Now leave me."

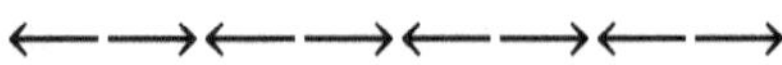

Out in the hallway, Ben took a hold of Argyle's arm and nervously jostled him saying, "We make a good team, don't we?"

Argyle was more than upset and shook Ben's grip off and then punched him on the arm. "What was that crap about Gilbert hiding something? We've got one week to come up with a plan. And it better be a good one." Argyle tsk'd in disgust and punched the elevator button.

The ride up to their office space on Sublevel Two was silent.

Ben rubbed his arm and wondered if it was going to bruise.

Argyle's thoughts were more serious. *Crap. If Gilbert is supposed to be hiding information about Meglamon, something important, what could it be? Maybe I'd better Google Professor Meglamon and see what comes up.* Turning to Ben, he said, "Not a word of this to Gilbert. Let's find out exactly what he knows first."

The doors slid open and the boys stepped off the elevator and made their way to their desks where Gilbert was waiting for them, idly passing the time trying to duct tape a wheel back onto his chair.

Argyle immediately fired up his laptop computer and leaned forward with concentration as he typed search words and looked at the glowing screen.

Several fruitless searches later, Argyle typed, "Meglamon Crime Bad" into his browser and 0.25 seconds later, one link appeared. It was a Wikipedia page address and Argyle was thrilled. *Wow! One web site, this is gonna be good!*

Clicking on the hyperlink, his expectations rising, Argyle waited as the page loaded onto his laptop screen.

For a split-second, his screen went black and then a tiny, wavering dot appeared in the center. Argyle leaned in closer to peer at the dot just as it quickly expanded and seemed to explode. Argyle jumped back at the suddenness as it enlarged into a grotesque and very menacing head shot of Meglamon laughing maniacally with a looping sound bite yelling loudly, "You've Been Hacked! You've Been Hacked!"

Argyle jammed his finger on the Sound Off key and sat there looking at the now mute laughing face on his screen.

Wonder if The Thrasher has a page like this?

Ben sat down at his desk and took a moment to watch Gilbert, who had broken a sweat over the whole duct tape repair job he was engrossed in. Eventually Ben picked up a rubber band and became fascinated with winding it around his fingers and snapping it on his thigh. This eventually bored him so he hooked the band under a fingernail, stretched it out as far as it would go, aimed at Gilbert's head and let fly.

Thwack!

"Ouch," yelped Gilbert, covering the spot with a hand and looking up at Ben with annoyance. "What'd ya do that for?"

Ben, ignoring Gilbert's protest, answered his question with a question. "What exactly was it that you did over at Meglamon's?"

Gilbert was not expecting this. He stood up and pretended to test his taped-up chair by moving it around and studying the movement of the wheels, noting that the one he just repaired didn't move at all. His thoughts raced, *These guys just got back from a meeting with Thrasher and now they're asking me about Meglamon. Stay calm. Act cool.*

"Oh, you know. The usual."

"Refresh my memory," Ben said, affecting a toothy smile.

"I did a lot of Accounting. Balanced money in with money out. Mostly it was out." Gilbert stopped talking. As the words left his mouth, he knew they made him sound boring and he thought to punch it up a bit as he continued, "A lot of really important receipts crossed my desk. I saw things." Gilbert fell silent.

Ben was twisting another rubber band around the end of a pencil and stopped his movements to look at Gilbert.

"What kind of receipts?"

I'm in trouble now. The best paperwork I saw was from a company threatening to sue Meglamon for non-payment of a water-heater repair bill. Gilbert moved his story forward, "Meglamon had legal troubles. He trusted me to straighten it all out." *He swallowed hard. I've got to shut up. I'm making it worse.* "Let's go to lunch!"

Ben smiled, "Not just yet."

Argyle added, "We're not hungry."

Ben continued, "Seems that Meglamon trusted you pretty good. What else did he trust you with? Besides his legal woes, that is," and sat staring blank-faced at Gilbert, hands frozen in movement waiting for a reply.

"Well, he never really confided anything to me. He wasn't that way, you see."

"What way was he?"

Gilbert gulped, "Secretive and cranky. Got angry if his lunch was late." Moving his look from Ben to Argyle, Gilbert had to wonder what they were after or were they just trying to make him look bad, again.

Argyle looked up, closed his laptop and stared hard at Gilbert. "Did Meglamon ever ask you to develop anything… weapons, poison gas, giant goo-monsters, anything… with your fancy Chem. degree?"

Sputtering, Gilbert replied, "No, no, nothing! I told you, I left Meglamon's stupid 'ol rickety organization to join Thrasher's corporation, to become a henchman, my life-long dream!"

Gilbert was truly shaken and glanced back and forth from Argyle to Ben and back as if half expecting either of them to jump up and pound him. Finally, he croaked out, "I've got to go to the bathroom."

Gilbert quickly got up and left but was back within ten seconds. "Forgot my change for the turnstiles."

When Gilbert had finally left, Ben addressed Argyle, "Seems Third knows nothing."

Argyle said, "I'm not too sure about that." And after a moment added, "Let's give it a couple more days. I've got to think."

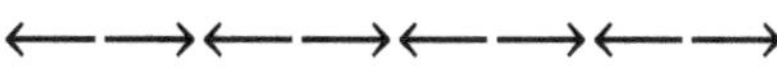

The last few hours of the day were painfully slow. Gilbert pulled out his Crime Manual and tried to look thoughtful and studious as he flipped pages and sipped a chocolate Yoo-Hoo.

Ben watched Gilbert until he became bored and eventually wandered off to goof around with some of the other henchmen.

Argyle was engrossed with his Meglamon search results. It looked like Meglamon had started out pretty strong when he inherited his daddy's crime business but managed to run it into near bankruptcy. His crimes, for the past year, according to the local paper's page eight articles, ranged from stealing gasoline from parked cars to bashing in coin boxes on Laundromat washing machines. Three times, the police picked up his men for running over parking meters and attempting to steal the coins that would spill out.

This doesn't sound like a super crime outfit, mused Argyle. *Looks like Meglamon is a poor manager. Or maybe he has other plans. Plans he may have mentioned to Gilbert. I'll bide my time, then...*

Ben bounded back, yelling over to Henchman Sperry, "Yes, we'll see about that!" interrupting Argyle's train of thought, at which point, Argyle looked up.

"Time to go home. Ben, stick around a minute. I want to talk with you."

"Sure thing, Arg."

Both men stared straight-faced at Gilbert and watched as he packed up his papers and stood up to leave. Both gave him a silent nod and he smiled and said that he would see them tomorrow.

Did they just give the silent nod to break my kneecaps? Gilbert shuddered and picked up his pace. By the time he got outside, he had a couple thoughts forming in his brain.

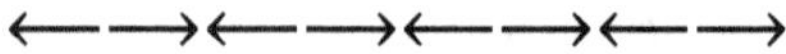

Ben made the easy walk from the seedy warehouse lair, through a couple of trash-strewn alleys, overgrown with tall weeds, to the stinky river shore where his camp cruiser (nah... it's a tugboat) was tied up.

Ben had bought the "Party-Oh" when he first hired into Thrasher's organization. He thought to save his money and eventually buy a real bachelor pad up on Fifth Street and live among the swanks and glittering storefronts. He pictured the beautiful babes that would fight to have one night with him and all the expensive beer he would buy. It was a good dream. Unfortunately, Ben wasn't very good at saving his money, nor was he good at working at his career. After two months completing his training and receiving his "promotion" because a henchman was careless on a caper, Ben returned to his lazy, slacker ways. The rest was history. Meaning, Ben still lives on the "Party-Oh" tugboat that is tied up on the stinky river.

Tossing his keys into a bowl by the door, Ben threw open some windows, grabbed a beer, and plopped down in front of his TV.

Gilbert had hidden himself behind a Dumpster and waited for Ben to leave work and then followed him at a discreet distance as he picked his way between buildings, making his way the few hundred steps home.

Now he crouched behind some weedy shrubs and watched as Ben slugged down beers. He was on his fifth one when Gilbert made his move.

Ben jumped when he heard the small rock hit his cabin door and heard his name called out. Setting his beer down and taking hold of his pistol, he rose from his chair and moved with caution toward the door, dimming the lights on his way.

No one has ever knocked before, thought Ben, and standing aside called out, "Who's there?"

"It's me, Gilbert."

"Oh," letting out a sigh, "Third!" Ben whipped the door open, "Did you miss your bus?"

"No, I just thought to visit you, that's all."

"Come in, sit down, can I get you a beer?"

"No thanks," Gilbert glanced around the shabby cabin. "Got any Yoo-Hoo?"

"Nope. Just beer."

The two sat for a nervous minute just looking at each other until Gilbert said, "So what was the third degree all about, today?" Gilbert put on his tough face and looked hard at Ben.

Ben noticed Gilbert's "deer in the headlight" stare and took it for what it looked like: Gilbert is clueless.

"Well, you see it's like this. We just wanted to get to know you better, that's all. Sure you don't want a beer?" Ben asked as he got up to retrieve another one for himself.

"No. I said no." Catching himself, Gilbert softened the hard edge of his voice, "Thank you." Gilbert thought to himself that it didn't go well the last time he had a beer. Best to stick with Yoo-Hoo.

Gilbert waited for Ben to return to his chair then continued, "It seemed that all the 'Get to know me' questions centered around Professor Meglamon and I want to know why. What is that all about? Especially after you two guys got back after your meeting with Barry." Gilbert gulped. *Ok, it's out there. He knows I know; let's see how he answers.*

Ben just smiled and said, "Oh, Third, you're imagining things. Oh look, a Gunsmoke rerun is on!" And turned the TV volume up.

How annoying. Gilbert had to raise his voice to be heard, "Is Barry mad at me? Is Argyle mad?" and waited for Ben to answer.

Ben took a sip of his beer and shushed Gilbert. "Wait for the commercial."

Gilbert sat quietly but his mind was a mess. *If Barry thinks I'm still working for Meglamon then I'm in trouble. Isn't it obvious that I'm not? Wouldn't I be driving a nice new Lexus instead of taking the bus? Really?*

Gilbert shouted over the TV sound, "Gotta get going, Ben, I'll see you tomorrow."

Ben smiled and raised his beer can in salute and went back to watching Marshal Matt Dillon sweet smile Kitty Russell as Doc Adams looked on.

Once outside, Gilbert felt nauseous and his head flooded with thoughts. *Those guys are up to something. What is it? Am I being set up? I'm going to need a plan.*

Chapter Two

They Show Up

Meanwhile, on the other side of town…

It was a few minutes past noon. The sun shone brightly, and the sky was a fantastic deep color that made one think of the word azure. One of those perfect, tranquil summer days.

All of a sudden, a brilliant light exploded, and little sparks flew out in all directions accompanied by a low rumbling noise, just as at its center, three figures suddenly materialized. They stood frozen, crammed closely together, shoulders uncomfortably hunched up to their necks, arms plastered at their sides, faces distorted in shock as they took a few seconds to seemingly get their bearings. You see, these men are so obviously from the future and that's how time travel works.

The few pedestrians who witnessed the light show gawked in surprise and slowly moved away from the apparition as if it was contagious.

Recovering their wits, the three men shook themselves out and relaxed a bit. The taller one smiled, tipped his hat to the crowd and said, "Thank you ladies and gentlemen. Show is at 8:00PM tonight. Don't miss it!" and took a bow.

The onlookers, recovering their own wits, smiled, laughed, and clapped, then moved on, thinking they had just seen a promotion for a magic show.

Grotcom, the tallest of the three men, surveyed the street corner they stood on and the intersection it faced. "Hey, Bintcom," he said, addressing one of his companions, "look up... " looking up at the street sign above his head, "Park Street and Second Street. Find out where we are."

Bintcom, an average looking guy in his mid-thirties, pulled a little flip-device out of his shirt pocket and busied himself with one-fingered typing.

Malcom, an older guy with a potbelly, immediately produced a little hand-held device and spoke into it. "Mid-century Western United States, corner of Park and Second, tourist mode, go!" The little device started talking, ⚡ ⚡ *On this spot in 1972, a guitar player, playing for tips, was arrested for panhandling. He went on to become the town sheriff, and...* ⚡ ⚡ Malcom pressed the "audio off" button, silencing the device. "Apparently my e-history book made it through."

Bintcom spoke, "According to this, we're close to The Thrasher's lair, but sources are vague at best because The Thrasher was good at conspicuous concealment."

Grotcom nodded and stood for a moment, arms akimbo, eyes searching the scenery. "Let's walk around for awhile, get the lay of the land, maybe talk with a few locals."

His companions agreed and Malcom switched his e-history device back on. ⚡ ⚡ *In the mid 21st century, malware became so prevalent that most young programmers quickly learned how to turn the evil code into harmless but fun games. Many got rich off this source code and...* ⚡ ⚡ Malcom turned the volume down and touched the "search" button. ⚡ ⚡ *Yes Malcom. How may I help you?* ⚡ ⚡ In response, Malcom said, "Tour guide: find the closest coffee bar."

Grotcom and Bintcom turned to look at him. Malcom shrugged. "What? Time travel always makes me hungry for sweetened bread products." Then affected a sheepish look of embarrassment.

The tour guide chimed out, ⚡ ⚡ *The closest coffee bar is eight blocks south of your current position.* ⚡ ⚡

The three stood for a moment then Grotcom said, "Ok. We'll start there, energize ourselves on healthy carbohydrates and plan our next step."

Bintcom added, "Try to look like we belong here, blend in."

Before his advice was fully heeded, Malcom had stopped a pedestrian and was engrossed in conversation.

"We're looking for The Thrasher. Do you know him?"

The pedestrian appeared not to comprehend what Malcom was saying.

"The Thrasher's lair. Know where that is located?"

By this time, the pedestrian had stepped back in alarm. "No. No one does."

Grotcom stepped up, "Don't mind him, he's a tourist." And took a hold of Malcom's arm and pulled him away. The pedestrian hurried on.

Leaning in close to Malcom, Grotcom said, "What're you trying to do? Get us caught?"

Malcom looked hurt. "Sorry boss. Thought I was helping. I'll be better after I load up on carbs."

Bintcom thumbed it down the street, "Carbs are that way."

As the three travelers walked on, they totally clicked into tourist mode, pointing out aspects of the "ancient architecture" and admiring a "large tree." Bintcom's device was telling them that the large tree, a Coast Live Oak… *Had gone extinct in the early 23rd century when a hybrid insect, one that escaped from a top-secret bio-lab, had taken a liking to oak trees. Scientists were unable to capture or eradicate the voracious little demons so just hushed the whole affair up.*

"Sure glad I upgraded my app to version 3406.1 with the full range expanded 720 terabyte knowledge socket," said Bintcom, smiling at his little hand-held device. "The stuff it comes up with."

The coffee bar destination is in three blocks.

The trio ambled slowly down the street, eyes agog, taking everything in. In short time they were standing in front of a pet store. Malcom had his face pressed to the store window trying to peer further into the store. Bintcom was studying a lizard that was laying on a rock under a lamp and was amusing himself by sticking his tongue out at the creature and waiting for a reaction, which never came.

Grotcom tried the door and it opened under his hand. "I have heard about 'Living Museums' of the 21st century but never thought I'd ever see one. I'm going in."

Inside, the three travelers stood spellbound. They could not believe what they were seeing. Just in front of them was a small wooden pen that corralled several puppies. Some were bouncing around, yipping with play. Others were snoozing on little blankets, paws twitching as they dreamed.

Bintcom whispered, "Is that one diseased? Look at it! It's spastic!"

The clerk had watched the men come in and waited to see what they were going to do. Sensing their confusion, he approached them, "Is there anything I can help you with? Are you here to find a pet for that someone special? A child perhaps?"

Malcom was taken back, "You sell children here?"

"What? No!" stammered the clerk, wondering if he heard correctly.

Grotcom quickly diffused the situation, "Don't mind him, he's a tourist."

The clerk looked relieved, nodded and said, "Yes, of course," and turned from the group. "I'll be over there. If you need anything, just ask."

Grotcom smiled, "Thanks," and led the little party further into the store.

Bintcom started taking a picture of everything. "When I get back, I'm going to post these to my Facecram page. My close acquaintances will be duly impressed."

The men spent the better part of an hour in the "Living Museum" store looking at everything.

There were rows of glass enclosures that housed lizards, turtles, snakes, and spiders. All warmed by lamps and set up to look like dioramas of the 26th century except that these creatures were alive! Not moth-eaten, hay-stuffed little replicas.

The birds squawked with indignation at seeing Malcom's face crammed right up so close, and all moved to the far side of their large cage.

Grotcom and Bintcom were both bent over peering into a fish tank when Malcom joined them.

The three were mesmerized and stood frozen for minutes staring into the little ocean scenes watching brightly colored fish swim back and forth.

They had not heard the clerk come up. "That one there is a Silver Arowana," he said, pointing at an eight-inch-long squiggly thing rooting on the gravel bottom. "And there's a bunch of little guppies."

His silent approach and the suddenness of his voice made the men jump.

Malcom blurted out, "Won't they drown in there?"

Grotcom straightened out and standing behind Malcom he couldn't help but notice the puzzled expression on the clerk's face and said, "Tourist," arching his eyebrows to show mild humor.

The clerk said, "Oh yes," nodded to Grotcom and in a fairly sympathetic voice addressed Malcom, "No, they won't drown. They're perfectly happy. See?" pointing to a fish that was swimming slowly by.

Malcom looked confused.

Grotcom then announced, "We should be leaving now," and strode to the door with Malcom and Bintcom following closely behind. Once outside he said, "Ok. That's enough goofing around. Let's get a coffee and some carbs, we have to make a plan."

Fifteen minutes later, Grotcom, Bintcom, and Malcom were ensconced at a back table at Neet's Coffee House. They had stumbled through ordering and paying for their coffee and snacks.

Bintcom was saying, "I thought we were made when Malcom tried to pay by cramming his forehead onto the credit card mechanism."

Malcom said, "Sorry fellas, I forgot where I was."

Grotcom said, "Well, at least the whole 'He's a tourist' thing works."

The three sipped their Triple Caf Quad Espressos and picked at their tasty carb icing rolls and considered their day.

Grotcom spoke, "I think somehow we need to capture The Thrasher and take him back with us to the future. He's a reasonable man. Once he sees what his time machine has done to screw up humanity, he'll just not invent it."

"Chaa, I don't know how sensible a guy named 'Thrasher' is gonna be," said Bintcom. "I think we should just flat out kill him. We sneak up behind him and POW! Kill him."

Malcom sucked the icing from his finger, "I think we ought to capture him, take him for a ride back to the dinosaurs, all the while explaining to him how his time machine created a commuter nightmare, and dump him out for a big Croc-O-Saur-Puss to eat." He picked up his other tasty carb icing roll, this one with banana chips in it, and said, "Say this is The Thrasher and I'm a hungry Saur-A-Puss," and took a big bite shaking his head and making monster noises to illustrate his point. "Simple."

"Even if he's not reasonable, he would be a man out of time," said Grotcom.

"A man in our own time!" argued Bintcom.

"Croc-O-Saur," sang Malcom, smiling at the other two.

The conversation went on like this for some time. None of the arguments won any of the men over but they were lively and wildly creative and outlasted two more cuppas and a sugar cookie. One could still hear them as they exited the coffee bar and walked on.

Chapter Three

Robots Are Gonna Take Our Jobs!

Day six without a good caper, thought Argyle as he sat at his desk surveying the rest of the office. It was noisy and filled with idle henchmen, all dressed in today's designated work wear all according to the ornate marquee in the locker room… a snappy pin-striped, light blue jumpsuit with one orange sleeve and the opposite orange pant leg. The collar flaps sported large Thrasher logos with red sequined eyes. Each man wore the required red socks and white sneakers, appropriately showing Thrasher logos at the ankle.

The spangled red eyes on the jumpsuit collars did not cheer Argyle up. Normally he would delight in seeing so many eyes glinting in the harsh glare of the overhead phosphorescent lights. He would imagine daring daylight capers where so many sequins would blind their victims, making the episode more manic and fearsome. But not today.

Today, Argyle sat feeling sorry for himself.

Yesterday, Thrasher loosed a few dozen "robots" into the henchmen's office space and the adjoining break room. Basically, every room on Sublevel Two was crawling with these little, rounded disks, all scurrying about the floors, bumping into walls, beeping incessantly, and getting caught in the tangle of cords and wires strewn under every desk in the main office room.

One particularly insistent little disk repeatedly bumped into Argyle's foot sputtering the phrase, "Hey, move," (bump) "Hey, move," (bump) "Hey, move" (bump). Argyle picked up his foot and when the thing squeaked forward, brought his boot down on the annoying little thing with such force that the top crushed in and two wheels were smashed. Argyle, with a huff of contempt, had kicked it two desks away where it lay on its back, disabled and whining, "Please, (whir,

whir) Please…," until Alexey, the gofer henchman, picked it up, gave it one good blow to its circuit underbelly, silencing it, and tossed it into a nearby waste can.

Today, the majority of these little domed annoyances lay silent, strewn haphazardly all about, their batteries drained, their blinky lights dull.

Argyle, Ben, and Gilbert sat at their desks waiting for something to happen. Waiting for the call to action, a caper demanding courage, a reason to shoot guns!

The minutes dragged on and on.

How much "In-A-Gadda-Da-Vida" can I tap out, thought Argyle, pencils frozen in mid-air, in mid-beat, *before I go stir crazy?* After a moment of non-thought, *Who am I kidding, I love that song!* and resumed tapping on this desktop, idly looking around the office.

Ben sat with his feet up, draped across a desk drawer, studiously picking at his fingernails with a penknife. He almost poked his finger with the knife's point when his cell phone rang. It was the sporting goods store over on Seventh. Four weeks ago, Ben had ordered some fifty-pound test fishing line and it was now ready for pick-up. Ben had heard that giant bass lived at the very bottom of the stinky river. Somewhere below the stink. He figured that he could cut his grocery bill down by fishing for his dinner.

Having pressed the Answer button and greeted the store clerk, Ben responded, "Oh, that's great. I'll be by after work. How late are you open?"

Nine. (click)

"Whoa. Hello! Hello!" Ben called into his now dead phone connection. He looked up at Argyle who shrugged with disinterest.

Ben dialed the sporting store's line and after a couple of seconds, said, "Hey! Did you just hang up on me?"

(click)

"I didn't get a 'goodbye' outta that guy," Ben announced to no one in particular.

Gilbert sat motionless, staring at a spot on the ceiling. Argyle had glanced up to see what the deal was but saw only a dark, rusty water spot that didn't hold his attention. He was more curious about what Gilbert found so fascinating about a stain on the ceiling. Gilbert sat, looking up, but jumped at the sound of a loud click that came from the waste can that held the dying remains of one of Barry's "Floor Bots", as the little pests had quickly become known as.

The gentle whirring of the surveillance camera alerted the office denizens to its scanning and panning, and Argyle had to suppress a small snort of laughter as he watched the other henchmen instantly straighten up, act busy, and smile as the camera's lens moved about the room.

As soon as the cameras settled back into their stationary position, Gilbert got up, went to the waste can, and stood bent over, peering down at the bashed-up mess that groaned every few minutes as it struggled through its last moments of battery life.

Just then the P. A. System crackled to life and the noise level of the office quickly dropped to zero as everyone came to attention…

> *I suppose by now, you all have noticed my little army of... ahem, robots, robotics, robotic creatures! Yes. My robotic-like creature-like mechanical things. Well, my sturdy henchmen, that was only the beginning.* (…Barry's voice starts to rise…) *Soon I will unleash the most fearsome robot army to ever have been conceived.* (…his voice approaching fever pitch…) *From the mind of The Thrasher! I will rain down terror on all those who oppose me! You'll see!!*

The P. A. System clicked silent. The henchmen were stunned silent until Sparry yelled out, "Robots are gonna take our jobs!" Then, the entire office erupted into a manic chaos.

Under cover of the boisterous disorder, Gilbert saw his opportunity. He seized the damaged Floor Bot out of the waste can and quickly stuffed it into his backpack that he had slung over the back of his chair earlier that morning. He then sat down like nothing had happened.

But Argyle had seen and sat with a sly smirk on his lips staring sideways at Gilbert. When Gilbert caught Argyle's look, he flushed with panic but recovered an outward calm and returned an awkward smile.

Argyle nodded a slight nod, raised two fingers to his eyes and turned his hand to point the two fingers straight at Gilbert, holding them there for at least three long menacing seconds.

Gilbert almost lost it. *Shit. Don't panic. Stay calm. Think of something.*

After Sparry's crazed outburst and ensuing disruption, Ben had gotten up and joined in the fray. He was just now returning to his desk to rejoin Argyle and Gilbert.

"This is really bad news. There's talk about our jobs being outsourced! That can't happen, could it? Where would we go, Argyle? What would we do?" Ben slumped down into his chair looking sad and dejected and, in a fading fairly whiny voice said, "What are we gonna do?"

A muffled clicking sound escaped from Gilbert's backpack.

Ben sat up, alert, "What was that? Did you hear that?" looking at Argyle.

"I didn't hear anything. How about you, Third? Did you hear something?" giving Gilbert a smirky look, again.

"No, no. I didn't hear anything. Must be rats, I guess."

By now, the office henchmen had settled down. Some were standing in small groups grumbling among themselves, others were on their cell phones talking in muffled tones behind cupped hands.

Argyle stopped his pencil thrumming and announced that he was going to lunch. He stood up and looking at Gilbert, said, "You stay here and answer the phone." Then turned to Ben and asked, "Hungry?"

Ben got up and followed Argyle into the break room and stood shifting his weight from left leg to right as he stared blankly into the candy machine.

Argyle dropped a series of coins into the Lunch-o-Matic's slot and selected a baloney and mayo with sweet pickles sandwich that dropped down into the pick-up tray with a noisy almost sickening thud. He then moved to the drink machine but came away empty-handed as the machine was empty… as it had been last week when he wanted a nice cold Bubble Up Lemon Lime soda, but the machine had been empty then too.

Ben stood staring at the last two malted marshmallow bars in the display window. "I can't decide."

Argyle moved to a small table near the corner and grabbed a chair. "Never mind, Ben, you'll figure it out. Hey, let's talk."

Ben, still stunned by Barry's announcement, flopped down in a chair and said, "Whazzup?"

"Forget that stuff about downsizing and outsourcing. It's not going to happen to us. We're fine. But just in case, Gilbert has an 'in' with Meglamon. Speaking of which… we've only got two more days until Barry wants some insider information outta Gilbert. What have you come up with?"

"Not much. I trapped him in the elevator yesterday and asked him a bunch of questions like, 'How often did you and Meglamon talk, what did you talk about, what's Meglamon's favorite color', you know, stuff like that." Ben was counting the change from his pocket and looking up at Argyle asked, "Got a dime?"

Argyle took a big bite of baloney and chewed on it while he thought, *Ben's near to useless. I've got to do everything myself.* Furrowing his brow, Argyle took another bite of baloney and continued thinking, *Gilbert is stealing a Floor Bot. Why? Is it for Meglamon? That's pretty ballsy, stealing from Thrasher and giving to Meglamon. Who would have guessed Third could be so clever? Wait a minute, if that's true, then Ben and I are in big trouble, Thrasher trouble, cuz we recommended Third for the job.*

Argyle swallowed the last bite of sandwich and got up. "We've got to come up with something. Fast."

The rest of the afternoon was depressing. Henchmen were grumbling and slamming desk drawers to release their growing frustrations.

The Gun Range, down on Sublevel Four, was filled to capacity by 12:30PM and booked solid for the rest of the day.

Argyle desperately wanted to shoot his gun but opted for two hours on the par course on Sublevel Three. He would beat his own time on the "Course of Obstructions", burning baloney calories and thinking about what he was going to tell Barry about Gilbert's secret relationship with Meglamon. Time was slipping away and as every good henchman knew, Barry waits for no man.

"Ben, take Third down to the Henchman Training Course on Sublevel Four and time him on the rope climb." Turning to Gilbert, Argyle pointed a finger and added, "You climb up and down until you can do it flawlessly and beat a time of 8.7 seconds."

Gilbert jumped up, "I can do that!" and made his way to the elevators.

Ben turned to Argyle, "No one can do 8.7 seconds. Baily holds the record at 28.3 seconds."

"Yea, well, then he'll sleep good tonight from the workout." Argyle looked after Gilbert who was stepping over a huge tangle of cables making his way to the elevators. "Keep him there for at least three hours then we'll meet back here."

Ben nodded. "I'll take my e-Padlet… gonna need my Jewel game and the Stopwatch app."

Argyle put everything he had into the first forty-five minutes of his workout. He was very proud of himself having escaped every trap, sustaining only a small cut from the ragged rusty knife that jabbed his calf from behind at par seven. It hurt and was going to leave a red, angry wound mark but Argyle had been through worse. And it was worth it as the seeds of a Gilbert - Meglamon story had started to germinate… *This is going to be good!*

Argyle had showered and changed into his street clothes and was waiting at his desk when Ben and Gilbert returned from the Sublevel Four training course.

"How'd Third do on his rope climb?"

Ben looked a little disappointed as he answered, "Not very good. His best time was…," looking at his note pad app, "72.6," and glancing over at Gilbert said, "Tell him how many times you fell."

Gilbert looked a wreck. His hair was matted down and there was a big red lump on his forehead. He looked at Argyle, his face twisted into a mixture of pain and embarrassment and said, "Eight."

Argyle asked, "How many of those were on the way up?"

"Six."

"Next week you'll go again, and again, and again until you don't fall," ordered Argyle.

The big locker room marquee had indicated that jumpsuits were required again today. Red Hammer pants, high-top sneakers with logos on their tops ($149.95 today only!), a white polo shirt with a huge Thrasher face emblazoned across the chest and belted down by a skinny black canvas belt.

Argyle was crestfallen. There were no pockets in the Hammer pants so there was no place to stash his gun. It was going to be another one of those days… no fun.

As Argyle settled into his chair, he glanced at his weekly schedule. There were no capers lined up all the way through next week and then it was a lousy office supply heist assigned to the night shift. This meant day shift was stuck doing maintenance. Crap. Argyle noticed a pencil note on next week's to-do list reminding him that he was supposed to meet with Audrey's father next Tuesday to talk about a job. Audrey had been nagging Argyle for months about how working in The Thrasher's organization was getting him nowhere but if Argyle worked for her father… well, everything would be fine.

Argyle let out a puff of breath and his eyes scanned the scheduler for the remainder of the week. *Today is Thursday. Thrasher expects information. He'll want to know what Gilbert knows about Meglamon. By tomorrow. Ok. I have the rest of today to fine tune my idea, add a little flair to it, and make it Barry-worthy.*

Ben called over to Argyle, "Hey, there's donuts in the break room!" and took his seat opposite Argyle.

"Yeah, saw 'em. No powdered ones left, and I hate the sprinkled ones."

"Arg, it's not like you to turn down a donut even if it does have sprinkles. What's up? Are you ok?"

Argyle pushed back in his chair, savoring the loud creaks the chair springs were making but even that didn't completely brighten his mood. "I've got a lot on my mind right now. I have tool maintenance duty down on Sublevel Three this morning. Should be done by 12:30PM. How about you, what are you doing today?"

"I've got to repair one of the foot traps on the Obstacle Course. Seems it didn't fire a round of buckshot when Mason stepped on it. Got away uninjured and Thrasher is very upset. Should be done by 12:30PM but if not, I can break for awhile and go at it again this after-noon."

Argyle said, "Ok. I'll meet you in the parking garage at 12:45PM. We'll do Taco Barn." Then added, "Where's Third?"

"I don't know. Climbing ropes, I suppose."

Morning dragged on. Argyle completed his chores and returned to his desk where he found a note reminding him about his meeting with Barry tomorrow. It was scheduled for 9:30AM in the Ted Bundy con-ference room just down the hall.

Ahh, that's okay. I have my story ready to go, Argyle mused as he wadded up the note and tossed it away.

His phone beeped a reminder of the time, so Argyle grabbed his sunglasses and keys and headed up to the parking garage to meet Ben and go to lunch.

The ride to the downtown was smooth and uneventful.

Argyle said, "What happened to your hand?"

Ben lifted his bandaged fist to inspect it and said, "Well. The foot-plate I was working on was stuck so I tried everything I could think of to un-stick it, but nothing worked. Finally, I just smashed it with my fist and the damn thing opened up like greased lightning and the sawed-off shotgun fired. Took the doc a half hour to pull about a dozen pellets out of my hand."

"Tough break," said Argyle.

"Yea, but it's my left hand so I can still shoot a gun. Should be back to normal in a few days."

Argyle pulled into the Taco Barn parking lot and found a place to park right in front.

Upon seeing the boys enter through the front doors, the kid running the cash register started furiously pushing menu buttons and as panic was building in his chest, stuffed a variety of items into a bag as fast as he could.

By the time Argyle and Ben reached the counter, the kid had spun around to face them holding two stuffed bags and two extra sized soda drinks, he knocked the cash drawer open, grabbed three twenties and a handful of quarters and was saying, "Gentlemen. Your order is ready. It's the usual but I've added extra sauce packets and napkins for you," and pushed the items and money across the counter. He stood nervously waiting for approval.

Ben said, "Thank you very much. You've been very helpful today," and scooped up a bag of food and a drink while winking at the kid.

Argyle made a pretense of counting the money and staring for a long second at the kid who seemed to visibly tremble in his shoes, then said, "Thanks," pointing a finger-gun at the kid before taking up his food and turning to leave.

Back inside Argyle's VW bug, Ben said, "They're always so nice here."

The ride back was more upbeat. Ben was munching away on his Beefy Taco-Rito and making slurping sounds through his straw.

Argyle, lost in thought, sipped on his drink and counted the green lights as he drove the short distance back to work.

Chapter Four

Argyle's Big Meeting

"Today is going to be a good day!" exclaimed Argyle as he placed his laptop on his desk and sat down on his chair, bouncing twice to make the springs sing. For good measure, he spun around in a circle and when he stopped, sat smiling and nodding with self-satisfaction.

My meeting with Barry is going to be great. I'm ready and my explanation of the whole Gilbert – Meglamon thing is sure to wow him. I may get a bonus out of this! Rudely, Ben interrupted his revelry.

"You're in a good mood this morning, Arg. Are there donuts in the break room?" and made to get his fair share of the donut booty.

"Nah," answered Argyle, "I've got a meeting with The Thrasher in about ten minutes. It'll be a good one."

Ben squirmed in his seat. "Am I supposed to go with you?"

"Nope. Only me. It's a private meeting between myself and Thrasher." Argyle could feel his smile widen as a few of the other henchmen in the office today, overheard his statement and looked his way. It was a very proud moment for Argyle.

The rest of the guys were thinking that it was better Argyle than any of them and looked quickly away.

Argyle slowly stood up, pushed his chair close to the desk, turned, and with what he thought was the grace of a panther, stepped over and around the tangle of power cords that littered the office floor as he made his way to the Ted Bundy conference room for his big meeting with The Thrasher.

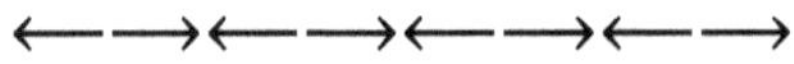

Miss Q was standing outside the closed conference room door and checked her watch as Argyle approached. She held up one finger to indicate that Argyle must wait a moment, and then at exactly 9:30AM, knocked lightly and announced, "Argyle Stevens to see you, sir."

"Yes, yes, yes!" yelled The Thrasher. "Show him in!"

Miss Q nodded at Argyle, opened the door and held it open as Argyle stepped through. "Henchman Stevens, sir," and silently left, closing the door with a quiet swoosh.

Argyle stood still trying to adjust his eyes to the low lighting of the room. *Should I turn the lights on?* he wondered.

Just as the thought left his mind, a glaringly bright light snapped on, spotlighting Barry, who was standing on a small platform at the head of the room. It made him seem eight feet tall and gave Argyle a fright.

Barry was dressed entirely in a skin-tight body suit made of a black semi-gloss material that seemed to phosphores a blue-black sheen as he moved. His hands were dark except for thin glowing white lines that sinewed from his wrist to fingertips that Argyle thought resembled skeleton bones. A form-fitting Thrasher logo mask that glowed an eerie shade of death-white concealed Barry's face.

Argyle was transfixed, staring at the apparition that stood before him. And then it moved.

Barry slowly raised his long thin arms, both hands clutching a long cape, unseen in the darkness, until now. As the cape unfolded it revealed a blindingly red sequined lining. As the cape inched upward, Barry started to emit a guttural sound. Quietly at first but building in intensity as he raised his cape until the whole drama culminated with Barry loudly screeching a maniacal laughing sound and fluttering his cape up around his head and shoulders. The specter transfixed Argyle to his spot.

It ended when Barry slammed his hands back down to his sides and stood silently, in his spotlight, staring at Argyle.

A very uncomfortable five seconds passed. Argyle's mind raced, *What does he expect me to do?*

Then, before Argyle could check himself, he started to clap as if he had just witnessed the best stage play ever performed, adding a whoop or two and praising Barry. "Oh boss, that was stupendous! That was astonishing! You look fabulous!"

Ohmygawd, ohmygawd, ohmygawd, please don't kill me!

Barry stepped down off the platform and pressed a couple of console buttons on the conference table, raising the room lights and cutting off the spotlight. Slowly he peeled the skull-mask off and shook out his dark, matted hair then raised his glaring eyes to look directly at Argyle. "Do you really think so?"

Argyle nodded with assurance, "Absolutely, you've outdone yourself this time," adding for good measure, "I was really frightened." And immediately wondered if he hadn't gone too far with that last statement.

"Do you think Meglamon will be frightened?"

Argyle thought to himself, *Doubtful, but best not to let on.* "Absolutely! He'll be scared to death!"

"Good. Sit down. We'll start today with your evaluation of Gilbert Alan Martin the Third and his relationship… with…" slamming a fist on the table and yelling, "Meglamon!"

Argyle took the chair closest to him, that is to say, the one that was farthest from Barry and was as close to the door as he dared, clearing his throat as he started, "Well it took me awhile to get anything out of Third, he's a tough little nut." Argyle hoped that a small buildup of Gilbert would make it seem that he hadn't hired a wimp into Thrasher's organization. And to impress Barry with his abilities as a clever henchman, added, "But I got it in the end. The whole story."

Barry was wringing his hands in delicious anticipation and nodding his approval.

Argyle continued, "Third was an accountant, and in that capacity, had access to certain contracts and receipts which he collected into a folder."

"Yes. Receipts. Continue."

"These contracts and receipts all indicated, to Third's sharp eye, that Meglamon was up to something big."

"Yes. Something big. Continue."

Argyle thought, *This is going well,* then continued. "This all made Third a little suspicious so he started asking a few innocent questions, like 'Why would Meglamon need a new anti-matter converter? Don't we already have one?' and eavesdropping at meeting room doors."

"Yes. Eavesdropping. Continue."

Wow, I'm on fire here... "It took determination but our little Henchman Third can be quite the feisty French bulldog if he has to. Very Fierce." Argyle noted the look of doubt on Barry's face so decided to nix the big talk about Gilbert. It couldn't possibly stand up to the test and might return to bite Argyle in the ass.

Continuing, "Well. Anyway. It seems that Meglamon is trying to develop a full-fledged cloaking device and may have a working prototype already built." Argyle smiled with pride at the story he had invented and at the masterful way he had just told Barry about it. Full of suspense and intrigue. He was not fully prepared for Thrasher's response.

"WHAT!!" Barry's voice was a shrill, high-pitched animal-like sound that paralyzed Argyle from head to toe.

Barry was up and pacing about the room, "He has not the brains to develop a cloaking device! What makes him think he can accomplish anything more technical than a waffle toaster?" And then rounding on Argyle, "Are you sure you have the story, right? That your little Gilbert-pup wasn't confused in some way?"

Argyle could actually feel Thrasher's glare burning into his face, but he gathered his wits and spoke, "Henchman Martin was very sure of his statements. They were backed up by receipts."

Barry exploded, "Receipts! Oh, yes, of course," his voice dripping with incredulous stickiness. "What else did he tell you?"

"Well... Meglamon's prototype works some of the time. He's cloaked a few frogs and one alley cat that got away before he could un-cloak it," Argyle's mouth was so dry his tongue almost stuck to the roof, but he pressed on.

"The good news is that the model runs on used vegetable oil. Meglamon can make things invisible but they stink." Adding, "Like the river, I'm told."

Barry sat down with a plop and gathered his billowy cape tightly around him. Argyle thought he looked like a death cocoon. They sat in quietude for minutes, Argyle silent and tense, Barry thrumming his fingers on the table, deep in thought.

Argyle's throat caught and he could hear his wristwatch ticking. Tick... tick... tick... *Wonder if Barry can hear it?*

After an excruciatingly long sixty more seconds, Barry slowly turned his gaze from his long sinewy fingers to Argyle's face. For a brief moment, Argyle thought he saw a strange mixture of fear and burning hatred in Thrasher's eyes.

Barry spoke, "This is very grave news, something I will have to consider. Now, there is one more matter I wish to take up with you at this time."

Fifteen minutes later, Argyle found himself out in the hallway headed back to the henchman office pit.

"Come on, step it up!"

Argyle was ushering a man-sized robot prototype down the hallway, eyeing it suspiciously and feeling embarrassed to be the keeper of the abomination.

Why me? Man this stinks… worse that the river… the other henchmen are going to go ballistic when they see this.

"Stop!" Argyle barked at the pile of metal and bolts. It stopped in its tracks. *Better check my weapon…* Argyle pulled his gun out of his belt and spun the cylinder ensuring that all the chambers were full before replacing it and snapping an order at the bot.

"Move!"

The bot moved clumsily forward, listing into the wall as it almost tripped over its own large metal blocks that were its feet. Thinking that it was walking forward, but still facing the wall, the bot shuffled its feet but made no effort to straighten itself out. The cloddy metal block-feet tapped out a rhythm as they banged against the kickboard along the wall.

Argyle had to grab at its arm and tug it straight, at which point, their progress down the hallway resumed.

The pair reached the wide entrance to the office pit and Argyle ordered to bot to stop, maneuvering it so that it faced the pit and the two dozen henchmen who sat silently staring at them, mouths agape, and eyes unbelieving.

Before anyone said anything or made any kind of move, Argyle, using as much command as he could muster, spoke, "This is THAM-1. It stands for: Thrasher's Humanoid Army of Mutilators… the first of many. The Thrasher has given me the responsibility for its testing. The Thrasher expects your full cooperation in this matter." Argyle thought the more he mentioned The Thrasher, the less crap would be blown him by the other henchmen.

He continued, "I will develop a testing plan and will enlist the aid of any of you, as the need arises. Any questions?" And waiting *NO* number of seconds, added, "Good."

Argyle commanded THAM to walk forward and after ten minutes of untangling its feet from the ever-present mess of cords and cables, made it to his desk.

"Stand there," Argyle said, indicating a spot next to his chair.

Gilbert had been sitting quietly, watching the show but was now up and eyeing the bot with admiration and excitement. Absent-mindedly, he raised a hand to touch it but froze as Argyle said, "Don't touch." Gilbert sat back down but sat nervously, waiting.

Ben had not said a word. He could tell by the scowl on Argyle's face that he was not in the mood to answer any questions or offer any explanations, so Ben sat, watching Argyle, and waiting.

Argyle sat glowering at the bot, his mind a tangle of disconnected thoughts.

The low murmuring that had started among the other henchmen as they began to realize that Barry had foisted a robot into their midst, was cut short by the loud static crackling sounds of the P. A. System coming alive. It was Barry. He was angry and screaming almost at the top of his voice…

> *If it's the last thing I do, I will see Meglamon destroyed! Wiped from the streets of this city, bones bleaching in the sun and then trampled to dust… DUST… under my boot heel! That amateur offends me with his mere presence. And how dare he dabble in the science of physics. I will crush him! I will destroy him! I will send my robot to annihilate him!!* (click)

Argyle gazed about him and when he was sure everyone was looking at him and the bot, spread his arms wide, and said, "See." Then looked at the faces turned his way, daring anyone to say anything.

Most of the henchmen caught themselves and looked quickly away, others gave Argyle weak smiles and thumbs-up, while a scant few got up and left the area.

Gilbert was infatuated with THAM and could not take his eyes off of it.

THAM stood as tall as Ben but shorter than Argyle. It had a rounded bucket-like head, a shiny metal body, big boxy boot-feet, and pincher-like things for hands. The face that had been painted on the bucket looked amusingly evil. Scowling eyebrows, beady eyes, and a toothy smile, that on closer inspection, looked like it was disguising a speaker – transmitter box. *Probably its ears and speech capabilities,* thought Gilbert. There was an antenna sticking out the top of its head and Gilbert wondered if it wasn't part of a GPS system. He was dying to get closer to this marvel, this brainchild of The Thrasher.

Ben was studying Argyle's face and when Argyle finally looked up at him, he said, "What's up, buddy?" and sat waiting for Argyle to spill the beans.

Argyle straightened up in his chair and looked from Ben to Gilbert and back. At length he spoke, "We're going to give this bot the Hench-man Test." He turned his gaze to THAM and fell silent.

"Good, Arg. Any variables to speak of?"

"Not yet."

The trio, well, now the happy little quartet, were quietly assessing their new responsibilities.

Argyle spoke first, "We'll start after lunch." And turning to THAM said, "Stay."

After taping a "Do Not Touch" sign to THAM's chest plate, the boys left for lunch.

On the ride up in the elevator, Argyle hit the Emergency Stop button, frightening Gilbert but only slightly concerning Ben.

Argyle turned and squarely faced Gilbert, glaring at him. *I should have done this to begin with,* and quick as a flash, grabbed Gilbert by the front of his work jumpsuit and flexed his bicep, thereby lifting Gilbert up off his feet.

Gilbert, surprised by the action, started to whine in protest.

"Quiet, you. Look. I know you have a dirty little dark secret.

154

Maybe one that Meglamon told you and I want you to spill it. Right now!!" Argyle frowned in anger and after shoving Gilbert a bit, let go his grip, causing Gilbert to fall loose-legged to the floor where he bent over coughing in an effort to catch his breath.

"Okay, okay. A few years ago, when I got out of college, I couldn't find a job so I did volunteer work for two years."

Argyle, flexing a fist, took a menacing step toward Gilbert, completely unnerving him.

"Wait, wait, wait! It was for Habitat For Humanity. I worked for Habitat For Humanity." Gilbert had crunched himself into the corner and now slowly looked up at Argyle, expecting to get thumped.

"That's it?" said Argyle. "That's your big secret?"

Gilbert nodded, "Yes. I'm sorry. I thought if you knew that you wouldn't hire me and I wanted to be a henchman so bad I needed to be a henchman it's been a dream of mine to be a henchman oh please oh please can I still be a henchman?" Gilbert sniffed then wiped his nose on his shirtsleeve but fell silent, looking at Argyle, who was staring hard and thinking.

Wagging a finger in Gilbert's face, Argyle said, "You owe me big."

Gilbert nodding with enthusiasm, "Yes, yes, I'll do anything, anything you need."

Ben leaned in, "Maybe a new habitat, eh?" and poked Gilbert in the chest.

Argyle pushed the Garage Level One button again and the elevator resumed its upward course.

Chapter Five

A Private Side of Thrasher

There have always been rumors about Sublevel Six. Some say that Sublevel Six is cavernous and spreads for miles in all directions, like the lost NY subway underground.

Others have said that Barry hoards a great mountain of wealth down there, made up of diamonds, rubies, bits of rare metal, and a thirty-foot diameter meteor ~ straight out of space!

Idle gossip speculated that Miss Q has been down there numerous times and has seen things with her own eyes. One time, one of the rookie henchmen stopped her to tell her that he had heard The Thrasher maintained a menagerie of live freak animals down there and asked if that was true, Miss Q listened courteously until the rookie was done speaking and then, with eyes wide in surprised innocence, told him that she had never heard that one before, then walked away shaking her head in disgust.

Whatever the rumors were, or are, or will become, no one but The Thrasher will ever know exactly what goes on in Sublevel Six.

Truth be told, Sublevel Six *is* a large cavernous space that only The Thrasher is truly familiar with.

The main introduction to Sublevel Six is through a small anteroom with several doors leading off in many directions. In this anteroom hangs a portrait of Barry's mother, Mrs. Teasdale, stern-faced and posed in her finest housecoat. She seems to be glaring straight ahead and conveniently, right at the observer. The portrait is lit from above, casting shadows across the painting that seem to make it appear grainy and unrefined. It's the first thing Barry sees when he enters Sublevel Six *(Hello Mother)* and the last thing he sees when he leaves *(Don't worry Mother, I'll be back soon)*.

There are four distinct work areas and one small area for living. The living area consists of a single sized bed, usually unkempt. A bedside table piled with technical manuals and notebooks crammed with ideas and pictures and manic late-night scribbling. A dresser stands against a wall next to an antique wardrobe where Barry's finest pieces of clothing are kept. The lighting in this space is quite modest with all the lumens provided by two table lamps that snap on and off by a wall switch.

The work areas that are currently set up are an office, an electronics work area, a machine shop, and a supply warehouse and depot.

Barry's office is crammed full of drivers and routers and things that blink. There is a wall of video monitors that have an almost constant video feed from all the cameras he had installed throughout the lair, including the parking garage and his exclusive rooftop. There is an extensive and powerful P. A. System that Barry uses for spur-of-the-moment henchman training, or as is whispered behind his back, "Barry Rants."

The electronic gadgetry is arranged in a loose circular fashion around the outside walls of the room. This surrounds a large hoop of a table that in turn, allows for a large fairly luxurious office chair to move about in the center. Imagine Barry at command central, turning this way or that, watching this monitor or that, pushing this button or that, listening to this conversation or that. Can be very scary.

When Barry is musing over a problem, he will either steal away to his rooftop where he can be alone and think, eying the city and dreaming of domination, or he will sit in his office watching… and listening… and thinking. Either way, he'll solve his problem!

The electronics work area looks cluttered at first glance, but it is anything but. There are many, mismatched, parts bins holding tiny transistors, spools of thin copper wire, gold tipped connectors, thermoelectric devices, batteries, flasher alarm lights, antennas of every length and style, cables, snap action sensors… just to name a few of the things neatly stored there. Each bin and cubbyhole has been meticulously labeled and parts are never mixed up or misfiled. A discipline Barry learned from his Mother.

When The Thrasher bends to his task, when he is on a roll developing his latest creative endeavor, the last thing he needs is to go searching for a 1.5 amp 200 volt full-range bridge rectifier!

The workbench is usually clear, with all tools and parts returned to their special places, although sometimes there is a work in progress left standing, especially if The Thrasher became distracted or had to attend to company business.

Down the hallway, a step or two, is a great room space that functions as a machine shop. This is where Barry's really big ideas are brought to life, like THAM-1. Here metal can be pressed and drilled or sanded with abrasives to remove spurs. Things can be welded, blasted, torched, pressurized, stress-tested, atomized, drowned, rolled, bent, vibrated, or tumbled. All that takes machines, big machines, and things like liquids, grit, and high-pressure air, as well as safety glasses, earmuffs, helmets, and explosive devices. THAM-1 didn't just happen in a vacuum!

The last workroom that was set up in Sublevel Six was the supply warehouse and depot. This is a biggie. It holds multiples of everything, stored and inventoried and organized.

As Sublevel Six was being excavated, it was discovered that it sat above an ancient, long-abandoned tunnel. Speculation at the time was the tunnel had been an attempt to build a commuter road underneath the stinky river sometime in the early 1700's but was abandoned because no matter what was tried, the stinky river always managed to seep through and, well, stink the place up. Efforts were abandoned, the tunnel sealed, and political ties cut and buried. Eventually it was forgotten.

The breakthrough from the supply warehouse proved fortuitous for Barry. It didn't take too much to unseal the tunnel out in one direction and begin delivery of his private supplies. He was also fortunate enough to find a small group of homeless, semi-mutant men camped nearby the tunnel entrance, who, when they saw the tunnel seal crumble down and Barry suddenly emerge into the full moonlit night, fell to their knees in humble praise, thinking him the living embodiment of Snalt, a grotesque god from outer space they assumed had come to save them.

Barry took advantage of the situation immediately. He turned them into delivery handlers who used hand-trucks and carts to wheel Barry's supplies to the supply warehouse delivery point. All for a few coins and the occasional glare. They were very grateful.

Sublevel Six was the home of developments such as the myriad of torture devices proudly displayed throughout the lair, it fostered the brilliance behind the par course and shark tank combo and grew the idea of robotic-like mechanical things (think Floor Bots) like his THAM-1 humanoid that was the prototype of his future Bot Army and a prime example of Barry's tenacity.

As of late, Barry had fallen deeper and deeper into a dark, black funk. It was not enough to create a bot that looked menacing. Barry needed to take his desires of world crime domination to the next step. The thinking and planning of this new adventure was compulsive. It drove Barry to parts of his mind where only true evil lived, it was a dark, reclusive place where his state of mind was hostile, quick to flare but at the same time reflective and imaginative. The more time Barry brooded in this dark place, the longer he was away from the daily business of the lair.

Barry emerged from one of these black funks, inspired by the bare seed of a world domination idea and began furiously scribbling his thoughts and drawing weird pictures in a notebook when he was interrupted by his phone ringing, which chased the thoughts from his conscious mind and caused him to explode with anger. He was so furious, he stomped to the machine shop and blew up five bags of grit to calm his temper.

After that, Barry drew up maintenance schedules, a few caper suggestions, and shift assignments and told Miss Q she was in charge and to only call if it was an emergency.

Now, Barry sat poring over his notebooks, aligning all the ideas contained within, measuring the progression of his mind, and mapping the future of crime.

Chapter Six

The Testing of THAM

Argyle wrestled THAM into the elevator and pushed the button for Sublevel Three. He decided to set up a bot testing area in one of the smaller unused rooms down the back hallway.

When the elevator doors opened, the boys stepped out. Argyle turned to THAM and said, "Follow me."

The bot took a few steps forward and then uttered its first words, "Thrasher is crime king."

This shocked Argyle, *It speaks?* "What did you say?"

The bot's bucket head swiveled a bit to the right, back to the left, and then forward again as it said, "Thrasher is marvelush."

Ben, who had stood by listening, said, "I think it means: Marvelous. Thrasher is marvelous."

"We have a lot of checkout and testing to do," Argyle pondered, rubbing his chin and looking suspiciously at the bot.

"Third," called Argyle, "Get paper and pencils, you're taking notes."

Gilbert had been standing several feet away, transfixed and staring wide-eyed at the shark tank, the 396,000-gallon habitat that took up most of Sublevel Three's great room. Barry's pride and joy.

Argyle and Ben stepped closer to see what Gilbert was looking at. What they saw was fascinating. Four of the six Great Whites were lined up in the tank in such a way that it appeared they were watching Gilbert.

Ben moved to Gilbert's side and buddy-slapped him on the back. "Seems the girls like you, Third."

Gilbert jumped. "Why aren't they moving? Don't they have to keep moving or die?"

Ben looked thoughtful. "Yes. Strange, isn't it?"

Argyle, with the bot close behind, interrupted their musings, "Let's use the Pillory Room."

Barry named his Sublevel Three rooms after torture devices. There was the Thumbscrew Room, the Knee Splitter Room, and the Head Crusher Room. But the Pillory Room would do just fine.

Ten minutes later, the quartet was ensconced in the Pillory Room. Gilbert took three minutes to run back up to the office pit where he grabbed a steno pad and four pencils. He was now sitting at a small table, pencil poised over paper waiting to take notes.

Ben had been dispatched to fetch miscellaneous items that would be needed for the battery of tests Argyle had thought up. As he returned from his errand, he noticed that Argyle was gone and as he dropped a length of rope, a large box of sidewalk chalk, and a pair of spandex leotards, size 3XXL, into a pile, asked, "Where's Arg?"

Gilbert looked up from his doodles, "He left ten minutes ago. Said he'd be right back."

Ben nodded his acknowledgement and then walked over to THAM. Peering at the hastily painted face he remarked, "Damn. This thing is ugly."

Just then, Argyle pushed the door open and dragged in a cart loaded with boxes and other items. "Help me unload this stuff. I'll tell you where." Lifting a box marked Guns-N-Stuff, Argyle indicated to Ben to move the other box, marked Jump-N-Run over to a point just past where the bot stood. Gilbert pitched in where he could.

It took the guys about half an hour to set everything up and when they were finished, they stood back to admire their handiwork.

There were five distinct testing areas set up: Strength, Agility, IQ, Weapons, and Caperware.

"Pretty impressive, Arg," Ben said, smiling at the scene, "But wouldn't it be better to just toss the bot into the shark tank and be done with it?"

"Yeah," said Argyle, "I thought of that, but let's do all this first. It took me a day to come up with it and I don't like to waste my brain power." After looking around to make sure all was ready, added, "Let's get started."

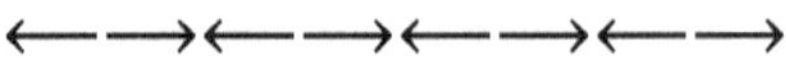

Strength testing was first.

Argyle brought out his hand-held Break Detector and set the little pressure pad on a spot on the floor. "Ben, draw about three circles around this, like a target."

"Third, let's call this the Drop Test," Argyle said, pointing a finger at Gilbert's notepaper.

Gilbert scribbled a few notes then added a little picture of a target in the right-hand margin.

Ben used a nice hot fuchsia pink colored piece of sidewalk chalk to draw circles that made the target about three feet wide.

Argyle ordered the bot into a man-lift and stood back as he worked the remote control to lift THAM about fifteen feet into the air, carefully positioning the bucket over the target and stopped.

Turning to Gilbert, he said, "Pay close attention and write everything down. Then addressing Ben, said, "Better stand back."

When everything was ready, Argyle looked up at THAM and barked, "Jump down onto that target."

THAM took a step forward but finding only air to step on, lost its balance and tumbled forward. Arms and legs flailing against its metal sides, down THAM came with a whooshing sound, to slam into the Break Detector's sensor pad, sending up a cloud of dust, bouncing once and coming to rest on its back.

Argyle stood slack-jawed in amazement. He fully expected the bot to bust up into a million pieces, but there it was, still in one piece and now starting to wriggle, like a fat dumb bug on its back. Argyle walked over to it and tapped it in the side with the toe of his boot, "You alright?"

THAM emitted the sounds of gears whirring and said, "Thrasher good," in a slowed-down slurred kind of way.

Ben, addressing Gilbert, said, "He said, 'Thrasher is good'. Did you get that down in the notes?"

Gilbert nodded. He was drawing a little picture of THAM tumbling through air about to hit his target.

"Okay," Argyle said, "Let's set up for test two."

Argyle and Ben hobbled together several hundred pounds of dead lift weights and wrestled it into the man lift bucket. Argyle raised the bucket and skillfully rocked it back and forth until the weights tumbled out and fell with frightening speed straight down onto THAM's chest. There was a jarring sound of metal on metal followed by silence, as the three men stared, not without some disbelief, at the results.

Upon impact, THAM's arms and legs sorta jerked up in the air, twitching wildly, and Gilbert thought he saw THAM's eyes widen in shock. The weights had bounced off and rolled over to the side and THAM had lain still for about sixty seconds. Now, however, the bot was trying to upright itself by flailing its arms and rocking back and forth. It managed to roll onto its side and was pushing itself up when it said, in a garbled undertone, "Thrasher, Thrasher, Thrasher," and fell silent, staring at Ben.

Argyle spoke, the suddenness of his voice making Ben jump, "Well done THAM. The Break Detector says you just took…" tapping on the meter to make the needle jump, "eight hundred thousand psi to the chest. If you were a car you would be totaled right now." Then stood smiling to himself, proud of his mathematical abilities.

Ben moved closer. "Look, Arg. There's not a mark on him. What's he made of?"

"Titanium."

"Let me help you up, chum," said Ben as he grasped THAM's arm and attempted to get him up onto his feet.

Argyle said, "I thought arm wrestling would be a good strength test but after this I think we'll move on to the dead lift."

It took all three men to get THAM onto its feet and a minute or two later the bot was standing in the ready position.

Argyle said, "Go ahead and dead lift the thousand pounds." Then made ready to time the effort.

THAM bent over at the hips and grabbed the bar in one of its pincher hands, lifting the weight with ease, even shifting the entire thousand-pound dumbbell to the other pincher hand while it futzed with its head antenna, trying to straighten it out.

"Holy crap," gawked Ben, "We'll never wreck the thing at this rate."

Gilbert was smiling to himself as he drew another little picture of THAM. In this one, THAM was twirling the dumbbell like a baton.

"Let's move on," announced Argyle.

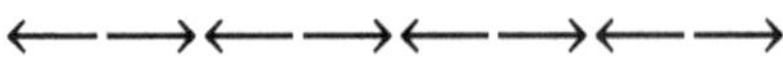

The Agility Test was second.

Argyle had Ben and Gilbert chalk out two patterns on the dusty stone floor. One was a quadrant jump test where THAM was to stand in square one, do a two-footed hop to square two to its left, a two-footed hop to square three just in front of it, and a final two-footed hop into square four to its right. THAM was to do it quickly and with grace.

Neither of which happened.

The second pattern, chalked on the floor, marked out a bunch of squares marked left and right. THAM was to run as fast as it could, placing its feet on each of the appropriate squares. This was the Quick Feet Test.

THAM had been at this test for an excruciating five minutes before Argyle called a halt to it.

Ben had been laughing so hard at THAM's efforts to "run" that he was holding his sides and tears were running down his face. "I have never seen anything so funny! Imagine THAM trying to outrun the cops! What a joke!"

Argyle had been laughing, too. It *was* a funny sight. THAM's big boxy feet trying to run.

Gilbert, however, was not amused. He felt embarrassed for THAM "At least THAM attempted to run," he said, trying in a small way to defend the bot.

Argyle turned to Gilbert with a look of mild annoyance and said, "Are your notes caught up?"

At which Gilbert busied pencil on paper, scribbling anything that came to mind but feeling Argyle's stern look on the side of his head.

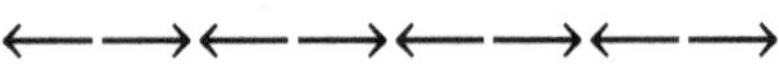

IQ Testing was next.

Argyle rummaged around in a box and came up with a large envelope marked "IQ" from which he produced a series of glossy 8x10 pictures. He held them up at arm's length so that THAM could see them.

"THAM, this is a Rorschach Test. It will tell us how smart you are.

Are you ready?"

THAM made a wagging movement of his head that Argyle took for a "Yes" and began by showing card V and waiting for an answer.

THAM spoke, "Thrasher."

Argyle showed card IV.

"Thrasher," THAM said.

Argyle showed three more cards in rapid succession.

"Thrasher, Thrasher, Thrasher," came the response.

Ben piped up, "It's a simple case of hero worship."

"Yes," Argyle said, "but is that a high IQ or is it just a dupe?" Turning to THAM, adding, "Count to ten, THAM"

THAM seemed to be struggling with that command. His head rotated left and right, and his clamper hands made little twitching movements. Finally, Argyle said, "Never mind," and THAM settled down.

Argyle turned his back on THAM, rubbed his temples with his fingertips, and muttered, "This is getting painful," adding, "Moving on, here."

Ooh, Weapons Testing!

Argyle cheered up a bit after consulting his notes and realizing that they were at the weapons portion of the test. He liked weapons. They were the best.

Argyle had Ben set up an easel and targets at the far end of the room while he produced a hand gun, a machine gun, a crossbow, and a flame thrower from a trunk and lay them in that order on the table where Gilbert sat taking notes.

Oh, the crossbow, thought Gilbert, remembering his clumsy and failed attempt to shoot the damn thing during his henchman training. *THAM will never get that one… I'll note that no one gets it anyway. That should help.*

THAM's clamper hand could not hold a handgun. On the attempt, THAM managed to clamp too hard, shattering the grip. Argyle soon realized that THAM had no real fingers so pulling triggers was impossible. He put the machine gun aside.

The crossbow was an exercise in hilarity with THAM constantly dropping the arrows and twanging itself in the face with the tightly stretched bowstrings.

It made for a very funny time and at one point, even Gilbert joined in, hearing himself as he laughed the loudest.

It was already mid-afternoon and Argyle sent Gilbert up to the break room to see if there were any donuts and to bring back several juice boxes. On his return, he found both Argyle and Ben intent on attaching something to THAM's arm. When they stepped back, Gilbert saw what it was.

"Good idea about the duct tape, Ben. It came in handy," Argyle said.

Ben was smiling ear-to-ear, "I get it by the case. It's very user-friendly stuff!"

The boys had used a half roll of the gooey backed silver stuff to tape a flamethrower to THAM's right arm and were admiring their efforts.

THAM was mumbling, "Thrasher knows all," and "Crime Lord," its head rhythmically tilting left then right. The boys ignored him.

"Third," snapped Argyle, "Make a note: THAM unable to correctly hold a flamethrower and not able to ignite it properly."

Gilbert eyed THAM more closely and noted a little scorched patch next to its left knee.

Ben saw him checking it out and said, "A little mishap with the ignition source." Then grinned.

Argyle said, "THAM, take aim at the target and fire at will."

THAM's head swiveled around to face the easel at the far end of the room, then coaxed its body to line up with its head.

WOOSH!! Blue-green flames shot out of the barrel and roiled down the room ending in a huge ball of yellow and white flames that incinerated the easel and caused big red embers to float up, up, and out of sight into the darkness.

"OK!" whooped Ben. "That's more like it!"

Gilbert said, "So. Do I have this right? If someone tapes a flame thrower to his arm, and someone else lights it, then he passes the test?" He sat, looking expectantly at Argyle.

Argyle scrunched his face in thought, then said, "Sure, why not. THAM passes flame throwing… with help." One minute later added,

"Third, you're setting up Test Five. Ben and I will be right back," and thumbed Ben to the door.

The Caperware Test

When Argyle and Ben returned from their little break, they found Gilbert sweaty and winded. He looked wiped out and was slumped back in his chair sucking greedily on a chocolate Yoo-Hoo, but by golly, he had completed Test Five setup and was damn proud of himself.

The sight was a little shocking and Argyle and Ben stood staring at THAM, neither saying a word for a long moment.

THAM stood stock still, on display. It was wearing a black skin-tight… nope… a metal-tight shirt with puffy pirate sleeves. There was a huge red Thrasher logo on the chest with glowing eyes that blinked and glared simultaneously back and forth. There was a Robin Hood-like cap duct taped on its bucket head and a large Thrasher logo taped to its antenna. It was obvious Gilbert had worked very hard to get a pair of 3XXL caper-tights onto THAM's beefy metal legs.

Gilbert basked in the moments of silence. It could only mean that Argyle and Ben were speechless with admiration. Then he spoke.

"Now, THAM"

At which, THAM raised its arms over its head and yelled at the top of its speech box, "Thrasher rules!" And waved its arms around in a manner meant to be menacing.

Gilbert beamed with pride.

Ben busted a gut laughing.

Argyle took a picture of it and immediately uploaded it to the company chat room page then said, "I have one last test."

It took five minutes to duct tape a four-ounce chunk of C4 explosive to THAM's chest and walk it to the far end of the room where it now stood, face into the corner, waiting.

Argyle ran the copper wire back to the doorway and connected it to a battery. "Cover your ears!" he said as he twisted the dial sending a charge of electricity down the wire.

The C4 exploded with a horrific boom, the force of which lifted

THAM up and projected it like a rocket across the space to land in a heap with a thud where it lay still, looking dazed.

Argyle walked up to THAM and stood studying it. There was not a mark on its shiny Titanium body but the caperware had been torn and scorched and stunk of burnt polyester.

THAM slowly started to move its limbs and tried to get up.

"Help me out here, Ben," said Argyle, making to get THAM to its feet.

"Are you ok, friend?" Ben asked THAM

THAM turned its head to look at Ben and said, "Yes. Thrasher rules."

"Yes, that's right, Thrasher rules, buddy."

Argyle stepped over to the table where Gilbert sat. "About done with those notes, Third?"

Gilbert answered, "Yeah, just now," putting a period at the end of a sentence.

Argyle scooped up the sheaf of papers and said, "Third, clean up here, then you can go home. We'll see you tomorrow."

Calling over to Ben, "Supervise, will you? And lock up on the way out."

Argyle thumbed the papers for a second or two, straightening them up and said, "THAM, you're with me."

THAM immediately followed Argyle out the door, down the hall, across the great room, and into the elevator.

A small group of henchmen, who stopped their par course workouts to watch the little parade pass by, saw two figures standing silently in the elevator as the doors slowly closed and gears and pulleys groaned as it began its labored ascent.

Chapter Seven

Time Travelers Plan Their Next Move

"Oh, bling on a stick I'm getting tired," declared Malcom as he flopped himself down on a bench seat and started undoing his shoelaces. "And why are History Shoes all looped around with strings?" Fumbling with the laces, Malcom was getting frustrated.

Grotcom was watching, with some measure of fascination, as Malcom fumbled with his laces and gave a snort-laugh when Malcom ended up tying a knot around one finger thereby tethering his hand and foot together.

In his agitation, Malcom started to pull and yank at his handiwork but only managed to get his foot out of the shoe.

"It says here," said Bintcom, waving his flip device, "that The Thrasher's henchmen routinely frequented this section of town," swiping the page forward, "because they found the (air quotes) 'fast food cuisine to be of the highest standard' (end air quote)."

"Amazing, isn't it," Grotcom said, "that it took humanity so long to realize that cholesterol, white bread, and peanuts were the most beneficial foods ever invented. The Thrasher's men were ahead of the game."

Malcom said, "Mind if we just sit here for awhile? My feet are tired from walking all morning and I'm dealing with this," holding up his hand that was hopelessly bound to his shoe, "right now."

"Yea, I guess we can use this bench as a base for awhile," said Grotcom. "Hey, Bint! Wander a few paces down that way and show that picture of those two henchmen, ask anyone if they've seen them lately." Grotcom pulled a folded and wrinkled photo out of his pants pocket and stared at it for a second. "I'll go this way," thumbing it up the street in the opposite direction. "Mal, hit up anyone passing by."

The travelers all agreed to the plan and with Malcom still studying his shoelace dilemma, Bintcom and Grotcom began canvassing the boulevard, flashing pictures of Argyle and Ben and asking questions.

Two hours later, Bintcom came rushing back to the bench base a little out of breath and very excited. He joined Grotcom, who had returned five minutes prior, and Malcom who had never moved but who, however, had freed his hand and now sat with both shoes properly laced *and* on the correct foot.

"Oh My Grute, I think we're in luck!" exclaimed Bintcom as he plopped down next to Malcom. "I showed that picture to a store clerk…"

"What kind of a store?" interrupted Malcom, "A soda pop store?"

A little annoyed, Bintcom answered, "No, Mal, it was a store full of paper cards and things." Then softening with the memory, added, "It was fascinating really, since paper went extinct… well, I guess… will go extinct in seventeen- and one-half years from now."

Grotcom was losing his patience. "Soooo? The 'lucky' part?"

"Oh, yes," Bintcom said, "The store clerk told me that these two guys are on this street every other week, Tuesday, for lunch. They come right about noon. You can almost set your watch by them." Then glancing at his wrist, "Not our proton watches, he meant the ancient carbon battery watches of this time period."

Malcom flipped through his device. "Hey, today is Tuesday."

"And the clerk said today was the 'every other' one," said Bintcom, smiling with self-satisfaction and leaning back on the bench.

Grotcom looked at his watch, "Noon is ten minutes away. All we have to do is wait until they show up. We'll approach them before they get their lunches and drive away. You guys remember our story?"

Both nodded but Bintcom spoke first, "We're here from out of town and heard The Thrasher was hiring."

Malcom added, "We have experience and would like to go with them to The Thrasher's lair for job interviews."

"Exactly," said Grotcom. "I'll offer to buy lunch so we can talk them into it."

The three travelers sat quietly together on the bench as each thought out the parts they were to play in the upcoming theatrical.

Chapter Eight

All About Gilbert

Gilbert felt he had tried, had really tried to do everything that was asked of him. He thought that his can-do attitude would win him points with the guys, Argyle Stevens and Ben Watson.

Didn't he suit up to clean the shark tank? Didn't he climb that blasted rope again and again? Who was it that always fetched donuts? Who always took last position when out on capers? Who always did the grunt work? Well, he could answer that: it was him, Gilbert, Gilbert, Gilbert. That's who. He was really starting to wonder if the guys weren't taking advantage of him.

A few weeks ago, Gilbert decided to stop feeling so sorry for himself and put a little distance between himself and the guys. To his surprise, they hardly noticed and his new life as an independent Junior Henchman became less stressed. He learned to navigate the lair, started to learn who's who among the other henchmen, and in general, stuck to his own business.

There was that time when he boosted that broken Floor Bot though. He thought he was being so stealthy. But Argyle had spotted him stuffing it into his backpack. Oh man, Gilbert thought he was a goner for sure, that Argyle would tell Thrasher, who, of course, would shoot Gilbert dead. But it was trash! It was in the trash!! Somehow Gilbert didn't think that small detail would matter much and had only hoped that his commemorative pile of donuts would be remembered with appreciation.

He sat on pins for days waiting for the worst to happen. But nothing did and office routines soon resumed. That was five weeks ago. During those five weeks, at home, alone every evening, Gilbert steadied his nerves by tinkering with the Floor Bot. He carefully disassembled it and examined its inner workings. When he found a part he was unfamiliar with, Gilbert did a detailed on-line search until he found explanations, descriptions, and functions. By the end of week two, Gilbert knew what he had, its limitations, and a solid plan for its improvement. He over-nighted a bunch of parts and was soon on his way to "fixing" the little bot.

When he was finished, his excitement level was very high. He had created a remote controlled, turbo-charged, big-wheeled, monster floor bot with heavy-duty nylon and aluminum suspension arms and oversized bumpers.

OMG!! Gilbert could make his MFB, his Monster Floor Bot, tear down the sidewalk, leave tire scratch marks for three feet, pop a wheelie for ten feet, and spit five seconds of sparks from a small port in the front grill.

It was a thing of beauty and gave Gilbert endless hours of enjoyment as he ran the bot up and down the local streets. Once in awhile, he would make it chase a pedestrian and would laugh out loud every time.

Last week, Gilbert modified his modifications to include the ability for the bot to right itself if in his exuberance he caused it to tip over. He got the idea when watching a PBS special on turtles. Gilbert added a tail that switched back and forth for no apparent reason other than it looked cool. After painting a scary face on the bot, Gilbert added a pair of dragon horns, just to make it more ferocious.

Good times. Yet. Gilbert wanted diversity. He needed it. While the MFB was fabulous and provided Gilbert with endless hours of pleasure, he felt he wanted more out of life.

Gilbert fantasized about being a great henchman. Greater than Argyle and certainly greater than Ben. He would spend some evenings pondering the question of how he was going to accomplish his life-long dream of rising in the ranks to be recognized and possibly honored and idolized as the greatest henchman ever.

This started to occupy Gilbert's mind beyond the mere question of it; it turned into a problem that must be solved.

Gilbert became obsessed and somewhere amid the all-consuming fever of henchmanhood, his brain concocted a plan: he would practice capers, secretly, to gain confidence and experience and when the time was right, demonstrate his newfound immensity, his strength, his grandeur, to his co-henchmen, thereby winning their respect.

Then, Gilbert was sure, it would be Ben cleaning the shark tank, not him!

But first things first. Gilbert would need caperware. He didn't want it to be as flashy as The Thrasher's caperware. He felt that sequins were a bit overused and not quite his style. He did need a good logo though and had been toying with one for some number of weeks. Thrasher's logo was a scowling skull, universally recognized as his brand. Meglamon had an evil eye inherited from his dad -- but still it was his brand.

Gilbert felt that his logo would top them all. It would strike fear into victim's hearts and stand for really bad things. Gilbert's logo was a… squid. A savage, predatory squid.

Squids where mythological, ancient, intelligent, squishy cephalonpods with chromatophores and ink-shooting capabilities. What other creature could say that? None, that's who. For crying out loud, they have chromatophores!

Gilbert worked meticulously on his squid villain caperware. He felt that embarking on a caper, he should look one way and departing from the caper he should change and appear different. Using this as a guideline, he created a figure-flattering moo-moo that was light beige all over and covered with dark brown spots and dots, those being grouped closer along the back and lightly along his front, giving him dimension. Down his sleeves were tufts of silken material that moved like fins when he walked. Gilbert was proud of that.

Now everyone knows that squids have eight arms. Gilbert's original design included six arms that were gathered around the hem of his moo-moo and used his own two legs to make up the difference. However, after hours of sewing and stuffing the caperware arms with cotton batting and fixing them just so, Gilbert took one step and fell right over onto his face. So, it was back to the drawing board to come up with a fix. After all, it wouldn't be very professional to stumble his way out after a caper.

After weeks of sewing and re-sewing, Gilbert finally finished his super good, super villain squid caperware and tonight he stood in all his squidness before a mirror, appreciating all his hard work.

Gilbert's head was tucked up into the squid's butt fins and his feet stuck out the head-arm end at the bottom. It looked as if the squid was doing a handstand and walking along like nobody's business but Gilbert was hoping that not too many people would notice that because it couldn't be helped. It was the only way to put squid caperware onto a human body. No matter.

The squid moo-moo was dotted perfectly, the stuffed squid arms raised and positioned faultlessly, and two little armholes placed so to look very natural, so he could brandish a squid gun with one hand and grab the loot with the other. Oh yes, the squid gun. Gilbert's own invention. It blasted out a dark brown cloud of mist, intended to confuse his victims while he escaped. Also, it didn't taste very nice. Very squid-like.

He added a dark gray cape at the back because he thought to wrap it around himself as he left a caper, to use it as a disguise, to disappear into the crowd as he made his daring escape. Like a squid would do.

The only thing left for Gilbert to do was to brainstorm a list of really cool capers. Once that was done it was on with the show!

Chapter Nine

All Hands Meeting With A Dusting of Team Building

The note read:

All Hands Meeting Today
All Henchmen are to report at 9AM
(SHARP!!)
to one of the following meeting rooms:
Jeffery Dahmer, Joel Rifkin, Leonard Lake.

Do Not Be Late... **OR ELSE!**

Alexey had placed a copy of this note on everyone's desk and had just finished taping the last one to the face of the Lunch-O-Matic when Argyle came in to get a cup of coffee.

"Hey," said Argyle.

"Yeah, hey," responded Alexey in his thick Russian accent, nodding in greeting. Argyle was just about the only henchman that didn't pester Alexey about his English pronunciations. Like saying "Vell," instead of "Well," that sort of thing.

Argyle asked, "So. An all-hands meeting. Know the topic?"

"Nyet," Alexey said, adding, "No one tells Alexey nothing."

"Yeah," said Argyle, "I suppose not."

Argyle grabbed his coffee and the last donut, half-buried under a pile of crumbs, clearly left over from yesterday's botched Cashco caper, and headed for his desk. He had five minutes before the All Hands and wanted to get there early so he could get the best seat.

As he pushed open the door to the Rifkin room, Argyle noticed two things: the henchmen already there were crammed close to the door, leaving the head of the meeting room virtually empty *(Chickenshits!)*, and two, there was a wide-screen TV monitor sitting at the head of the table, occupying the leader's position.

I'll just take a seat right up front – I'll show them who's unafraid... Argyle walked, head held high, past the crowd of henchmen to take a chair right up next to the monitor and sat grinning, as if he had just traversed through a minefield... and made it!

Suddenly the monitor came alive with a little boing noise and The Thrasher's face, a full two-feet-wide came into focus. Several of the henchmen flinched as The Thrasher spoke.

⚡ ⚡ *Attention! Attention! If you recall my announcement of several weeks ago, I ever so politely requested that everyone take a moment to consider crime enhancements, to think outside the box as it were. To add a certain je ne sais quoi to an already highly delectable process of caper performance... Yes, Miss Q, that's French... After making my heartfelt request, I waited, somewhat impatiently, for the myriad of suggestions I felt sure were going to flood in.* (...a long and awkward pause rippled through the room, made especially uncomfortable by the fact that Barry's gaunt, almost colorless face seemed to be scanning the audience right through the screen...) *Well. After an excruciatingly long amount of time, two rather interesting suggestions were submitted. I shall read them to you at this time.* (...ahem, ahem. Barry cleared his throat...) *Suggestion number one simply states, "Ditch the funny caperware."* (...angry yelling...) *WHAT! Ditch the part of my crime legacy that has greatly contributed to my reputation as the most splendiferous crime lord ever! EVER!!* (...Barry had been waving his gun around and then suddenly...Bang! It went off with a deafening sound and in a cloud of smoke, freezing the henchmen in various looks of stunned silence... Barry looking off camera, said,) *Oh stop whimpering Miss Q, you'll be fine.* (...continuing...) *Suggestion number two seems to have been more thought out. It reads, "What if a henchman were to carry another henchman on his shoulders, with length altered caperware to hide this fact. Wouldn't we look more ferocious during capers?"* (...Barry's voice is gently parental...) *Yes, I agree that a group of nine-foot-tall villains all showing up to a caper would strike fear into the hearts of those on the receiving ends of said caper. However.* (...his voice rising...) *Certain problems would arise.* (...his voice louder and filled with anger...) *How would these lofty henchmen... get... through... doors?!* (...Barry is mumbling to himself and shuffling papers about, then under his breath...) *Sometimes I think I should shoot the lot of them and start over.* (...speaking in a normal voice...) *Get to work!*

BOING! The TV monitor snapped to black.

Argyle sat back in his chair, *So my suggestion about nine-foot tall henchmen was well thought out,* and smiling to himself, *I'm a genius!*

The sound of shuffling feet brought him back. The crowd of henchmen at the back of the meeting room had all moved to get out through the door at the same time, clogging the exit with grumbling bodies. As Argyle joined them, he heard one chap say, "Well, that went better than expected," and another ask, "Will we be getting donuts later on?"

By the time Argyle gained the hallway, most of the henchmen had dispersed and he found himself walking next to Sparry.

Argyle smiled a good morning and said, "That nine-foot henchman suggestion was really something, wasn't it?"

Sparry scrunched up his face into a "You gotta be kidding" look and was about to say something when little shoe-heel clicking noises came quickly up the hallway behind them, interrupting the conversation and causing the men to step to either side and turn in anticipation.

It was Miss Q. She held a great wad of paper napkins against her left arm and had clearly been crying. She still was. Her eyes red and puffy and her nose running even as she sniffed. A few steps on, she disappeared into her office and quietly closed the door behind her.

Argyle and Sparry were dumbfounded. Argyle spoke first, careful to keep his voice down, "Thrasher shot Miss Q. Unbelievable."

Sparry raised his eyebrows in astonishment and turned to walk on, saying nothing, but raising a hand in a "See ya" gesture as he stepped away.

The rest of the morning was fairly uneventful. Argyle was assigned to refill the Lunch-O-Matic machine with the meager quantity of deli goods procured from yesterday's poorly performed Cashco caper. Truth be told, there was only one case of sandwiches, bologna and mayo on white bread. Argyle was not thrilled with the prospect of eating Lunch-O-Matic bologna for the next several weeks because the next Cashco caper wasn't scheduled until late next month.

The thought was depressing.

When Argyle finished his task, he returned to his desk where he found another note. He picked it up and looked around. There were notes on all the desks.

The note read:

All Henchmen!
You are to report to Level Three Parking Floor at
4:30PM today for my ingeniously thought out, newly
formed, first annual
Team Building Re-
quirement!

Attendance Will Be Taken.
*Do Not Be Late... **OR ELSE!***

Argyle was just finishing up reading it for the second time when Ben and Gilbert came in.

"Where've you been all morning?" asked Argyle.

"Oh, we were assigned to check all the men's rooms for paper products. Some had more, some had none. We were supposed to share the wealth, so to speak," answered Ben.

Gilbert added, "We got to work after the meeting this morning," and after glancing at the note on his desk, said, "Hey, what's this?"

Argyle shot a look at Ben. "Apparently some of the other henchmen have a morale problem, they're not team-like and some training is in order." After a moment of reflection, added, "I hope we can shoot our guns."

4:30PM came soon enough and the boys found themselves queued up with the rest of the dayshift henchmen as they crowded into elevators that were shuttling everyone up to Parking Level Three.

The elevators emptied everyone out into a typical parking structure floor. The seedy warehouse housed Thrasher's lair in the bottom six sublevels and was host to three above-ground parking levels, an abandoned and broken-down warehouse on Level Four, and a remodeled roof area that belonged to Barry only – no one was allowed on the seedy warehouse roof! No one!

The first thing Argyle noticed as he stepped out of the elevator was that the space had been sectioned off into three areas labeled: Trust Me, Fix This, and Do This.

The second thing Argyle noticed were the four henchmen, grouped together in the center of the space. It was Sparry, Williams, Mason, and Cehtov all dressed in costume, each with a huge letter on their shirts. As they stood there, the letters spelled out EATM.

EATM? Is that a word? Thought Argyle as he walked over to them.

"Hey, Argyle!" called Williams. "Long time, now see!"

"It's… No see. Long time, no see," countered Argyle.

"No. I see you… now!" guffawed Williams.

"Say," said Argyle, "Together you guys spell out EATM? What's that?"

"No," said Sparry, "We spell out TEAM. It's a team building off site, so we spell out TEAM."

"Oh, I see," said Argyle, rolling his eyes to himself.

"Hey, Arg, check this out," said Chetov and moved over to Sparry's right. "Now we spell MEAT!"

The four henchmen started laughing and gently shoving each other around which instantly caused Argyle to lose interest. He started to wander away when a rapid succession of loud beeps sounded, calling everyone to order. The P. A. System, temporarily propped up around the garage, crackled to life…

> *Attention! Attention you mopes! Today we will team build. By the end of this meeting… you will be one big happy team! (…there was a brief moment of silence then Barry yelled…) I mean it! (…causing everyone to twitch nervously…) Anyone not deemed team worthy at the end of this exercise will be demoted and I'm sure you all know what that means. As you build your team, you will realize that your co-henchmen are more than just lug nuts, they are your wing-men. Not that they can fly. (…ahem…) Be bold, not cocky. Combined, we will achieve my greatness and I know that's what you want. So. Succeed in being a team. Win one for The Thrasher!!*

The P. A. crackled briefly and emitted a horrible voltage feedback noise before going silent.

Everyone stood staring at each other, wondering what they should be doing. Eventually small groups of friends gathered together to talk about their predicament.

Argyle, Ben, and Gilbert soon found that Davis and Carter had joined them and stood idly watching as a team of seven henchmen grouped up at the Trust Me station.

One guy was already climbing up to the top of the drive ramp while the others formed a tight group just below him. All of a sudden, the guy jumped off the ledge and the others tripped over themselves and each other as they scrambled to catch him. The result was a mess! The jumper went down feet first, crashing into two of the catchers, clubbing them with his heavy work boots. They winced in pain and withdrew their joined hands which caused the jumper to twist around and bang heads with another catcher, who howled like a kicked bear and dropped the jumper to the ground with a dead-sounding thump. The jumper lay in a lump, moaning.

Argyle glanced at Davis, who glanced back at him then spoke, "We can do that one later."

Gilbert, who had been watching with mild curiosity, said, "Yeah. They probably did it all wrong, anyway."

Davis added, "Yeah, look who jumped first… Anderson… really?"

Ben tapped Argyle's arm. "Let's do the Fix This station."

"Agreed."

The Fix This station instruction card read, "Each team will choose a chair and take seventy-five paper soda straws from the dispenser. You will take two minutes, as a team, to come up with the one and only way to repair the chair using only the seventy-five straws. You will have fifteen minutes to implement your strategy."

The men stood looking at a virtual sea of broken chairs.

Argyle let out a puff of breath and said, "It would be easier to just go to Office Most."

Mason approached the group, the giant "T" on his shirt glittering in the dull gray parking garage light. "Hey guys. I have to time you on this. Do you have a team name, yet? Gonna need it for the logs."

Argyle thought, *a team name? No one said anything about a team name,* and then blurted, "The Thrasher Five."

The others just shuffled a bit until Ben spoke, "Very nice. We're The Thrasher Five!" and raised his hand in a high-five gesture.

There were no takers. "Seriously?"

With the chair chosen and the seventy-five straws in hand, The Thrasher Five stood in a group around the chair, discussing.

"What's wrong with the chair?"

"No glue."

"No duct tape. Damn. I love duct tape."

"The chair is missing one of its wheels."

"How about that rip in the seat, do we have to fit that, too?"

"Nah, that's not broken. You can still sit on it."

"We could use the straws to build a wheel."

"Who ever heard of straw wheels?"

"Time's up!" yelled Mason. "Your fifteen-minute repair time starts…" and grinning maniacally, screamed, "NOW!"

The team, clearly startled and in a panic, shuffled and bumped into each other as someone grabbed the chair as others grasped at the straws, sending a bunch of them to the floor.

Ben, panic in his voice said, "What do we use for glue?"

Argyle was shaking his head, looking at the mess of men and straws. Then he had one of his brilliant ideas.

"We'll have to use spit."

"Yes. Spit!" echoed Ben, and hoiked into his hand, offering it to the group, who looked at him and his proffered hand with a mixture of disbelief and disgust that gradually turned into acceptance.

The group hunched over the chair, ripping off straw wrappers and spitting into little balls of crunched straws and paper, wildly fixing them to the broken chair leg.

Mason yelled out, "Two-minute countdown!"

This caused the group to pick up their pace from panic to frantic. The men grunted under their labor of spitting and paper packing and when Mason called, "Time's up!" the sounds of relief they uttered were audible.

The men stepped back to survey their repaired chair. It stood before them, slightly tilted to one side but upright on a huge ball of slimy wet straws, tightly packed in a huge wheel-looking thing around the end of the chair leg.

The sound of a digital camera aperture made Argyle look around.

Gilbert was snapping pictures of the chair with his smart phone.

Argyle looked at him, his expression asking, "What are you doing?"

Gilbert shrugged and said, "It's for my Facecram Page."

Mason addressed the group, "Tag it with your team name and place it over there. You can move on to the next station when you're ready."

After completing the Trust Me exercise, resulting in only one black eye and three broken fingers, The Thrasher Five moved on to the third and final section, the Do This challenge.

The Do This challenge was a tug-o-war game against one of the other teams, which in this instance was The Raging Maniacs, a group of five guys headed up by Milford, an overweight henchman from the maintenance crew.

Williams, the cheerleading henchman wearing a giant "E" on his shirt was standing, clipboard in hand, at the Do This instruction card. "Welcome to Do This. Teams 'The Thrasher Five' and 'The Raging Maniacs', you will have one minute to complete this challenge. The Thrasher thinks that it's all the time a real team would need to vanquish their enemies. So strap on those roller skates and let's get to this!"

The men sat on their rumps on the parking garage floor tying up their skates, taken from a pile, carelessly dumped in a big tangle of wheels and laces.

Gilbert found a right-foot skate that was in his size but could not locate its mate. He was spending too much time rooting in the pile with no luck and was forced to take a left-foot skate two sizes too large. When he complained to Williams about it, Williams told him that he didn't really care, that Gilbert needed to have two skates and had better just move it.

"Your one-minute starts in ten seconds!" announced Williams. "Line up."

Both teams of men, half of which had clearly never been on skates before, slipped and hobbled to the test area where a one-inch thick, thirty-foot length of rope lay along the floor.

With The Thrasher Five lined up on one side and The Raging Maniacs on the other, Williams blew a whistle signaling that the tug-o-war had begun.

Argyle and Davis both gave a violent jerk on the rope, pulling one of the Maniacs off his feet, who then fell back with a crunch.

"You're out Lewis!" cried Williams.

Lewis got up and made his way to the sidelines rubbing his left rump as he went.

Carter, inspired by The Raging Maniacs loss, cried out, "Again, Thrasher Five!" and gave a good pull on the rope, aided by Davis and Argyle.

One more Maniac went down amid the unsteady footing of the remaining three Maniacs. He scrambled out of the way but not before his hand was stomped by a teammate trying to steady his flailing skate-shod feet.

The Raging Maniacs yanked back on the rope, catching The

Thrasher Five off guard.

Gilbert went down, twisting his ankle and landing in a heap at the rear of the rope line.

"You're out Martin the Third," cried Williams. "Come on you henchmen! You've got fifteen seconds!"

With roller-skated feet slipping this way and that, The Thrasher Five yanked and pulled and jerked and tugged at their end of the rope sending two more Maniacs down.

The sudden non-resistance from the other end of the rope was enough to start the men off into a foot slipping free fall just as the whistle sounded.

TRILLLLLL! "Time's out!" cried Williams. "The Thrasher Five takes it!" At the exact second before the team collectively lost their footing and tumbled into a twisted pile of skates and men.

"We did it!" cheered Gilbert, jumping up and down with glee.

As the two teams were shedding their skates, the elevator doors slid open and Miss Q stepped out.

Argyle took note of her bandaged arm, now cradled in a sling, and watched her as she scanned the group, found Sparry and made her way across the parking garage to where he stood chatting with Williams, Mason, and Chetov, who now spelled out the word, ATME.

This puzzled Argyle and he watched as Miss Q handed Sparry a slip of paper, say a few words Argyle couldn't hear, and then continued to watch as Miss Q walked back to the elevator.

Momentarily, Sparry called out for everyone's attention.

"Ok you gumps, listen up! Thrasher sends his regrets for not being here to personally witness your feats of team greatness. Seems he had a more important matter to attend to but looks forward to seeing the team scorecards." And after a moment's hesitation added, "That's all. Go home."

Chapter Ten

At McClusky's

Ahh McClusky's Eight Ball. Voted the "Best Dive Tucked Into a Dank Alley" of 1987. That was a good year for dives and McClusky was very proud of the award. The newspaper article announcing the big win was cut out, framed and hung with pride right there next to that fifteen-year-old bottle of barely used vermouth.

Argyle was the first through the door, followed by Ben and trailed, a respectable five-foot distance behind, by Gilbert.

The bartender, Max, looked up as the door swung open and waved the boys over to three open stools about halfway down the bar. Before they had taken their positions, Max had set up three drinks and a bowl of mixed nuts in a nice straight line. A Dirty Martini for Argyle, a Rancid Sponge for Ben, and a Virgin Shirley Temple for Gilbert.

"I am glad this day is done," said Argyle as he lifted an olive out of his drink and eyeballed it suspiciously.

Ben had gulped half of his Rancid Sponge in one big swallow and now sat choke – coughing on the libation. "The jalapeño - lemonade combo," (choke, choke, wheeze) "is so smooth."

Gilbert sat sulking, turning his drink around and around in the ring of water his sweating grape jam jar of a glass had made on the bar.

Ben turned to Argyle and said, "Cheer up, Arg, THAM will be a rusted-out hunk of junk before too long. Look at how badly it scored on the Agility Test you gave it."

"True," said Argyle, "but having it try to climb a rope after having to explain what a rope was may not be enough. I'm going to have to think about this some more," and fell silent.

Ben had finished his drink and ordered another. Halfway through that one, he caught sight of a woman sitting at the far end of the bar.

She was staring at him and smiling.

Fulana Ramera was on the prowl tonight. She wore her most flattering outfit: a skin-tight miniskirt (even if it was stretched a little too snug over her plump thighs), and a buff-brown blouse with black animal stripes and spots that had the cutest faux fur around the collar and cuffs.

She had rat-combed and hair sprayed her over-bleached blond hair up into the most provocative style she could manage and took care to put on extra eyeliner because, as everyone knows, if one doesn't overcompensate for the low, mood-setting lighting of a bar, one will always look washed-out.

Fulana had watched the two men and their chubby little sidekick enter McClusky's and decided the dark swarthy-looking one was just her type. She waited until he had finished his second drink and then made her move, sliding seductively off her stool, just in case anyone was watching, and after tugging her miniskirt back down, she made her way over to Ben.

Standing just behind him, she leaned forward to whisper in his ear, "Care to dance?"

Ben had indeed noticed her slinky walk toward him and felt a tingle on his ear as she pressed her lips close. *Is that strawberry scented lipstick?*

Swiveling his barstool around, Ben came face-to-face with an angel… or was that the two Rancid Sponges talking? No matter.

Smiling, Ben said, "Fast or slow?"

Fulana took him by the hand, "Both," and tugged him toward the jukebox.

Moments later, La Bamba by Los Lobos blared out of the little tin speakers of the Rock-Ola as Ben and Fulana hopped around like clumsy teenagers.

Meanwhile, Argyle had ordered a second martini and sat ignoring Gilbert.

Gilbert thought he had better get back on Argyle's good side and took the opportunity to ingratiate himself.

"Max, put that on my tab," Gilbert cheerfully said.

Max limped over and glared his one good eye at Gilbert and barked, "What tab you talking about? The one with *all* the drinks on it?"

indicating the empty glasses in front of Argyle and Ben's now empty stool.

Gilbert swallowed hard. Max always unnerved him. "Yyyyes, please. And would it be possible to get another Temple? This time with a shot of Jameson Vintage in it?"

Max was stunned. He never would have guessed that Gilbert had any taste whatsoever, let alone for whisky. "Sure. From my own stash," and moved down the bar to ready the drinks.

The music was a bit loud and Gilbert had to raise his voice to be heard, "Argyle, have you ever thought about doing your own crime startup?" He sipped the last of his Virgin Temple.

Argyle turned his head and looked doubtfully at Gilbert as if seeing him for the first time. "What?"

"I mean, I hear there's lots of entrepreneurial shady money to be had. Maybe you could start a good pyramid scheme."

Max set fresh drinks in front of the boys and one for Ben, as well, leaning over and winking at Gilbert as he slid the bill across the bar.

Was that a 'wink' or a 'blink'? Gilbert smiled.

Argyle studied Gilbert for a second. "My career path is up… not out."

Ben, with his arms around Fulana, came laughing back to his stool, grabbed his third Rancid Sponge and called to Max, "Another Loaded Paisley Martini for the lady!" Then turning to Argyle, he said, "We're gonna sit over there," and staggered away.

Gilbert said, "I'm just saying. You have the brains and the brawn. You could do it. Start-up costs could be minimal, and I bet you could easily poach half The Thrasher's henchmen. They're already trained and own their own guns, some of them actually like you. It might take a couple weeks to find a good lair and outfit it with state-of-the-art crime computers, maybe a couple of days to move desks and chairs in, another day to shop Cashco for break room supplies. The way I see it, you could be up and running in three weeks for less than fifty thousand, and you could make that back in two, maybe three capers."

Argyle had quietly listened as Gilbert yammered. *He hasn't said that many words in as many weeks. Sounds like he's given this some thought. Wonder what else is going on inside that little skull of his.*

Gilbert took a long pull of his non-Virginal Temple, sat back in an expression of relief and gave Max the thumbs-up.

Max nodded in acknowledgement.

Encouraged by the warmth that was now spreading through his chest, Gilbert tapped the edge of his glass on the bar. When he got Argyle's attention, asked, "Have you thought of a Super Villain name yet?"

Argyle was thinking over what Gilbert had just said about guns and capers and the question he just put to him made a bit of sense. Argyle made a, "Hmmm," sound and thought for a moment. "I think that if I were to become a Super Villain, and I'm saying… *if…* I might call myself something like The Deranged Viper. Or maybe, The Crazed Gunner. Something that would invoke fear and loathing. Although maybe not loathing. Maybe anxiety. Nothing beats a victim that is deep in fear and anxiety." Argyle fell quiet and eyed his glass.

Gilbert started to say something, he wanted to open up to Argyle, to tell him about his secret dreams of becoming a great henchman but changed his mind. Maybe it was too soon. And Gilbert wasn't sure that Argyle wasn't really out to make Gilbert into a goat, it was still way too soon to know for sure. So, Gilbert simply said, "Just think about it. I could help."

Argyle caught Ben's eye and yelled out, "I'm leaving." Under his breath he added, "Have a job interview with Audrey's dad tomorrow. Fun."

Ben stumbled over, "Ok best pal of mine. I'm gonna have one more dance then call it a night," and turning to Fulana, "Ready baby?" He grabbed her and spun her around, making her giggle in drunken delight, as his last coherent thought flowed past…

Oh, I just know I'll be in pain tomorrow but I'm having such a good time tonight!

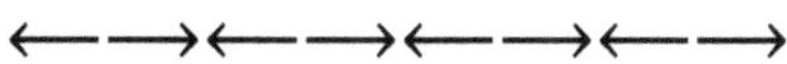

As the evening wore on, the Loaded Paisley Martinis and the Rancid Sponges flowed like nice cool water, a welcome thing when you've worked yourself up into overexcited, sticky hot dancers as Ben and Fulana had done.

Fulana would not let Ben sit down. She managed to change one of his twenties into a huge pile of coins and fed the Rock-Ola like there was no tomorrow. And by the looks of Ben, that might just be true.

McClusky's had filled up with patrons by mid-evening and Max lost count of how many drinks Ben had slugged down. By the time he cut him off, Ben was barely able to hold himself up. The last Max saw of him, he and Fulana were staggering out the door together with Ben bellowing out, in his worst drunken and slurred voice…

♪♪ "In A Gadda Da Vida, Honey

Don't You Know That I Love You?" ♪♪

Chapter Eleven

They've Run Into The Boys

WHOOSH!

"What was that?" Malcom exclaimed as he jumped from surprise.

"Check that out!" cried Bintcom, leaping to his feet and pointing down the street.

Grotcom, shading the sun from his eyes with his hand, peered down the street. "O… M… Grute," he slowly enunciated, "That's a prototype MFB. They were used as senseless entertainment in their early years but were soon retrofitted with Taser-like weapons that struck citizens down by numbing their feet."

"I can't believe we're seeing one live!" exclaimed Bintcom. "Let's follow it!"

Grotcom said, "We can't. We're on a mission and shouldn't get sidetracked."

"Hey," Malcom puzzled, "isn't that Gilbert Alan Martin III? The inventor of the MFB?" pointing to a chubby little guy standing across the street, working a joystick device and laughing to himself.

"He looks dangerous," Grotcom said, studying Gilbert as he weaved and bobbed his way down the street.

"We should talk to him," added Bintcom as he started forward.

"Bint, wait! We have a mission," said Grotcom.

"Too late anyway," intoned Malcom, "He's gone."

And just like that, Gilbert had moved away and disappeared into the lunchtime crowd, guiding his Monster Floor Bot out of view of the travelers.

At exactly noon, Argyle turned his VDub onto the street and drove slowly, looking at the storefronts on either side. "So, what's it gonna be today, Ben? Burgers, tacos, dogs? The choice is yours cuz today I'll eat anything."

Ben scrunched up his nose in concentration. "Let's see. I had a burger yesterday and a to-go pizza the day before." And thinking further, said, "Let's do dogs. There's the Pup-n-Bubbles down the other end."

"Okay, dogs it is."

"Look! Look!" said Malcom. "There's the signature 1958 yellow Volkswagen Beetle. That means Argyle Stevens!" His excitement was palpable.

"Okay, this is it. Remember your roles: we're here from out of town and looking for jobs," cautioned Grotcom. "Don't blow this!"

Argyle pulled his Bug into the Pup-n-Bubbles parking lot just as the travelers crossed the street to intercept him and Ben.

Grotcom put on a big smile as he approached the car and said, "Argyle? Argyle Stevens? Is that you?"

Argyle was taken back. He eyed the trio with suspicion and moved to exit the bug lest he needed to shoot his gun. Ben was right with him.

Grotcom pushed forward, "We have heard so much about you. My friends and I," flourishing an arm at Bintcom and Malcom, "love your work. We've been admirers for ages!"

Argyle was dumbfounded. *My work? What the hell… ?*

Grotcom, smiling almost maniacally, certainly on the verge of looking like a lunatic, said, "Let us buy you lunch, please, it would be an honor and our pleasure."

Bintcom leaned into the conversation, "Whadda ya think? Up for a bite at Benny's?"

Argyle thought, *what the heck* and relaxed a bit.

Ben chimed in, "Oh, Benny's. They have that mile high ham pile sandwich, Arg. Whadda they call it? The Piggy's Flying Now?"

"Ok," said Argyle, "I'll drive."

With Grotcom, Bintcom, and Malcom literally stuffed into the back seat, Argyle steered his Bug for Benny's.

The ride over gave Malcom a leg cramp. He tried to be brave but his limp into Benny's said it all: the back seats of VW Bugs were not made for humans.

The waitress sat them at a large booth in the back and set them up with drinks before leaving them to decide their food order.

Grotcom smiled and said, "We've heard of you two but you, I'm sure, are wondering about us." He pointed at Bintcom. "This is Bint McDougie, and that," pointing at Malcom, "is Mal Circafrat," and sticking his thumb on his chest said, "and I'm Grot Zealbot. We're from out of town."

"Yes," said Bintcom, "we have been hearing, for years, about the good henchmen jobs you two do and felt we would like a change. We would love to work for Thrasher Incorporated."

"We hear all the time about your courage and your street smarts. You are an inspiration to us," said Malcom.

Grotcom took up the point, "The capers you go on are so well thought out, not like the crappy capers we have to do."

"Yes, we're jealous," Bintcom said.

Malcom added, "Any openings at Thrasher Inc.?"

"Any openings?" asked Grotcom.

Ben sat sipping on his sixty-four-ounce Sidewalk Soda special and looked over at Argyle, who had been holding his coffee cup listening. Then Argyle spoke, "I'm having a little trouble with this. Who did you say you worked for?"

Grotcom answered, "Oh, our boss doesn't like us to say his name in public, therefore, let's just say he's a big shot in the next town over and he loves crime."

Ben said, "Oh, we know him, don't we?" turning to Argyle.

"Yea, isn't he the one who pulled that big jewel heist last year?" mused Argyle.

"That's him exactly!" exclaimed Grotcom, "Good. So, you've heard of him."

Malcom added, "In spite of his notoriety, he's a crappy boss. We want to work for The Thrasher," and sat smiling.

"Yes. Thrasher," added Bintcom.

"Any openings?" asked Malcom, hopeful as always.

Ben made end-of-drink straw sucking noises and waved the waitress over, "Set me up with another Sidewalk Soda and I'll have the Pulled Pig and Mayo on toasted sourdough with pickles and tomatoes. Two sides of fries and one side of potato salad. My friend, Grot, is paying."

The next somewhat awkward moments were filled with chat about the weather and late-night TV shows then mercifully the lunch plates arrived.

After the lunch bill had been placed in front of Grotcom, Argyle cleaned his hands on his napkin and made to get up. "I know you'll understand if my partner and I decline to hook you up with job interviews. It's against Thrasher policy to bring strangers around." Argyle stood up and Ben quickly followed. "Stay where you are fellows, we've got to be going. I'm sure you can find your way about town." And the two boys walked out of Benny's.

The waitress came by to collect the check and Malcom asked her, "Do the sodas come with free refills?"

The travelers sat for a few moments in silence, then Grotcom spoke, "Well, that didn't go too well. We're gonna need another plan."

No one spoke for ten more minutes then Bintcom snapped his fingers, "I've got it! We go back to our bench base, downtown, and watch for Gilbert Alan Martin III and follow him to The Thrasher's lair!" Oh, Bintcom was pretty proud of his idea and sat smiling at his fellow travelers.

"Then what?" asked Malcom.

Bintcom gave it a half of thought, then crestfallen, just shrugged. His idea was only half a plan.

"Then," said Grotcom, "we wait for Argyle Stevens and confront him with the truth."

"Yes. The truth," said Bintcom.

"I don't know. The truth has never done anyone any good," said Malcom. "It always seems to bring trouble."

One hour later…

"I know I saw Martin III ditch down that side street right there," pointed Bintcom. "Let me go take a quick look. I'll be right back," and strode away.

Malcom was back on his bench watching Bintcom cross the street and cut between two parked cars before he disappeared from view. He turned to Grotcom and said, "What if we don't find The Thrasher's lair? What if we're here for days and days?"

Grotcom, swiping through his e-device reading old articles about The Thrasher raised his eyes and idly looked around before answering. "We'll find the lair. We're pretty close. Those guys wouldn't drive for miles just to eat fast food no matter how good it was."

Bintcom came back. "Nothing but garbage cans over there."

A commotion across the street made the three travelers turn and look.

Two people had burst out the front doors of the Third Hand Clothing Boutique and were running down the street, wildly waving their arms, and yelling unintelligible things to the pedestrians they passed.

Suddenly, a short, stocky, costumed character came slamming out of the store to the sidewalk, stopped and looked to the right, then to the left and made his decision. He ran straight across the street, seemingly straight to the travelers.

But no. As the character ran, he wrapped himself in a dark gray cape and appeared, somewhat, to blend in with the gawking pedestrians. Still, he walked very quickly past the travelers and down the street.

The owner came out of the store yelling, "Help! HELP!! I've been robbed!" And frantically fluttered his arms about gasping for breath. "Somebody call the cops!"

Malcom calmly turned to Grotcom and said, "Say, wasn't that The Squid?"

Bintcom had already searched his e-history book and produced a picture. "It sure was. Says here he started as a junior henchman with Thrasher Inc. and became the greatest Crime Lord of the 21st century!"

Grotcom was on his feet, "Quick! Let's follow him!"

Gilbert decided that he should practice capers. He would get very good at pulling capers and would show Argyle and Ben what for. He would be included, he would be heroic, and they would stop laughing at him. He would sure show them.

The take from the Third Hand had been small but that didn't matter to Gilbert. He was perfecting his craft; it wasn't about the money, although having some walking around change never hurt.

The caper went well enough. He surprised everyone and had used an accent on his voice to disguise it. Clever. His Squid gun hadn't worked as planned, though. It shot a mist of brownish liquid but didn't leave the cloud of blinding squid stink like he thought. He would have to work on that some more.

Gilbert noted that his runaway was a bit awkward as the squid arms attached to his moo-moo sorta flopped around and threatened to trip him up. He made it a block or two away and slipped out of the costume easily enough and stuffed it into his backpack fairly quickly.

He was pretty sure he got away with it, but thought now to pick up his pace, he was late getting back to work after his lunch break.

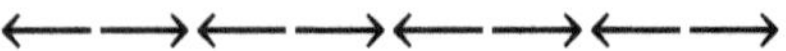

The travelers tailed Gilbert for several blocks, keeping a discrete distance so as not to be made.

Malcom started falling behind, his pudginess taking a toll on his stamina. He waved Bintcom and Grotcom on. "I'll catch up!"

They watched Gilbert as he doffed the squid suit and kept up with him for three more blocks before he slipped from sight and they lost him.

"Wow!" said Bintcom. "You know what this means, don't you? Gilbert Martin III is The Squid! Who knew?"

Dialing up an e-map of the district, they calmly studied the buildings around them.

Malcom caught up, puffing with the effort. He doubled over, holding his side, "I think Benny's is coming back on me."

Grotcom said, "There's only two warehouses in use in this area. That one right there," pointing to a two-story wooden building to the left where a few workmen stood around the loading ramp smoking. "And this one," pointing to a spot on his e-map. "A seedy old warehouse four blocks that way."

The three travelers stood quietly looking in the direction Grotcom was indicating.

Chapter Twelve

Meetings Never Go Well

Argyle's alarm blasted to life at 7:01AM and almost immediately his phone rang. The contact photo appearing on the screen told him that the caller was Audrey.

"Hello, sweetie." (pause) "Yes, I'm up." (pause) "Picked it up from the cleaners last night on my way home." (pause) "Yes." (pause) "The blue one." (pause) "Not the blue one?" (pause) "Ok. Green." (long pause) "We've gone over my job objectives so much I think I dreamt about it last night." (pause) "It'll be fine. You'll see, I'll wow your dad all over the place." (pause) "Meet me at Valley Café at 10:00AM for coffee." (pause) "Love you. Gotta go."

Argyle pushed the End Call button, and his phone went silent. He sat on the edge of his bed rubbing the stubble on his face, thinking.

This has been a long time coming. Today's the day I sit in front of Audrey's father and talk about my career goals. This one's for Audrey. She's gonna owe me big for this.

Audrey's father is a big shot supervisor for the Vellum Corporation. He runs the crew responsible for producing and shipping Translucent #17-Pound, a very fine paper. He's been supervisor for as long as Audrey could remember, and she has been talking Argyle up to him for a couple of years.

Mr. Eckhart doesn't approve of Argyle. He thinks he's too common. The feeling is mutual because Argyle doesn't approve of Eckhart. Thinks he's too pompous, always bragging about shipping quotas and fewer accidents than the other crews. Well, stuff his allotment percentages anyway!

Argyle shuffled into the bathroom and began his morning like he always did, by splashing cold water on his face.

Audrey has mentioned her father's company to Argyle at least fifty times. Always in a slightly different way but basically the same old song.

Audrey wants to get married, settle down, have at least 3.8 children (the National average) while her fertility rate was still working, and she wants all this and security, too. She didn't think Thrasher Inc. was secure. It didn't have a pension plan or a 401K. Audrey thought Argyle could do better if he worked for her dad at Vellum Corp. How could he not? Look at her father. Working the same job, his nose to the grindstone, for the same company, year after year after year. It was the perfect life!

Argyle stood in front of the mirror as he tied his tie. The green one, as Audrey had instructed. When he finished, he took a moment to look himself over and was very pleased.

I sure do clean up good!

And looking at his watch, *The interview is set for 9:00AM, shouldn't take more than thirty minutes, then I'll ditch the suit coat and tie, meet Audrey for coffee at 10:00AM and be to work by 10:15AM. I'll blame the traffic.*

On the ride from the apartment to the vast work yards of Vellum Corp., Argyle reviewed his meeting strategy.

Go in, shake hands, smile, and take a seat. I'll let Eckhart blither for a few minutes, smiling and nodding, whatever. Then I'll talk.

Argyle arrived on time and was issued a sticky visitor badge that he affixed to his suit lapel as indicated. The receptionist led him down a hallway lined with closed doors on one side and banks of heavy glass windows along the other. The view through the windows was into a large warehouse cavern that was bustling with activity. Men scurried about in little forklifts moving large rolls of paper from little lifters on the yard side of the building to shelving among rows of industrial racks and from there, onto trucks waiting on the drive side of the building.

Argyle watched in disbelief. *They look like ants.*

The receptionist halted a few feet from the end door and, directing Argyle's attention to it said, "This is Mr. Eckhart's office. Knock and then go on in." She turned and strode back down the hallway, her sensible shoes barely making a sound as she went.

Argyle knocked and opened the door and was momentarily dumbfounded at what he saw. It was nothing of what he had expected. What he had expected was a large plush office with a big oak desk, over-stuffed chair and a couch to comfort all the serious big shots that surely sought Eckhart's advice and counsel. The way Audrey spoke about her dad, how could it be otherwise?

Well, it was otherwise.

First of all, the door, when opened all the way, banged on a dented metal cabinet that was stuffed with paper-backed industrial manuals and dozens of Material Safety Data Sheets, all of which had dog-eared pages and dirty edges from all the handling. The office couldn't have been any bigger than ten foot by eight foot, it was windowless, had one florescent light fixture that buzzed, and was stuffed to the ceiling with "stuff." The walls were decorated with taped up schedules, thumb tacked pie charts, with the odd Certificate of Completion tacked up here and there.

Audrey's father sat behind an old looking beige surplus desk, white shirtsleeves rolled up, green tie loosened about his thick, sun-mottled neck, pencil raised over a stack of papers. He looked up, recognized Argyle, and motioned for him to take a seat. The only chair available was a short, straight-backed one tucked up close to the desk and wedged between the desk and a stack of cardboard boxes.

"I'll be right with you, Mr. Stevens."

Argyle nodded and sat down, trying to look professional. In the minutes that passed in silence, Argyle looked around at the cramped, over-stuffed office. His eyes lit on one of the certificates tacked on the wall behind Eckhart. It was awarded to Mr. Eckhart for a one-hour forklift class he had attended six years ago.

Argyle almost felt sorry for him. Eckhart looked pudgy, out of shape, older than his years, and tired. He definitely looked tired. Then he spoke. His voice gruff.

"So. What makes you think you're qualified for a job here at Vellum Corporation?"

The slight shred of sympathy Argyle had felt for Audrey's father vanished immediately into thin air.

200

"I can run a par course without sustaining injury," Argyle said, in his defense, adding, "and I can power lift 350-pounds."

"Can you drive a forklift?"

"No."

"Have you operated a Fordrinier machine?"

"No."

"Do you know what vellum is?"

"No."

Eckhart leaned back in his chair, that is to say, back about three inches before the wall behind him stopped his chair. A smirk of a smile came across his face and for a moment froze there, twisted and insane-looking. "Then I think we're done here," said Eckhart and started to stand up.

Argyle, confused, asked, "When do I get to talk?"

"I believe you just did. Thank you for coming in." Eckhart came around the desk, holding out his hand to Argyle.

Argyle stood up and yanked at the front of his suit to straighten it out after the crumpling it received at the slight of having to sit in a tiny chair. He looked at Eckhart's outstretched hand, sniffed a sort of derogatory noise, opened the door, stepped out and snapped the door shut behind him.

Outside in the hallway with the bustle and beeps and loud calls coming from the warehouse floor, drifting faintly through the wall of windows, Argyle thought, *Audrey's not gonna like this.*

On the other side of town, Gilbert was sitting in a back booth at the local Benny's anticipating a meeting of his own.

After his promotion to Junior Henchman, Gilbert felt rather giddy and one of the first things he did was to update his résumé. He took his time, chose his words carefully, and when he was completely satisfied that the résumé had captured the essence of his brilliance, without too much overstatement, he posted it to LinkedUp.

Gilbert was sure that his phone would ring the second he hit the Done button on his LinkedUp page. The world would see his true genius and beat a path to his door. But as the following hours ticked past, and no calls came, Gilbert's enthusiasm waned and faded until he lost interest completely. Eventually, his attention turned back to his own business and he forgot about LinkedUp altogether.

That was until yesterday when a headhunter representing "a very important client" called and asked for a face-to-face meeting.

This took Gilbert by surprise and he energetically agreed but only if the meeting would occur way over on the other side of town, away from the seedy warehouse and any Thrasher employees who may spot him.

Gilbert had called in early that morning, leaving a message on Miss Q's phone, saying that he had a doctor's appointment. He said that in order to free up his morning and to save himself from having to find some excuse to leave work for a couple of hours.

Gilbert agreed to a 10:00AM meeting at Benny's and here he was, sitting in a back booth, sipping a hot chocolate, nervously awaiting the arrival of Gene, the headhunter guy.

Ultimately, and fifteen minutes late, Gene came rushing through the front doors, gazed around the almost empty restaurant, lit eyes on Gilbert and blustered and huffed his way to the table.

Calling to the waitress, "I'll have a hot tea and a piece of pie, any kind will do," and jammed into the seat opposite Gilbert, flopping a loose stack of papers down on the table as he did.

"Hello. I'm Gene, we spoke briefly on the phone," and sat smiling at Gilbert.

Gilbert said, "How did you know it was me?"

"Oh, that was simple," said Gene, "you look like a Gilbert."

The waitress arrived with the tea and pie and the check, didn't say a word, and walked away.

The tea was tepid and the pie looked to be some kind of berry concoction, or maybe not. It was an indistinguishable slab of blue-purple stuff sitting in a slurry of purple-gray liquid.

Gene's attitude darkened. Speaking loudly so the waitress could hear, he declared, "This does not look like the full-color fantastic picture on the menu! I ought to sue the pie right outta this establishment. Yes... I... should."

Gilbert sat dumbfounded. It never occurred to him to shout out about Benny's misleading menu photos. He always thought to himself, *think where you are, man,* and he always calmed down about the cold pancakes.

Nevertheless, Gene had picked up his fork and was stuffing a huge bite of the ugly pie into his hungry maw. Without acknowledging, in spite of his outrage, that he was eating the pie, Gene started the conversation with Gilbert.

"Your résumé is very impressive. Junior Henchman in less than four years. Very well done."

Gilbert smiled, "Thank you. I worked very hard…"

"Yes, I can see that," said Gene, cutting Gilbert off mid-sentence and riffling through the mess of papers strewn about the table. "Ah, here it is."

Gene pulled a sheet of paper to the top of the pile and Gilbert got a quick glimpse of it. It was typed and had pencil notes in the margins. There was a title of some sort, bolded across the top, and yellow high-lighter pen all over it.

Gene studied that page with a furrowed brow then looked up at Gilbert. "Yes, I think you'll do fine."

Gilbert was glad and smiled in his "Aw shucks" way.

Gene continued, "My client, The Clawer, thinks you are exactly the man for this job. He likes your employment history, in fact, one might say, it's what interests him the most." Gene sipped at his tea, made a face and continued. "The Clawer L.L.C. is a start-up, in its early stages. Clawer would like you to get in on the ground floor, be part of the team, build an empire," and pausing, trying to read Gilbert's face, added, "Does any of that sound appealing to you?"

Gilbert looked down at his hands, trying to form thoughts. "I like the 'empire' part. Will there be a stock option grant and a signing bo-nus?"

Gene looked mildly shocked at the questions. "Wait. I think I have that information here somewhere."

Gilbert watched as Gene made a big show of moving papers around, patting his hands on them, and looking thoughtfully at his food ticket before he answered, "No," and sat staring blank-faced at Gilbert.

Embarrassed, Gilbert asked, in a sheepish voice, "Do you have a job description?"

Becoming more animated and smiling a broad and toothy smile,

Gene said, "Yes, I do. The Clawer thinks you would be the perfect candidate to work as a mole in Thrasher's organization." Gene waited for that to sink in then continued, "He would like you to observe everything, maybe take some pictures, and report to him on a regular basis."

"Gee, I don't know," Gilbert stammered. "Thrasher is pretty strict about his employees working outside the company. I heard about this one guy who worked weekends mowing lawns and when Thrasher found out, well, it was donuts in the break room!"

Gene, wearing a look of mild contempt on his face, said, "Do you need a minute to think about it? Yes. Think about it. I'll be right back," and wriggled his way out of the booth and trundled off to the men's washroom.

Gilbert was stunned. He really didn't know what to do. On the one hand, a start-up opportunity and with a company with a cool name like The Clawer. On the other hand, he may have to work too hard and most likely couldn't count on his anonymity to keep him safe. He would be right out there. In plain view.

Gene was back but didn't sit down, instead, he busied himself with gathering the papers into the semblance of a pile, grabbed up his food ticket and, partially winded by the effort, straightened up. "Well, what's it going to be, champ? Going to make the leap to greatness?"

Gilbert slowly shook his head as he spoke, "It's a very tempting deal and I'm grateful to Mr. Clawer for taking the time to think about me but I'm afraid I'll have to pass." Then smiling a very faint smile, quickly added, "Maybe in a couple years when The Clawer goes public, we can talk again?"

Gene shrugged and made a tsk sound through his teeth. "Have it your way," and abruptly turned to leave, but then he stopped and turned to Gilbert and said, "How 'bout another proposal. Have you ever heard of The Thwarter?"

"The Thwarter?" Gilbert asked with a puzzled look on his face. *Wow, what a cool name!* "No, who's that?"

"Well, it's more along the lines of a law enforcement career. It's a startup and The Thwarter is looking to put together a team. Crime fighting is the wave of the future!"

I don't know about that, thought Gilbert, but he tried to keep an open mind. After all, there was that whole Habitat For Humanity thing from a while ago. "What are the perks? What does it pay? Is there travel required?"

"It's more along the lines of a contract position. It's a non-profit."

Gilbert didn't like the sound of that. Non-profit? That's not why he decided to get into crime. Crime fighting is a dead-end. But, still, if there are really cool costumes and exciting missions… maybe.

Finally, Gilbert came to the conclusion that this sort of job was not for him, and so he politely declined. "Sorry. I think I'm pretty happy with where I'm at right now."

Gene frowned and shook his head. "Well, if you ever change your mind, give me a call," and then he walked away. Gilbert watched as Gene stopped to pay his tab and rush out the front doors, then looking at his watch, Gilbert jumped. *10:45AM! Crap! I've got to get to work!*

Gilbert barely made it to his desk before Argyle and Ben strolled in. *I think I got away with it!*

It was obvious that Argyle and Ben were in a conversation and as they came closer Gilbert heard Ben ask Argyle, "How did the meeting with daddy go?"

"Ugh. Not good. I wouldn't work for that company for all the (finger quotes) Vellum (end finger quotes) in China."

Ben, his face screwed into confusion, asked, "Does China have Vellum?"

Argyle ignored the question and said, "Now Audrey is all upset with me. Thinks I've blown a huge opportunity and is determined to speak with her father about it." Shaking his head in total disbelief, he then said, "How can it get any worse?" and took his seat.

"Here's how," said Ben as he handed a slip of paper across to Argyle. "There's two clogged toilets on Sublevel Three that need our immediate attention."

Suddenly the P. A. crackled.

Attention, my vast number of minions. My loyal and (ahem) well regarded, ruthless subordinates! ATTENTION!!

Now you know that in my last public service announcement I asked you to contemplate the future of crime and to submit your well! thought! out! suggestions!

Before we move on, I need to put one idea to rest: "Casual Fridays" are not going to happen. Whomever is stuffing my suggestion boxes with this ridiculous notion, take note… I will get you.

Next point of business. Conquer Space. I like it. I will dominate crime and expand my business to Mars and Jupiter.

Next. Billboards. Used as brand marketing and as a warning to lesser crime bosses… like Meglamon! (cough, cough) Miss Q a sip of water if you please. Not for you! FOR ME!

Moving on. Guest appearances on late night talk shows. This is good. I could show the world that I am a crime lord of fashion; I'm witty and deep. I could tell stories from my interesting life, and threaten everyone! Yes. Good.

Finally. Clone myself. Okay, now we're talking. A veritable mob of me! I like it. I like it a lot!

A goodly number of suggestions, my henchmen. I'm looking forward to more ideas for improvement, so keep 'em coming!

Now, until next time… get out there and market my brand!

The P. A. System clicked silent.

Chapter Thirteen

The Henchman's Ball

It's that time of year again. The company party, or as any henchman worth his gunpowder would refer to it as: The Henchman's Ball. Most everyone looked forward to this night. It's a time when everyone can relax and have fun. It's a night to dress up, feel special, and be courteous.

Argyle especially loved the Henchman's Ball. He loved the anticipation of a night full of surprises, the glamour of the evening filled with fancy dress suits and the pride he always felt as he walked around with Audrey on his arm. She always looked high class when she wore her glitter gown and fixed her hair up all nice and curly.

The Ball would be held on a Saturday night as always. That morning, Argyle would take his vintage VW Beetle down to the self-serve car wash, gently soap and dry his little baby, and detail the interior from the headliner fabric right down to the floor mats. He and Audrey would be going in style.

And tonight is that night!

The VDub was pristine. Argyle was on time to pick Audrey up (and she looks stunning in her slinky tight glitter gown and those high, high heels), and he remembered to bring the orchid flower wrist corsage, too.

The route to the party was well known to Argyle. He had driven it every day for more than a handful of years. As always, it's held on the fourth floor of the seedy warehouse, just above the parking garages, one floor below Barry's private (!) rooftop.

Argyle parked his bug and ran around to Audrey's door to hold it open for her. Like the gentleman he thought himself to be. Audrey had smiled and giggled in her wonderfully girlish way with the special attention.

They both stood on the rickety old freight elevator, Audrey holding her gown up so as not to get any questionable goop on it. *Is that severely decomposed watermelon?* The elevator shivered upward, the sounds of gears and motors groaned under the labor.

As the elevator inched and shook its way up, the transformed and beautifully decorated party hall was slowly revealed.

Miss Q, Feartha Wolf, and a host of others had most certainly outdone themselves this time.

This year's party theme was Under the Sea.

The entire space had been made over, swept and mopped clean. The rows and rows of paned windows that traversed all four walls had not been washed. Feartha thought the opaqueness of the centuries old grime added to the illusion of being under water. And indeed it did.

There were plenty of tables, each dressed with a shimmery, turquoise organza fabric and blue fish netting that draped to the floor, spilling into little mounds. The centerpieces were made from children's plastic beach pails and filled with sand. Each one had a stick or two poking out of it, each of which had a plastic seashell glued to it. The pails all sported large Thrasher logos done up in blue and green glitter. Sticking out of the sand were bits of rubbish, a gum wrapper or a bottle cap. Just the sort of thing one might find on a real beach.

The tables were set with the best plastic cutlery money could buy, ahem, that a caper could procure. Very heavy duty. And the paper plates were almost cardboard – you couldn't beat that.

There were yards and yards of sea green material suspended from the ceiling all the way to the floor that most certainly represented seaweed floating in the ocean and there was lots of glitter strewn about the floor in an attempt to make it look like the ocean bottom.

But the real bang for the buck lay in the dozens of huge plastic blow-up fish suspended in various poses from the ceiling.

But not just any fish. These creatures all had sharp pointy teeth.

There was an Angler Fish with rows of long, thin white teeth. Very frightful. There were several large Stingrays floating about the space and at least two schools of Piranha, one of which was in the act of attacking an unfortunate… something… that had gotten too close.

One of the bigger, toothy creatures appeared to be a Tiger Fish.

Gee, that looked pretty mean. But the best of the bunch of plastic blow-ups were the Great White Sharks. Barry's favorites. They were huge! One was poised, jaws agape, as if it were swooping down upon one of the tables about to chomp on a person or two.

Sparry and his date and their friends were at that table. Sparry was up on a chair, sticking his head into the shark's mouth and making distress noises and waving his arms around. Everyone was laughing and taking pictures of him.

Speaking of pictures, there was a small staged area off to the right where couples could pose to have their formal picture taken… to commemorate their good time. The curtained backdrop was made of sky-blue fabric and looked vaguely like an ocean scene. There was a giant Thrasher logo centered on it. The logo was made to look as if it were constructed of seashells and shrimp and, of course, sequins, one of Feartha's favorite and most famous things. The couples were posed off to the side so as not to obscure the logo.

The rest of the warehouse was festive with balloons and lit entirely with blue and green lighting. Like under the sea. Get it? Truth be told, it made everyone look a little sick. Oh well.

Argyle spotted a table fairly close to the dance area and the stage that had been erected off to the left, so gently indicated to Audrey, by a light touch at her waist, to head in that direction.

When Audrey understood that Argyle wanted to sit right in front, she quickly steered them to another table tucked comfortably off to the side away from too much foot traffic and center stage. She fell for that last year and then got stuck with a huge dry-cleaning bill when an overzealous magician's trick went very wrong. Nope. That wasn't going to happen again this year.

The invitation said, "Bring your own bottle," and Argyle brought two nice romantic bottles of André champagne for Audrey and him. It would be the best $8.52 he would ever spend!

Argyle and Audrey had been at the table for about twenty minutes, sipping at their plastic tumblers of André and soaking up the atmosphere when Ben and his date arrived with a flourish.

"Hello, you two lovebirds, don't you look nice tonight," exclaimed Ben, making a big thumping sound as he dropped his plastic gallon container of vodka in front of two available chairs. "This is my date,

Fulana Ramera. Arg, you remember her from the other night, right?" asked Ben, facetiously.

Argyle could feel Audrey's eyes on him but didn't dare look at her. "Yes. McClusky's. I remember." Argyle put his arm around Audrey's shoulder and drew her near, "And this is my beautiful fiancée, Audrey," hoping to deflect any questions he didn't particularly want to answer.

The couples smiled and greeted each other, and Ben pointed to one of the empty chairs and Fulana sat down.

She was decked out in a long tiger print caftan that billowed out with miles of sheer silk-like material. Her makeup was thick, and her perfume hung heavy about her, like the vast number of discount store jewelry bracelets piled up her arms and the bulky chains around her neck.

Fulana immediately wrapped herself around Ben as if guarding him from any other females. She took up her tumbler and jokingly showed the empty bottom of it to Ben. "Can we have a little drinky-winky, sweetie?"

"Yea, yea! Let me just get this opened up and away we will go!" said Ben, reaching for his vodka.

Audrey was about to ask Argyle something when Gilbert walked up to the table, alone and looking embarrassed. "Hello. There's an empty seat right there. Mind if I take it?"

Argyle was thinking… no, but before he could say it out loud, Ben cut him off, "Sure! Why not?" and looking around, "Where's your date? Did you bring a date? Can't wait to meet your date."

Gilbert maneuvered his way around to the other side of the table and took the seat next to Audrey. He lifted a small Styrofoam cooler onto the table in front of him. Trying to look nonchalant and shrugging his shoulders a bit, Gilbert replied, "I couldn't think of anyone I wanted to bring so I came by myself."

Ben was looking at him, his face crunched into a look of doubt but shrugged a "so what" gesture and asked. "What's in the cooler, a sixer of exotic beer?"

"Nope. A sixer of chocolate Yoo-Hoo… on ice."

Ben just laughed and asked, "You want some vodka in that?"

"No thank you. I'm good," Gilbert replied and sat quietly hoping he wouldn't have to answer any more of Ben's inane questions.

The theme music to the 1975 thriller "Jaws" was playing softly throughout the warehouse as more henchmen with their wives or dates trickled in and slowly filled up the other tables.

Mason came over with his wife Sadie and their niece, Dysphora, who looked over the group with a certain level of disdain, then took the seat next to Gilbert. She immediately pulled out her phone and started texting, tsk-tsking and periodically making little grunting sounds.

Mason, addressing no one in particular, said, "Couldn't find a babysitter," wagging his thumb at Dysphora.

"Don't mind her," Sadie added, "She's fifteen."

Gilbert noticed that small groups of party-goers were making their way to the buffet tables and remarked that he was going to join them and get some food before it was all gone.

Argyle turned to Audrey, "Shall we?" She nodded yes and they got up to join the ever-growing numbers headed for the buffet.

The tables were full of cold cuts and cheese sticks. There was mozzarella, Swiss, cheddar, and a creamy jack cheese from down south somewhere. There were piles of submarine sandwiches of all types. Salami with mustard, baloney with ketchup and mayo, some sort of beef-looking stuff with pickles, and a nice imitation crab (Fluke?) with capers and tomatoes. All the choices came on either a hard Kaiser roll or a soft French roll with lettuce and onions. What a feast! And if that wasn't enough, there were salads, too! Argyle couldn't decide between the Ambrosia, although it looked a little beige and not too fresh, and the Haggis, a hearty sheep's heart, lungs, and liver mixture with spices and oatmeal. How could he decide? He couldn't! So, he helped himself to a big quantity of both.

Dinner hour went smoothly enough. As the minutes ticked on and the more food and alcohol that were consumed, the noise levels among the dining tables went up. Everyone was having a good time and feeling in the mood of the evening. Argyle was feeling so good that he told a joke…

"Thrasher's at the door. 'Knock, knock.'
I answer, 'Who's there?'
Thrasher says, 'You know.'
I answer, 'I know Who?'

Thrasher says, 'Exactly!'"

Mason and Ben started laughing to beat the band. You'd have thought it was the funniest thing they had ever heard. Argyle was laughing, too and eventually Gilbert joined in. Audrey just looked at Argyle, you could almost hear her thoughts, *Oh my gawd, what am I getting myself into here? I should reevaluate my life. What am I doing? I've got to get Argyle out of this.* And turning to Argyle said, "May I have another full glass of champagne?"

A four-piece band took their places on the stage and struck up the "Jaws" theme until the overhead music was turned off. One of the men stepped to the microphone and welcomed everyone to the Henchmen's Ball, made a comment on how nicely everyone cleaned up and then cracked a joke (no one laughed) before introducing The Thrasher.

"Ok folks, put your hands together and let's give a nice loud welcome to your host for the evening… The Thrasher!"

The band struck up a nice energetic ditty and the audience clapped as vigorously as they could. The house lights went down and a few seconds later a spot snapped on over the microphone at center stage… and there he was! Thrasher!!

He was dressed in an elegant Italian made Kiton tuxedo with a men's vicuna cape draped about his shoulders. His pale face looked sickly green, a shade of chartreuse and lime and not very pleasant. His eyes dark but sharp. No matter where he looked, his gaze was penetrating, evil. It could chill you to the bone.

Audrey leaned over to whisper in Argyle's ear, her voice dripping with condescension, "Ok, here we go."

Argyle jumped. *Hope no one heard that*! And stole furtive glances around him.

The room settled down and was now perfectly quiet. In the dim glow of the spotlight, Argyle could see all the faces in the crowd turned to The Thrasher, rapt and enthralled.

"What a night so far. Am I right?" yelled Thrasher. And in return, clapping and whoop-whoops resounded.

Continuing, "Let's hear it for Miss Q!" (claps and hurray's) Miss Q was standing off to the side and when everyone turned to look at her, her face started twitching so much that she put her hand up to try to smooth it down. "And how about Feartha! She and her crew did a magnificent job decorating," turning to Feartha and lowering his voice as if he was speaking only to her, "with my favorite Great White Sharks! Feartha… you're very good!" Feartha was sitting at a table up front and stood to take a bow, her usual stern face twisted into a sort of smile, well, it was hard to tell actually what she was doing with her face, so let's just say she was smiling with pride at the recognition. "You know you're my favorite!" said Thrasher.

Thrasher gave a big grin to Feartha, so big that a row of white teeth shown but it didn't look like a smile, it looked like he was starting to growl. Feartha sat back down.

"We owe a big thanks to last night's swing shift henchmen for the successful caper on the 82nd Street Deli over on Irvine Street. Without it, we would now be sending out for pizza!" (clap, clap, clap) Thrasher eased his hands up and down signaling for quiet before going on.

"Thrasher Inc. has had a good year thanks to my benevolent leadership and steadfast guidance. Just look at all the donuts," directing everyone's attention to the mile-high stack of them on the dessert table. "This year saw the most capers done in one year since 1987."

Thrasher took the mic out of the stand and started walking up and down the stage. "We completed dozens of Cashco capers without losing a man," pointing out into the darkness, "And how many successful Office Most capers did we do?" waiting a second before he answered his own question, "That's right… many! Think back with pride at all the capers that were accomplished this year but look forward with excitement at all the capers and plans I have for the year to come. More capers! Bigger capers! Better capers than ever before!!"

The audience erupted into a deafening roar of applause and hoots and whistles. The henchmen were obviously very excited about the caper news.

"I would like to see all of you henchmen step up to the challenges. Maybe contribute more crime suggestions or fix that leaky faucet without a maintenance order."

Silence from the audience.

"This next year will bring many special opportunities but there is one exceptional situation I have in the works. I am in the middle of developing a very useful marketing tool. I will be filming one of our capers. I will use this film to promote Thrasher Incorporated and it will be designed to strike fear into the hearts of caper targets and inspire all henchmen to greatness. But beyond all of that, it will showcase me, The Thrasher." (cheers and clapping) "If we all work together… remember your team building exercises… next year will be an even better year than 1987. Thank you everyone!" Barry took a bow and straightened up staring around the room. You could hear a pin drop. Then he held the microphone out on front of him and dropped it to the floor with a bang just as the spotlight snapped off.

The henchmen and their families and dates went wild! There was a standing ovation and loud cheers from almost everyone. Well, not from Audrey.

The house lights came up and everyone started to chatter, again. Several folks started to make their way to the donut table, joined by Argyle who was determined to snag at least six little powdered ones for his dessert.

Returning to his seat, Argyle asked Audrey what she thought of Thrasher's speech.

"I thought it was self-serving," she said, "with a hint of sociopathic personality disorder."

"Really?" replied Argyle, "I thought it was very humanitarian of him to create an upcoming caper to be filmed… for our own good."

"Oh, Argyle. You are so gullible. Your credulity is off the charts. Maybe that's why I love you so much." *Was that the champagne talking?*

"So," Argyle said, "Credulity's a good thing, right?"

Audrey could only smile at him. Then she spotted Barry easing between tables and her face darkened.

In reaction, Argyle looked around, saw Barry coming nearer, and sort of nicely manhandled Audrey to her feet as she was saying, "I have half a mind to say something to that man. I ought to… "

Argyle cut her off, "Let's dance," and steered her to the dance floor barely skirting Barry's visit to their table.

Just as Argyle got Audrey to the dance floor, the band started playing a salsa. This took Audrey's mind off of talking to Thrasher and on to dancing with Argyle. She took his hands in hers and started to one-two-three step her feet in time to the music, swaying her hips, teasing Argyle to join her.

The dance floor was crowded and the air close. Audrey and Argyle had danced for half the song when the crowd started to push against them, moving them to the edge of the floor.

The other dancers were trying to move away from the couple at the center, to give them more room and Argyle and Audrey stopped dancing and turned to see what the fuss was all about.

Holy crap!

It was Ben and Fulana and they were doing a very vodka-soaked version of Dirty Dancing… salsa style. The crowd around Ben and Fulana were cheering, which did nothing but encourage them. Someone yelled, "Get a room!"

Argyle couldn't find the words to describe what he was seeing. Audrey looked at him with raised eyebrows and said, "That's nasty," and turned to go back to their table.

Argyle took a fast look to see where Barry was but didn't catch sight of him. When they got back to their table, only Gilbert remained still sitting there. They both sat down and right away Gilbert tried to start up a conversation with Argyle.

"So, have you heard about this new guy, The Thwarter?"

Argyle screwed up his face and said, "The what?"

"The Thwarter. Supposed to be some sort of vigilante. Know anything about him?"

Argyle just shook his head and glanced around the room, looking for Barry. "No. Is he supposed to be some sort of cop or something?"

"I've heard he's out to get us. Hey, do these vigilante types actually make any money? I just have to wonder what's in it for them."

Argyle thought for a second and finally came out with, "I don't see how. Bunch of do-gooders. Believe me, the real money's in crime. That's the future right there."

Audrey just rolled her eyes and looked toward the door.

"Besides," said Argyle, "what kind of a name is 'The Thwarter'? You can barely say that without spitting."

"I guess it means 'one who thwarts', as in thwarts crime. I think it's a cool name, myself."

Argyle smiled and said, "Third, there can never be a cooler name than 'The Thrasher'. Don't ever forget that!"

"Speaking of The Thrasher," said Audrey, "here comes Barry now.

I just might have to say something… "

Argyle put his arms around Audrey, "Let's leave. Go get an ice cream. Whadda you think?"

Audrey already had her coat over her arm and her evening bag in her hand. She was smiling, "Let's just go home."

Just then, Ben and Fulana came back to the table and sat down. "Where are they going?" Ben asked Gilbert.

"I don't know. Something about ice cream. Say, Ben, have you ever heard of… The Thwarter?"

Chapter Fourteen

For Morale & Posterity

⚡⚡ *Attention all henchmen. Attention! To-day's subject is morale, or more specifically, lack thereof.* (…gentle, soothing voice…) *Now, I know that we all have a bad day now and again* (…loud and agitated…) *like I did yesterday when I read in the local paper that Meglamon hit that pawn shop over on Garrison Street! How dare he!* (…calmer now…) *As I was saying: Lack of Morale. Most of you are lacking morale even now!* (…cameras go nuts panning back and forth, zooming in and out...) *And it becomes all too apparent when out on capers. There's no enthusiasm for the work, men. If you're going to be henchmen, you're going to have to step it up!* (…voice rising, like a cheerleader…) *So, give it up, give me a loud Henchman Booyah!* (…yelling…) *I can't hear you!!* ⚡⚡

There's an audible click as Barry ends his broadcast but no one hears it because the office is almost in a riot as henchmen jump up to yell "Booyah" and pump their fists in the air. Two henchmen are chest-bumping and yelling at the top of their lungs. It's a regular testosterone-fest!

Almost immediately, Alexey appears holding dozens of slips of paper and begins distributing them to empty desks and handing them to henchmen as he makes his way around the office area. His progress is slowed by the tangle of cords and wires piled up everywhere and little groups of henchmen standing around energetically discussing Thrasher's reprimand regarding their lack of enthusiasm.

"I think I do get worked up when out on a caper."

"Maybe I'm the stoic type. All business."

"If Thrasher was referring to that convenience store caper last week, well, who could work up any morale for that?"

"I displayed morale when we hit that ATM last month… I worked that crowbar with a lot of morale!"

"Is that the caper where Thorne tore his leotard and his Tighty Whities hung out? That was funny!"

Eventually, Alexey made his way around the office and stopped in front of Argyle's desk, extending his hand, offering a slip of paper.

Argyle reached for the paper but felt a bit of resistance as Alexey kept a hold of it for a second until Argyle met his eyes. "You good henchman. Not like these other guys. You full of morale," said Alexey.

Argyle studied Alexey's face for a second to make sure he wasn't trying to punk him. When he decided that Alexey was on the level, Argyle gave a curt nod and said, "Thanks. I try to set a good example."

Alexey, nodding more to himself than to Argyle, shuffled away to finish his deliveries.

Argyle held the slip of paper up and peered at the undersized font…

> The following henchmen are to report to Sublevel Five: Stevens, Davis, Milford, Watson, Thorne, and Lewis. Ms. Feartha Wolf is standing by ready to distribute caperware #23. Henchmen are then to proceed to Sublevel Four to gear up for a very special caper. Report, armed and fully caperwared to the Leonard Lake meeting room at precisely 2:00PM.
> **Do Not Be Late.**

Argyle lowered the paper slip and as he realized that he was about to go on a caper, a smile crept across his face. He dreamily thought about the pending adventure and that he was to, "report armed and fully caperwared." Armed. Argyle was a very happy man and walked on air all the way to wardrobe.

218

Milford was the last to enter the meeting room. It was 1:59PM exactly. Henderson, who was standing at the head of the table looked up from his meeting notes and said, "Milford, pull the door closed, would ya?"

When everyone was settled down, Henderson began. "Thrasher will not be attending today. He's off on some very important business and has tasked me with taking charge of this group and this afternoon's activities."

Henderson looked around the table of men assembled there. Each wore a tight silver Lycra body stocking with large Thrasher logo shoulder patches. The Thrasher skull had large 3-D eyes that seemed to follow you. Unnerving. Just below the logo hung epaulets with several gold cords that dangled down almost reaching the elbow. Strung across the chest from one epaulet to the other were four gold-colored chains of different sized links and lengths. Bright red work boots and a bright red sequined belt almost completed the look. On the belt, cinched tightly at the waist, were two black holsters, one for the henchman's choice of handgun, the other for a peculiar looking device of Thrasher's creation. Each man was to wear a black facemask.

Argyle had removed the odd device and was turning it over in his hands wondering just what the heck it was when Henderson spoke, "Careful with that, Stevens. It's very sensitive, has a hair-touch trigger."

Too late. Argyle had looked up as Henderson was speaking and must have man-handled the device because it fired, making the weirdest beeping noise that modulated up and down in frequency as it sent out two taper thin wires that attached themselves to Milford rendering him rigid, unable to react.

Milford, his face frozen in shock, sat sorta jittering, eyes unblinking, staring at the ceiling until one of the little wire barbs gave off a tiny shower of sparks and dislodged, falling into Milford's lap.

Henderson broke his curious attention and commented, "Ok. Good lesson learned. Thrasher's device houses an electroshock mechanism capable of delivering a walloping twenty million and one volts. He calls it the Scary Thrasher Device or STD for short. Don't any of you guys get any funny ideas about this STD, it's patent pending."

Argyle had watched Milford twitch for a minute then turned his attention to the device still warm in his hand. The beeping had run down but the blinking, colored LED lights that sequenced up the barrel were going strong. "I have two questions," he said, "How long will Milford stay incapacitated and will he be a brain-tard when he comes to? He owes me ten dollars. I'd like to get that back."

Ben nudged Argyle under the table and when Argyle glanced at him, gave the thumbs-up and mimed, "Good one."

There were sniggers around the table, but all went quiet when Henderson answered.

"Milford will be indisposed for about fifteen minutes. There's no data to explain post-shock brain activity. Thrasher only cares about knocking 'em down, not about their future well-being. So. Let's just say that Milford is now a part of the grand experiment."

Reaching under the table and pulling out a box, Henderson placed it in front of him and opened it up, eventually producing three motorcycle helmets, all sporting little devices mounted on top.

"Today's caper activity is special. Each of you have been hand-picked to participate because of your unique caper abilities. In Milford's case, well, I guess we'll see."

Milford's body had relaxed, his head now slumped forward to rest on his chest. Periodically, he made a little mewing sound and was still drooling so it was presumed that he was okay.

"Stevens, Davis, Thorne, these are for you," said Henderson as he passed the helmets down the table. "Each of these helmets have a top-of-the-line GoCam mounted on them that will be used to record today's caper."

Ben piped up, "Will it be a good caper?"

"Yes, it is," replied Henderson. "We're going to rob a Binks armored transport vehicle."

Ooohs and aaahs were heard around the table and excited whispers grew in intensity.

Argyle spoke up, "Don't you mean Brinks Security, not Binks?"

"Nope. It's Binks. They're a small-time operation over on the east side. They have a fleet of two used mini-shuttles. It's reported that the Binks brothers have retro-fitted their used shuttles with…" Henderson broke off talking while he shuffled through his note pages. "Here it is. They bolted three layers of thin aluminum alloy on the sides and back, stenciled fierce-looking hedgehog logos on them and have fostered a myth of secure transport through aggressive on-line marketing tools and spam. Thrasher expects this to be as easy as… Thrashing a hedgehog."

The men sat quietly, not quite getting the humor, looking around at each other and waiting for Henderson to continue.

"We know that Binks has one client, a pawn shop on Nope Street and that they pick up cash and credit card vouchers every Tuesday afternoon at 4:40PM for 'secure transport' (Henderson made air quotes) to a bank over on Third Street. They pass an alley on the way down Baker Street and that's where we'll be waiting in two unmarked vans. One van pulls out in front as Binks starts to pass, the other speeds out in back to block its escape. Everyone jumps out and we rob 'em."

Excited chatter erupted as the men talked among themselves. Henderson let it go on for a minute before continuing, "Now, this is the important part. Stevens. Davis. Thorne. You must activate your GoCams before the vans move out of the alley. Hold your heads steady, no unnecessary jerky movements. The goal is to record the robbery in total. Record anything and everything but at all costs, hold your heads steady! Is that understood?"

Just then, Milford gulped in some air as he raised his head and with glazed-over eyes, looked about.

Ben said, "Buddy. You alright?"

Milford gazed uncomprehendingly at Ben for a second and said, "Did I fall asleep? What did I miss?"

The men started laughing as if Milford had told a good joke. Milford smiled and looked sheepishly around in confusion.

Lewis chortled, "Oh, not much, Mil, not too much at all!"

Argyle shouted over the laughter, "Got that ten bucks you owe me?" Which triggered another round of laughs.

"Ok, ok, settle down," Henderson called out, motioning his hands to indicate that the men were to quiet down.

"This caper and its recordings are very important to The Thrasher. He intends to use all the footage to create the most fantastic recruiting and marketing campaigns ever produced. I believe special effects and voice-over will be added to enhance the action. Any questions?"

Henderson pulled his notes into a messy pile and began to tap them into order.

Milford looked impressed but confused so Henderson asked Lewis to bring him up to speed.

"Hearing no questions, I can only assume that we're all ready to go," said Henderson.

In unison, as if by rehearsal, the entire group of men stood, thrust a fist in the air and yelled, "Booyah!"

Oh. The caper. Most of it went well, exactly as Henderson had outlined at the meeting.

The vans surrounded the Binks mini-bus and the henchmen jumped out, shouting for pedestrians to "Beat it!" and waving their guns in a menacing manner. There was a moment, just before the back door of the mini-bus was forced open when Ben got in Argyle's face to smile and wave into the GoCam mounted on his helmet. Argyle had brushed him off and muttered a derogatory epithet before remembering about the GoCam and hoping that he hadn't been recorded.

Argyle was recording the henchman who was shooting the handle off the back door and trying to pull the door open. This proved to be harder than imagined when the tangle of shredded handle seemed to jam the lock. It was taking too long. Finally…

The mini-bus door was forced open and the tearful cries of the driver flowed out as he pleaded for his life, punctuating every other word with loud snot-filled sniffles. It was pathetic, but in they went.

Davis was up in front, GoCam-ing the henchmen holding their guns on the driver through the windshield. They looked fierce and determined until the cries of the driver started to get to them, then they relaxed their stances and looked at one another with a classic WTF? expression, shrugging their shoulders.

Thorne was busy walking around the scene recording everything and managed to catch the part where Milford dropped his STD causing it to fire its wire barbs into one of the back tires of the mini-bus, flattening it immediately.

As Lewis held his gun on the blubbering Binks driver, Ben started spray-painting stylized Thrasher logos on the mini-bus along with the slogan, "Thrasher Was Here."

Milford was inside the bus stuffing cash and vouchers into a duffle bag and Thorne was busy recording the action surrounding the scene. He was just bending over, recording a lump of gum on the sidewalk, soft and shapeless in the sun, when Argyle yelled for everyone to load up into the vans and move out.

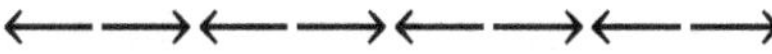

Argyle, Davis, Milford, Ben, Thorne, and Lewis were asked to stay late that evening. Henderson told them that Thrasher wanted to see the GoCam footage then possibly congratulate them for a job well done.

Argyle waited, very satisfied with his caper performance even though he didn't get to shoot his gun and his STD had been useless since, after plugging Milford, he did not have time to recharge it. But he felt he had held his head steady and captured the essence of the caper.

Ben, on the other hand, was nervous about *any* meeting with The Thrasher. Even good news was never all that good.

The men congregated in the break room and chatted amicably about the caper, but as time ticked away, the conversation wore thin.

"I'm hungry," said Ben. "Anyone got change for the candy machine? There are two malted marshmallow bars left."

Davis spoke up, "They're the same ones that have been in there for months."

"Oh, too bad," said Ben, frowning and looking dejected.

Henderson popped his head in and said, "You fellas go home. Thrasher's too busy to look at the GoCam footage right now. Says he'll deal with it later."

Everyone got up to leave except Milford, who appeared to be day-dreaming.

Ben poked Argyle in the arm, thumbed attention to Milford and said, "There goes your ten dollars."

Chapter Fifteen

A Dream Come True

Ahh. The future of crime. It had come to him in a fevered dream. Barry remembered that he had tossed and turned as he lay in his bed, his mind more restless than it had been in the weeks previous. Usually, when he could not sleep, he would get up, prowl the labs, stare at his video monitors, or scribble in his journal. But that night was different. That night, Barry had been exhausted, really bone-tired when he lay down. The tossing and the random disconnected thoughts had haunted him well into the early hours.

He recorded that dream in his journal the moment he awoke and sat now, on the edge of his bed, with the leather-bound journal open in his lap, reading the words he set to page all those months ago.

A scene of a city materialized around Barry. He was standing on a rooftop, not unlike his sanctuary atop his seedy warehouse, and he was surveying the city around him. The buildings were tall and shiny with garish neon marquees set randomly about their sides. The traffic on the street below was congested and noisy and the sky was full of strange flying craft buzzing this way and that.

Barry wondered at all he saw and puzzled it out that he was in the future. That the stinky river had been dammed up and the city, his city, had grown up to fill in all the spaces with buildings and people.

He thought to take a step, but his right foot would not move. It was stuck to a large disk that glowed orange and green. As he looked down at it, he noticed a black box protruding from his chest. It appeared to be made of metal and had wires that were attached to his body. The box had a dial on it and when Barry turned the dial, he was instantly transported to his lab. In a great flash of light and accompanied by a whooshing boom, Barry found himself in his machine shop, momentarily stunned and speechless.

The dream swirled and faded like all dreams do, and Barry woke up, his heart thumping in his chest, knowing his future was assured.

Barry got up from his bed, carefully placed the journal on his nightstand, and smiling to himself, strode to that very machine shop.

The future that his dream presented was almost a reality. It had consumed his mind, spurred his creative side forward, and filled his days with meaning and purpose.

And here it was. The fruit of many months of labor, of development, of problem solving, of countless sleepless nights, of sweat, of blind rage, of tears, of joy… Barry's Time Machine!

It dominated the center workspace of the lab. There was a thick, four-foot metal disk on the floor. Directly overhead hung a large patio umbrella, missing the canvas cover but festooned with sensors, wires, lights, a Jacob's Ladder, a camera, and battery transformers.

The tangle of wires that were attached to the umbrella structure and those that protruded from under the raised disk platform, all led to a huge and cumbersome looking console situated several feet away. The face of the console was complicated with VU meters, dials, switches, blinky lights, and buttons, all flanking a large screen computer console and extended keyboard. There were three computer mice all lined up in a neat row to the right, a large executive office chair pushed up, and Grute help us all, a Keurig coffee maker just to the left of the keyboard.

In the days following the completion of the construction of this… dream come true… Barry set about testing it. To begin a test, he would place an object on the metal platform. The first thing Barry chose was a pumpkin that he had carved to look like his scowling skull logo. Barry thought it hilarious that at some time in the future, a large carved pumpkin with his logo on it would materialize, hopefully in the midst of a fancy crowd of well-to-dos and scare the bejeezus right out of them!

After placing the object on the platform, he would activate the time machine and perform a systems check.

The platform would light up a bright orange at first and when it had warmed up, would pulsate from orange to green all the while making a whining sound to indicate that it was working.

The wired-up umbrella structure would hum and vibrate and once in a while, sparks would rain down from one of the seven transformers that ringed its outer edge.

Barry could never quite figure out why it threw sparks but since it didn't appear to interfere with the overall operation, he didn't worry too much about it.

The first trial of the time machine, its maiden run, was that of the carved pumpkin.

That didn't go so well.

The pumpkin sat in the center of the glowing and pulsating platform, the overhead structure came to life and hummed like a champ, Barry sat at the console and when he was satisfied that all was working as it should, typed in a future date and time and held his breath as he pushed the large green Go button on the panel just above the computer screen.

Power surged through every component of the system, lights blinked brightly and furiously, and the whirring sound of electricity being sucked from the source rose to an almost deafening pitch. Everything accumulated in an explosion that rocked the lab and pitched Barry to the floor.

When he regained his feet, Barry surveyed the scene. The pumpkin had exploded, spewing tiny bits of flesh and seeds everywhere. But for a few frayed wires, the machine looked okay.

It was a very disappointing test.

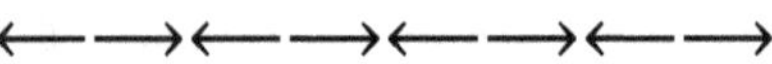

In the intervening months between that first test and now, Barry worked diligently to fix the machine, tweak this function and fine-tune that sequence. The result of all his hard work came together last week when Barry hit the large green Go button and the Thrasher bowling ball that stood silently on the glowing platform, twinkled out of existence.

Barry sat dumbstruck and when the implication of the now missing bowling ball finally sunk in, Barry sprang from his chair and danced with joy, prancing and high strutting in his exuberance all over the lab. He ended his dance of joy by standing on the platform, arms outstretched, gazing upward in ecstasy, thinking of the future and how he was going to dominate it.

Then it hit him. Was the bowling ball really in the future? How could he know for certain that it wasn't stuck in another dimension or if it had not in fact been blasted into outer space?

Further tests were needed. He might also have to go himself but needed assurance that he could return to the present whenever he wished.

Barry paced back and forth, his mind wrestling with his latest problem. He was not aware of time, he was not aware of thirst or hunger, and he was not aware of his own exhaustion until he flopped down on his bed, his mind still consumed with possible solutions, dragging him deeper and deeper.

The deeper he went into his mind, searching, searching, the more frustrated and angry he became.

Why couldn't he solve this problem? Why?

He may have slept, he couldn't tell, he sat up on the edge of the bed and in the building emotion of disappointment, slammed his fist downward where it landed on his journal.

Then the chaos started to calm. Ah ha! Of course! The dream that started it all. In it, Barry was shown a small metal box protruding from his dream body. Turning a dial on the box transported Barry back to his lab.

Simple! He would invent a Time Positioning System, a TPS device that would find the trip's point of origin, somewhere along the time route Barry had gone on, and simply return him to it no matter where he was. Easy, peasy.

Barry focused on the task and worked tirelessly until he managed a decent prototype. He decided that it was unnecessary to actually wire the device to his chest but chose instead to equip it with a really powerful antenna and two 16-volt batteries. It would strap around his chest, just in case.

Integration testing highlighted another problem. The object, or in this case, Barry, would already have to be standing on the time machine's platform… before… system activation. If placed after, nothing happened correctly. So, don't ask what happened to all Barry's test subjects. Don't ask.

Barry was almost beside himself when he figured that out.

Crap! Rubbish! Slam! Bang! And damnitall!

Barry was going to need a second person, an assistant, someone he could trust. But who?

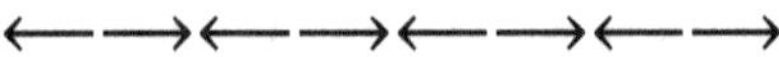

Argyle was a bit surprised to find a slip of paper on his desk when he returned from lunch. He looked around the office and noticed that there were no slips of paper on any of the other desks. *This can't be good.*

It read: A. Stevens, you are to report to Sublevel Five first thing tomorrow morning and wait there until summoned. Keep this confidential. Signed, T. Thrasher.

Argyle was stunned that Thrasher had requested his presence. *Requested? Nay, I've been summoned.*

His confusion shortly gave way to fear. He searched his mind trying to think of anything he may have done to provoke Thrasher's attention but came up blank. He was the model employee. Did whatever was asked of him, usually without griping. Tried to be a loyal henchman, except that time when that Liberty Bell caper went bad and he ran to save himself. Argyle was an obedient guy, he was always willing to do as Thrasher asked, except sometimes when he felt it necessary to bend the rules a bit.

Oh! Of course! That was it. Argyle was going to be rewarded for his model henchmanship. Thrasher had finally took note of Argyle for his stand-up-man-ship. *Is that a word?*

Argyle sat smiling to himself and rehearsing his acceptance speech. He could almost see it now…

Thrasher would expound, in elaborate detail, all that Argyle had ever done to deserve recognition: bravery, honesty, loyalty, length of service, and humility, don't forget humility. And after a long and eloquent speech, Thrasher would present Argyle with the coveted Scowling Skull trophy and ask Argyle to say a few words.

Thank you Thrasher, for this prestigious award. You do me a great honor by recognizing all those cool virtues that I strive daily to put forth in my work. I hope I am an inspiration to all other henchmen and

228

I vow to continue in my goal to elevate Thrasher Inc. to the highest villainies possible. Thank you.

Argyle imagined all the jealous henchmen that would gather around him to admire the Scowling Skull and clap him on the back. This sure would show Audrey that Thrasher Inc. was the best career path for him.

This was going to be good.

Chapter Sixteen

Argyle's Dilemma

Argyle sat at his desk with his feet up, his hands were clasped behind his head and he was lost in his thoughts. *Tomorrow morning I will be the envy of everyone. I will smile because I now know that I am Thrasher's favorite. Wait 'til I show Audrey my award, she will have to admit that this is better than forklifting for her father. Ahhh… I can't wait!*

People came and went, and the office buzzed at the normal rate, but Argyle hardly heard any of it. It seemed to swirl past in fast-forward while sugarplums danced in his head.

"Arg! Arg!" shouted Ben, nudging Argyle's foot. "Wake up! It's time to go home!"

"Uhh, what?" stammered Argyle as he focused on his surroundings.

Men were packing up and leaving, scrapping back their chairs, waiting in line for the elevators.

"Oh yea, thanks," said Argyle, "See you tomorrow." His foot had gone to sleep, and it took a moment to shake it out. By then the office was empty and quiet. The cameras had stopped panning about and the night shift guys were straggling in.

Argyle packed up his desk and made his way up to the garage and was just putting his key into the VDub's door lock when he heard someone call his name.

"Argyle Stevens."

He turned and scanned the area. Approaching from between the next row of cars were the three guys he met at lunch. The ones looking for jobs.

"What the hell?" said Argyle, thinking he may have to shoot these clowns. "Did you follow me?"

Grotcom raised his hands in a defensive gesture, "No. But the game has changed, Argyle. We've got to talk."

Argyle agreed to talk and drove them to an abandoned and dilapidated warehouse about three units away where they could talk without being seen or overheard. Argyle drove in and parked inside the cavernous main floor. Everyone piled out and Argyle locked the passenger side door, leaving his door unlocked… just in case.

The travelers spent the next fifteen minutes doing an information dump, each eager to show-n-tell Argyle all about why they were there in his time and what they were trying to accomplish.

Argyle's head started to swim. "Wait!" he said, holding his hands up to stop the three men mid-yammer. "Let me get this straight. You guys are from the future. You've come back to stop Barry from making a time machine, which you all have used to get here, and if you can't stop him then you want to kill him." Argyle looked from Grotcom to Bintcom to Malcom and said, "Right?"

"I know it all sounds fantastic, but I can assure you it's the truth," Grotcom said. "Thrasher's time machine, and make no mistake about it, he's got one. Thrasher's time machine will make the future absolutely miserable. There are time machines all over the place being used for all manner of things. Some people use them to transport to their mailboxes and back! It's crazy!"

Bintcom picked up the litany, "The commute traffic on time machine lines is killing us. The wait is too long, and the networks are so slow, they hang up and have to be rebooted all the time which only adds to the commute time."

Malcom added, "It's a nightmare. Sometimes we're stranded on the other side of town."

Grotcom said, "It's so obvious what needs to be done. Thrasher's time machine must be destroyed."

Argyle shook his head with confusion and a small, tiny thread of belief. "Why me? Why are you guys talking to me?"

"Well, for one thing, you're hanging with The Squid," said Grotcom.

"The Squid?" said Argyle. "Ewwww! What are you talking about?"

"The Squid. The greatest Crime Lord of the 21st century. He's working for The Thrasher. Don't you know that?"

"Yes, Gilbert Alan Martin III. The Squid. Here, take a look at this," said Malcom as he handed Argyle his e-history device.

Argyle took the device and held it up close to his face and squinted at the tiny print. There on the screen was an article in a future newspaper that reported on the latest crime activities of the dreaded Squid. He blinked and scratched his head, and then said to the travelers, "There must be some mistake. There is no 'Squid' working here." Then he handed the device back to Bintcom.

"Be that as it may, there is yet another reason why you should consider our offer." Bintcom handed the e-history device back to Argyle. "Read this."

Across the screen was the title of a magazine article dated nine years in the future. It read: "Thrasher loses all in a bid for world crime domination," and several sentences into the paragraph, after mentioning that The Thrasher had been seized at the scene of a botched caper, Argyle spotted his name. "Since The Thrasher's arrest, Thrasher Inc. underwent a management takeover and quickly transitioned under the guidance and leadership of Argyle Stevens." There were more words and a picture of The Thrasher behind bars, but Argyle didn't bother reading further.

Oh... My... Golly! It's mine! All mine!!

"So," said Grotcom, "Are you in?"

Chapter Seventeen

The Summons

Argyle Reported to Sublevel Five as soon as he had changed from his street clothes into today's designated work clothes. A quick glance at his reflection in the shiny elevator doors assured him that he looked good in his beige cargo pants, the ones with all the pockets. Argyle loved cargo pants pockets. He filled them all with interesting things: his keys and wallet, phone, his gun, a pen knife (one never knows when one will need to clean ones fingernails... does one?), breath mints, two dollars worth of change, a compass, bandages, and a few other items he felt were necessary. The black polo shirt with "Thrasher Inc." on the pocket and large, rather gaudy Thrasher logo on the back, showed off his muscular chest, which Argyle puffed out further in an attempt to look more pumped up. Fortunately, the required footware today was simply steel-toed work boots, Argyle's boot of choice.

Feartha Wolf, the all-encompassing and very imposing manager in charge of Sublevel Five, looked up when Argyle stepped off the elevator, and spoke, "Please wait here, Mr. Stevens, it will be just one moment." She then lifted the receiver of her desk phone and spoke in a whisper.

In three minutes time, the small ding of the elevator bell sounded and Miss Q stepped out into the foyer.

She walked straight over to Argyle, smiling, "Good morning Mr. Stevens. Thank you for being on time." She held out her hand in greeting.

Argyle was a little surprised, Miss Q had not spoken that many words to him in the seven years he had been with Thrasher Inc. "Good morning, Miss Q. So nice to see you," and took her hand gently in his. Miss Q's hand was small, delicate, warm, and soft, and Argyle didn't want to hurt her. He quickly let her hand go and said, "I see your arm is better," referring to the whole Barry-Rant-Gone-Wrong incident.

Miss Q blushed and waved it off. "It was only a scratch," and hurriedly looked down at her scheduler. "If you're ready, would you follow me, please?"

Argyle nodded and Miss Q took a step, Argyle fell in behind her and trailed along.

She led him into the caperware fitting room area and over to one of the changing rooms. When they were both inside, Miss Q pulled the curtain closed and turned to face Argyle. "You are not to divulge any of what you are about to see or experience to anyone. Not to co-henchmen, not family, not friends, not your girlfriend, no one. You are not to record this in any form including, but not limited to: paper, social media, video, or audio. There are dire consequences to any of these actions, possibly donuts in the break room. This is The Thrasher's directive. Do you understand the terms?"

Argyle knew all about donuts in the break room. "I totally understand."

"Good." Miss Q produced a slip of paper and handed Argyle a pen. "Would you initial here?" indicating a small box among the sentences, "And sign on the line at the bottom?" Argyle initialed and signed and handed the pen back to Miss Q.

Miss Q stashed the paper in her scheduler and said, "Well, ok. Let's begin," and turned to face the changing room mirror. She ran her fingers behind the right-hand side edge until they touched a lever. She released the lever and the mirror swung slowly out on its hinges to uncover a huge, heavy-looking wooden door with thick iron bolts and a massive locking mechanism.

Miss Q lifted a set of keys from her skirt pocket and fingered through them until she produced one odd looking key, which she then fit into the door lock, turning it, with a bit of effort until an audible click was heard.

She put all her petite ninety-eight pounds behind it and started to push. Argyle quickly stepped up, "Oh, excuse me," and moved in front of Miss Q. He put his brawn against the door and pushed. It creaked slowly open. Argyle felt he was pushing against rust but eventually the door opened all the way to reveal a darkened hallway that faded off into the black shadows.

Miss Q stepped over the threshold, "There's a light switch here somewhere," she said as she ran her hands over the rough-hewn wall. "Oh, here it is."

The switch made a loud snap that echoed up and away before lighting a succession of low-wattage bulbs strung down the middle of the ceiling and leading down into a sort of gloom.

Argyle peered ahead. The hallway looked as if it sloped downward and took a turn some thirty or forty feet into the dim distance.

"Ready?" asked Miss Q.

"Ready," said Argyle. And with Miss Q leading, down the hallway they went.

As they walked the hallway, Miss Q's tapping heels and Argyle's thumping boots echoed eerily off the walls adding to the already mysterious nature of the atmosphere.

Argyle thought he heard dripping noises but couldn't place where it was coming from. They had just passed another heavy wooden and overly padlocked door when a manic squeaking noise made Argyle jump and goose bumps to rise along the back of his neck. Instinctively, he moved his hand to his gun, stashed in a side cargo pant pocket.

Miss Q turned her head slightly in his direction and said, "Oh, yes, I'm sorry, I forgot. There are rats down here. I've never actually seen one, but I imagine they're pretty big judging by all the noise they make." She never missed a step.

It took Argyle a moment to relax but he didn't let his guard down for a second. He hated rats and was prepared to blast the hell out of the first one he saw.

The dimly lit hallway sloped gently downward and curved this way and that. At one point there was a stone staircase leading fifty steps down to a landing and from there, another fifty steps that ended in front of another hallway that continued on.

"How deep underground are we?" asked Argyle, his voice all but swallowed up by the shadows.

"I really don't know," answered Miss Q, adding, "It won't be long now, maybe another two hundred feet."

The dim lighting and the stale air were starting to get to Argyle. *What have I gotten myself into?* But just as Miss Q had said, they quickly came to the end of the hallway that terminated at another door. This one, though, wasn't wooden like the others. This one was steel reinforced with rivets and metal slats and sat upon four huge, very huge hinges. It reminded Argyle of the vault doors at Fort Knox.

Miss Q again retrieved the set of keys she had used earlier, thumbed to the right one and easily slid it into the well-oiled lock. It turned smoothly under her hand. Argyle moved to pull the vast door open, but Miss Q had already pulled it wide. Argyle became aware that it slid effortlessly, making only the slightest of whooshing sounds as air rushed between the dank hallway they were standing in, through the widening doorway, to whatever was beyond.

Argyle froze in his spot. He stood looking through the now open vault door wondering what was next. *Yea, what's next?*

Miss Q turned to face him, "You'll go on alone from this point. Follow the passage until you come to a door. It's unlocked, so go on through into the anteroom. You are to wait there for The Thrasher."

It was all Argyle could do to nod his understanding, say, "Thank you," and cross the entrance. A few steps in, he heard the door start its swing and turned to watch as it made its way back across its arc and heard the muffled click as it latched closed.

Argyle could hear his blood rushing in his ears and placed a hand on his chest to feel his heart beating rapidly. *Breathe it out. Calm down. You can handle this.*

The hallway Argyle now found himself in more resembled a tunnel than a hallway. It had been roughly hewn from dark gray rock. The ceiling was shrouded in blackness, the floor rough but flat, and the few bare bulbs strung along the wall provided only dull lighting.

Argyle stepped carefully along, lacking the confidence that Miss Q had shown as they traversed the previous hallway. Eventually, a door came into view up ahead. It was a plain door, nothing extraordinary, no succession of fancy locks. Just a plain door.

Argyle steadied his nerves, placed his hand upon the knob and turned it.

It opened up to expose a somewhat dimly lit anteroom. Argyle helped himself in and quietly closed the door behind him. As he turned into the room and his eyes adjusted to the change in lighting, he jumped in fright, real fright, as he came face-to-face with Barry's mom.

236

The portrait, in all its glory, glared down, stern-faced, right at Argyle. He had flinched with the scare and now stood, a little unnerved, staring at the painting. *Oh... My... G. I can see the family resemblance.*

Barry was in his office watching Argyle on the hidden camera he had installed recently in the picture's frame. It made him feel good to see Argyle so nervous. One should rule through fear and intimidation. It always made for subservient workers. Barry chuckled at his profound thought.

At just the right moment, when Argyle was starting to sweat, Barry calmly stepped from his office into the anteroom.

The sudden movement caused Argyle to turn quickly, expecting trouble. When he recognized Barry, Argyle smiled and said, "Hello. I'm here."

Barry stared for a long three seconds then said, "Yes. I see. Come with me."

"My work is intense and often takes a toll on my well-being. I sometimes sleep there," waving an arm at his living quarters, "My office is there," waving his other arm at the open doorway.

Argyle stopped to peer inside and was amazed at the stacks of electronic gear that climbed up every wall. The humming and clicking sounds it all made were definitely audible and almost annoying. *It can't be good to sit in all that electromagnetism.*

Barry had not stopped walking or stopped talking and in fact, had disappeared through a doorway down the hallway. Argyle stepped quickly to catch up.

"...but this is where my creative forces come to fruition," Barry exclaimed with pride. He was standing inside the threshold, surveying his electronics lab.

Argyle didn't know what to think let alone what to say. It hadn't really occurred to him that Barry's torture device collection and robotical mechanisms had to have begun somewhere. Now he knew.

Barry turned and stepped around Argyle, his thin, sinuous body breezing past and out into the hallway.

"I chose you, Argyle Stevens, for this assignment because you are trustworthy."

Argyle had stepped lively to keep up but all of a sudden Barry halted and turned around to face him. The quick move had surprised Argyle and he almost ran head on into Barry.

"You can keep your mouth shut," Barry was saying, "You can think on your feet." Barry stared. "Was I wrong?"

Argyle gulped, "No, boss. You were not wrong." Argyle started to stammer, "I mean, you *are* not wrong."

"Good."

Barry turned and resumed the tour. "Also, I felt that your testing of THAM-1 was thorough and inspired. You were worthy of the task."

"Thank you." Argyle liked to hear The Thrasher's praise and smiled inanely as he thought, *So. I'm inspired! Alright...*

Barry led Argyle to the supply depot and briefly waved his arms about at all the racks and stacks. "I find it handy to keep supply levels up."

Argyle walked around in amazement, looking at the racks and racks of spare parts and stockpiled components. He had never seen such a collection. It was as if The Thrasher had built his own hardware store, but bigger.

"Watch your step, Stevens!"

Argyle had been looking up and had inadvertently wandered too close to a small pyramid of plastic gallon jugs, all of which contained an iridescent chartreuse liquid and sported a warning skull and cross-bones and a picture of liquid drops burning a cartoon hand. Argyle froze mid-step. *That can't be good.*

"My precious stash of 4-Methoxybenzylamine. Very hard to come by," Barry intoned, adding, "This way, Stevens," and made for the door.

"All that you have seen is merely in support of this..."

Barry and Argyle stepped out of the short hallway and into the machine shop. Argyle was on the verge of overload. First, all the electronic surveillance gear, then the robotics lab, and that supply warehouse with its machine parts and caustic liquids. It was all so amazing. Never in one hundred years would Argyle have been able to guess that any of this was going on in Sublevel Six.

But this! This machine shop! It was fantastic, it was over the top, and it was very professional looking. It was all Argyle could do to keep his amazement in check as he looked at The Thrasher and thought, *Who are you?*

Barry's face was happy, or appeared so to Argyle, as he gazed upon his dearest creation that sat squat in the middle of the room. Thrasher reached over to the wall and snapped a switch that illuminated three huge spotlights, all pointed at the marvel.

Barry spoke clearly, his voice calm and steady. "This is my greatest achievement so far. Behold, Stevens…" (his voice rising) "My Time Machine!"

Barry walked to the console and laid a hand on the cool metal and stood looking at Argyle who quickly surmised that he had better say something complimentary.

"It looks complicated and shiny," was all he could come up with. *O.M.G. Those three travelers were right! The Thrasher has a friggin' time machine!*

Barry started speaking as he walked dreamily around the machine's various components, "With this, I will be able to achieve my dream, the one goal that has driven me forward, almost driven me mad, Stevens. The goal always just out of my grasp, illusive, seductive, tempting me… until now. Now I will dominate crime. I will be (voice rising) the one and only… (rising) Crime Lord… (reaching a crescendo) of the… (almost shouting) UNIVERSE!" The Thrasher stood puffing air, wild-eyed, and manic, adding "It's Indisputable."

Oh crap, not the universe, too? thought Argyle. As the moments passed in relative silence, Argyle thought to say, "That sounds like a worthy goal, one that seems you may be able to reach. Exactly what is it you need me to do?"

The sound of Argyle's voice snapped Barry out of his silent revelry and back to reality. "I've conducted a series of tests, some successful, some not, some with unknown consequences." Barry was walking in a slow circle around the transport platform as he spoke. "Each test inched me closer, closer to success, but the closer I got, the clearer it became that I need a second body." Barry stopped pacing and looked at Argyle. "I have to go into the future myself. Each trip is two way. I will travel to a destination and perform a bit of reconnaissance, maybe take a photo or two and come back." Barry had absently-mindedly walked around to the console chair as he had been speaking. He stood now with his hands on the back of the chair, and slowly started turning it in Argyle's direction.

"That's where you come in. I need you to start the travel sequences, monitor the events, and record everything while I'm gone. I may need you to do this several times over the next several weeks or months." Staring steadily at Argyle, "It will take time to set up my future crime empire. Everything must be perfect."

Both men stood looking at each other.

Argyle was absolutely flabbergasted. His body was in a kind of immobile shock, but his mind raced. *The way it's supposed to work, the way it's always worked, the way I was counting it to work is that you work hard, start at the bottom and work your way up to Senior Henchman. You enjoy bossing guys around for a while, supervising capers and then one day you find you're the big crime guy head of your own corporation. Not like this. Not being offed from the future...*

"You may be wondering, 'What's in this for me?' and you would be right to wonder. Here's my generous allotment to you. I will make you First in Command during those times when I'm away. With my future crime empire virtually assured, I can give you a liberal stock option grant, let's say fifty thousand stocks initially and another fifty thousand when my work is done. I am also prepared to hand over an unselfish, but as of yet, undecided amount of hush money. To seal the deal." Barry was idly fiddling with a dial or two but stopped and stared at Argyle.

Argyle's thoughts were conflicted and started to cause him anguish. It may have shown on his face.

Barry said, "Good. I see we are in agreement." Waving Argyle closer, Thrasher indicated that he was to sit in the console chair. It took ten minutes to explain which buttons to push at what time and in what sequence. Argyle scratched a note or two on a spare Post-it and tried to make sense of it all.

Barry ended the tutorial with, "...and when all is ready, push this big green Go button, here," pointing above the console screen.

"Ok, but what should I do if you don't come back?" asked Argyle.

"Well, that would imply that I made a mistake somewhere," he said in a slightly sarcastic tone, "And I didn't." Adding, "I will launch myself into some indeterminate year in the future, and then I'll be gone initially for thirty minutes in that future time, at which point I will return to the present. It's a test. I'll begin my work in earnest on the next trip."

Barry hurried to prepare himself by strapping the Time Positioning System remote around his chest and donning a pair of safety goggles. He stepped up onto the sensor platform and faced Argyle, who sat at command waiting to begin the test.

Barry said, "I am ready." And signaled with a thumbs-up.

Argyle carefully went through the launch sequence exactly as shown and when it had completed, he hesitated long enough to steal a glance at The Thrasher, standing on the glowing platform with a backdrop of little sparks falling from one of the transformers above.

Argyle held his breath and pushed the big green Go button and sat motionless watching the machine whirr up to speed and, son of a henchman, The Thrasher began to twinkle and glow and then he disappeared! Just like that.

Argyle jumped up and said, "I've got thirty minutes!"

And what a thirty minutes it was.

Argyle, with the help of his multi-pocketed cargo pants, had brought several bricks of C4 explosive with him. He hurriedly ran around Sublevel Six setting the little blocks and wiring them together as he went. One C4 block in the living quarters, one in the office, and one in the robot room. The supply depot got four of them, enough to damage the crap outta the place, with a fifth one tucked neatly underneath the convenient tower of highly corrosive chartreuse liquid.

With only ten minutes left, Argyle uncoiled the copper wire, which connected all the C4 blocks, across the hallway and into the time machine room. He quickly, and with the steady hands of an expert, wired up the remaining three blocks to the little cascade of fire-power he had already laid down throughout the facility and finally to a hand-sized timer that Argyle then set and taped to the underside of the console table.

The timer had started the second Barry twinked out on his trip. It would trigger the C4 explosives in exactly twenty-eight minutes.

The plan was to prevent The Thrasher from returning, no sense allowing him to return to mess up Argyle's plans.

The timer was ticking down and when Argyle had completed the setup it read six minutes.

Out loud, Argyle said, "Time to go!" and bolted down the hallway to the anteroom. He took one half second to rip the portrait of Barry's mom off the wall and toss it with force down the hallway into the fire zone, before bolting out the tunnel door, slamming it behind him.

Argyle ran like the devil himself was chasing him. Dull bulbs along the wall were a blur. He ran until his chest hurt and then ran some more. He gained the high staircases and still he ran. He ran down the hallway, the dim ceiling lights whizzing past. He ran until...

KABOOM!! The C4's exploded... Boom! Boom! Boom!

Argyle could only hope that the explosions had taken out the labs, the tools, the journals, all the supplies, but most of all and of the utmost importance – destroyed the time machine.

The explosions rocked the hallway, bringing dust and cobwebs raining down. Argyle reached the secret door in the changing room and clamored out, shutting the massive wooden door then the mirror door behind him. He took a moment to catch his breath, brush the dirt off, and to calm down before he stepped out of the fitting room into the foyer.

Feartha Wolf and three of her seamstresses were standing still, silently looking at each other and waiting for something to happen. At Argyle's sudden appearance they turned their shocked and questioning looks on him.

Argyle calmly walked to the elevator, pushed the call button, turned to the ladies and shrugged...

"Must have been an earthquake!"

Epilogue

"The Sock will see you now."

Both Ben and Gilbert had been waiting to see Argyle in his new office ever since the disappearance of The Thrasher threw the entire organization into turmoil. The last they had heard, Argyle had been given temporary (and perhaps permanent?) command of the Thrasher organization, and they were curious to find out what he had in mind for his fellow henchmen. Was Argyle even a henchman anymore? It seems he's been given a promotion – and no henchman, as far as they knew, had to die in order for it to happen. Excellent!

Argyle was not entirely sure what happened to The Thrasher. He knew that the time machine was still experimental, so how certain could he be that Barry correctly calculated the time element of his experimental journey? Barry had said that his test destination was indeterminate, so where was he? Could it have been thirty minutes? Could it have been thirty years? Or could it be thirty centuries??? Was there a possibility that he might run into him again in the near future? He had to be ready in any case.

He was also thinking about the travelers from the future. If Argyle had indeed been successful in destroying the time machine – which he was certain he had – that would mean that the travelers never arrived to the past, but Argyle certainly has a solid memory of talking to them. That's why he destroyed the machine in the first place. This time travel stuff was sure confusing! One thing he knew for sure: they were nowhere to be found. He made a point of seeking them out in order to hire them for his organization. They seemed like a bright bunch of fellows, and he was sure that he could find a use for them, especially with their knowledge of future events. Finally, he came to the conclusion that since he was unable to find them, that must mean that it's because the time machine was never invented. Is that how time travel works? His head would spin whenever he would try to think of it. Best not to go there.

Then there was the matter of "The Squid". Gilbert, a great Crime Lord? It was almost too absurd to contemplate, and yet he saw for himself what was displayed on the travelers' e-history device. Could there be more to Gilbert than meets the eye? Nah! But still…

Both henchmen stepped into the office of what used to belong to Barry Teasdale (AKA The Thrasher) and remained silent for a few moments. Then Ben broke the ice. "The Sock? Really?"

Argyle smiled and said, "It's just a working title. I'm still trying to think up a really good crime name. Any suggestions?"

Gilbert started to say something but stopped himself. There would be plenty of time to brainstorm really cool crime boss names, so for the time being he chose to remain silent, pondering what may be in store for him now that The Thrasher appeared to be out of the picture.

"How about 'The Dervish'?" said Ben. Argyle shook his head and just said "No. That name doesn't make any sense. Anyway, I called you guys here to update you on the status of the 'new' Thrasher organization. Barry is on leave, and we don't know when we may see him again, but in the meantime he has appointed me First in Command, his right hand man! to lead the group in his absence. Any questions?"

Gilbert raised his hand and waited for Argyle to acknowledge him. Argyle looked slightly annoyed. "What?" he said. Gilbert spoke meekly, "What is THAM doing here?" Gilbert was looking at THAM standing in the corner of the office about five feet behind Argyle. Its eyes were blinking a glowing red.

"I'm glad you asked that, Gilbert!"

He called me Gilbert, not Third, thought Gilbert. *What could that mean?*

"Gentlemen, let me introduce you to the latest member of our team. I'm sure you're already well acquainted with THAM." Argyle gestured toward THAM who then stepped forward in a shaky fashion and stood next to Argyle.

"Greetings, fellow Henchmen!" THAM uttered in a broken mechanical voice. Both Ben and Gilbert were taken back in amazement.

"How did you get it to do that?" asked Ben, incredulously.

"A little help from the IT department, and it was fairly easy to program the bot," said Argyle, "but I know what you guys are thinking. You're thinking *robots are gonna take our jobs!* But don't worry. This is the last of the THAM bots, and that brings me to you, Gilbert. I want you to take charge of THAM. Show him the ropes, as it were. Think you can do that?"

Gilbert's heart jumped. He would love nothing more than to mentor THAM. Of course! He gulped and said, "It would be my honor. I will make a Henchman out of it, I mean *him,* yet!" Gilbert was so happy that he could barely contain himself.

Ben was still a bit skeptical of THAM, but nevertheless was determined to accept it. Maybe he could use THAM to clean up his boat or fix the plugged sewage line in the henchmen's lounge. He could see some potential there.

Argyle turned to Ben and said, "Ben, I want to put you in charge of break room snacks. You will be Director of Donuts. From now on it will be donuts in the break room every day! Not just when we lose a henchman or two, but every day."

"Whoa!" said Ben. "Daily donuts? I'm on it!" Then he added, "Will there be any cool capers?"

"I have big plans. Big! We're gonna have some real first-class capers, not just the dumb Cashco capers we always got stuck with. I can't say yet what those capers are going to be, but trust me. You're gonna love 'em!"

"Booyah!" yelled Ben. "About time. I was getting antsy waiting for some good capers. Are we going after Meglamon?"

"Yes! We will *crush* him!"

After a brief pause, they all burst into laughter. After an awkward silence, Argyle suddenly got serious and said, "But one thing's for sure."

"What's that, Arg?"

"The future is never what you think it's going to be."

The Future of Crime
N. K. Hart

TEST
(You Were Warned)

1. In chapter one, how many bullets were on the table and how many were in the gun's chamber?

2. Thrasher is toying with the idea of taking his organization public with shares to be traded on the open market. He has thoughts of becoming a super-rich start-up. Study the NY Stock Exchange symbols below and choose the one Thrasher might use. Choose wisely.
   _____ (1) FEAR.ME
   _____ (2) DOOM.UR
   _____ (3) TINC.IM

3. Every Crime Lord should have a Crime Lady, and Thrasher is no exception. Should this be Helen Mirren, Helen Hunt, or Helen, the daughter of Zeus?

4. In chapter four, where was Thrasher?

5. Explain, in 500 characters, what you believe Thrasher is trying to accomplish.

6. Solve for x if sin $(x+36^\wedge)$ = cos x

7. Quantitative Aptitude Question #1:
   Ten years ago, Thrasher was thirty years younger than Meglamon, who at the time was sixty-five. How old is Thrasher now?

The Future of Crime

BOOK THREE

MISADVENTURES IN CRIME
Further Tales of THE HENCHMEN

N. K. HART

History is indeed little more than the register of the crimes, follies and misfortunes of mankind.

Edward Gibbon (1737 - 1794)

Chapter One

Hard Start

It's been several weeks since Sublevel Six was destroyed by the "earthquake" that preceded Argyle proclaiming to be appointed Number One by The Thrasher. He thought that the transfer of power from the absent, where-abouts-unknown Thrasher to himself, the new leader, would have been smooth and uneventful, but he was mistaken.

The henchmen took the news of The Thrasher's sudden sabbatical rather badly. Several wandered the hallways looking lost while others became frightened and edgy, reaching for their guns at every sharp noise or sudden burst of laughter. Many henchmen decided they were getting paid to do nothing and sat with their feet up on their desks periodically calling out bawdy jokes and laughing out loud while others played stud poker for serious stakes. Most were grumpy and started to complain about the lack of capers. Nerves were on edge and last week several of the henchmen started a riot over the lack of donuts in the break room that started when Clark pulled his gun on Carter and was heard to yell, "You want a donut?" and thrusting the barrel of his snubnose into Carter's face, "I'll show you a donut!" It took three henchmen to tackle Clark to the floor and fifteen minutes to calm him down.

Argyle knew he had to do something. He decided to call a meeting. Sitting in his office, that is to say, the Lizzie Borden meeting room on Sublevel Four that Argyle appropriated for his office, he carefully considered what his talking points should be. He opened his laptop and launched the 2003 version of PointyPower and chose a template. It was one giant glaring bloodshot eyeball, lightly faded so it didn't overpower the applied text. *"Cool,"* Argyle thought, completely happy with the choice.

He sat for several quiet moments tapping his chin with the eraser end of a dull pencil, then had an inspiration. He laid the pencil down and started to type.

Three hours later, Alexey delivered little slips of paper to all of the henchmen...

There is a meeting this afternoon at 3PM in Argyle Stevens' office, the Lizzie Borden meeting room. It's mandatory. Don't be late.
Or else!

As he handed them out, he found himself fielding questions. "What's this?" (A meeting notice.) "What's it about?" (I don't know.) "Why?" (Still don't know.)

Argyle liked the "or else" part. It made him sound tough. He sat at his desk, pretty happy, as he looked over his presentation slides...

Slide #1. The giant glaring eyeball that would greet the henchmen as they filed into the meeting room and took their seats.

Slide #2. The organization's new logo.

Argyle had come up with some doozies. The Deranged Viper and the Crazed Gunner. The Viper didn't work out so well. Every time Argyle drew it up, it didn't look deranged. It looked cross-eyed. He ditched the Crazed Gunner idea when he decided that he should just be a "Crazed Gunner" anyway. But then, after weeks of agonizing over it, Argyle came up with the perfect logo. The Psychotic Weasel. It featured a psychotic weasel's head on an argyle print background with the byline, "Look out...The Psychotic Weasel...will kill you" or some such catch phrase encircling the wonderfully creative graphic. The weasel's eyes were laser red! Argyle could just hear all the ooohs and aaahs as the henchmen admired it.

Slide #3. The talking points. Organizational Attrition (Audrey helped Argyle with this one). Recruitment and Training, Financial Stability, and Capers.

Slide #4. The giant eyeball with the words, "Get Out!" written real big and in bold that announced that the meeting was over.

Argyle could see himself leading the meeting. He would walk back and forth at the front of the meeting table, looking thoughtful as he patiently explained each talking point and what exactly it was he expected from each and every henchman. They, in turn, would listen appreciatively and nod their heads in agreement. They would hang on his every word and at meetings end, explode into loud applause. Argyle would bask in the moment.

This was going to be good.

Ben Watson had been sitting at his desk when Alexey had come through handing out the meeting notices. As Alexey handed the slip of paper to Ben, he said, "Here you are Mr. Ben."

Ben sucked in a breath and abruptly took his feet off his desk and, as he sat up straight, reached for the paper, saying, "I'm no longer Ben, Alexey. Apparently, I've fallen from favor. It's back to Watson for me. Plain ol' Watson."

Alexey hesitated a moment. "You seem unhappy, Watson," and following Watson's gaze to Argyle's now empty henchman desk, added, "Oh, I see. You miss Mr. Argyle. Tell me, you no longer friends?"

"It's not that," Watson almost spit the words out, "everything is great. Argyle is the boss. Fulana has left me and Gilbert quit." Watson's voice was getting louder. "Everything is just peachy, Alexey, *peachy!*"

"Oh," Alexey said using his most empathetic voice, "You know, there's always hope that things will get better."

Watson rounded on Alexey, "Hope?" his tone aggressive. "That's what you're going with? Hope?" his voice rising. "Well, hope blows!"

Chapter Two

The Retrofitting of Gilbert

Gilbert Alan Martin III had not been happy with how things had been going at Thrasher Inc. for some time. First, the whole joke about the crossbow and then he almost died in the shark tank!

Gilbert had thought he should have been promoted to full henchman level *months* ago. Hadn't he done everything he was told to do? Hadn't he displayed grace under fire? Of course he had. Time and time again. But he had had enough of being made the goat and had quit.

That was weeks ago, but to Gilbert the time seemed to fly. He immersed himself into developing "The Squid." He worked very hard to remove a technical kink or two with the squid gun. It was now housed in a very threatening casing that Gilbert practiced brandishing. There were four pressurized squid ink pellets that, when pierced by a patented process, would shoot a fine black mist several feet forward. The mist would spread into a six-foot cloud around the victim, was laced with a mixture of sulphur chemicals that stunk like a skunk and would stop an attacker dead. Just ask that smart-alecky clerk down at the 24-hour Quick Shop.

His squid suit, while notably a fine piece of art, would threaten to trip him as he "ran away." Gilbert had to admit to himself that the suit had to change. It was a hard-pressed decision at first but became easier with time. The suit, with its foam legs and wondrous colored markings restricted Gilbert's gait. Sure, he could walk into a convenience store and command respect, but running away after seizing the booty was really awkward. Once he had tripped over one of the suit's foam legs when it had caught on a bent railing spindle that sent him straight down into a heap at the bottom of the stairs. Besides bruising his knees and scraping his chin, Gilbert was embarrassed to the point of humiliation.

Someone had recorded his ungraceful heist exit and uploaded it to Me-Tube where it immediately racked up sixteen thousand views and was laced with comments like, "This is the funniest robbery I've ever seen!" and, "I can't stop watching this in slow motion…hilarious!"

After that it was easy for Gilbert to "let go." The suit was retired to the back of a closet where it now hung in a dry cleaner bag.

From tragedy comes something favorable, or some such thing, and Gilbert rose to the occasion and developed a completely new super villain suit.

His new suit was form-fitting, which would allow for unrestricted get-away. At first Gilbert worried that wearing spandex would accentuate his pudgy figure but thought he would work that issue later, after he finished munching potato chips and sipping a chocolate Yoo-Hoo. Shaded and colored like a squid, the suit was almost perfect. It was only missing one thing.

Across the chest piece of the new suit was the masterpiece, the magnum opus, the tour de force of Gilbert's creation…his logo…introducing…The Squid!

It was terrifyingly beautiful and guaranteed to strike fear into all who dared to oppose. Gilbert sat for moments after the last sequin had been sewn into place, just smiling and basking in those thoughts.

Putting it all together and slipping a dark gray ski mask over his head, Gilbert admired himself in the mirror. But before he could run a beta test of his new look and technology, and by that Gilbert meant robbing the 24-hour Quick Shop again, he needed to complete work on his super evil surveillance drone, aka the floor bot he swiped from Thrasher Inc. all those months ago.

Gilbert slipped out of his wondrous suit, folded it nicely, and got back to work.

Chapter Three

Show 'em Who's Boss

As Argyle peered down into his brownbag lunch sack, his mind drifted back to the carefree days of lunchtimes past when he and his buddies would drive over to the Pup-n-Bubbles or to the roach infested food truck parked on 8th, where they would score a decent meal and spend an hour relaxing.

Now it was fried egg and bell pepper on white bread. Every day. It was all Argyle knew how to make and he felt that as the new boss, he had to spend time doing boss things, not lunch things with friends.

"Just eat the damn thing," he thought, *"and get back to work, the meeting is in three hours."*

After Miss Q had shown him how to load his slides into the projector, Argyle had instructed her that at 2:50PM she was to station herself outside his office door to prevent anyone from entering until precisely 3PM. She was also to take "roll call" and to especially note which henchmen came at 2:59PM, which he considered late.

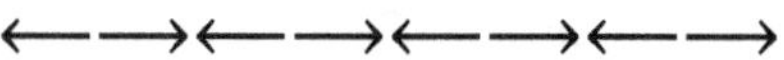

At exactly 3PM, Miss Q knocked lightly at Argyle's door and upon hearing him say okay, opened it and stepped in holding the door wide open so the large group of henchmen, crammed together in the hallway, could enter.

The giant eyeball slide blazed brightly in the dusky darkness of the room. Argyle stood just under the projection, a single spotlight from above casting shadows down his face that made him appear to be a bit menacing, accentuated by a slightly satisfied smile that crept across his face when he thought, *"See. I did learn a thing or two from*

Thrasher."

Argyle's satisfaction was short lived. As the crush of henchmen flooded through the doorway, those first in, not being able to see very well through the darkness, stumbled into chairs sending them screeching across the floor into the path of other stumbling henchmen, some who tripped and unceremoniously fell to the floor. The room was filled with groans and protests and threats as henchmen bumped and battered their way in.

Finally, someone found the light switch and the huge industrial shop lamps suspended from the high dark ceiling flared to life, blinding everyone. More groans were emitted as men covered their eyes and waved their free hands back and forth as they tried in vain to find a seat at the meeting table.

Argyle stood at the head of the table waiting for the henchmen to take a seat and come to order.

Finally, everyone managed to grab a chair and pull it up to the table but there was no order. Davis threw a wad of paper at Carter that hit him in the side of his head catching him by surprise and making him flinch. The henchmen sitting with Davis all started laughing, which embarrassed Carter, who then retrieved a menthol lozenge from his shirt pocket and fling it back with such force that it nailed Anderson in the eye. Anderson yelped in pain and that sorta started a mini riot with henchmen taking sides and hurling threats.

Argyle had had enough. He stepped back and made a claw with his right hand and raked his fingernails down the whiteboard all the while keeping his eye on the fray. He expected the resulting ear-splitting nerve chilling noise to stop the henchmen cold and bring them to attention. To Argyle's surprise there was no sound. So, he raked his nails downward once again but harder this time. Not one sound.

"Humph," Argyle thought in slight confusion, *"It always worked in the movies."*

He stood for half a second, came to a decision, pulled his gun from his pant waist, took aim at the henchman nearest to him and pulled the trigger.

BANG!

That did it. That got everyone's attention. The room went silent as everyone froze. Except for Lewis who was holding his left leg and writhing on the floor. Argyle had kneecapped him.

Argyle stood glaring at the rabble. "If I was The Thrasher, you would be dead now." He continued to glare as he brought himself down a bit. "You're welcome," was all he could think to say in the moment.

Finally, he slammed his gun down on the table and said, "Let's get on with this meeting."

Four long and sometimes painful hours passed but by golly, Argyle's first official meeting came to a close.

His new identity, that of Psychotic Weasel, was a hit! What a rush it was to have the meeting start on such a high note. It pleased Argyle to no end.

However, the "high" was short-lived.

Argyle's talking points had each turned into a painful struggle to make himself understood while fielding an onslaught of inane questions.

Point One: Organizational Attrition. (He's going to have to speak to Audrey about this one.) There's no denying this. Since Argyle assumed power, about twenty percent of the henchmen force had quit. Most of them were concerned for their futures while others should have been fired long before anyway. Someone asked, "Why did twenty percent leave?" And this started fifteen minutes of everyone telling everyone else about what they had heard.

Argyle listened with care because he did not know why anyone would leave such a prestigious workforce. But as conversations progressed, he slowly started to realize that it may have been because of him. He was too tame, too nice, and not psycho enough. Rumor had it that if they stayed, they would eventually become bored and soon after, and worse yet…soft.

Argyle took notes.

Point Two: Recruitment and Training. Basically, staff numbers have to come back up. Several Cashco and Stiples capers must be scheduled soon and there were simply not enough maintenance henchmen to do the jobs efficiently.

Ads must be placed, résumés reviewed, interviews held, and training done.

Argyle could tell he was dealing with rookies. "What would an ad say?" (Henchmen needed for Psychotic Weasel LLC.) "What's an LLC? Little Lucky Cuties? Ha! Ha! Ha!" (It's professional.) "Would you actually say Henchman Needed?" (Yes.)

And on it went until Argyle literally wrote the ad out on the whiteboard, turned back to the meeting and, laying his hand on his gun, asked if there were any other questions. There were not.

Point Three: Financial Stability…refer to talking point four: Capers.

After Argyle announced that he had big plans for big capers, the men became very animated and excited about the possibilities. "Are jewels involved?" (Possibly.) "Gun play?" (Hopefully.) "Will there be a caper bonus?" (Maybe.) "How about robbing Binks Brothers again?" (Probably not but I'm keeping my options open.)

Argyle held up his hands motioning the men to settle down. "When I have worked out all the details, I will convey the capers to those that will carry them out. Until then, stay calm."

"When will that be?" called out Vincent.

"Well," responded Argyle feeling that he was finally in control of the meeting, "Feartha and her wardrobe team have been very busy rebranding all of the caperware. When she is satisfied and when *I* am satisfied, we will make our move."

The henchmen were stoked and chattered wildly among themselves.

Argyle raised his voice to be heard, "And don't go to wardrobe to ask how's it going. Leave them alone! I'll tell you when things are ready." He looked around and knew he had been understood. "I have one last slide," and flicking a button, Slide #4 came into view…

GET OUT!

Chapter Four

A *Big* Learning Curve

Davis had moved into Argyle's abandoned desk and now sat with his feet up passively watching Watson do an impression of a working man as he shifted in his seat randomly opening his desk drawers and scratching a dull pencil across a piece of paper.

Finally, Watson ran out of busy work and sat back in his chair.

Davis spoke, "You look lost." Staring at Watson, he waited for an answer.

Watson looked over at Davis and pursed his lips into what he thought was a pout before saying, "The boss wants me to begin interviewing henchmen recruits, so I'm preparing."

"Recruits, eh?" Davis nodded in acknowledgement. "Let me see your job description and list of questions," and held out his hand, wagging his fingers in a "hurry up" gesture.

Reluctantly, Watson handed him the piece of paper he had been fiddling with.

Davis held it up so he could read it but instead of studying it, he started laughing. "What kind of question is this?" he asked, pointing at a specific scribble.

"It's a doodle of me hanging from a showerhead in the locker room after the boss…Psychotic Weasel…learns that I don't know one thing about interviewing anything let alone henchmen wannabes." Watson was frustrated and depressed and banged his forehead down onto his desk. "Just kill me now," he mumbled into his desktop.

"Well, well, well. Aren't you the lucky crime?" Davis smiled a big toothy grin. "And you thought I was encroaching on sacred territory by claiming this desk."

Watson lifted his head to look at Davis. *"Is this a joke?"* he thought, "What do you mean, Davis," he quietly asked.

"I mean, my new friend, that you are in a pickle and that I can help. I have extensive interviewing experience."

Watson immediately lightened up and smiled in relief. "Really?"

Davis continued, "I helped my son get into a Saturday tutorial on spot welding. I coached him for weeks!" Davis looked so proud, that his chest was actually all puffed out.

Watson was so excited he jumped out of his chair. He couldn't control his elation at being pulled from the brink of destruction and stood nervously jitting from one foot to the other as he sputtered, "We'll need questions, we'll need statements, we'll need diagrams!" He caught his breath and looked at Davis, "Partner?"

"Sure, why not?" Davis decided and stood up holding his right hand forward toward Watson. "When do we start?"

Watson grasped it and shook it exclaiming, "Right after lunch!"

On the way in from lunch, Davis, with Watson trailing close behind, stopped at Miss Q's office to inquire if the ad that "Psychotic Weasel had so carefully crafted," had generated any interested parties.

Miss Q listened patiently as Davis acted out the part of intelligent guy and then explained that the ad had just been uploaded to FredsList and responses would be forthcoming. She sorta dismissed Davis and Watson with, "I will be sure to let you know as soon as I have something."

Back at their desks, both men goofed off for an hour before deciding that a flood of résumés was imminent, so they had better prepare.

"First question up," Watson said, "is to ask what do they like better, Star Trek or Star Wars."

Davis answered, "Or Star Gate." He sat looking at Watson like Watson was clearly out of his mind for omitting the most beloved TV franchise ever.

Watson stammered, "Uh, maybe we'll leave that question for last."

The two men sat and discussed for an hour, got up and discussed some more as they made their way to the break room to raid the vending machines, and discussed even further as they returned to their desks.

"Finally, we agree," said Davis, "that the most important thing to ask an applicant is, how many confirmed shootings have they accomplished."

Watson added, "That and the Star Trek, Wars, Gate question."

Davis ignored the comment. He scratched a note on paper. "It's the only way we can judge their level of professionalism. Low number of shootings means rookie and therefore in need of more training."

"Training can be a fun experience," smiled Watson, "especially since the shark tank needs cleaning again."

"True that," said Davis adding, "Maybe a couple of new rookies would be okay."

Satisfied that they had adequately prepared for interviewing, Davis and Watson goofed off for the rest of the afternoon, said good night and left for the day.

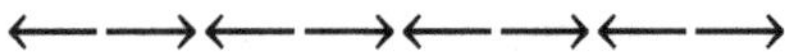

When they arrived to their desks the next morning, they found that Miss Q had left a response résumé to the FredsList ad, one copy for Davis and one for Watson. It took a minute for the men to understand what they were looking at. The paper was folded in half and when opened, revealed a large gaping shark's mouth with hand-written words scrawled inside. The men then sat quietly reading…

> Dear Psychotic Weasel LLC,
>
> I am responding to an ad I read on FredsList. My name is Morgan Taylor and I am the person for your job.
>
> Looking forward to hearing from you.
>
> Signed, Morgan Taylor

Watson lowered the résumé and looked over at Davis. "Wow. I'm impressed."

"Me, too," said Davis, adding, "We should meet with this

applicant."

"Agreed. And soon before they're snapped up by another super villain organization."

"Like Meglamon," Davis whispered under his breath so as not to prompt the devil to appear.

A look of fear momentarily shot across Watson's face but quickly composing himself, he said, "I'll ask Miss Q to set up an interview."

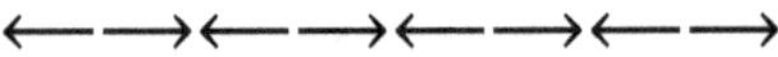

Miss Q notified Davis and Watson that the interview had been scheduled for the day after tomorrow, which to say, is today.

The men were very excited about this meeting. They had both dressed smartly, were prepared with questions, and had practiced their whiteboard skills. As they approached the Charles Manson Room that Miss Q had reserved for the meeting, Davis slowed his pace and touched Watson's arm in an attempt to slow him down.

Speaking very low, Davis said, "Remember. If this goes really well, we could get a bonus or at the very least, high praise from the boss and quality recognition from everyone else!"

"Yes," agreed Watson. "Argyle, I mean Psychotic Weasel," he quickly corrected, "will be thrilled with us, no doubt."

On Davis' nod, Watson turned the meeting room doorknob, swung the door open and stepped in. He froze in his tracks.

Davis was starting to come through the doorway and when Watson stopped short, Davis completely ran into him. Confused, he uttered, "What the…" before Watson backed up, forcing him back out into the hallway. "Hey!" he protested, giving Watson the stink eye.

Watson turned to face Davis. "There's a woman in there. She's sitting at the head of the table."

"A woman?" Davis asked.

"Yes. She's sitting at the table. Alone." Watson hurriedly answered. "What are we going to do?" he sputtered in a hushed tone.

Just then a knocking came from the door, the shock of which caused both men to jump and step back away from the door.

Davis exchanged a questioning look with Watson and then addressed the door, "Yes?"

A soft voice replied, "May I come out?"

"Oh, oh, oh," Watson said, then stared at Davis wide-eyed silently pleading for him to take over.

Davis stepped up, "Yes. Absolutely. Please do."

The door slowly opened and the woman that had been sitting at the table appeared. "Are you here to interview me?" she asked, looking from Davis to Watson and back to Davis.

Davis felt that he had been put on the spot and all he could sorta choke out was, "Interview you?" as he pointed at her.

"Yes," she announced. "Shall we get started?" she said as she held the door wide and beckoned the men to come in. Following them, she directed them to take that chair and that chair, which they, in a dumbfounded state, did, and she resumed her seat at the head of the table.

"Shall we begin?" she asked.

Davis and Watson slowly nodded their agreement.

"Good," she smiled. "I'm Morgan Taylor."

Chapter Five

Meanwhile...

Argyle sat at his desk going over a monthly report. The numbers were not good. His fledgling LLC was in the red and if he didn't do something quick, it would sink into the mire without a trace.

His thoughts ran away with him.

"I'm losing staff. Rumor has it that I'm too soft. We're low on toilet paper. Lack of donuts. Need capers."

On and on his mind rattled until he called out, "Stop!"

Argyle leaned back in his chair and made a decision to fix all the problems that vexed him. *"After all, problems are really only inconveniences. Right?"*

Taking each...*inconvenience*...one at a time, he worked through several points.

Staffing. This one was easy. He had assigned the task of recruiting to Watson who had Davis helping him, so that was in progress.

Weak leadership. Argyle had honestly thought that eliminating Thrasher's rants and explosive behavior would reduce workplace stress. Apparently not. Okay. He could fix this. *"I will become more unpredictable. I'll stare at henchmen more, but not Miss Q, she's too sensitive. I'll stop using the words please and thank you. I'll send henchmen on difficult capers that may solve the donut problem. I'll yell out orders more often."* Then Argyle had another idea. He reached for his phone and punched up the number for Feartha Wolf's office. She picked up on the eighth ring.

"Yes?"

"Argyle here. Have you completed converting the caperware logos?"

"Just finishing up now. Have about a dozen pair of socks left to do."

~ CLICK ~

Argyle hung up without saying goodbye. *"That was fun!"* Immediately his phone rang. It was Feartha. Argyle did not pick up because, honestly, he was a little afraid to.

Capers. Argyle thought that he had better get going on this one and soon. *"I'll ramp up the maintenance capers,"* and he started a list. *"Vending machines, toilet paper, hand soap, pencils, printer ink. Looks like Cashco and Better Buy first."* He sat for a moment then thought about big capers. *"Need cash to pay the electricity bill. Hmmmmm. Wonder if the Binks Brothers are still in business..."*

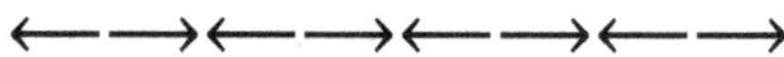

Argyle sent two squads of henchmen out on maintenance capers after first going to Sublevel Five for caperware. Argyle met the men after they had changed. He wanted to "inspect the troops" so to speak.

"Well okay. Cashco caper guys you look good."

Five men stood there in khaki pants and white polo shirts emblazoned with Psychotic Weasel logos on the front pockets. Argyle turned to Feartha who was standing nearby inspecting her handiwork. "You've done a fine job, Feartha."

She turned to Argyle and suspiciously eyed him, "So you're happy with the red sequin eyes?"

"Yes," Argyle answered, "they look like little laser beams." Smiling, he waved the Cashco caper guys off and stepped toward the Better Buy caper guys who looked much the same as the Cashco crew, so, Argyle waved them off too. Finally, he came to a third group of caper guys and took his time admiring the caperware.

The men were dressed in light brown faux leather body suits embellished with large Psychotic Weasel chest-plates that made the men look something like oddly dressed ancient Roman soldiers. They wore masks that had been made to look like fur so that each outfit resembled a weasel-like creature. It was quite the sight.

Argyle smiled and nodded and then addressed the men. "Today is a big day. It will be the official launching of Psychotic Weasel LLC. The first time our organization is introduced to the city, and you all have been specially chosen for this mission." Then Argyle stopped walking and talking and stood with his fists resting on his hips. "Get this straight," he barked, "it's important that this caper is carried out exactly as I have outlined it. You are to burst through the front door of Maymen's Silver Exchange, scaring and menacing everyone in there. Grab all the booty, not the cheap crap he puts in the front window, the good booty behind the counter. Understood?" he snapped, giving them his best impression of a tough guy.

The men shifted their weight as they all murmured their agreement, but otherwise stood and listened.

Argyle continued, "Brandish your guns and yell our new slogan, 'Weasel Forever!' got that?"

"Yes", "Okay", "Of course" responses came from miscellaneous directions.

"Let me hear you yell that out one time…with fervor!"

The men clenched their fists like professional wrestlers, waved their guns and yelled "WEASEL FOREVER" so loud their faces turned red.

Argyle was pleased. "Any questions?"

"We got this, boss," Johnson said and the others, starting to feel the pep talk, smiled in their growing excitement. Johnson pumped his fist in the air and turned to encourage the other henchmen. "Caper! Caper! Caper!" he repeated until the others joined in and the group bumped and bounced their way to the elevators and out of the seedy warehouse and into fame.

Oh, Argyle was so elated. He thanked Feartha for a job well done and returned to his office on Sublevel Four to plan more capers.

Meanwhile…

Watson and Davis were "interviewing" Morgan Taylor in the Manson Room on Sublevel Two.

Morgan sat at the head of the table, her hands folded in front of her. She looked at Davis, who tried to hide his embarrassment by quickly looking over at Watson. She followed his gaze, resting her look on Watson and said, "Tell me a little about yourself, Watson." And waited, nodding her encouragement.

"Uhhh, uhhh, uhhh," he sputtered.

"Take your time," Morgan said.

"Okay," Watson relaxed. "I'm a full henchman. I've been on many capers and I…"

Morgan interrupted, "How many capers?"

Watson stopped short and answered, "What?" he was so confused.

"How many capers?" Morgan indulgently repeated.

"Oh. I suppose dozens and dozens."

"You don't have an exact number?"

Watson looked at Morgan, who was now taking notes on a pad of paper she had produced. "Let's say five hundred," he answered, leaning forward to try to get a look at what she was writing.

"I see," Morgan smiled. "Please continue."

Watson sat for a moment in slight bewilderment then rushed on. "I-can-train-henchmen-and-I-like-donuts." He sat back and managed a smile.

Morgan thought he was grimacing. "Are you okay, Watson? Do you need a drink of water?"

"No, no, I'm fine," he assured her.

"Then how about you, Davis. Do you like it here at Psychotic Weasel?"

Davis was startled at being addressed and to cover, he reached for a bottle of water, made a show of opening it up, and slowly sipped at it as he formulated an answer. Finally, he said, "Yes, I'm happy here," then huffed out his breath to relieve his stress and sat back smiling.

"Well, that's fine," said Morgan. Continuing, "Have you both read my résumé?"

Watson perked up. "The one inside the shark's mouth?" he asked.

Morgan smiled, "Then you've seen it?"

Davis said, "Yes we have, and we were very impressed."

"So clever," added Watson forming his fingers into teeth that he held up in front of his mouth as he made fierce growling and chewing sounds, then laughed at his own antics.

Morgan gave a polite little laugh then said, "So you both know all about me."

Both men looked confused.

"And you have convinced me," Morgan continued, "to take the

job of henchwoman here at Psychotic Weasel. I can start immediately." Then, "We should celebrate," and looked at Davis then at Watson. "Who's buying lunch?"

Meanwhile…

Argyle had been rummaging through an assortment of papers and small widgets that Thrasher had left laying about the lair and that Miss Q had collected into a large box and delivered to Argyle a few weeks back. He found that he had a few minutes so took advantage of it.

There were three college ruled notebooks among the mess, the first was dedicated to the development of fantastical devices. It was full of weird drawings that depicted a bizarre array of machines that would launch arrows, rocks, rockets, and one that was shown launching little stick men in caperware.

As Argyle thumbed the pages, he found that he was more than a little impressed with Thrasher. *"He certainly had an active imagination,"* Argyle thought. He slipped the notebook into his briefcase. (A gift from Audrey.)

Notebook two was very interesting. It contained a collection of capers. Each one was fully realized right down to explicit details such as what size rope to use to tie victims up with. As Argyle slowly turned the pages, he became more inspired, *"Some of these capers actually look doable,"* he mused. *"Well, of course not all,"* he added.

One caper involved the Henchman Catapult™. Thrasher had drawn the catapult outside the city's largest bank, the Bank of Trust, out on S.W. 87th Blvd. The moment was frozen in time on the page but clearly showed a succession of henchmen being launched, one quickly after another, up into the air and onto the bank's roof. Argyle squinted closely at a little detail penciled in the background. It was a henchman who had obviously missed the roof. The drawing showed a little figure that had splattered on the side of the building with the note "calibrate catapult first", penciled next to it. *"Ok, good to know,"* thought Argyle. Scribbled handwriting all over the page noted things like, how much cash would be available at what times, number of guards, number of henchmen needed (give or take a couple), and what caperware would be worn.

Argyle was very impressed. *"So creative,"* he thought as he closed the notebook and slipped it also into his briefcase. *"I'll read this later tonight."*

Notebook three was a collection of past and future Barry rants. *"Now this is interesting..."* Argyle's curiosity had been piqued. The rants contained within the notebook were not written in some haphazard manic way with words shot out in a random manner. Each rant was written with intention, structured, grammatically correct, and all were labeled with subject titles and dates.

Argyle had to wonder, *"These rants do not appear to be the ravings of a lunatic. They easily could have come from a fifth grader but are clearly written in Thrasher's script."* Argyle read a rant that happened to appear when he stopped thumbing notebook pages. It was titled, Fear is The Boss of the Dim, and dated for a public rant later this year. After reading the rant, Argyle closed the notebook and sat dumbfounded. *"Was Thrasher so insane that he was sane?"* he asked himself before answering, *"Whatever,"* and before he put notebook three into his briefcase next to book one and two, a thought came to him. He got up to leave his office and taking the notebook of rants with him, made his way to Miss Q's office on Sublevel Two.

Argyle slipped unseen down the hallway that joined Miss Q's office with the henchmen's office pit. He stepped into Miss Q's office and closed the door. Miss Q had looked up at his entry, but Argyle stopped any questions by putting a finger to his lips and quietly shushing her before slipping past her desk and into the secret P.A. system room that lay beyond a bookcase on the wall.

Once inside, Argyle fired up the cameras and watched all the monitor screens jump to life. He studied the visuals for a minute before fiddling with the sound levels. What he saw on the monitors was a bunch of idle henchmen. Half had their feet up on their desks in different stages of napping, others were shooting dice and still others were surfing the dark net. Argyle leaned closer to study one of the screens. *"Is Miller job hunting on FredsList? Damn!"*

Argyle flipped the audio switch and yelled into the microphone,

⚡⚡ Hey you mooks, get your feet off those desks! ⚡⚡

Then fiddled the camera joy sticks sending them into a flurry of pan-n-scan.

Most of the henchmen froze in terror, the others quickly tried to hide what they had been doing and assumed smiling faces and attentive postures…aka Thrasher style. One of the nappers shot awake and, in his shock and frenzy to look innocent, jumped up and immediately tripped on loose cables and fell in a grunting heap to the floor.

Argyle was pretty sure he had everyone's attention so thumbed the rant notebook pages, chose one at random and began…

> *Ahem, ahem.* (Argyle cleared his throat then assumed a tone he thought conveyed authority but in actuality was just his loud voice. Continuing…) *Psychotic Weasel here. I believe the future of Thrasher Incorporated…(louder)…I mean Psychotic Weasel LLC!* (Okay, I think I covered that well.) *will be full of opportunity for those who work hard in the pursuit of my dream of becoming the biggest most feared crime lord the world has ever seen! I will crush Meglamon…or…or…or some other crime wannabe!* (Then as an added incentive…) *And we will shoot our guns!*

Argyle looked at the monitors. The henchmen were smiling and nodding and looked genuinely happy. It made Argyle feel good. Continuing…

> *Well, that's it for now. GET TO WORK!*
> (He shouted and then snapped the P.A. system off.)

Noticing that the spy cameras had been shut off, the office full of henchmen burst into laughter. Some tossed wads of paper at the now still cameras. "What a joke!", "So funny!", "Really sad!"

Argyle hadn't seen or heard any of it.

Meanwhile…

Watson, leading Morgan and with Davis trailing behind, had come back from their celebratory lunch at the Suds-n-Tots and took a moment to stop by Miss Q's office to introduce the new hire.

Miss Q had taken it all in stride. She greeted Morgan and fished out several pieces of new hire paperwork from a file cabinet along with a copy of Thrasher's Golden Rules that had Thrasher's name crossed out and Argyle's hastily scribbled on the front page. She handed the little pile of papers to Morgan and, with a smile, welcomed her to Psychotic Weasel.

Watson led the little group down the hall to the office pit, explaining that Morgan could take any available desk, adding a note about the crappy chairs and to watch her step so as not to trip on the mess of cables. "We're not sure where some of them go," he had said.

Morgan scanned the pit and immediately moved through the space grabbing a decent chair as she went. She moved with such determination that Watson and Davis just watched as she picked a desk, Argyle's old desk, the one Davis moved into last week. Morgan plopped down the sheaf of papers, sat down, and immediately started looking in the drawers, picking certain items out and tossing them into a nearby trashcan.

Davis knocked Watson's arm with his elbow, "Hey, that's my desk," he said.

Watson looked at Davis. "You gonna tell her?"

A look of confused fear shot across Davis' face. "No! Not me!"

The men stepped forward, Watson took his seat and Davis took Gilbert's old place at a dilapidated, duct-taped mess of a desk. They sat quietly as Morgan filled out her employment forms and took note of the reactions of the other henchmen to finding a woman among their midst.

Davis leaned over to Watson and whispered, "This is going to be interesting."

Meanwhile…

Chapter Six

Maiden Flight of the Cephalopod

Oh, Gilbert was so pleased with himself. He had worked very hard to retrofit his floor bot with remote voice control circuitry and modify the little spinner motor, first by boosting the RPMs then by welding four sets of rotary blades to its top so it could fly.

After mounting camera gear to its sides, Gilbert found that it had a bit of space left in the dead center of its belly, so his evil genius mind came up with a lighter-launcher. After carefully applying for a patent, he built a prototype and feeling pretty good about that, refined his design and built a full-scale model.

Gilbert manufactured little explosives, the size of M80s but a lot more, well, explosive. He called them pods. He then conceived and refined a little launcher that would light the pod's fuse with a laser flash then hit it with a tiny hammer that would launch the lit pod through a short, fat tube, much like a bullet through a gun barrel, except this device shot lit fused pods at its targets. And it was pretty accurate.

Gilbert named it Tentacle One and planned to build seven more. He saw himself with eight lighter-launchers, one in each tentacle. Get it? Squids have eight tentacles, Gilbert was a Squid…oh, never mind.

The beta test flight of Tentacle One and the debut of the reimagined squidware were set for next Tuesday at 11:30PM. There was to be a new moon, that is to say no moon at all, and Gilbert thought it would be the perfect time. He was sure that his flying floor bot would perform as expected but just in case, and to be sure, he scheduled Saturday in the park as Test Flight Day.

Tuesday night 11:15PM

Gilbert positioned himself in an alley across the street from the 24-hour Quick Shop and watched the store through the large brightly lit front windows. When it looked quiet enough, he powered up Tentacle One and released it as it gently floated upward.

"Move forward to within two foot of the windows," Gilbert commanded, "Stay at six-foot height." The drone, its little blades whipping the air, slowly moved forward. Gilbert followed at a discreet distance.

The drone hovered at the window awaiting further orders.

As Gilbert moved to the doors, he commanded, "Follow me."

The drone whirred just behind Gilbert as they both entered the store, now only peopled by the same smart-alecky clerk that Gilbert had shot with his squid ink gun a few weeks back.

The clerk looked up in surprise. "You again?" he asked without really asking. "What's with the chubby suit?" he smiled before starting to laugh out loud.

"Kick his ass," Gilbert commanded, and Tentacle One loosed a lit pod that sailed upward and over to land behind the counter. The clerk, who was fast on his feet, dove for cover just as the pod exploded sending sparks and smoke in all directions.

"Hey!" he yelled, "That hurt!"

Tentacle One had moved closer and after adjusting the barrel to focus on the clerk, Gilbert spoke. "I am The Squid. I will spare you...*this time*..." he menaced, "if you tell the world that there is a new crime lord in charge here...*after*," he emphasized, "you give me all your cash!"

The clerk, fairly subdued by the whirling drone that was looking right at him, said, "Okay." He stood up slowly and pushed a button or two to make the register drawer open and scooped out a few bills. Keeping his eye on the drone, he handed the cash over to Gilbert, who, by the way, looked resplendent in his body suit and was now holding his shiny, powerful squid ink gun pointed steadily at the clerk's head.

Gilbert grabbed the bills and took a moment to count it. "What??" he screamed. "Thirteen dollars? Where's the rest of it?" he yelled as he thrust the squid ink gun closer to the clerk's face.

"The night's receipts are vaulted at 10PM every night," the clerk choked out. "The only customers since then wanted two big slurps and a large box of donuts. I swear, Squid, it's all there is." The clerk started to cry.

Gilbert was so angry. Thirteen bucks wouldn't even pay for the lithium battery that powered the drone. Gilbert spun around and started for the door, calling out as he went, "Tentacle One! With me!"

Chapter Seven

The Unholy Past

Argyle had taken the three notebooks home with him last night and studied them until his eyes hurt. By evening's end, Argyle thought he now understood The Thrasher pretty well, probably better than anyone alive right now. *"He's a complete mess,"* he mused as he put the notebooks back into his briefcase.

Argyle found that he had a few minutes before climbing into bed so thought to call Audrey. Audrey and Argyle have been engaged for two years. She picked up on the second ring, "Hello?"

"Hi babe, are you busy?"

"Oh, it's you," she said, "No, not too busy. How about you? Are you busy?"

Argyle loved their love talk. "No. Not busy. Wanted to say good night and ask if you would like to have dinner with me Friday night?"

"Hmmm…which restaurant?"

"The Village Spot on 29th, down the street from McClusky's Eight Ball. We could go dancing after."

"Then I should wear my puffy skirt and high heels," she hesitated, "Okay. It's a date!"

~ CLICK ~

"Oh!" Argyle was momentarily shocked. Audrey had hung up on him. He immediately called her back, but it had gone to message.

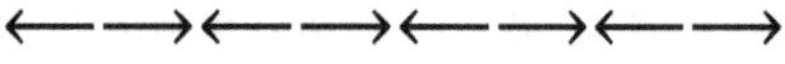

The next morning when Argyle arrived at work, Miss Q met him at the elevator. She had a small wheelie cart with her that carried two more boxes of Thrasher stuff that she dutifully turned over to Argyle. He had pushed the cart into his office and started removing items from the top box.

First and foremost was an ancient video tape recorder. Argyle guessed it to be from the early 1960's. It was housed in a suitcase and weighed a ton! He pulled it out and got it to the meeting table and opened it up to take a look. There were a few buttons to operate it, a six-foot-long power cord, a clunky CRT display, and spindles that sat either side of a wide record/play head. The box also contained a dozen or more reels of magnetic film tape. None of them labeled.

After getting a cup of coffee and spending way too much time getting this mechanical wonder set up, Argyle finally sat down, loaded a film tape on the play spindle, threaded it past the head, secured the end to the take up reel, and fired it up.

The tape started to move and the display lit up. Argyle thought, *"I should have brought popcorn,"* but that thought faded quickly as the video played.

It was The Thrasher. His face filled the screen with menace and poise. Slowly the camera rolled back until it revealed The Thrasher sitting at the head of a meeting table.

Argyle mused, *"Could have been recorded here in the Lizzie Borden room!"* He smiled, *"My office."*

Then the camera moved closer to The Thrasher and he spoke. "You!"

Argyle jumped at the sharp suddenness of Thrasher's voice, something no one had heard for many months.

"Yes you, Argyle Stevens." Thrasher leveled a look at the camera before continuing. "I've been watching you."

Argyle snapped the machine off and sat frozen, his heart making jerky thudding movements in his chest. When he calmed down enough to breathe, he got up and canvassed the room looking for a microcamera or a microphone or a something. He found nothing. His office was not bugged. He sat back down and reluctantly pushed the play button.

"Stevens," Thrasher spoke, "I've had something on my great mind for some measure of time, now. I'm becoming distracted from the everyday business of running a crime mob. The ongoing tasks of henchman maintenance and the constant demand for my caper creativity are taking me away from my real joy… (Thrasher's voice had been laced with annoyance but had slowly started to increase in volume.)…finding a way to smash Meglamon!"

Argyle nodded at the screen. He knew how much Thrasher hated Meglamon. A lot. That's how much.

"All of this has brought me to the conclusion that I need someone I can trust to take over the daily operations of Thrasher, Inc. Someone to carry out my orders. Someone with very little creativity. Someone who can shoot guns. (A slight pause while Thrasher leaned in) And! That! Someone! Is! You! Stevens!" Satisfied, Thrasher sat back and folded his arms across his chest, and with a calm voice, continued…

"However, I find you slightly lacking in two aspects of your personality. One. You will need to psycho it up a few notches. Work on that. Two." And here the camera pulled slowly back as Thrasher stood up. One could see his anger rising as he pulled in a breath of air, placed both hands on the table, leaned forward and yelled, *"MAN UP!"*

The film tape had run out and now made flapping noises as the take-up reel spun in circles.

Argyle sat stunned. It took him a full minute to come to an understanding of what he had just heard and witnessed. When it finally hit him, Argyle joyfully jumped up from his chair and in one smooth movement drew his gun from his belt, raised his hand over his head and in near ecstasy, squeezed off three rounds that disappeared into the deep darkness of the room's cavernous ceiling. As he stood in his joy, little clumps of dirt and rock briefly rained down from the dark ceiling.

"By Grute," he said aloud, "I can't wait to tell Audrey. She'll be sooo glad that I am not working for her father." And to himself, *"I won't mention that I wouldn't have done that anyway."*

"It's celebration time! I'm going to the gun range and shoot my gun!"

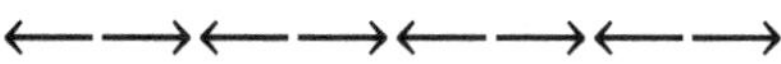

Argyle met Audrey for lunch and joyfully told her all about his confirmed destiny as a crime lord. She had smiled as he told her all about his plans and had offered advice on how he could "Fix up" the seedy warehouse and paint the break room in festive colors.

Audrey let Argyle ramble on and on until he got to the part about ratcheting up on the psycho bit.

"Wait. Go back a bit," Audrey interrupted Argyle's narrative. "What's that about becoming a psycho?"

"Oh no, babe, not *becoming* a psycho," Argyle's voice was sweet and low, "I'm to bring out my *inner* psycho. See the difference there?" he innocently asked.

Audrey stared at him for an uncomfortable moment then said, "I swear on somebody's mother's grave that if you start turning into a Thrasher junior, I. Will. Leave. You."

"Oh," Argyle laughed and took her hand and as he gently patted it, he added, "but I'm The Psychotic Weasel now and I'm okay. Right?"

Audrey considered Argyle's words and relaxed a bit. "Yes, of course. You're right."

"You'll see. I'll be the same big ol' lug that loves you. I promise." But just as the words left his lips, a voice in his head murmured, *"Ahhh, that promise won't hold."* Then Argyle smiled sweetly and dug into his melted oily tuna sandwich with jalapenos and barrel aged pickles with renewed gusto.

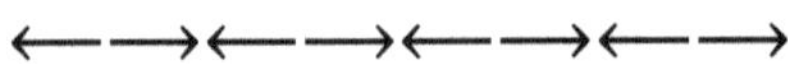

Back in his office after his lunch date with Audrey, Argyle thought that he should work on marketing his new company. He agonized over several ideas he had that seemed brilliant at the time but now that he needed to add details, seemed way too difficult. For instance…

Marketing Goals: to become the top crime boss, feared by all.

The Plan: advertising. Brochures? *"Yes."* Business cards? *"Nah, would need too many. That's a no-brainer."* Billboards? *"Yes! A 50-foot Psychotic Weasel would be way cool!"* A web page? *"Absolutely! However, I'll need a Russian hacker for that. I know! Alexey! He's Russian!"*

Argyle reached for the phone and punched up the number for Brown who answered right away, "Yeah?"

"Psychotic Weasel here. You're on Marketing now. I want you to create a company brochure that contains my logo…big and in color. You are to write the main text." Argyle listened then said, "How do I know what text? That's your job!" Changing the phone to his other hand, Argyle continued, "and include the company slogan, 'Weasel Forever!' in big bold lettering. Got that?"

"Yes, CW."

"What did you just call me?"

Brown answered, "CW. It's short for Cycotic Weasel."

"Spell that."

"C Y C…"

"Stop!" A nervous moment passed, then Argyle sighed, "It's Psychotic Weasel. P S Y C H O T I C Weasel. Oh, never mind."

~ *CLICK* ~

Argyle then called Ross. "You're on Marketing now. I want a billboard, maybe seven of them. They will feature Psychotic Weasel and promise mayhem."

~ *CLICK* ~

"Alexey," Argyle said into his phone, "build a web page for me. One that will sniff out the credit card numbers of whoever browses it."

"I'm not sure that's possible, Mr. Argyle," Alexey replied.

"Well, look into it and do the best you can."

~ *CLICK* ~

Argyle sat back in his chair, *"Not saying goodbye sure saves a lot of time,"* and smiled even though his head was spinning from all the thinking he had been doing. *"Maybe an hour on the par course will help."*

Chapter Eight

Something Happened To THAM

Argyle decided he needed a break from managing company business so scheduled a two-day stay-cation with the IT Department, that is to say, a makeshift space on Sublevel Three. Months ago, he had given them Thrasher's Humanoid Army of Mutilators, better known as THAM-1 and a requirements list of upgrades and was anxious to see how it was going.

The IT Department consisted of two guys, Jones and Tanner, who seemed to know their stuff and were always talking about bits and surge protection and a lot of other in-depth subjects that Argyle couldn't follow. He had thought that spending time with them would help and today was day one.

After exchanging pleasantries with Jones, which consisted of him gushing about the boss' visit, Argyle asked to see THAM.

"Of course, PW. You don't mind if I call you PW, do you?" Jones hesitantly asked.

Argyle looked at him and said, "It's fine. Very endearing," then thought, *"Well, at least this guy can spell."*

Jones looked relieved then stepped toward one of the work areas, waving an arm and saying, "This way."

As Argyle approached the benches and storage racks, he got his first look at the revised THAM. It was overwhelming. THAM was so changed. Argyle walked up to THAM and stood examining the robot up close.

THAM looked so different. Instead of the makeshift mass of metal with a wash bucket for a head and clunky metal boxes for feet, THAM was now a thing of beauty.

It was broad shouldered and sleek, stood over six-foot tall, closer to seven, and was made from several types of shiny metal. Its head was humanoid shaped with one big Cyclops eye in the center, screens for ears, and a lighted speaker for a mouth. Argyle could see a jumble of wires and cables behind the moveable metal plates that acted as skin. *"I think I see blinky lights in there,"* he thought as he peered inside its chest. The bot had feet that reminded Argyle of a weird combination of battle tank treads, springs, and large ball bearings. Very complex.

Tanner had joined them and stood with Jones as they silently watched Argyle and waited for his initial reaction. Would it be elation and a bonus? Or retribution and a bullet?

When Argyle had seen enough, he turned to the two men and with a smile said, "Wow," adding, "Love the Psychotic Weasel patch."

Tanner huffed out the breath he was holding, and Jones clapped his hands and exclaimed, "Alright!" and immediately launched into twenty minutes of Show-N-Tell.

"We renamed it DOOM," Tanner said. "It stands for Dangerously Ominous Omnipotent Machine," he smiled with pride.

Jones leaned in, "What do you think? Is that a killer name or what?" But rushed on in his excitement, not waiting for Argyle to answer.

After the two men had pointed to this and had explained that, Tanner announced that it was time for a demonstration. He took up a remote controller and held down the power button until the unit lit up and DOOM reacted by whirring and sputtering to life.

Argyle took a half step back, unsure of what to expect.

"DOOM," Tanner spoke, "meet Psychotic Weasel."

The bot straightened up to his seven-foot height and held his metal clamping hand thing out as he attempted to step forward toward Argyle. It didn't go so well.

DOOM lifted a roller tread foot and swung it forward, but it had folded limply causing the robot's first step to fail. It was saying, "Greetings Psychoooo," as it fell forward, "tic," it screamed on the way down and BANG! it landed face down on the stained concrete floor, "Weasel," it mumbled as it tried in vain to right itself.

Jones and Tanner leapt forward to help DOOM get back up on its feet. Argyle joined them when he saw how much trouble they were having. After several minutes of struggling, they managed to get DOOM standing back up where it raised its clamper hand again, turned to look at Argyle and said, "Greetings Psychotic Weasel."

Argyle took his claw and slowly moved it up and down, and said, "Thank you, DOOM. Are you alright?"

Audible whirring and clicking sounds emanated from DOOM's head. Finally, DOOM spoke, "I seem to be fine."

Tanner was whispering to Jones, "Maybe springs for ankles wasn't the best idea."

Jones nodded. "Better try a hinge joint."

"Yeah."

Turning to Argyle, Jones said, "We have a few kinks to work out," then rushed to add, "This is only the beta version, beta DOOM if you will."

"Yeah, we'll get this," agreed Tanner.

Argyle nodded that he understood as he remembered all of THAM-1's training and how that played out. "Okay. We know it can't walk so good right now, but can it shoot a gun?"

Jones became very animated, "You bet DOOM can shoot!" and turning to Tanner, said, "Another demo?"

"Yes!"

Tanner started rummaging around the supply shelves in an intense search while Jones repositioned DOOM to face the far wall of their workspace. Tanner called out, "Here it is!" as he pulled out a vintage Winchester model 777 bolt action rifle and made his way to where DOOM stood. DOOM took hold of the rifle and opened the chamber, noted that it was loaded and slammed the bolt closed.

Argyle was impressed.

Tanner spoke, "DOOM." And DOOM swiveled his head to look at him "See that target down there?"

DOOM swiveled his head back. "Do you mean Jones?"

Jones had been setting up a paper target that had the scribbled likeness of Meglamon on it and hearing DOOM speak, jumped back and yelled, "No! Not me!" his eyes wide in terror.

Tanner assumed the gentle tone of a mentor and patiently explained to DOOM, "No, not Jones. The paper target he has set up for you."

DOOM looked at Jones, "Sorry," then looked at Tanner, "Yes, I see the target."

Meanwhile, Jones had handed Argyle and Tanner earmuffs before putting on his own.

Tanner yelled out a command. "Blast the hell out of it, DOOM!"

DOOM took aim and loosed the round. A big puff of smoke distorted the scene but as it dissipated, Argyle got a look at the Meglamon target. It had been kneecapped!

Tanner pumped his fist in the air and Jones ran to DOOM who lifted his clamper hand in the air and a big high five was delivered by a joyous Jones.

When the hilarity calmed down, both men and DOOM stood looking expectantly at Argyle who then knew he was supposed to say something. Looking thoughtful he said, "Okay," then asked "What else can it do?"

A thought flew through Tanner's mind, *"Not elation. No bonus."* He ventured to say, "The requirements list is a good document and we've been hard at work developing each condition on the list in order of priority."

"Yes," added Jones, "Giving it language and some level of rationality took a lot of time and parts."

"And we spent a huge amount of time on his target shooting practice. We're almost out of bullets," added Tanner.

"Okay," said Argyle putting his hand up to calm them. He could clearly see they were stressing out. "Maybe I should add some detail to the requirements items. Would that help?"

"Yes," said both men in unison, looking a little better.

"Yes," said DOOM making Argyle, Tanner and Jones turn to look at him in surprise. DOOM's head whirred to look from one to the other to the other. "It would help."

Chapter Nine

Liberating the Men's Club

Business was slowly getting back to normal except for a change or two that had crept in.

Maintenance capers had resumed and followed a reliable schedule. Smaller capers, whose purpose was to generate income, were somewhat regular but did not generate the required amount of capital necessary to float operations. Larger, more daring capers were becoming necessary and were under consideration.

The staff was getting restless. Complaints of boredom were heard and gossip was shared.

It took two days for the veteran henchmen to get used to having Morgan Taylor…*a woman*…in their ranks. At first, everyone just glanced at her and talked to each other in hushed tones or behind their hands.

Morgan ignored it and had gone about the business of settling in. She easily found the par course on Sublevel Three and took to working out daily. She had also inquired as to which henchman was the best at completing the Training Center Course. As it turned out, it was Davis, so she immediately challenged him to a timed competition. All three courses: Night Infiltration, Find the Booty, and Swamp Assault.

This was huge! On challenge day, the training center was packed with expectant henchmen all loud and chatty with excitement. One of the guys had wheeled in a whiteboard to set up an odds chart and was taking bets on which contestant, Morgan or Davis, would win which course and who would take the day. The odds fluctuated madly as money changed hands at a rapid pace.

Finally, the hour came and the two competitors appeared.

Morgan was the first to step through the doorway from the hall.

Her backers raised a whoop whoop and jostled each other to get a look. She was wearing a black unisex shiny spandex body suit with black high-heeled boots that came up to her knees, and a tunic cinched at the waist with a bright red sash that she had knotted at her hip. The tunic had a Psychotic Weasel logo on the chest, done in black sequins, except for the eyes that shone laser red in the light. She wore black fingerless long gloves and a black face mask that hid everything but her eyes. Most of her long auburn hair was tied back in a pony with the rest hanging loose and flowing. Most of the onlooking henchmen were instantly smitten.

Davis had joined the crowd virtually unnoticed and was trying to push his way forward when someone finally spotted him and yelled, "Hey, it's Davis!" at which most of the men turned and cheered him on… "Good man!" and "You can do this!"

Davis wore a tank top that did not hide the beginning of a dad bod and a baggy pair of basketball shorts that hung down past his knees. He had on a pair of steel toed boots and a Thrasher ball cap that he had altered by pulling out some of the threads so that it now read, "T-rash."

Davis stepped up to Morgan who smiled at his approach, and said, "Hi" before they shook hands.

The noise level in the room had gone up as excitement grew. The Bookie called out, "Last call for bets!" and several men gathered up.

Morgan turned to Davis, "Quite the happening, isn't it?"

"Yeah," Davis said as he looked around. "Quite the to-do."

"I guess these guys were starved for entertainment."

"Well, there hasn't been anything noteworthy to talk about since the boss replaced the turnstiles with a security guard that sat in a chair and asked everyone if they had concealed weapons, you know, guns or knives."

Morgan looked surprised. "Really?" she asked.

Davis nodded, "Yeah. Imagine a big crime organization without guns or knives," shaking his head in disbelief. "He was here for two days before the turnstiles were reinstalled."

The Bookie yelled out, "That's it! No more bets!" and walked over to the first test course. "Davis! Morgan! Step over here, if you will." When the three stood together, he continued, "First contest. Night Infiltration. Now you both know how this is gonna go. The course is dark and full of obstacles. You will be issued night vision glasses and will have ten minutes to grab all the booty you can…*without!*…getting hurt. The one with the most valuable booty wins."

The course was darkened, and the night vision glasses were on. The Bookie turned to the onlookers and shouted, "No help from you mooks! I…will…evict…you!" he warned, pointing a finger at a few of the onlookers. Then turning to Davis and Morgan, "Ready?" They both nodded. "Your ten minutes start now!"

Off the contestants flew to encouraging cheers from the crowd of henchmen now crushed against the course railings in an effort to see the race through the darkness.

The minutes ticked by and the excitement grew. Finally, the Bookie's stopwatch chimed, and he yelled, "Time!"

A moment or two later, both contestants stepped out of the darkened course, arms loaded with stuff.

Four henchmen had been chosen at random to tally up the booty and now stood doing exactly that. When they finished their count, they handed little slips of paper to the Bookie who read them and then announced, "The winner by 12.25% is…Morgan!"

Half the henchmen rushed forward to claim their winnings. The other half moaned at their losses.

"Course two!" the Bookie called out. "The Blindfold Challenge."

Here the contestants would have a canvas bag over their heads thereby making them unable to see anything. This course included the Rope Climb and the dreaded Fast Feet Run. Contestants were to make their way through the series of obstacles, again, without bodily harm. The one with the best time and the least number of injuries would win.

Morgan and Davis stood at the entry point. Davis was determined to win this one after feeling the sting of defeat for course one.

The canvas hoods were secured, and the bookie called out, "Go!" and Davis plunged in like a bull in a china shop.

Morgan entered a bit more carefully, noticing sounds and measuring distance, paying attention to what was underfoot. In the background she could hear Davis sorta thrashing about, making "Ow" sounds. Once she became familiar with the smell and feel of the course, she moved stealthily forward, ducking when a wooden pole swung overhead and bypassing pressure plates that would have sprung up under her step.

Davis was several feet in front of her and making his way fairly well when all of a sudden he missed a step and his leg sunk into a hole causing him to drop to the ground.

Morgan made the distance to where Davis was struggling to get up and said, "Give me your hand," whereupon she tugged him up to his feet, then said, "There you go. See you at the finish!" before turning and leaving.

Davis was dumbfounded but quickly recovered and moved on.

Morgan managed to exit the course first with little more than a bloody scratch on her upper arm. Davis stumbled out a few minutes later having sustained a banged-up shin, a twisted wrist that throbbed with pain, several bruises, and a cut on his forehead.

The Bookie looked at Davis with pity. "Wow man, you look bad." Turning to Morgan he added, "The winner of course two!"

When the bets were cleared, everyone moved to course three, the Swamp Assault. No one has ever made it out without some kind of injury. Broken bones, sprained ankles, alligator bites. This was going to be exciting.

Henchmen lined the fence around the course, calling out encouragement and cheering their favorite contestant on.

The Bookie addressed Morgan and Davis, "What can I say except stay away from the 'gator bites'," adding, "Start now!"

In they went without hesitation. Nimbly they ran on shaky rocks, across murky water, and up and over felled tree trunks.

Davis took a patch of Spanish moss to the face and tussled to get it off of him. The distraction caused him to slip off a river rock and sink to his knees in sticky muck, but he pitched forward to grab at a low tree limb and managed to pull himself out.

Meanwhile, Morgan got one of her spiked heels caught on something that made her fall forward. As she plopped to the ground, she raised her eyes and right there, not twelve inches in front of her was the toothy, leathery snout of an alligator. The beast was staring right at her. She froze, thinking that any sudden movement would cause it to attack. She stared into its unblinking beady eyes then, almost without thought, round-housed a powerful punch that landed on its nose. The alligator shot its head up and opened its hissing maw but, in its shock, wriggled its way backward to submerge into the dark water and disappear.

Morgan wasted no time getting to her feet and tore forward like the devil was chasing her. She shot through the finish gate so fast she ran into the crowd of cheering henchmen knocking four of them and herself into a heap.

The Bookie was at the finish gate calling to Davis, "Come on man. You're almost here," and when Davis was out, the gate was slammed shut.

Davis limped over to Morgan, who had gotten herself up from the floor, and said, "Congratulations! Nice job," as he extended a hand.

Morgan shook hands with Davis and managed to say, "Thank you, Davis. You're a good competitor," before the crowd of henchmen crushed in to give their cheerful hurrahs and clap everyone on the back and make promises to buy beers at McClusky's Eight Ball.

Needless to say, Morgan won each of the three courses and took the VIP trophy for overall win. It definitely elevated her status among the other henchmen. Or is it henchpeople, now? Anyway, the trophy stood about fifteen inches tall. It was an inverted wineglass super glued to a nicely stained piece of wood. Perched on top was a little stuffed alligator toy and trapped inside the glass were hazard bits like broken glass and rusty nails. The words, "Training Center VIP" and the date were carved into the base. It now sat on Morgan's desk for all to see.

Chapter Ten

Speaking of Morgan

Morgan did not rest on her stunning victory of the training center challenge, for the very next morning she was asking Miss Q to set up two interviews with persons she had found on FredsList.

The first one looked promising. The résumé had a long list of firearms experience and a personal collection to match. It listed promotions from low-ranking recruit to Caper Leader in just over two years. Morgan thought, *"This applicant's résumé is brimming with experience. Maybe a little too much,"* but thought it was worth a shot…pun intended.

The second recruit was pretty junior but like Watson said, "Someone's gotta clean the shark tank."

Miss Q set up an on-site interview with applicant number one for tomorrow, first thing.

The rest of the morning was spent with Davis and Watson brainstorming questions and the list was getting long and included a lot of crazy spitball questions. For example: Would you say you were lucky or crazy? Do you know any good jokes? Have you ever been chased across rooftops?

When the conversation seemed to stall, Morgan called for a lunch break. "Davis, I know that you have a maintenance caper this afternoon and Watson, you've been tasked with repairing a leaky sink up in the locker room. So!" she said as she gathered up her notes, "first thing tomorrow morning, you both are to meet our candidate upstairs and escort him to Miss Q and then to the Jeffrey Dahmer meeting room." She shuffled her note pages into a neat pile. "Eight AM sharp, boys," and smiled as Davis and Watson affirmed her words and made ready to leave for lunch.

Morgan ate lunch in the break room and spent most of that afternoon on the par course before leaving for the evening.

At precisely 8AM the following morning, Miss Q knocked on the Jeffrey Dahmer meeting room door, quietly opened it and ushered the recruit, followed by Watson and Davis, inside.

"Ms. Taylor, this is Dan Hansen, your 8AM interviewee. Mr. Hansen, Ms. Morgan Taylor."

"Good morning Mr. Hansen. May I call you Hansen?" Morgan asked.

"Yes, I prefer it, and nice to meet you," Hansen smiled.

"Please call me Morgan."

"Thanks, I will."

Morgan indicated a chair and Hansen sat down. She turned to Davis and Watson and said, "That side of the table, if you would," and took her chair at the head of the table.

An hour before the scheduled meeting, Morgan made a visit to the Weapons Storage Department on Sublevel Four and had checked out two Glock 43 handguns and two rounds of ammo that now lay disassembled on the meeting room table. One in front of Hansen and one at the head of the table.

"I'd like to start with a series of round-robin questions, starting with Davis and moving around the table," Morgan said as she nodded with her words. "We'll end up with my question. Sky's the limit!" She smiled at Davis and said, "You're up."

"Okay," Davis acknowledged her and scrunched up his brow in serious concentration as he turned to look at Hansen, then asked, "What was the worst caper you've ever been on, and why?"

"Oh," Hansen did not hesitate, "that would have to be the one last year when the hit was on for the Ring-a-Ding Brothers circus that was nearing the end of its tour and was supposed to be brimming with cash." Hansen rolled his eyes at the memory. "Turned out they were in the red. No cash, no coin, only a lot of dancing bear shi...." he caught himself, "Uh, excuse me, fecal matter. Very disappointing."

Morgan nodded at Watson. He shifted a bit in his chair before asking, "What spirit animal do you have?" Watson smiled at his question. It was a good question.

Hansen looked a bit skeptical but answered, "A spider," and sat quietly looking at Watson who now was acting all upset.

"That's not an animal. A spider isn't an animal," he protested.

Hansen replied, "I like to stay unexpected."

Watson did not know what to say so just huffed out a breath and sat back, thrumming his fingers on the chair's arm rests.

Morgan spoke up, "Okay then. Hansen, do you have a question for any of us?" She waited and watched.

"Yeah, thanks," Hansen replied as he turned to look at Davis. "What is the cosine of 30°?"

Davis just stared at Hansen in disbelief for a moment before speaking, "What difference would that make? Who would even care?" In his frustration he leaned forward in his chair and leveled a stink-eye at Hansen. "Want to arm wrestle?" he sputtered as he banged his elbow on the table with a thud, wriggled his fingers in a challenge, and glared daringly at Hansen.

Hansen just laughed. Watson put his hand up to his mouth to stifle a light laugh.

Morgan tapped the point of her pencil on the table. The little tapping noise hushed everyone and brought them to attention. "My turn. Hansen, what you see before you is a disassembled Glock 43 and one bullet. I chose this weapon because you listed it on your résumé as one of the many handguns that you own." Hansen nodded and Morgan continued, "I'm going to challenge you to a little competition. We're both going to reassemble these handguns, load it, and when finished, take aim and fire."

A look of incredulousness flashed across Hansen's face. "Fire at what?" he asked.

"Why, each other," Morgan answered in a matter of fact. "And here's my question: Think you can manage that?"

Morgan sat patiently as she watched Hansen struggle with it and then look over the gun parts scattered in front of him. Finally, he answered, "You're on!"

A timer was set and as Morgan pressed the start button, she said the word "Go" and they were off!

Both Morgan and Hansen's hands flew to the parts, taking slide and barrel, firing pin and recoil springs and expertly fitting them together before quickly moving on. Within minutes, Morgan had her Glock 43 assembled and slamming the magazine tube into the frame with the proper amount of force, picked up her one round, loaded it in the chamber and with a flourish, pointed it at Hansen.

He, at that moment, had just slid the magazine of his weapon into position and was reaching for his bullet when he noticed the barrel of Morgan's Glock 43 steadily pointed at his head. He froze.

Morgan fired.

Davis and Watson were shocked! They sat wide-eyed staring back and forth from Morgan to Hansen who had yelped in pain and now sat holding his left ear, blood running down his hand, little painful murmurings escaping from his lips.

Morgan leaned forward leveling a look at Hansen's ear. "Watson will take you to a doctor to have that treated," adding, "You will be hearing from me in a day or so." She pulled in a breath and slowly let it out. "You know, Hansen, if you and I were opponents out in the field, you would be dead right now." She had a very serious and very scary look on her face. "You're welcome."

Chapter Eleven

Always Something

After spending two days in the IT Department, Argyle's mind was spinning with confusing gobbledygook technical stuff. Half of what the techs said was far above his head and at times it seemed that they spoke an alien language only they understood. He was sorry that he committed to two days and was relieved when his time was up. Argyle thanked Jones and Tanner for their time and expertise but left quickly at the end of day two.

Today he was back at his desk. Back among the clutter and chaos that was his job. Now his only decision for the day was which mess to tackle first.

Ahhh. Morale.

Of course.

A big number of weeks ago, Argyle created a pseudo-name for himself so that he could logon to #LairChat, the company-only chat room, to read gossip and make comments. He had chosen the name Venom. It sounded scary, it was a super villain, and Argyle felt it fit him.

He logged on and noted that there were about a dozen henchmen currently online with two chat threads active. Thread one…

> Mutt: Had anyone else heard that caper drivers were going to be outsourced to China?
>
> Cowboy: Last week it was weapons repair to India. Now the drivers?? How does that work?
>
> Flytrap: Remote control.
>
> Mutt: That's not good. Suppose they remote control a whole van of us over a cliff?

Flytrap: We go BOOM!

Argyle switched threads…

> Speedy: Better avoid Watson today. He's in another
> one of his bad moods.
> Troll: Still? Geez man, let it go already.
> Quat: They seemed so good. What happened?
> Schmoo: Rumor has it that Watson only wanted to
> party and Fulana wanted a cushy life.
> Speedy: Not on that tug boat.
> Schmoo: Not on that stinky river.

Argyle hadn't talked with Ben Watson for a very long time. His promotion to boss had intimidated Watson, who thought at first that he would naturally tag along. You know, because of their friendship. But Argyle thought differently. He knew he was destined for greatness and as Audrey had pointed out, Watson was a liability.

Argyle decided to chime in…

> Venom: Everyone knows it's a true fact that all major
> crime lords have pets. What pet should Psy-
> chotic Weasel have?

#LairChat lit up!!

> Mutt: A fish. Possibly a piranha.
> Quat: A mouse. Could name it Rat to make it feel good
> about itself.
> Cowboy: A cat named Mouser.
> Speedy: Gerbil. It's fresh, never been done before.
> Quat: Who ever imagined that a weasel would have a
> gerbil as a pet!
> Speedy: I know, right?
> Troll: An ant farm.
> Venom: Really? An ant farm? Why?
> Troll: Thousands of pets for the price of one.
> Venom: Oh.

Venom, ahem, Argyle, stayed online for another hour reading lots of comments that could be summarized as henchmen morale was pretty low right now. It gave Argyle an idea, but a new thread sidetracked him. The subject was superheroes…

> Cowboy: What if Batman, Green Lantern, and Robin Hood were all rolled into one. What would that look like?
>
> Troll: A green bat in a forest.
>
> Quat: A very mean guy with a bow and arrows.
>
> Mutt: A chartreuse very muscular guy who can, with his mind, will arrows to fly and who wears a cool hat.
>
> Venom: A flying super evil guy with a patch on his chest that depicts a sword stuck into a bloody blob. He's comin' atcha very fast. He has a laser beam mechanism on the back of his hat to blind you as he left the scene.

(silence then…)

Cowboy: Okay.

Argyle leaned back in his chair, *"Good chat,"* he smiled as he logged off. *"Back to work."*

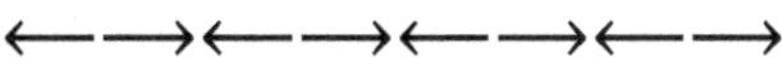

One hour later Argyle had worked out his idea. He would cure the henchmen morale problem once and for all. He would institute Friday Beer Busts. Well, maybe just one to see how it would go.

Argyle immediately scheduled three capers. The first group were to rob two or three ATM's. It would impress the henchmen and give them something daring to do. The ready cash would fund party decorations and pay the power and water bills. The next group would hold up a couple of liquor stores. This should happen on a Wednesday night.

Nothing exciting ever happens on Wednesday nights so no one would be expecting it. The last group would hit a deli or two. This should happen the day of the big bash, so everything is fresh.

After checking with Miss Q, the Beer Bust was scheduled for the following Friday, which happened to be the last Friday of the month.

The ATM capers went okay with only one interruption. A bank security guard, who had been monitoring the ATM visual monitor, noticed when two henchmen crowded the view and blocked the camera feed with a gloved hand. Thinking he was some sort of hero, he charged out the bank's doors waving his pistol and yelling, "Hey you two! Knock it off!"

Smith, who had been using a crowbar to pry open the front of the ATM, turned to face the guard and in his panic, chucked the crowbar at the quickly approaching guard, smacking him in the chest, essentially knocking the wind out of him. The hard-hitting thud of a crowbar to the chest forced the guard's gun hand to jerk upward and squeeze off a round before he fell backward by the blow and landed in a leg spayed heap.

Smith's partner, Blair, kept bashing at the ATM in his determination to rob it empty.

The stray round from the guard's gun shattered the customer convenience outdoor light above the ATM, causing nasty shards of broken glass to rain down on the two henchmen just as Blair got the ATM opened up.

Both men dove forward grabbing at the bills all nicely lined up in the counting chute, emptying the ATM before driving away into the night.

Both men sustained a substantial number of bloody cuts and as part of their debrief to Argyle, strenuously declared that their injuries more than qualified for donuts in the break room. Argyle agreed and picked up the phone to instruct Miss Q that a box of two dozen non-sprinkled donuts was warranted.

"Yes. Tomorrow morning would be nice," he had said, looking over at Smith and Blair and nodding as if to say, *"I've made it happen."*

Argyle did not hang up on Miss Q. He never did. She's too sensitive.

The liquor store capers went better. The henchmen team hit three stores in rapid succession before fleeing safely away. The take was horrendous! Their getaway van was stuffed to the roof with kegs of micro-brew and cases of scotch and whisky, and not the harsh rotgut stuff either. This was the real thing. This was Canadian.

As the week ticked down to Friday, all Psychotic Weasel employees became energized by the news that a Beer Bust was in the works.

Feartha Wolf and her trusted team of seamstresses had put together a wonderful party plan and started to work first thing Friday morning transforming the 4th floor of the parking garage into a fun zone.

The area had been swept and all the cobwebs knocked down before dining tables and chairs were arranged.

Per Feartha's plan, a stage had been erected at one end of the large rectangular space. It was raised about three-foot high with little steps on either side with a curtain across the back proudly displaying a seven-foot diameter Psychotic Weasel logo. Feartha had envisioned Argyle standing behind the curtain waiting to be introduced, a bright spotlight would flick on and Psychotic Weasel would emerge to thunderous applause.

Feartha had lined up two other acts. The first was a comedian who, she thought, would be light and funny and set the pace for the remainder of the party. The second was a magician of some repute. Very exciting.

There was a little stage set up at the opposite end of the space that would be used for karaoke with a loaded play set mixture of Death Metal, famously rough with hints of disease and gore, and Outlaw Country, very popular among the henchmen.

Between these two venues, against one wall, was a walk-up bar that would be tended by two barmen. They would be tasked with pouring drinks in a civilized manner. Flanking the bar on both sides were six self-serve brew stations, where the giant beer kegs would be set up.

Across from that would be the food station. Feartha was informed that a caper was scheduled for noon, actually today, that would procure deli type food. The goal was to have premade sandwiches and wraps and chips just for the taking. No mess, no fuss.

Feartha included one very special party favor. Two axe toss cages. She wanted to mark Psychotic Weasel's very first employee Beer Bust as something special, something everyone would remember for a very long time to come. And what would be more memorable than tossing axes?

Feartha and her team were just putting the finishing touches on the party space, floating balloons, streamers, signage, and Psychotic Weasel logos, when the sound of squealing tires racing up the drive ramp made everyone stop and turn to look.

It was a huge food truck being driven by Davis. He pulled to a stop and rolled down the window grinning, as he called out to Feartha, "Where do you want this?"

Feartha stood akimbo with a look of impatience on her face inspecting the food truck with its sides emblazoned with a company name, The Demented Taco, surrounded by flames and cartoon beans being chased by a two-legged butcher's knife.

Her first thought was, *"What the??"* before she rolled with it. "Park it there," she said, indicating the space she thought would be occupied by deli sandwiches, "as soon as we move the tables."

And it was done.

As Davis jumped out of the taco truck, he explained, "We went to two delis and they were both closed. Must be a holiday." He looked a bit confused and scratched his head but continued, "After a moment of discussion on whether to break in and take everything in pieces, we decided not to. Someone had the brilliant idea to boost a food truck and someone else called dibs on tacos." Davis stepped back and swung his arm out to introduce the truck. "Ta da!" he sang out, waiting for a congratulatory remark.

Feartha huffed out a breath and before stepping away, said, "It'll do."

It's exactly what Davis needed to hear and a huge happy smile on his face said it all.

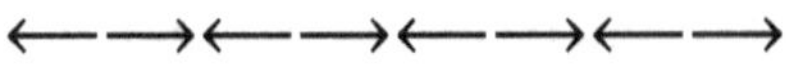

Argyle spent his Friday lunch break closed up in his office memorizing the speech he planned to give at the 3PM Beer Bust kick off.

Recently he had read through Thrasher's notebook of rants, carefully marking the ones he thought he could use by placing little strips of Post It ® notes that stuck out along the pages. Today he was reviewing those marked as possibilities, determined to choose one and modify it for a custom fit.

Finally, he had one.

It was a few minutes past 3PM and henchmen had been drifting in one, two, and three at a time. Some found the serve-yourself brew stations and now stood in small groups here and there passively watching the scene as more persons arrived and the noise levels and joviality slowly increased.

Two men stood at the bar ordering shots of Canadian Club and ceremoniously dropping them into their pints of ale then, on the count of three, chugging the mixture down in one take.

Clearly these two men would be passed out by 4PM.

Around 3:30PM, Miss Q stepped onto the stage and positioned herself at the microphone. She cleared her throat and steadied herself before speaking. "Hello everyone."

No one heard her above the rowdy laughter and loud talk.

"Hello," she spoke a second time, tapping the microphone with a finger.

Watson had grabbed a table close to the stage and had watched as Miss Q struggled to be heard. He got up, leapt onto the stage and nodded to Miss Q that he would like to use the microphone. Miss Q smiled and stepped back to give him room. Watson grabbed the mic and called out rather loudly, "Attention all you mooks!" The parking garage fell silent as everyone turned their attention to the stage.

Miss Q smiled at Watson who then jumped down off the stage and resumed his seat at the front table.

"Welcome everyone to the first Psychotic Weasel Friday Beer Bust. (Raised beer cups and sounds of approval rippled across the room.) As will become a regular feature, our leader will say a few opening remarks. (silence) Please join me in welcoming Psychotic Weasel!" Miss Q politely clapped as she backed away from the mic and left the stage.

The parking garage lights dimmed down a bit just as a spotlight came into brightness pointed at the seven-foot diameter Psychotic Weasel logo in the center of the closed curtains that now parted as Argyle stepped through.

Waving to everyone, Argyle began.

"Welcome henchmen, and by that, I mean henchmen and henchwoman! (awkward applause) First, let's thank Feartha and her team for all the hard work they put into the planning and their efforts to make this party a success!" Argyle burst into clapping in an effort to lead the attendees into doing the same. "Also, a round of applause to the caper teams' successful acquisition of food and drink!" (wild applause and whistles) "And speaking of capers, I have several very important ones in mind. Extortion! Mayhem! Robberies galore! Never a dull moment so get ready to be busy, keep working, and never let up."

Argyle paused to bask in the moment of applause, then, taking an ominous tone, he continued, "Never forget that you represent me, Psychotic Weasel, when on capers. You must be poised but tough. You must be brave," (raising his voice...) "never afraid!" (glaring about him...) "Never!" Relaxing a bit, Argyle took three steps across the stage before continuing in a calm voice. "Remember there are donuts at stake." Argyle paused and scanned the faces turned toward him. "That's right. Donuts." Argyle walked back to center stage and stood for a moment organizing his next thought. "I'm seriously considering instituting a bonus policy as a way of recognizing those who demonstrate the best Psychotic Weasel practices." (Henchmen all happily looked around at each other at the news) "Only the best will qualify." (Argyle stated loudly) "THE BEST!" (he yelled) "Okay, on the count of three I want to hear everyone yell Weasel Forever! And you had better give it all you've got." Argyle did an impression of The Thrasher's scowling evil eye...

"One. Two. Three!"

The parking garage reverberated at the thunderous noise of all the voices, in perfect synchronization...

"WEA...SEL...FOR...EV...ER!!"

Argyle stood indulging in his feel-good moment then stepped down from the stage to mingle with his employees.

Within minutes the karaoke stage fired up as three henchmen started belting out a corrupted version of some song that stated that gloom was a virtue and all anyone could hope for was a death by zombies. Geez, who would've guessed so many in the crowd would know the lyrics and sing along?

By 5PM the self-serve brew stations were pumping ale and it was three deep at the bar. Everyone was getting their rowdy on and feeling just fine.

Davis and Johnson took charge of the food truck and were dealing out tacos as fast as they could. The tacos didn't look all that good, what with burnt ground meat (is that really meat?), a shred of lettuce, and a small hacked up cube of cheese on top. But they were being consumed just as fast as they went out the window, so Davis and Johnson more or less assumed they were doing just fine.

The Bust's first main stage entertainment act was being introduced and many henchmen made their way to that end of the parking garage.

"…a comedian of some repute, straight from a gig one town over, let's all welcome, the arrogant, the scurrilous, the disrespectful, Jimmy 'The Big' Pylon!"

A mild smattering of applause rippled across the front four tables where six or seven henchmen, including Argyle, were relaxing.

A man with a black hood over his head was being handled roughly by two henchmen who tugged him forward to the microphone and who then ripped the bag off his head. Jimmy "The Big" Pylon stood blanching in the spotlight glare squinting and shading his eyes in an effort to focus. He sputtered, "Wha, wha…where am I?"

Someone in the audience yelled, "Be funny, comedian!"

Jimmy, now able to see better said, "Well, well, well, I guess this is what I get for trolling the very dark web for gigs. Next time I'll use the dusky dark web instead." He peered through the darkness. "So, what's your name?" he directed at a guy up front.

No answer.

"Okay, I'll call you Bob." Turning to the man next to him, "And yours?" Nothing. "Okay. Bob, again." Next man. "You?" Again, silence. "Another Bob. Sooo, who's the boss here?"

Jimmy scanned the front tables and noticed two men pointing at a man who, fatefully, was Argyle. Pointing at Argyle, Jimmy asked, "That guy?" and directing his comments to Argyle said, "Did you know you've hired a whole pile of Bobs?" then busted up into peals of laughter at his own joke.

No one else laughed, in truth most of the audience looked confused.

Jimmy continued. "Psychotic Weasel, eh? Run out of aardvarks?" A smattering of faint laughter.

Argyle was annoyed and could feel his jaw tighten.

"I heard the beavers said 'no', although I understand the skunks were up for it!" Jimmy laughed out loud and slapped his thigh in mirth. Then he peered through the darkness to focus on Argyle, "Oh, I see you now. Yes, a weasel!" and about doubled over from laughing.

The audience was silent.

Jimmy stood for a second collecting his thoughts. "The other night I was watching the sports channel when the cage match championships came on. Did anyone catch that?" Silence. "Well, the featured show, the main event, was two guys that looked about the same, all bulked up, masks, and whatnot. One was wearing red speedo shorts and the other black. When the bell rang to start the match, all they did for the first two minutes was circle each other grunting and lunging in an effort to scare the other one." Jimmy had been pacing slowly up and down the stage as he spoke but now stopped and addressed the audience. "So, who would win in a hand-to-hand combat? A weasel or The Thrasher?" He stood smiling…waiting…

That was it. Argyle held his hand up and snapped his fingers. Immediately three henchmen leapt up onto the stage frightening Jimmy, who cowered as he stumbled backward. Two of the three men grabbed Jimmy and he cried out, "Was it something I said?" The third man bagged Jimmy's head and Jimmy cried out in fear, "No, no, don't hurt me!" just before one of the men said, "Shut it funny man," and punched him in the stomach. The henchman glanced over at Argyle, who sneered and nodded his approval.

The three men then manhandled Jimmy "The Big" Pylon off the stage and away down the drive ramp.

Feartha took the stage and announced, "There will be a thirty-minute intermission."

The clock ticked toward 6PM and the parking garage Beer Bust was an animated show of laughter and loudness that reverberated off the concrete walls that at times seemed to set up a kind of rhythm.

The karaoke stage was a constant flow of doom, death, and metal alternating with sad country songs about lost loves and endless highways. The men on stage vacillated between rage and tears. It had to be the alcohol. There was no other way to explain it.

Feartha had shut down the axe toss cages a little past 5PM and actually pad locked them shut. The competitions that started out as friendly "Who can hit the bulls eye" bets, seemingly within minutes, turned into "Hey Smith, go stand in front of the target!" Smith almost lost a hand. It came this close!

As the clock struck 6PM, Feartha took the stage to announce the main attraction, Edwin The Extravagant, a magician that was sure to entertain.

Lots of henchmen crowded to the main stage area in anticipation of the show. It's a well-known fact that all henchmen love magic acts, and this act was sure to please. They jostled each other in an effort to get a good view of the stage and joked and laughed as they waited.

Someone up front called out, "Quiet!" and a couple of the guys started shushing everyone. The sound levels dropped to a hush as all eyes turned to the stage. The spotlight came up and the Psychotic Weasel logo parted as Edwin The Extravagant slowly stepped forward.

Earlier, Edwin had watched in horror as Jimmy "The Big" Pylon was attacked by three very large, mean men and dragged screaming down the drive ramp. He trembled in fear at remembering Jimmy's pathetic cries for help fade into the distance. Edwin imagined that Jimmy was stuffed into the trunk of a car, driven to wherever cement was mixed and was now probably part of a stadium support column.

Now Edwin stood mid-stage facing dozens of these men determined to survive the evening.

"Good evening," Edwin said to focus attention on his act. He parted his cape enough to reveal his right hand. In it was a bright red, rounded object that he held up for inspection by his audience. He turned his wrist slowly around in little circles to display the red object, which seemingly mesmerized everyone looking at it.

The parking garage was dead silent, all eyes were on the stage.

Slowly, Edwin raised the red ball over his head and in one swift movement, brought it down with great force, slamming the ball at his feet. A loud bang accompanied by a brilliant flash of light and a huge cloud of black smoke that roiled upward, shocked the henchmen watching. When the smoke cleared, Edwin The Extravagant had disappeared.

The crowd went wild with "Wow!" and "Oh!" and clapped loudly and enthusiastically and waited for Edwin to walk back out on stage to take a bow. The clapping slowed down and still they waited. The clapping stopped and they waited. Disapproving murmurs started to ripple through the crowd until eventually one of the men jumped on stage, parted the curtain and looked behind.

Three seconds later, he turned to the crowd and said, "He's gone."

Groans and cursing were tossed about, and it seemed about to erupt into a melee when Feartha took the microphone and told everyone to, "Knock it off, go have a beer."

Less than thirty minutes later, when the taco truck had been shut down, the liquor was gone, and the ale ran dry, all henchmen left for home, except for four men Feartha told to help with cleanup.

Chapter Twelve

The Cephalopod Makes Another Move

Gilbert's test of Tentacle One was so successful that he busied himself making two more drones. He loved the idea of having drones as henchmen. They did as they were told and didn't stop for lunch. They were perfect employees.

Gilbert, as The Squid, robbed a couple of Mom-n-Pop stores to practice working his drones. The total take was nothing to laugh at but certainly nothing to celebrate. The big lesson he learned during the trials was that under the stress of the moment and the fact that all three drones looked so close in appearance, he would have to color or mark the drones as individuals. Gilbert experienced momentary confusion when he would order the drone he thought he was looking at to do something and another drone would move.

The problem was now solved. Gilbert stenciled numbers all around the drone bodies so he could tell at a glance which one he was ordering to do what bit of havoc. The test was this…

Squid decided to rob a liquor store. He chose a Friday night after the big rush of working folks had bought up their weekend intoxicants when the store register would be full. Squid waited until the store was empty of customers and commanded Tentacle Two and Three to guard the door while he and Tentacle One went inside and robbed the joint.

Tentacle Two and Three did a wonderful job. Anytime a prospective customer approached the entry, the drones would buzz and harass them like bees, effectively driving them away. Meanwhile, Squid and Tentacle One were collecting all the loot and together, the little team of four would escape into the night. Squid's take was $1722.00. What a night!

Emboldened by the liquor store heist, Squid stopped at an ATM on the way home and boosted another $2900. He was on a roll and felt he couldn't miss so drove across town and hit a second ATM netting $3140.

Squid's Friday night labor of love earned him a whopping $7762 dollars!

As he sat in his apartment gazing at the pile of bills on his table, he had to ask, "So my little tentacles, what shall we do with all this boodle?"

The answer came the next morning over a sourdough olive and bleu cheese bagel and orange juice down at the corner deli.

Gilbert sat munching his breakfast and reading the daily newspaper. He was trying to find news of his Quick Shop robbery that was not on page one. *"That little fink of a clerk had better follow through or I'll..."* There it was! All the way back on page twelve squished between an ad for woman's shoes and a story about lawn seed. It simply read…

A man wearing a calamari suit and babbling about crime lords robbed a Quick Shop late one night three weeks ago, making off with $13 dollars of the cashier's personal money. Police are not interested in spending public monies to chase a lunatic.

Gilbert was incensed. A calamari suit?! He slammed the paper down and, in his anger, yelled out, "I'll get him for that!" causing everyone around him to pause in what they were doing and stare at him. In his embarrassment, he left.

However, the riddle of what to do with the seven thousand dollars was easily answered. Gilbert needed a house, preferably one on a dead-end street, few neighbors (if any), and space to build a shop. And (!) explore his right to claim himself Big Crime Lord Boss.

He would call Lonesome Trails Realtor in the morning.

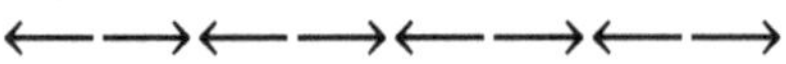

The realtor Gilbert tried to reason with was a jerk. There were several listings available that Gilbert agreed to look at and while on the drive to the first house, he patiently explained to the realtor, let's just call him The Jerk, exactly what he was looking for: someplace in the middle of nowhere, cheap, and available.

Instead, The Jerk took him, to a 6785 sf, 5 bd, 5.5 ba, split level Mediterranean home worth well over $4,000,000.00! And it was on a private gated court with three other mansions! Gilbert was so enraged he wouldn't get out of the car. He yelled out, "How many banks is *that* gonna take!"

The Jerk tried to calm him with soft banter. "I was only trying to show you what a little more budget would buy," and, "I understand this isn't quite your style," and other soothing phrases until Gilbert quieted down enough to finally stop glaring out the car window.

For the next two hours, The Jerk completely wasted Gilbert's time until Gilbert had lost what little patience he had and told The Jerk to hit it.

Later that evening, Gilbert sent his three drones out to look for a house that fit his requirements: an isolated one-story home (he hated stairs) with a good roof.

It took them several hours but by golly they found one! The pictures they sent back got Gilbert so excited he got himself another chocolate Yoo-Hoo.

The place was perfect. It was at the end of an overgrown dirt road that was at the end of an unused gravel road. It was a one story 2 bd 1 ba 1920's style bungalow house that appeared to be level and still had the majority of its glass windows intact. There was a bonus. There was a big garage/barn structure just steps from the back porch and it was only two miles out of town. And if it couldn't have gotten any better, Gilbert's internet search on the address said that the property had been abandoned thirty years ago and had remained vacant ever since.

That was all Gilbert needed to know to decide that he was moving there this weekend.

*** Flash forward three months ***

Gilbert moved in, stole utilities, set up shop and is now officially a squatter, although he prefers the term homeowner.

Chapter Thirteen

Now What?

Argyle couldn't wait to get to work Monday morning. He needed time alone. To think.

When he got home Friday night, all he could do was collapse into bed. He had drank way too much Canadian booze, ate way too many bad tacos, and had a screaming headache.

He popped awake Saturday morning and reached for his phone to call Audrey. That's when he noticed that she had called eight times between last night and this morning. *"Oh, oh. I may be in trouble,"* he thought as he hit the dial button.

"So where have you been?" Audrey asked after picking up without saying hello.

"I was late getting home last night. I had a headache…"

"Why?"

"Oh, the company Beer Bust ran late."

"The what?"

"Beer Bus…"

"I heard you. What I meant was why didn't you invite me?"

"It was a Psychotic Weasel company only gathering," he had said weakly, his head starting to throb again.

"Oh."

~ *CLICK* ~

Argyle looked at the blank screen of his phone. Audrey had hung up. *"Just as well,"* he thought. *"Where are the aspirins?"*

Sunday was lost to recovery and here we are now…Monday morning…

Argyle sat motionless at his desk staring at the rough-hewn wall opposite, just thinking…

"Friday Beer Bust. I think I'll let that one go. Although Feartha and her team did an outstanding job, I'm not sure that liquor is the best ingredient for team building and camaraderie. And that comedian, that Jimmy 'The Big' Pylon. Geez. What an obnoxious rat faced little…" Argyle couldn't think of anything bad enough to describe Jimmy so let it pass.

"What else can I do to improve morale?" and out loud he said, "I've got to think," and got up from his desk to walk about his office, the Lizzie Borden meeting room, straightening chairs and brushing crumbs off the long table onto the floor. Thinking, thinking, thinking.

Finally, he sat down. The only clear thoughts he had were this: Argyle sincerely hoped his henchmen crew did not like the Beer Bust, although in the back of his mind he knew he was crazy for thinking so. *"Who wouldn't like free food and hooch?"* And two, he should take their minds off of morale by stepping up the number of capers. *"They're bored, they have too much time on their hands."*

Argyle got serious and put pencil to paper and came up with a slew of capers. Some junk, some daring, but all worthy of donuts in the break room!

The announcement was made via the P.A. system in the secret room hidden behind Miss Q's office.

Argyle decided against using one of Thrasher's rants because honestly, he was too busy to "crazy" it up and besides, he wasn't convinced that it was really his style. He was more of a manager, more of a straight no-nonsense kind of guy. He decided to stick to giving orders.

Wake up out there! (he commanded) Everyone assigned to maintenance crews – get at it. Everyone else – heads up. I want three teams of two to report to Wardrobe immediately. Don't care which six. You are to immediately embark on a crime spree. Two to knock over ATM's, two to hit retail, and two to pry every last coin out of every last meter in this city. (Argyle looked at his notes) Alexey! (he barked) I want you to hack into police closed circuit spy cameras and replace their live feed with a video of cute kittens playing with string. (Argyle was sure that would distract the cops from his capers) Davis! Watson! Thorne! Milford! Morgan! Report to my office in fifteen. (Argyle raised his voice…) that's it! *JUMP!*

Fifteen minutes later…

"Okay," Argyle stood at the head of the table addressing the five henchmen seated before him. "I've chosen you five because you have proven yourselves *very* capable and trustworthy. What I am about to introduce to you is a new and daring type of caper." He looked at the expectant faces turned toward him. "We're starting a new franchise. As of immediately, we're going to boost luxury cars and SUV's" He moved quickly on to add details.

"Morgan, Thorn, Milford. You're drivers. You will scope out high-end luxury autos using one of these pass keys." Argyle reached for the leather sack laying on the table to his left, turned it out and dumped a bunch of keys whose fobs displayed the logos of Mercedes-Benz X1 and E400, BMW 740, Porsche Macon, Audi Q7, Jaguar F, and Tesla Model S.

"Davis, you and Watson," glancing at Ben with barely a flicker of remembered friendship, "will procure two tow trucks. Good ones. Sturdy ones that operate smoothly. Your job will be to hook up and tow any expensive vehicle identified by the drivers, that can't be driven for any reason given."

Argyle picked up the Tesla Model S key and held it up. "This car is worth over $205 thousand," and handing the key to Morgan, he said in a teasing tone, "No scratches."

Nods and laughter.

Argyle continued, "I have contracted with a very high-end chop shop. They will pay on delivery. Their job is none of our business but FYI, they disassemble, retrofit, or repaint and resell whatever their client base wants.

"Your job will be to deliver a steady supply of autos, not so fast that we attract attention to our enterprise, get paid, don't ask questions, and leave." Argyle paused and smiled. "Any questions?"

There were none.

"One other thing: this isn't a secret operation but it's not to be freely talked about and certainly not outside Psychotic Weasel. Yes?"

Argyle now stood arms akimbo and waited.

Morgan sat twirling the Tesla Model S key round and round on a finger. She smiled, and looking directly and unblinkingly at Argyle and said, "This is going to be fun."

Later that afternoon, after Argyle had launched a bunch of capers, he sat and thought about, *"What else? What else will bring in the big bucks?"*

He sat. He paced. He thought, *"Where is the money?"* then he looked up the word epiphany. Yhup, he had had one, a moment of sudden insight.

The Rolling Stones were playing at the Aardvark Stadium one town over, less than five miles from here. He would assemble a caper team to kidnap Mick Jagger and demand a million-million dollars for his safe return. His crew would mosey unobserved backstage and into Mick's dressing room, drug him, bag him like laundry and bring him to the seedy warehouse.

Simple!

Argyle briefed his five stealthiest men and sent them off into the night. He decided to stay at the lair to wait for their return because, he smiled to himself, he was a huge Mick Jagger fan. Huge! Maybe he could get an autograph *and* a selfie!

The clock seemed to move too slowly and round about five hours later, Argyle started to worry but he held steady.

To busy himself, he ran the par course, fed the sharks, and shot his gun.

At approximately a quarter past 1AM his henchmen returned, and he rushed up to Sublevel Two to meet them.

Argyle burst out of the elevator barely able to contain his excitement at meeting Mick Jagger, but his joy quickly faded to confusion when he ran into the empty-handed henchmen, his worst fears realized. They did not have Mick Jagger. Mick Jagger was not there.

Argyle stopped short, feet planted, fists balled at his sides. "What happened?" was all he could croak out.

The henchmen hemmed and hawed and pleadingly looked at each other until Vincent stepped forward to take the lead.

"Well boss it was like this. The parking was a nightmare; we ended up so far away it took us twenty-five minutes to walk to the stadium. Security was tight, they were crawling all over! There were too many for us to take," Vincent turned to the others, "Right men?" he asked as he nodded in agreement with their yay's and yeses.

Argyle stood absolutely still looking at them.

Vincent continued, "We broke in through an outside service door and pushed our way through packed hallways until we made it to the guest rooms on a lower level. It was still very crowded down there. Who knew there would be so many people?" he asked no one in particular. "Anyway, Miller here," Vincent thumbed in Miller's general direction, "he sees a sign indicating that the band is all clustered in one dressing room. Well, that made everything different. We didn't plan to nab all of them, just Mick Jagger, ya know?" He looked at Argyle for some flicker of sympathy for their plight.

He got none.

"Okay, we agree to mill around the hallway and wait. The crowd upstairs was starting to stomp their feet and demand that the show begin. They're chanting, "Stones, Stones, Stones," so loud that it started to vibrate the stadium." Vincent took a breath, "Well, finally the dressing room door flies open and the band steps out. To our luck the lesser Stones come out first, trailed by Mick and that's when we made our move."

Vincent had been getting into the spirit of his own story and now was standing a bit crouched with his hands out in front of himself posed in a grabbing kind of motion. "So's we grab him, see, but he's shocked by the sudden pawing-over we're giving him and he twists and squirms and calls out for help." Vincent looked at Argyle, "Ya know boss, he's a wiry little guy...and deceptively strong. You wouldn't know it to look at him." Vincent paused to think, *"Crap. Got nothing."* Then continued.

"Anyway, we couldn't secure him. The hallway was too tight, he wouldn't stop yelling, "Help me! Help me!" and the place started to fill up with Security. Fortunately, Miller sees an exit door to the outside and yells over the noise for us to follow him, which we did. We broke out into the parking lot and took off running. We hightailed it to the van and bee lined back here without," Vincent paused to emphasize the word, "*without* being followed."

The henchmen stood still, no one said another word, just stood still and watched Argyle.

Argyle's mind was buzzed at the news and he stood as still as a statue for a moment before mumbling, "A million-million dollars," then he turned and walked away.

Vincent, Miller, and the others silently watched as Argyle waited for the elevator to arrive, get on when it did, and silently wait as the doors closed.

The next morning, as Argyle drove his classic 1958 VDub to work, the radio station that he had been listening to stopped playing music and they began their hourly news broadcast. Argyle was about to switch stations, when he froze in mid movement.

> This is KPUP news. Last night there was an attempted kidnapping at Aardvark Stadium where a number of unidentified individuals tried to nab Mick Jagger. That's right! *The* Mick Jagger. Mick was too stricken to speak with us this morning, but Keith Richards appeared to be just fine and agreed to talk with us. Here's our interview… So, Keith, without Mick Jagger, The Rolling Stones would be lost, isn't that right? No, Marley, we wouldn't be lost at all. (he laughs) We would just replace him with Graham Parker. Wouldn't miss a beat!
>
> Well, there you have it. (Marley went on) The Rolling Stones new front man would be Graham Parker. Stupendous news!
>
> This is Marley for KPUP news.

"Oh, crap," Argyle thought, *"Who would have known…"*

Chapter Fourteen

Dangerously Ominous Omnipotent Machine

After Argyle's two-day visit to the IT Department, Jones and Tanner waited about a week for Argyle to supply them with a budget and a truckload of electronic parts. It didn't come. This concerned them greatly for several reasons, the main one being their jobs. No budget equaled no work. No work equaled now what?

The two men decided to go in search of answers and eventually made their way up to the henchmen office pit where they encountered Morgan Taylor. They told her the long sad story of scrounging parts and patching and splicing and how that wouldn't meet Psychotic Weasel's requirements list.

Jones lowered his voice and admitted that he had boosted twelve dollars in quarters from one of the turnstiles up on Sublevel One to buy a spool of copper wire and a small ball of solder alloy, "Just to keep moving forward!" he had said in hushed tones, looking around to make sure he wasn't overheard.

Morgan listened then offered this, "Psychotic Weasel does not have an excess of operating funds right now, but I think I can help. I have an idea."

Three days later, a third IT guy was hired. His name is Harris and when Morgan introduced him to Jones and Tanner, she said that his job was Marketing of the IT Department, but more specifically, the newly reorganized Robotics Development Laboratory, still housed in a dark little space on Sublevel Three.

Harris was very eager to get started. He was given a tour around the lab and knew exactly what needed to be done. He scouted around until he found a virtually unused room, or better described as a huge cavern with a nice flat concrete floor located down the hall. A nameplate on the door announced that this was the "Torture Room" but no one could remember the last time it had been used, so Harris popped the nameplate off and relabeled the room, "Robotics Lab 1."

It took all of two hours for Jones, Tanner, and Harris to move their meager collection of solenoids and wire racks down the hall. DOOM had to be moved on a dolly because his spring-loaded ankles had not been updated...*yet*...to nice titanium stabilizers.

Harris immediately established internet connections and got on #LairChat to announce that the Robotics Lab needed a good cleaning, better lighting, and a big, really big power panel.

Morgan made that happen by assigning several men to all the tasks and the work was completed within two days.

Meanwhile, Harris created an account on the GoFindMoney.com website that he had located out on the dark web. It took him a few hours to set up the pitch and after running it past Morgan (who was now the defacto manager of the lab) and getting her approval, he launched PW Robotics offering three levels of donorship for specific dollar amounts funded.

Level One sponsorship, for funding $1k or more, would be entitled to have their company logo (not to exceed four inches in diameter) affixed to DOOM at the conclusion of the retrofit. They would also receive, free, a six-month 3½" x 2" ad space in PW Robotics' new monthly publication. And if that weren't enough, Level One patrons would also receive a nice cloth Psychotic Weasel patch.

Level Two sponsorship, for a $500 dollar minimum, would receive the Psychotic Weasel patch and a one-time honorable mention in the monthly publication.

Anything under $500 would be Level Three and in seven to ten days would receive a letter of appreciation.

Feartha's wardrobe department started cranking out Psychotic Weasel patches in anticipation of the big launch and all the fervor it was sure to create.

And within days of the launch, dollars started rolling in. Slowly at first but as Harris' marketing blitz took off, sponsorship soared.

Meanwhile, Jones and Tanner put together a list of specialty parts that were needed for DOOM's retrofit and with their budget growing by the day, decided to go all out, to exceed even their own expectations.

They ordered their electronic supplies online, additional stockroom racks to hold the booty, four huge workbenches, bins, chairs, laptops, three drafting tables, and a coffee maker. They were off and running totally energized by their good fortune and the beautiful, slick, modern, new Robotics Lab 1.

Toward the end of week three, Harris felt that he understood the Lab's main goal: DOOM. But his mind was cranking out ideas about expanding. Not just another android. Not just a group of robots walking around. Something else. Something that would generate interest *and* income for the Lab.

Then lightning struck and Harris had an "Ah Ha" moment. He practically ran to an impromptu meeting upstairs with Morgan and the outcome of his brilliant idea was this…

Meet Smitty. He was hired after presenting his résumé and a short video of his latest project – a remote controlled robot that was shown demonstrating extraordinary capabilities such as speed, agility, and strength. He called it Fred.

Smitty settled into the Robotic Lab with ease. His job title was Robot Master Builder, and his job description was simply to build more robots. Fun, fast, fiery, deadly, armored, little fighting machines.

Morgan put him on a three-month deadline, with bi-weekly text updates, to produce one robot as a display of his skills.

"I'm loving this!" was all Smitty said before getting to work.

As Jones and Tanner drew up schematics for DOOM and Smitty started building a bot body and stuffing it with electronics, Harris took his marketing skills very seriously.

First, he drew up plans for several billboards that announced PW Robotics to the world, he ran advertisements in two local papers and one big city paper that claimed a distribution of 34,258 and created a Psychotic Weasel logo stencil that a crew of stealthy henchmen could use to spray paint all over the city.

After setting those marketing ploys into motion, Harris started work on his main project. He was going to create, write, edit, and possibly star in his new magazine-like publication…are you ready?... CYBORG! The Very Dark Side of Electronics.

When the Robotics Lab had settled into a sort of routine, Morgan requested a meeting with Argyle and soon met him in his office.

They did a minute of friendly chat then got down to business.

Morgan began, "I know you've been busy, but I wanted to catch you up to what I've been doing lately."

"Yes, I've been in a real trial and error phase for a few weeks," Argyle said.

"First off," Morgan's face lit up, "I'm having a blast running luxury vehicles to the chop shop. It's like owning a variety of high-end luxury cars without having to insure them. So, thank you for that!" she exclaimed.

"You know," Argyle was a little embarrassed, "I'm glad I put that plan into action. So far, I've received about a quarter of a million dollars from that little venture," he smiled as he added, "Psychotic Weasel is nearing solvency!"

"That's great, boss!" Morgan leaned in for a high five.

There was a knock at the door that was answered with Argyle calling out, "Yes?" and in stepped Miss Q with two cups and a French press full of nice dark coffee. She smiled as she put the small tray down and Morgan thanked her for her effort then Miss Q quietly stepped out.

Morgan served both cups and when finished, she pushed back in her chair, holding her cup to her lips for a nice easy sip. After a quiet moment she spoke.

"Every once in awhile I find myself with a little spare time on my hands, and early last month I found it so. (A sip of coffee) Usually I run the par course or visit the gun range, but that particular day neither of those activities interested me. I decided to just leisurely walk around the lair, take in the sights." Morgan paused to study Argyle's face and seeing nothing upsetting, continued. "Eventually I found my way to the IT Department and spent time with Tanner and Jones."

Morgan segued into a story about how the IT Department was failing, to hiring a marketing guy, another robot techie, and generating operating funds for the department.

Argyle had quietly sipped at his coffee as he listened and when Morgan appeared to have finished her story, put his cup down and merely said, "Really?"

"Yes," Morgan smiled, "Want to go see?"

Fifteen minutes later Morgan and Argyle were standing at the door to Robotics Lab 1. Morgan invited Argyle to open the door and step in. She followed.

Argyle took a step or two forward and stopped as he silently gazed all around the lab. In truth, he was in shocked amazement at what he saw.

The lab was well lit, organized, clean, and shiny. Tanner and Jones were busy in one section of the lab, heads down, fussing with a bunch of circuit boards and a man he didn't recognize was working at another bench further back in the lab space.

"Let me introduce you," said Morgan, touching Argyle's arm to pull him out of his mild shock. He followed her, still looking at all the changes. "Smitty! Have a minute?" she called out.

Smitty looked up and smiled at their approach. "Of course!"

Morgan introduced the men, and they shook hands. "Smitty's been here nearly two months now," she said to Argyle. Turning to Smitty, she asked, "Care to show us what you're working on?"

"Absolutely!" he replied. Smitty was always happy to talk robots with anyone that would listen, so off he went on an excited one-sided chat to explain this and point to that. At one point he asked Argyle if he would like a demonstration. "Keep in mind that I'm not done yet." He quickly added.

The little robot was the shape of a footlocker with solid rubber wheels, saw blades on each side, and a scissor lift undercarriage. Smitty made it race up and down the aisle, make fast turns and raise up on its lift, threatening everyone with its saw blades.

"I plan to put full armaments on it soon. Blowtorch and bullets. Should be very formidable when I'm done," Smitty said with pride.

Argyle was nodding his approval. "Very impressive, Smitty. Very nice job. Can't wait to see your bot in full action."

"Oh, that reminds me," Smitty said mostly to himself. "Morgan," he looked at her, "I've been meaning to tell you." Smitty now looked concerned and embarrassed. "I built two small prototype robots, more for proof of concept than anything else," he rushed his words in a show of assurance, "They seemed to have escaped."

Morgan raised her brow in surprise at the news. "And?" she asked him.

"And I've searched every inch of the lab and they're not here. They must have gotten out somehow."

Morgan said, "Well, I'll get a few of the men to help look for them."

Smitty looked relieved. "Thank you. The feral bots are fully armed, so mention to the men that they shouldn't sneak up on them or surprise them in any way. They will interpret it as an aggression and will fire at will."

"Okay," Morgan said. "Good to know." She turned to Argyle, "Want to visit DOOM?"

Tanner and Jones had stopped work when Argyle and Morgan came through and now waited at their workbenches in anticipation of briefing Argyle to their progress.

DOOM was in parts collected on three workbenches. His shins/ankles/feet were there, his hands/wrists/elbows over there, and his head/neck sorta opened up and laying on the bench right here.

"I see you're upgrading some parts," was all Argyle could think to say.

Tanner took the lead answering, "Yes," and outlining what it was they were trying to accomplish. He ended his "short" dissertation with this...

"Just online search for 'Killer Robot Images,' find the one that looks the most dangerous, and that should give you an idea of what we're up to here."

Jones was smiling from ear to ear. "A fully loaded bad ass!"

Chapter Fifteen

Up the Ante

Gilbert, as The Squid, was honing his skills. In any given week he would hit a random ATM and, just for practice, a small family restaurant. He loved the look of fear on everyone's faces when he entered a store with his drones that would immediately fan out to spy out anyone cowering in the aisles or under tables. It made Gilbert feel powerful. It made him feel in control.

This week Gilbert would hit an armored truck and decided on Binks Brothers Transport as his target.

In preparation, Gilbert sat in his shop with his three drones all hooked up to charging stations. He smiled with pride as he gazed from one to another, watching the chargers blink and the drone's indicators gaining power.

"Oh, my little henchbots," Gilbert said aloud, "you are the best." He looked from Tentacle One to Two to Three before continuing. "My life has improved one thousand percent since I built you." Gilbert felt genuine affection for the drones, and it was shown on his face.

The drones just stayed on their chargers.

Gilbert actually wanted to interact with the drones, wanted it pretty badly. He grabbed hold of his controller and tapped Tentacle One's attention button making it jump in response. It was good enough for Gilbert. Tentacle One loved him.

Gilbert knew that Binks Brothers made their transport runs on Tuesday. They followed a route around town, ending up at the First City Bank where they would move big overstuffed bags of cash to the bank vault.

There was a stretch of road between the last pickup and the bank where Gilbert decided the heist would occur. It was less travelled with few retail stores and a small number of pedestrians.

He would run into the road just as the armored van turned the corner. He would stand there facing the van, looking very menacing, ready for action. Tentacle One would be with him while Tentacle Two and Three would swoop down to cover the driver and the rider guy in the back.

After securing the area by launching lit explosives and scaring the bejeezus out of any strangers and glaring threateningly at the Binks guys to freeze them with fear, Gilbert would demand the cash... "Or else!"

Then he and his henchbots would disappear into the night.

Weeell…everything went according to plan right up to the point where the van stopped because The Squid was in the street blocking their way.

Gilbert demanded the massive bags of cash and the Binks guy in the back complied by handing over what looked like a high school pencil case. Gilbert was shocked.

"What exactly is this?" he demanded, thrusting it in the guy's face.

"It's cash, it's all the cash for bank deposit," the guy squeaked in fear, his eyes glued to the oversized squid ink gun pointed at him.

Incensed, Squid shouted at the driver, "You! Get over here," and when the two Binks guys were standing together, hands in the air, Squid commanded, "Empty your wallets!"

The drones moved closer and now hovered, warning the men to comply. Which they did without hesitation.

He was getting more angry by the minute and restlessly shifted from one costume tentacle to the other. "Hurry up!" he ordered, then grabbed the small handful of bills offered, turned, and stomped away.

Without turning his head, he ordered Tentacle Two to, "Shoot out their tires." And it was done.

At home, later that evening, Gilbert counted the cash. The pencil case contained $308.25 and the Binks guys had $82.00 between them. The Squid managed a big armored van haul that netted $390.25.

"What rubbish!" was all he could manage before explaining to the drones, using soothing tones, that it was not their fault. They did fine.

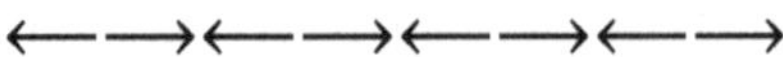

News of the Binks Brothers robbery made headlines and was the lead story on most radio news broadcasts, none of which escaped Argyle's notice.

Someone snapped a phone video that had been provided to the police and the two town papers. Still photos of The Squid had been printed with the robbery article and the public was asked to volunteer whatever information they had.

Argyle sat in his office reading both papers and the longer he stared at Squid photos, the more bothered he became. *"I'm pretty sure this is Third,"* he pondered. He remembered what the time travelers (you know, from the last book?) told him about The Squid. It was strongly implied that Gilbert, himself, would become a great crime lord called The Squid. He didn't really believe it at the time, but now he was convinced.

Argyle cut the articles out of the papers and taped them to the wall then sat looking at them, curiously asking himself, *"Just what is he up to?"* over and over again until he decided that if The Squid was starting up another crime organization…in his town!…then he should probably find out more about it.

Chapter Sixteen

Recognition

In the one-year since Argyle superseded The Thrasher there have been many changes. Some of them fast, some of them slow, but all of them helped to move Psychotic Weasel forward.

As the one-year anniversary approached, Argyle found himself sitting quietly in his office contemplating exactly what that meant. He looked back over his desk schedule and noted the highlights. Completely skipping over his first month of bumbling around trying to find his way, he noted with some satisfaction...

Psychotic Weasel's first woman recruit.

Creation of capers, an IT Department, and marketing strategies.

THAM-1's conversion to DOOM.

Friday Beer Bust, a morale booster, for sure!

Outside the box capers: luxury plus.

Okay, the Mick Jagger thing didn't pan out, but it was his brilliant plan!

Argyle stopped writing and sat for a moment looking at his list of accomplishments. Slowly he became aware of two things. One, all the notes on the page were about his accomplishments, and while it made him happy to see them all neatly lined up on the notepad, all they did was to say he was the idea man, not the brawn. And two, he was using two pencils to tap out "In-A-Gadda-Da-Vida" on his desktop.

Argyle smiled with satisfaction, put the pencils down and turned his thoughts to his crew. While all his henchmen were good solid workers, Argyle asked himself, *"Who stands out?"* While doodling notes and drawing circles, Argyle did a lot of thinking and after twenty some minutes, came to a conclusion. *"It's Morgan. Morgan Taylor stands out."*

This took Argyle completely by surprise. *"The standout henchman is a woman."* It almost shocked him into silence. Almost.

"First of all, she's personable and persuasive and a little intimidating as she quickly assimilated into Psychotic Weasel life. Oh! And there was her stunning victory over Davis in the training course competition." Argyle nodded at the memory. *"I heard about her interviewing technique. Brilliant."* Tapping his chin with a pencil, another point occurred to him. *"And look what she did for the IT guys. New digs, new equipment, and a huge budget. A truly promising outcome. Hmmm. She's making me look good."*

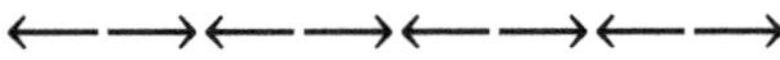

It took Argyle two days of thinking to come up with a type of reward program that he considered viable. He had dismissed the notion of a bonus system. He felt that cash rewards for good behavior would have a negative effect and shouldn't everyone be operating at peak performance anyway? *"Of course they should,"* was his answer.

Every time a possible solution to the "rewards" question popped into Argyle's head it was shot down. A system where points were accrued and levels of gifts are given? *"No. The accounting alone would be a nightmare."* Weekly meetings where standouts are named and applauded? *"Meetings? Really? No."*

On and on Argyle's mind tossed until he hit on it. He found the solution. He was so happy that he spent an hour in the shooting range before going down to Sublevel Five to speak with Feartha Wolf.

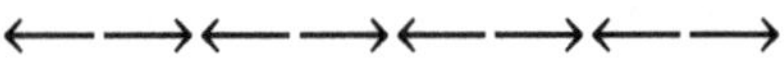

Working with Feartha was a dream. She never said "No" unless the answer was really "No" but otherwise she was flexible and could "roll with it." Argyle appreciated that.

"So," Argyle said, "it's settled. The ceremony will take place one month from this Saturday. That's the 27th. It's on for 7PM up on Parking Level Four," he summarized.

Feartha had been jotting notes throughout their conversation and now looked back over them to confirm that date and time. "That's correct. The invitations will say that the affair is formal, and employees may bring a 'plus one' and their own bottle. Correct?" She looked up at Argyle and waited for confirmation.

"Yes," Argyle smiled, "and maybe bring two bottles!" He winked at his little jokie comment but Feartha just looked at him.

Feartha nodded and closed her notepad, glanced at Argyle and said, "I've got this."

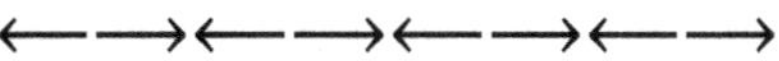

As usual, Feartha and her team of seamstresses did a bang-up job of transforming Parking Level Four into a black-tie event venue.

There was a large, rather impressive stage at one end with a speaker's podium adorned with a 3-D Psychotic Weasel logo whose eyes seemed to follow you. Very disturbing. Sky blue curtains decorated with translucent logos were draped artfully across the back of the stage and just in front of the curtains was a projection screen, recently pilfered from a local movie theatre. Feartha had collected mug-shot pictures, caper news articles, and had ordered pictures taken of the shark tank and training course alligators that she intended to stream onto the screen throughout the evening as interim entertainment.

The table of honor was gorgeous. It was the largest table there, would seat eight, and was draped with a royal purple cloth accented with white. The centerpiece was a grouping of four champagne ice buckets surrounded by a floral collection of roses, irises, and carnations. Certainly worthy of being called a table of honor.

There were a number of other tables set about the space, all were tastefully decorated but none as regal as the nice big table up front.

Lots of chairs had been set up along the two walls that bounded the tables so that stragglers and singles had a place to sit during the ceremony. A nice touch.

At the opposite end of the parking garage were a series of long tables set up for a buffet line service. Ahem, self-service. Feartha planned to have only finger foods, so small plates and napkins only. No sporks or other utensils required.

There was a dessert table but only cookies were planned. Again…no utensils, only napkins.

Clean up *might* be a breeze.

Saturday the 27th came along just as expected, following the 26th.

Fancy dressed henchmen started arriving alone or with their plus ones, who all looked stunning in showy cocktail dresses and corsages.

Argyle had arrived at Audrey's place a few minutes early to pick her up, but she wasn't anywhere near being ready. She wasn't dressed yet and was futzing with her hair and makeup. Argyle immediately stressed out. Weeks ago, when he invited Audrey to the ceremony, he had patiently explained that he was expected to arrive early to greet everyone. This was a milestone event. He was the boss. That was it. Period.

On the (late!) car ride to the seedy warehouse, Argyle had said, "You've had weeks to plan your makeup and now I'm late." That started an argument that included way too much for Argyle to take in at the moment, but one thing was clear: They were both upset and angry. And twenty-five minutes late.

Argyle seated Audrey at the table of honor, introduced her to the small group already there and left to mingle with his henchmen and their dates.

The mood was festive and getting more lively as bottles were opened and little quiche cups eaten. The buffet line moved right along and there were plenty of bruschetta, cheese balls, and jalapeno poppers to go around.

By the time Argyle rejoined Audrey and took his seat, Morgan was there as well as her plus one, who turned out to be Smitty, the robotics engineer from the lab. Argyle hadn't given much thought to who Morgan's plus one would have been, but this surprised him a lot.

Small talk monopolized the conversation at the table, and it was abundantly clear to Argyle that Morgan and Smitty were not a thing. Quickly it became evident that they shared a love of robotics because it was almost all they talked about.

As Argyle sat at the table of honor with Audrey, Morgan, Smitty, her date, and others, he thought back to three days prior when he had frantically searched through Thrasher's book of rants looking for something he could appropriate and customize into a speech honoring or at least recognizing Morgan Taylor for all she's contributed to Psychotic Weasel during her first year as a henchman. *"Oops,"* Argyle stopped short, *"better not say that out loud. Hmmm,"* he thought about it. *"The term is henchperson. Yes, from now on, if I can retrain my brain, it's henchperson."*

It was a fruitless search through the rant book and by the time he had read almost all of Thrasher's crazy rants, Argyle knew he would have to write his own speech. It terrified him right down to his shoelaces but by golly he did it. His speech, written down on a little packet of cards, was now tucked safely into the inside pocket of his formal suit. He patted it to make sure.

An hour into the munching and drinking, Feartha approached Argyle and whispered that it was time he made his grand introduction speech. "I'm sure you'll do fine," she had said.

Argyle steeled himself, brushed the crumbs from his lap, stood up, buttoned his jacket, and stepped to the stage. *"This is it,"* was all the encouragement he could muster.

He now stood at the podium, fished his little packet of cards from his pocket and cleared his throat. And after standing for a moment looking out across the faces that were now turned his way, he began.

"Welcome everyone to the First Annual *Henchperson* of the Year Award ceremony. We've come a long way in the fifteen months since reorganizing into Psychotic Weasel and each and every one of you have certainly proven your worth." Argyle was smiling. "Give yourselves a nice round of applause!"

The parking garage reverberated with clapping and whistling that eventually quieted and Argyle continued.

"It's not been an easy fifteen months. Fiscally we started out so red that it looked hopeless. Morale was at its lowest. The lair was in disrepair. And there was a severe shortage of donuts." (To this, the audience groaned and murmured their agreement.) "It all added up to this: more capers, more donuts!" Argyle yelled out. (The crowd exploded with whistles and cheers!) "Was I right?" he called out. (Yes! was the answer.) "Slowly the tide of red receded, fading into black ink that gained speed with the passing weeks, all of which has brought us to here." Argyle stopped speaking and looked around at staff and crew who were smiling and attentive. He pointed at Davis, sitting off to the right and said, "You look good in a tuxedo." (Davis smiled brightly as he smoothed down the front of his coat.) Argyle looked around, "You know, we all (!) look good tonight, don't we?" (Cheers!) Argyle cleared his throat. "But back on point…" Flipping through his cards, he said, "We're here tonight to honor one among us who has exceeded all expectations of the henchperson job description, one who has contributed new ways of doing routine tasks, one who had innovated new and exciting ventures, all of which serve to enrich Psychotic Weasel. Please welcome to the stage," Argyle's voice was raised, "Morgan Taylor!"

The crowd so thundered its approval that little rivulets of dust and cobwebs floated down from the ceiling.

Morgan got up from her chair. She wore a low-cut black spandex cocktail dress, tight to the waist then softly flowing down to her knees. Here and there were metal studs adorned with Psychotic Weasel logos. She wore strappy black dress shoes with four-inch heels that upon closer look were revealed to be handgun barrels.

Well-wishers sorta mobbed her as she made her way forward. You would have thought it was a scene taken straight from the Oscars! Eventually she made it to the stage and joined Argyle, who had been handed a trophy by Miss Q even as Feartha rolled in a bigger, albeit different trophy on a cart that she positioned just behind them.

Argyle stood holding the smaller trophy as Morgan came to stand next to him.

"I'm happy to announce that a Henchperson of the Year Award ceremony with a very classy black-tie celebration will become a recurring thing, and in preparation for that, a large trophy will stand as inspiration for us all." Argyle swept an arm to present the 3-foot-tall hefty looking trophy sitting on the rolling cart. "Every year the winner's name will be added to the metal placard. The trophy itself will be housed in a soon-to-be-built glass display case in the office pit on Sublevel Two." Turning back to the audience, Argyle continued.

"Morgan, to commemorate your extraordinary year," he lifted the smaller, yet still hefty, trophy he was holding so as to show it off, "This trophy is for you. Display it proudly." Argyle offered her the trophy and asked, "Would you like to say a few words?"

Smiling, Morgan accepted the little trophy as she took in its details. It stood about 16-inches tall and, she thought, about 8-inches wide. The base was square and heavy and the supports on it were snub nosed 38s welded between that and another base upon which a very cool looking killer robot replica stood. The robot was holding aloft a luxury vehicle on top of which stood a doll dressed in…you guessed it…black spandex, whose long hair was pulled up into a pony. The entire piece was gold plated and sported a name and date plate on the base.

It was a thing of beauty.

Morgan cradled the trophy in her arms and turned to the partygoers. "This means a lot. I know that the beginning of my employment with Psychotic Weasel was rough for some of you." She cocked her head and chided, "Don't deny it!" and gave a little laugh. "However, we all made it through and here we are. Most of us friends but all of us comrades. Thank you," she said holding up the trophy.

And the crowd went wild! (⇐ C'mon, you saw that coming, right?)

Feartha came forward and staged Argyle and Morgan for formal pictures and periodically grabbed others and made them smile, explaining that she was starting a Hall of Fame on Sublevel One outside the locker room.

Suddenly there was a loud ruckus back by the buffet that made everyone turn to look.

One of the plus one wives was gasping in fear and shying away from the dessert table.

Smitty called out, "Oh no!" as he leapt to get through the stunned crowd. "Don't make any sudden moves!" he yelled in a panic as he scrambled toward the cookies.

There, on the dessert table were Smitty's two lost prototype robots, tearing up cookies as they rooted down to the tabletop. One had taken offence at being interrupted and had started pitching cookie bits at the persons closest to it. The other one was emitting high-pitched grinding noises as its tread feet spun without traction, sending cookie dust wafting in all directions.

Smitty warned those closest to the table, "Back away slowly, carefully. No eye contact!" as he addressed the two robots in calm and soothing terms. "Larry, Bob, everything's going to be fine. You trust me, right?"

The robots stopped their cookie destruction and swiveled their weird turrets to "look" at Smitty.

"Hi guys," he continued as he inched closer to the table. "I've missed you," he smiled as he offered his hand to them.

Parking Garage Level Four was dead silent.

"I have something for you back at the lab," Smitty cajoled, hoping that their curiosity would take over.

One robot moved to the table edge, grabbed the tablecloth hem with a pincher and swung itself down to the floor. It rolled over to Smitty, stopping at his feet, "looked up" at him and made a purring sound. Smitty bent down and affectionately patted its turret. "Now, now," he murmured.

"What about you, Larry?" Smitty watched the other robot grind its tread feet in the cookie dust as it made little whining sounds. "I can help you with that, buddy," Smitty reassured the robot and reached to clear the tablecloth stuck in its treads, after which, he carefully lifted the robot up off the table and set it gently on the floor.

Addressing both robots, Smitty asked, "Ready?" and taking hold of one of each of their "hands", led them slowly down the drive ramp and further, back to his lab.

When Smitty and the robots had faded away, the deafening silence of the parking garage broke with what could be described as one collective exhale quickly followed by excited chatter.

Argyle took the stage and addressed the party. "Well! That was one hellava finalé! Raise your glasses to Psychotic Weasel Robotics Lab, everyone!"

Chapter Seventeen

The Squid Hits It Big

It was splashed across the front pages of the local papers and two of the nearby town papers, "Terrifying Bank Robbery!"

Argyle had stopped at the downtown newsstand on 7th to buy the morning paper but had picked up all of the different publications to read all he could about the Locally National Bank robbery. It wasn't one of his capers and his curiosity had gotten the better of him.

He sat now, in his Lizzie Borden meeting room office, with a large mug of hot coffee carefully reading through each article…

ALL THE NEWS

LOCALLY NATIONAL BANK HIT!

NEW CRIMINAL SPOTTED
By Ivy Smart

Artist's conception of bank robber

"There's a new crime guy among us. Described as some sort of chubby criminal, wearing a sea creature outfit, who entered the Locally National Bank yesterday evening at its busiest hour. A dozen or more persons were inside the bank at the time. One witness described the scene as manic after the costumed robber rushed through the front doors with five flying machines yelling for everyone to freeze and then told everyone to lay on the floor. Someone yelled out, 'Which is it? Freeze or get down?' To which the sea creature blasted him with some really stinky black ink stuff. 'That was all the motivation I needed!' said another witness.

The rest of the scene played out like any bank robbery would. The flying machines guarded the area as tellers stuffed cash into bags. Police have since identified this costumed robber as The Squid who is usually accompanied by three drones but as of yesterday, the count is now five drones.

The Squid and his drones fled with $17,040.00 but not before terrorizing everyone by lobbing explosives and smoke bombs. One witness told police that they heard maniacal laughter as the robber retreated out the doors. Police have put out an arrest bulletin and expect to have results soon."

Argyle made his way through the other news articles and pretty much had all the available information at hand. He took a nice sip of his still hot coffee and sat back. *"Well, well,"* he smiled to himself. *"Looks like Gilbert Alan Martin the Third has grown up."*

THE CITY NEWS

ALIEN TAKES CASH!

IS THIS THE NEW FACE OF CRIME?
By C. Itall

Argyle carefully clipped out all the articles and arranged them artfully on his stalker wall next to the news bits from week's prior. As he taped and pinned the bits of newspaper up he, had to smile again, *"Can't help to think that I had a hand in this,"* and then something like mixed feelings of pride and dread flooded his mind and chilled the pit of his stomach.

His desk phone rang, and he picked up. It was Miss Q. Would he be available for a short meeting with Tanner and Jones in the Robotics Lab? Say in half an hour?

Not a problem.

When Argyle reached the lab, Tanner and Jones met him at the hallway door asking him for patience as they took thirty seconds to tell a little story.

"Well," Tanner began, "you remember what DOOM looked like the last time you saw him. Pretty sad, right?" He asked rhetorically. "Then Ms Morgan hired Harris…"

Jones excitedly interrupted, "Who is a genius, by the way!"

"Yes," Tanner admitted before continuing, "Harris dove into marketing like…well, like henchpeople dive into a tray of donuts!" Tanner smiled at Argyle who was looking a little thoughtful at that very apt description. "Anyway," Tanner rushed on, "our budget exploded! We couldn't believe it!"

Jones said, "So we went back to your requirements list and revised it to include some elegant features…"

Tanner added, "Upgraded hardware."

"State of the art processors."

"The latest AI software."

"Video equipment."

"Advanced speech capabilities."

"And, and," Jones stammered, almost out of breath, "it's shiny!"

Tanner, now a bit more composed, looked at Argyle and said, "Now, get ready to meet your Dangerously Ominous Omnipotent Machine!" And slowly opened the lab door to reveal the new…the improved…DOOM!

Argyle stepped into the lab completely flabbergasted, almost speechless, but recovered enough to say in a hushed and reverent tone, "Wow."

DOOM had been completely transformed from the bogus robot he had been, into an annihilator! A huge smile spread across Argyle's face.

Tanner and Jones had been holding their breath watching, waiting for a sign. They looked at each other and slapped a high five. Tanner was sure there was a bonus for this one!

DOOM stood over eight feet tall. He had a gladiator helm for a head, a huge broad chest, and massive arms with fully articulated fingers on his very large hands. He had powerful looking legs and broad, well balanced feet.

Tanner and Jones stayed quiet and observed Argyle as he looked at the detail of DOOM. When Tanner guessed Argyle had had an eye full, he spoke, "DOOM has laser eyes, in honor of your Psychotic Weasel logo. He also emits a laser beam from his chest plate."

"Yes," added Jones, "it can cut through concrete and melt steel."

Tanner nodded, "DOOM can hold and shoot guns and see this little box on his right thigh?" He pointed so Argyle would take note. (Which he did.) "There's a very thick, very sharp knife in there."

"And DOOM has flame throwers in the palm of each hand!" Jones quickly added.

"And GPS and radar," Tanner almost shouted, "Radar!"

As Argyle studied DOOM closer, his attention was grabbed and held by a myriad of logo stickers that almost literally covered DOOM's metallic plating. He leaned in for a closer look. Tatts-n-Beer, read one. Another, Binks Brothers Security. "Hah!" Argyle huffed out loud. The rest appeared to be Mom-n-Pop stores, realtors, and restaurants. Curiously, most of them were located downtown.

Argyle took it all in and turned to face the two ITs, the smile still plastered on his face. Almost at once, both men said, "So what do you think?"

"I think," Argyle announced, "I think this is the greatest thing ever! You two have outdone yourselves and should be very proud of what you've produced here."

"And that's not all!" exclaimed Jones, who was over the top excited that Argyle was pleased. "We want to demonstrate for you that DOOM is articulate, accurate, and unafraid!"

"Yes," added Tanner, "we've reserved the Sublevel Three par course for tomorrow morning. DOOM will run, jump, tuck-n-roll, handle a variety of weapons, and absolutely amaze." He pulled in a breath. "Is 8AM good for you?"

"It is now!" said Argyle as he turned back to study DOOM a bit more.

Tanner nudged Jones with an elbow and jerked his head toward their drafting tables. Jones smiled and snapped his fingers as if in sudden memory and trotted away, soon returning with several drawings.

Tanner spoke, "We can't tell you how happy you've made our day, today. And to that we say…" (crinkling the drawing paper in his hand) "we have schematic designs of additional robots," he said as he offered one of the drawings to Argyle. "And would like your permission to continue."

Argyle smiled.

Chapter Eighteen

Oh, Professor

For the next handful of weeks, Psychotic Weasel LLC, operated by schedule. Maintenance capers became routine and lair repairs finally seemed under control. Argyle had managed to organize two wonderfully executed capers that netted three months of operating costs with only one incident of donuts in the break room.

Things were looking rosy and as Argyle found a rhythm to his management of staff and admin, he happily noted that a lot of the stress he carried in his shoulders and stomach had faded away. He was feeling pretty good about that until today's mail came in.

As usual, Miss Q had delivered the incoming mail to Argyle's office about mid-morning. The lair bills were always opened, and Miss Q would pay them and mark them as such for Argyle's information. Everything else was delivered unopened.

Today, among the paid bills and an advertising flier for a funeral home, there was a very ornate envelope addressed to Argyle Stevens, PW LLC c/o Seedy Warehouse. Argyle picked up the envelope and noted it was a high-quality cotton fiber paper. This made him very suspicious. Also, he found it noteworthy that it was addressed to the "Seedy Warehouse." *"Isn't that odd that the post office knows that I'm in the seedy warehouse,"* he pondered.

The envelope had no return address on it. That was very concerning, so Argyle donned a pair of latex cleaning gloves, safety glasses, and a dust mask before trying to open it, which he did very carefully using a straight edge razor blade.

"Can't let my guard down. This could be full of powdered cilantro!" Argyle thought. "I hate cilantro!" he said out loud.

Slowly, slowly, Argyle nudged the razor blade down the top edge of the highly suspicious envelope. *"Mustn't get careless, "* he told himself. He picked up a pair of tweezers, opened the envelope's cut edge, gingerly tweezed the paper contents, and lifted it out little by little until it was completely free of the envelope.

"Phew!" was all he could think to say to himself.

He set the tri-fold on his desk, put the tweezers down and pushed his chair away. Argyle realized that he had been holding his breath and in one quick move, exhaled and sucked in a big lungful of air. He shook off the tension in his arms and neck and then sat back down.

His phone rang, scaring him with its jarring sound. He picked it up, said, "Not now," and before the caller could speak, hung up.

Argyle stared at the tri-folded paper until he worked up his nerve to open it. With gloved hands, safety glasses, and his dust filter mask pushed firmly against his face, he ever so carefully unfolded the paper until it lay flat on his desktop.

"What the Lake of Fire is this?!" Argyle huffed. He slowly read the tri-fold. Here's what he was looking at…

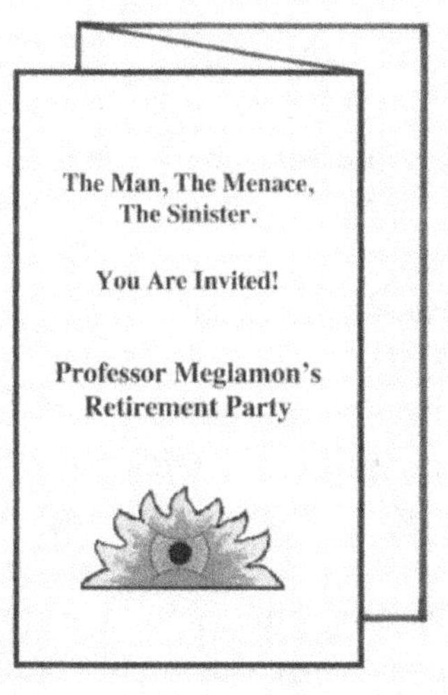

Date: 9th Month, 8th Day,
15th Hour.
Where: The Haddock
Room in the Faraway Hotel
Located Off Of Chubb Alley.
Bring Your Plus Three
and BYOB's.
Come On Time But
Leave Early.
RSVP Now!

"Meglamon's retiring!" Argyle said with a great amount of doubt. "Unbelievable." But the more he thought about it, the more he started to think it was an elaborate ruse to lure him and his plus three into a trap. *"It has to be,"* he questioned. Then he felt the need to talk this over with others, get their opinions and hear their take on it.

Twenty minutes later, Morgan, Miss Q, Davis, and Watson were seated at the meeting table.

Argyle had inspected the tri-fold for any trace of cilantro and finding none, took off his protective gear, brushed the tri-fold flat and presented it.

"This came in today's mail," Argyle explained. "Go ahead and read it and tell me what you think."

Miss Q said, "The paper's expensive. It appears to have been printed up professionally."

"From everything I know about Meglamon," Morgan said, "I've never heard of anything like this before. Makes me suspicious."

"That's what I thought," agreed Argyle. He then looked to Davis.

"If this is a trap, you have two choices: Don't go," Davis offered as choice one, "or go but blast 'em to smithereens!" He then slid the paper over to Watson.

Morgan added, "If you do go, go fully armed and stay alert. Keep an eye on your surroundings, 'back to the wall' sort of thing."

"I have to ask," Miss Q said, "If Professor Meglamon was setting a trap. Why would he use a professional printer and why meet in a public place? Why not just spring a trap as you drove home some night?"

"Hmmm," mused Argyle, "That does seem more menacing than being invited to a party."

Watson, who had been studying the invitation, spoke up, "You know, boss, there has been an increase in postings on FredsList from guys whose résumés mention employment with Meglamon's organization." He looked over at Davis, "Remember last week we had a big laugh at that one guy who bragged about his basic plumbing skills and we made cracks about him going out on capers with a wrench?"

"Yeah, that's right. I remember that now," Davis touched his chin in thought.

"So, maybe Meglamon *is* falling apart," noted Morgan, "and

losing employees."

"Maybe he really is retiring," said Davis.

"Then there's only one way to find out," stated Argyle, "and that is to RSVP."

September 8th, that is to say, today, proved to be a sunny, partly cloudy day. A perfect day for a retirement party.

Argyle volunteered to drive himself and his plus three to the Faraway Hotel and borrowed a PW LLC van for the task. His plus three were Audrey, Morgan, and Davis. All but Audrey were fully armed with micro guns, poison darts, tiny popper bombs, and other unobtrusive weaponry that could be stashed about their clothing and not be observed by any of Meglamon's stooges. Argyle refused to call them henchpeople, as it was an insult to all henchpeople.

At a quarter to 3PM, everyone, in their best preppy casual outfits, boarded the van and Argyle slowly drove away from the seedy warehouse district.

They arrived at the Faraway Hotel at approximately 2:56PM and followed the signs to designated parking. After they alighted from the van and gathered up their bottles of hooch, everyone grouped up for a last pre-Meglamon briefing.

"Remember, we're not here to have too much fun," Argyle stated. "Keep your eyes and ears open."

Morgan said, "Did everyone do a weapons check?"

"Yes," answered Argyle.

"Absolutely," answered Davis as he patted his jacket pockets.

Morgan smiled and nodded.

"We don't know what to expect," instructed Argyle. "So, expect the unexpected."

"Stay sharp," added Morgan.

"Geez people," Audrey said in her best and most frustrated valley girl tone. "You would think you were headed to the principal's office." Then rolled her eyes.

Argyle, Morgan, and Davis just stared at her blankly.

"Okay," Argyle said, "let's go to a party."

One of Meglamon's stooges was at the door to the Haddock Room asking names and checking them off a guest list before letting anyone in.

The small group took about five steps into the room and stopped to get a look at the layout.

Argyle was the first to spot this bent over old man who was doddering his way straight towards them. It took him a long moment to make the distance, but finally he made it. He stood right in front of Argyle, winded. It took another painfully long moment for him to steady down and when he finally did, he looked up at Argyle, smiled, grabbed at the bottle of Sikkim Old Gold whisky Argyle was cradling in his left arm, took it, said, "Thank you," turned, and doddered away.

Argyle looked over at the others, a scowl clearly marking his features, "What was that?"

Davis leaned in and in a lowered voice, answered, "I think you just lost your whisky."

Audrey said, "It's okay, dear, we still have the champagne," and gently tugging his arm, said, "Let's get a table."

The Haddock Room was fish themed. Go figure.

The walls were painted blue up to a point where a sky scene was introduced. Great schools of haddock were painted swimming around the room, through kelp and around rock outcrops, as seagulls flew through the air above them. It was almost too much.

It was a nice big room with several large round tables that each would seat a dozen people. However, only one of the tables had been set up with a paper table covering that had cartoon balloons around the skirt, plastic cups, and napkins. The only thing redeeming enough to be talked about was the centerpiece – a large glass bowl filled with sand that supported a plump little 3-D plastic Meglamon Evil Eye icon on a stick surrounded by twigs and dime store succulents.

Audrey steered the little group to this table, and they took seats that basically put them at the best advantage.

As the minutes passed, three more people took seats. They introduced themselves as another of Meglamon's stooges (a lesser one) and his wife, and the wife of the "door" stooge (the head one), who came to join them less than five minutes later, saying that, "Everyone's here now so the party can begin!"

The statement that everyone who was coming were actually all in the Haddock Room, at this moment, seemed very incredulous. Argyle cut a glance at Morgan who was steadily looking at the others seated around the table. She turned to look at Argyle and slightly shook her head as if to say she didn't quite get it either.

Davis had brought a six-pack of German beer, Grün Fisch, and now the sound of him popping the cap off a beer bottle gave a slight pause to the concentrated nothingness going on at the table. The head stooge nodded his agreement to Davis, lifted his own glass of bloody Clamato® beer and said, "Cheers!" This set in motion a series of popping, uncapping, and pouring sounds as everyone opened their bottles and guardedly smiled at one another.

Morgan, seated next to Argyle, tapped a finger on the table to get Argyle's attention without actually speaking. He looked at her as she jutted her chin to get him to look across the room.

There, slowly, ever *sooo* slowly, was the bent over old man, doddering toward the table. This act was enough to command the attention of all the party attendees. Another "younger" old man who wasn't quite as bent over but still didn't look like he was capable of walking any faster trailed him. As later introduced, this gentleman turned out to be Pavlov.

Finally! The doddering old man made the distance. He stood behind an empty chair trying to catch his breath. His walking buddy stood silently at his side, watching. When it seemed the old man was collected. Pavlov took the seat next to him.

Argyle's hand had gone to his jacket pocket and now rested on the mini-pistol he had stashed there. This was questionably the most bizarre party he had ever attended. He wasn't even convinced it was a party. The whole thing had his thoughts wavering between confidence and doubt.

The old man cleared his throat and spoke. "Welcome to all twelve of you…"

Pavlov jumped up to whisper in his ear but since the old man was a little deaf, ended up kind of shouting, "There's only ten of us, dad, there were two no-shows." After which he sat back down.

The old man straightened up to his full bent over self and resumed speaking, "All ten of you," smiling and nodding to everyone around the table. "My name is Professor Meglamon, and this is my retirement party." He then went into a coughing fit.

Argyle was shocked to say the least. Davis had said, "What?" at the old man's pronouncement, Morgan was steadily eyeing the scene, and Audrey looked unaffected by any of it as she poured a second glass of warm champagne for herself.

Meglamon finally cleared his coughing with a big gulp of Sikkim Old Gold and said, "I think I will take my seat and continue from there." Which he did right after up-ending the Sikkim bottle one more time.

"Okay. Again, welcome," he began. "A ham sandwich walks into a bar and orders a beer. The bartender says, Sorry, we don't serve food here."

Meglamon chuckled and looked around the table. No one laughed.

"Tough crowd," he mumbled before continuing.

"Oh, what can I say about my 62-years in villainy? It's been fun, I've had fun riding this rollercoaster we call an empire. But let's go back, back to when life was simpler. Hmmm. (Looking off into the distance as he searched his memories.) I'm a Professor…"

"Of what?" Audrey interrupted, sincerely wanting an answer.

Meglamon just stared at her then turned to the group and continued, "I found that I had ambitions beyond just being a full-time accredited and tenured," he gave Audrey a stink eye, "college professor, grading papers and dealing with immaturity. I have an IQ of 183. Did you know that?" He directed the query to his son, who nodded and smiled indulgently. "One afternoon, I remember it was a beautiful spring day, puffy clouds, slight breeze…Oh my, what was I going to say?" He turned to Pavlov and shrugged his shoulders, silently asking for help.

"You had ambitions, pop," he said.

"Oh yes, of course. I had read about a big unsolved heist. I believe it was of a famous painting taken from the Louvre museum. Anyway, I thought, 'I can out-do that,' and got to work planning, on paper mind you, (pointing a finger at Argyle) the crime to beat all crimes! The theft of the Liberty Bell from its home in Philadelphia…Pennsylvania! I spent many weeks designing, thinking, revising, and drawing the perfect theft. And I sold that plan for a *very* large amount of cash to some schmuck who then screwed it up."

Davis and Argyle looked at each other in surprise at that statement, because that was one of the earliest capers they had been on with Thrasher Incorporated.

"That," Meglamon emphasized, "to borrow a phrase from the young folk…kick started…my hobby of planning and selling crime descriptions on the dark web. Yeah, those were exciting days…" he was waxing sentimental.

~ *Fizzst* ~ broke the silence.

Davis had opened another beer, his third. The head stooge smiled at him and raised his fourth bloody Clamato® beer in salute.

Meanwhile, Meglamon, lost in his pleasant memories, had nodded off, his chin resting on his chest.

Pavlov gently rested his hand on Meglamon's shoulder to rouse him. Meglamon jerked awake very confused. Pavlov said, "It's okay, dad, we're at your retirement party."

Sputtering, Meglamon spoke, "Ah, yes, of course. Then I built an empire and…yadda, blah, blah, yadda, and so forth…I'm the crime lord of the century!"

"Excuse me, Professor," Argyle said, "Why did The Thrasher hate you so much?"

Meglamon scrunched his face in thought, then answered, "I've never met the man, son, I think it was purely because I existed," was all he could think of. Smiling, Meglamon asked Argyle, "You know why you were invited to my party?"

"This is it," Argyle thought just as Morgan thought, *"Here it comes,"* as both she and Argyle reached for their weapons. Argyle answered, "No, Professor, none of us could guess the answer to that question."

"It's because," Meglamon said kindly, "Psychotic Weasel LLC is crime royalty. That's why."

Dumbfounded, Argyle loosened his grip on his tiny gun. All he could come up with was, "Thanks."

Meglamon had moved on. "The last five years haven't been kind to me. I suppose it's only fair that a younger, more crime savvy generation of criminals take the reins of power." Meglamon looked at

Morgan, "I've slowly been going bankrupt. I've put my lair up for short sale." He pointed at her, "Want to buy it?" Morgan slowly shook her head no. Meglamon then looked at Argyle, "I'll make you a good deal? No?" Argyle politely declined. "Well, okay. That concludes my speech. How about cake? I like cake."

Pavlov got up, patted his dad's shoulder and said, "Good job." He then went to a side table and came back with a cake. It was a two-layer cake, not unlike one from a home kitchen, it was lopsided but decorated with a nice Meglamon logo. Two lit candles topped it off.

Pavlov placed the cake down in front of Meglamon.

~ Fizzst ~

Davis opened his 4th Grün Fisch beer. The main stooge smiled and nodded his salute.

After retrieving what looked to be a ten-inch-long butcher's knife, Pavlov carefully handed it to Meglamon so he could cut the cake. Meglamon took the knife, fumbled it and immediately it dropped to the floor in front of him. He and Pavlov bent to retrieve it and bumped heads. Startled, they both jerked up and felt their heads with a hand.

In the mean, the head stooge ducked under the table saying, "I'll get it, I'll get it," but Davis, not trusting any stooge, ducked under the table too, saying, "I'll just help with that if you don't mind."

Eventually, Davis popped back up, knife in hand, "Got it!" and handed it to Pavlov.

Pavlov decided that a butcher's knife probably wasn't a good cake-cutting tool, put it down and instead, told the lesser stooge to go to the kitchen and ask for a butter knife. Which he did.

An uncomfortable three minutes was spent waiting for the lesser stooge to return. Finally! he did.

Pavlov cut the little round cake into ten equal slices and passed them around, serving Meglamon first. By the time everyone had munched a bite or two of the vanilla lemon cake, Meglamon was snoozing again, softly snoring and making quiet mumbly noises. Pavlov let him sleep.

"I want to thank all of you for coming," Pavlov addressed the table. "It meant a lot to dad that you had enough trust and respect to do so." He smiled, looking at Meglamon with the love of a son.

Argyle, Morgan, Davis, and Audrey quietly gathered their

belongings and made their way out of the Haddock Room and continued on out into the sunshine of late afternoon.

Argyle had driven back to the seedy warehouse to drop everyone off and return the van to Parking Level Two.

The conversation on the way was animated, everyone had an opinion or an observation they wanted to share.

"I had always thought that Meglamon was *the* super villain," Argyle said. "Tough. Deadly. Unpredictable."

Morgan added, "It seems we've believed a fantasy version of him. Even if age has softened him, I didn't get the impression that he was any more ruthless in his youth."

"Yeah," Argyle added, "based on Thrasher's focused hatred of Meglamon, I've always believed they were equals." He fell silent for a moment then voiced a thought, "I'm thinking now that Thrasher built this all up in his own mind…without facts."

Davis said, "What's the term now? Fake news?"

Audrey just stared out her door window.

"And did you get a load of the two stooges?" asked Davis. "They didn't look in caper shape to me."

"Well, business has been failing for several years," Morgan spoke. "Could be they're just maintenance at this point."

The group fell silent, probably out of pity for how the mighty have fallen.

At the seedy warehouse, everyone said good night and dispersed. Argyle held the VDub door for Audrey then fired up the bug for the drive to her place. She was strangely quiet the entire way.

Argyle stole a glance or two of Audrey on the way and decided that she may have had too much champagne (In fact, the entire bottle!) and too much excitement and just needed to rest.

He pulled up in front of her house, parked and in the silence, studied her face.

"Shall I walk you to the door?" Argyle softly asked as he reached for his door latch.

"No," Audrey replied, her voice level and clear. "We need to talk, or I should say, I need to talk."

"Okay," Argyle said and quietly waited with growing concern. "*Hmmm*," Argyle thought, "*this never means anything good.*"

Staring straight ahead, Audrey began…

"We've been together for over three years now and we've had our share of ups and downs. Don't get me wrong," she rushed on, "There's been some very fun times. I've had a blast." Audrey hesitated for the briefest of moments to gather her thoughts. "I was very happy when Thrasher was crushed in that earthquake. I never liked him. Anyway. It was such a good day in that you were promoted to the lead position, the CEO of the lair. I was so proud. But," she looked down at her fidgety hands, "this last year for us has been…has been…I don't want to say bad…but it's been…unstable. Yes! That's it. Unstable. And I don't see that changing in the foreseeable future." She looked over at Argyle, who looked confused. "I want a husband who works 9-5, like daddy. I want a home and 2.75 children. But no. Today, looking at Meglamon, I realized how pathetic it is that he's come to this. I see that that's you in 30-years Argyle, and I can't do it. I won't do it. I have to break up with you." Audrey unlatched her door and swung her leg out. She turned her face back to Argyle, looked him squarely in the eye and said, "I can see clearly that crime doesn't pay."

Chapter Nineteen

CYBORG!

"The Very Dark Side of Electronics"

Harris was very pleased with the first issue of his magazine. It was slick with color pictures and filled with articles and interviews. He had written a two-page introduction that he ran under the heading, "From the Editor's Desk," where he talked about what readers could expect in upcoming issues. He teased them by listing possible interviews of prominent robotics engineers, articles on the future of cybernetics, and humorous stories of how some electronic experimentations had gone terribly wrong. He cited as an example, the one robot of note that had been designed to use lasers as weapons but upon beta testing, it instead shot sprays of fire retardant all because two lines had been crossed in the manufacturing process. What a surprise that weapon was! So funny. Back to the drawing board for that engineer!

Harris also encouraged, "Letters To The Editor," and promised big things, including exclusive in-depth interviews with the current generation of inventors and detailed discussions with robotic industry leaders. He also hinted at including a "How To" section for all those DIY'ers out there. Harris felt that the first issue of CYBORG! would mostly be about marketing and that after that, a wave of excitement would float the new publication for months.

After signing up many paid advertisers and securing DOOM's sponsors, Harris had found a small but efficient printing company that also handled mailing lists and then launched the very first issue. DOOM's hulking dangerous embodiment graced the issue's cover giving the magazine a special flair. Harris couldn't stop handling it and analyzing it. He felt that this was a winner.

Four days after launch, letters to the editor started rolling in. All were supportive with many of them suggesting future articles featuring something they favored. Harris was so hyped he started working on issue #2 almost immediately after pitching his current idea to Morgan…

After Harris said hello, he set two mugs of tea down on Morgan's desk. "Nice and hot, no sweetener. Right?" he asked.

Morgan nodded yes and thanked him for the treat. "What can I do for you today, Harris?"

"Okay," he started, "You've seen issue #1 of CYBORG! What did you think?"

"I liked it. The look and feel was good and the articles carried their own. Did you have contributing journalists?" Harris shook his head no. "Really? You wrote the entire mag?"

"Yes," he smiled, "and took all the pictures."

"Well, that's impressive."

"I wanted to keep the costs down in case it was a bust, no sense overspending right out of the gate." He took a sip of tea then continued, "I'd like to pitch an idea of mine, one that I think will solidify us in the field of crime bots."

Morgan looked intrigued. "I'm listening."

Harris launched into his narrative. The way he had it figured, in three months time, Smitty will have built two fighting floor bots. "One is nearly ready now," he had said. "Soon they will need to be tested beyond the beta testing to ensure all their systems are functional. I mean *really* tested."

Harris outlined his idea like this… "Using CYBORG! as a communication platform, I announce that a short movie, documenting these two bots being fully tested, will be available for download for the sum of, let's say, $49.95. We won't give away their full potential, just enough to scare the pants off any competition Psychotic Weasel may have."

Morgan listened to Harris' pitch and then her mind took off. "Well, how about this? Instead of a high-level show of what we've got…we issue a challenge to any and all of our competition to come up with their own fighting bot and we arrange a fight off to see who has the best crime bot."

Harris' eyes widened with excitement and he practically blurted out, "Yes! Death Slam!"

The featured story in CYBORG! issue #2 was Smitty and his two warrior bots, Kill-Va-Nader and Psycho Bomb. The cover was a glossy photo of Smitty, arms crossed in front of him, one hand holding a remote control, the other, a complex bundle of wires and blinky lights. He was perched on a workbench stool and, honestly, looked as regal as an Egyptian Pharaoh would have looked in 2589BC.

Holy moly! The dark web lit up with excitement and tons of email and snail mail piled in. The consensus: The fight is on! But! It should be held in an arena in front of an audience. So many people wanted to actually attend a crime bot fight.

Death Slam took off like a high-speed rail system. Smitty was energized beyond words and his competitive juices started to flow.

Morgan and Harris had several development meetings as well as briefings with Argyle, who was on board with a bot fight as soon as he heard about it.

Several venue ideas were bandied about and the positive and negative of each were discussed down to these details: crowd capacity, security, illegal activities and how to keep the cops out, and large-scale betting. For instance, the Aardvark Stadium where the Rolling Stones played has crowd capacity but was not low key enough to keep the cops at bay, and holding the event in an open city park afforded no crowd control and a security nightmare.

Finally, several decisions were reached that Argyle, Morgan, Smitty, and Harris all agreed upon:

1. Death Slam would be held on Parking Garage Level Four.
2. A limited number of elite reserved seating attendees would be allowed to watch the live performances at $950.00 a seat. No pictures or video recordings allowed.
3. The event would be recorded by several in-house professional cameras for paid streaming later at $79.95 a pop, shown as pay-per-view, and/or downloaded directly from PW LLC servers.

4. It would be nationally televised to hundreds of betting parlors with Psychotic Weasel selling licensing.
5. Security would be supplied by Psychotic Weasel and kept low key.
6. Betting could be set up on site and controlled by PW LLC for a cut.
7. A concession stand would be provided.

It was a well-known fact that local police never bothered with crime activity in the seedy warehouse district so there was no threat of their interference.

All this planning solved the venue problem. Now, on to the competition.

Harris said he had filtered all the responses he received from CYBORG! issue #2, tossing out the crazies, the unprofessional, and the amateurs and came up with one very viable possibility.

"I received a very impressive submission from the Di Lombaretti crime family three towns over." Harris handed around copies of a document. "I've dark web searched them, and they have been a well-known crime family presence for sixty-two plus years who have been perfectly happy operating in their own town. Apparently, there's a grandson interested in robotics who has built a pretty good roll-around bot that they would like to enter into our competition. Look there on page three," he pointed out.

Page three was a picture of a crime bot that looked formidable enough even if its weapons looked a little goofy.

Smitty peered closely at the picture, titled, At'em Smasher. "This doesn't appear to be a careless array of parts. It has three types of weapons, two cameras, and very advanced wheel traction." He looked up at the others. "I think it's a good bot and may be a worthy competitor." Smitty was smiling pretty brightly.

Morgan said, "Okay. That brings us up to three bots, including your two, Smitty." Turning to the table, she asked, "How many crime bots are we going to allow?"

Harris offered, "To keep the entire competition contained to one, let's say, long afternoon show, we should keep the number of bots to four."

"I agree with the 'one afternoon' aspect," offered Argyle, "Too much longer and henchpeople and guests might become fidgety. We don't want that."

"Good. I'll find one more contestant and close the entries down," said Harris. He then asked, "What is the big prize for winning Death Slam?"

"Oh!" exclaimed Smitty. "I've always wanted a Big Bullet trophy. Is that doable?"

"I think that is totally possible," Morgan added.

Harris quickly added, "A Big Bullet trophy *and* an exclusive feature in CYBORG! should please anyone."

The meeting continued…

Morgan quickly reviewed the points agreed upon so far. "We've got the venue, the prizes, and we need one more robot. We should come up with a date and a marketing strategy." She looked around. Everyone had pulled out their electronics and were searching their calendars. "And contest rules," she added.

"Let's set it for two months out," said Argyle. "That gives Harris time to put out one more issue of CYBORG! and find one more submission. It also gives us time to organize and build the venue," he looked thoughtful, "And time for Feartha's team to pretty it up."

"Smitty," Morgan said, "How about you and I meet later to discuss contest rules?" Smitty nodded and Morgan continued, "If that's acceptable to the rest of you?"

It was agreed and the meeting was adjourned.

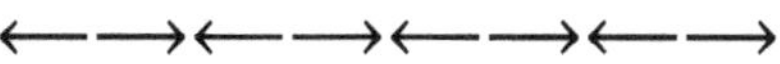

One week later, Harris forwarded an email with an attachment to Morgan, Argyle, and Smitty, with this note as lead in, "This email just came in. As you will see, it's from The Squid. He wants to enter a crime bot into Death Slam and the attached .jpeg is a picture of his entry. Please advise. Will wait before responding. – H"

Well, this caused quite the stir.

Morgan took herself straight down to Robotics Lab 1 to discuss it with Smitty and Argyle immediately printed it all out and pinned it up on his Squid stalker wall.

After everybody spoke to everyone, the four agreed that The Squid could enter his crime bot, Raging Blender, in Death Slam. It fit the rules criteria so what the heck. Raging Blender was in.

Harris released the next issue of CYBORG! announcing the competitors and how the venue was going to work. The reserved seating sold out almost immediately and betting parlor requests for broadcast licensing skyrocketed. They were literally coast-to-coast and every state in between.

This was going to be good.

Chapter Twenty

Death Slam!

Parking Garage Level Four was a hub of construction noises, excitement, and serious consideration as the Death Slam venue took on its form.

After the very impressive job Feartha had done to bring about a gorgeous Henchperson of the Year Awards venue and in real appreciation of her skills as a designer and a construction foreman, Argyle promoted her to Event Planning Manager. A position she took with grace and also in stride.

Feartha's skills were more than evident. By now, Level Four was as familiar to her as her Wardrobe Department. Feartha knew its strengths and its limitations and wasted no time capitalizing on one and covering the other. The Death Slam venue was perfect.

The arena itself took up half of Level Four's space, with the exact 50'x50' center designated the fight zone. This zone was raised a few feet off the floor for two main reasons: eye-level viewing for two rows of tiered seating and space for a number of recording devices to maneuver and capture the action.

There was a ramp to be used to move the fighting bots in and out and two reserved areas for the bot handlers. The fight zone would be enclosed in a black powder coated chain-link fencing material, guaranteed to keep the bots inside. It reached all the way to the ceiling. The floor of the fight zone sported a huge Psychotic Weasel logo that from any vantage point, looked very intimidating. A cool final touch was the lighting. Moveable spotlights that could change color from harsh white to soft white to yellow, green, blue, purple, red, and to orange, if one desired, were generously used throughout.

As explained in CYBORG! the tiered seating was reserved for

high rollers at $950.00 a seat. Very elite. And apparently highly desirable because all eighty seats sold out in two days. There were a limited number of overflow tickets available, but those folks would have to mill around just outside the arena and see what they could see…for $550.00 a pop. Who would have known those tickets would also be snapped up! It motivated Feartha to install two monitors out in the lobby area.

The remaining Level Four space was used up by a control booth (operated by Carter and Hansen), three betting booths (Psychotic Weasel charging a "handling fee"), a competitor staging area (no showing off!), and five large vending machines fully loaded with chips, chocolatey goodness, various baked goods, salty nutrition, and soda. Feartha had forbidden alcohol at this venue. She knew all too well what happens when alcohol and rowdy henchpeople are mixed together. Yhup. Nothing safe.

All around the walls, casting wonderful shadows on the ceiling and floor were the cutest Psychotic Weasel logo sconces. What a touch!

Feartha fired everything up for her final walk-though. The arena lights glowed softly, and the spotlights focused on the floor logo. The monitors relayed perfect pictures and the vending machines hummed and invitingly lit up their contents. She stood, arms akimbo, looking with her sharp eyes, seeing all the finished details, and feeling happy.

"Ladies and gentlemen!" Morgan called out from her position at the center of the robot fighting zone. "The event that you have eagerly awaited, the event that has caused a buzz among the ones in the know and stirred the imaginations of us all, is finally here. Put your hands together for Psychotic Weasel's first…" Morgan slowly turned to scan the faces of those packed into the arena, an inviting smile slowly lighting up her face, "annual…(wait for it)…Death Slam!"

The arena and those packed just outside, altogether close to 160 persons, burst into enthusiastic applause and loud whoop whoops.

After the tumultuous reception started to quiet down, Morgan spoke. "We would like to take a moment to introduce you to our players today." She turned toward the ramp and beckoned, with a wave of her arm, that the contestants were to come on up.

"Psychotic Weasel's own Kill-Va-Nader!" Kill-Va-Nader rolled in through the wide doorway, its buzz saws spinning and its one-thousand-volt taser emitting blue flashes of snapping electricity waving around at the end of a six-foot snake cord. Kill-Va-Nader started a slow parade around the fighting cage as it raised itself up and lowered back down on a scissor-lift under its carriage. Was that a blowtorch hose flexing out the back?

Laughter rippled through the crowd. Morgan turned and gave a little laugh and said, "Oh! Here comes Larry, our little nuisance bot," she smiled and bent down to speak to Larry, who, being no taller than three foot, was looking up at Morgan and listening. "Hello Larry, where's Bob?" she asked.

Larry looked around the cage and then beeped a response as it pointed. Morgan followed the direction indicated by Larry's clamper-cup hand and said, "Oh there he is!" Giving the crowd a minute to appreciate Bob as he zipped into the cage and spun in circles on his four wheeled legs around the floor.

Meanwhile, Kill-Va-Nader had almost completed its circuit and with Larry and Bob hovering near, they made their way out of the cage.

Morgan said, "Let's welcome At'em Smasher!" Loud claps and yea's from the audience. "At'em Smasher belongs to the Di Lombaretti family from three towns over." At'em Smasher looked formidable enough with its huge smasher hammer moving far back overhead and smashing forward. The weaponry was complimented by two nasty looking butcher knives, one jabbing in and out, the other chopping up and down. And if that weren't enough, there was a fully loaded 9mm handgun mounted on the front as well as whirling blades of death protruding from each wheel hubcap.

As At'em Smasher circled the cage, someone was heard to yell out, "That's my grandson's robot!" This was followed by a small section of spectators all standing up and pumping their fists in the air chanting, "At'em Smasher, At'em Smasher, At'em Smasher!"

Morgan turned to face them saying, "Alright, we have an At'em Smasher fan base with us today!"

Next up the ramp was Raging Blender, or more correctly, through the ramp door. Raging Blender was a flying drone that had been entered into the competition by The Squid.

Raging Blender was about four foot in diameter and was held aloft by one large and three smaller rotary wings that also served as battle blades. Raging Blender could flip itself upside down and use its blades to slice and chop…whatever…to pieces. In addition, it sported three popper cannons and two large caliber guns affixed to its "head". The large and angry looking Squid eyeball logo on the side also shot a laser beam. Eight foam tentacles hung down and floated in the wind as Raging Blender flew about, but their only purpose was to distract and confuse, and of course, look especially cool.

Morgan called out, "Last but never the least, here's Psycho Bomb!"

Oh, Smitty was so proud of Psycho Bomb. In honor of Morgan, Psycho Bomb had been outfitted with two grabber "hands" at the end of eight-foot snake cables. Both "hands" were replicas of a shark mouth complete with teeth but with an added surprise weapon: flamethrowers. Truly diabolical. Sweeping across the back was a Gatling style machine gun (very cool) and on the front, lazily moving and bobbing was a large, soft pink lotus flower bud, but look out! Don't smell this flower! It shoots an acid that will take your paint off! And to honor Argyle, the Psychotic Weasel logo, predominately displayed at the front so that it's the last thing you will ever see, shoots powerful red laser beams that can cut steel, melt glass, and freak you out just before slicing you in two!

Psycho Bomb completed its slow parade around the cage and made an exit down the ramp to return to the competitor staging area.

Morgan stood gazing after it. "Now, who isn't impressed with our Death Slam competitors?" she called out, beaming from ear to ear. The crowd erupted into wild clapping in its appreciation. She looked at her watch, "You've got fifteen minutes, friends. Get your break on, your bets placed, and your munchies procured, and we'll see you back here in fifteen."

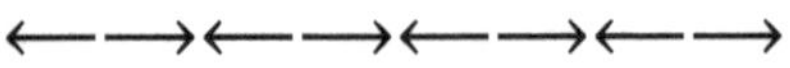

"The order in which all contestants will compete has been decided by the luck of the draw," Morgan announced. "Please welcome to bout one, Kill-Va-Nader and At'em Smasher!" she called out.

As the two crime bots rolled up the ramp, the overflow crowd could be heard calling out encouragement to their favorites and as the bots entered the cage, the high rollers broke into cheers. The bots lined up on either side of the cage, restlessly waiting to begin.

Morgan positioned herself by the ramp gate then spoke, "The fights you are about to see have been deemed No Holds Barred." She turned to address the bot owners, "Are you gentlemen ready?" Both nodded yes. "Then there's only one thing to say…" as she stepped out of the cage and slammed the gate closed before loudly calling out, "Let the mayhem begin!" to which both bots lurched into action.

For a few suspenseful moments the bots did a little sparring as they sized each other up, each one flexing their weapons. Kill-Va-Nader's saw blades were whirling as it raised itself up a foot or so then lowered back down. At'em Smasher was waving its hammer in a threatening manner and jabbing the air with one of its butcher knives.

Suddenly Kill-Va-Nader spun around and loosed a brief second or two of blowtorch flames that hit At'em Smasher's jointed arms that held the knives, turning the meat cleaver a sooty black. At'em Smasher ran forward, but Kill-Va-Nader was quick to sidestep just moments before the big hammer smashed down to the floor jarring the air with a loud bang. That gave Kill-Va-Nader the opportunity to rush past At'em Smasher, sawing the cleaver's support in two, sending the blade spinning across the floor.

At'em Smasher wasted no time turning to meet Kill-Va-Nader's next drive-by and swung the hammer down to connect soundly with one of Kill-Va-Nader's saw blades, bending it pretty badly. Kill-Va-Nader spun around and took a good whack at the hammer's support sending sparks flying but doing little damage.

The crowd was noisy and excited, pumping fists up into the air and yelling, "Get 'em!" and "Kill 'em!"

It took a minute for Kill-Va-Nader to recover its balance before it brandished its blowtorch in an effort to slow any attacks. However, At'em Smasher was quick and circled around to hammer the life out of the other saw blade, missed, but bent two gun barrels sticking out of Kill-Va-Nader's side causing two of the other gun barrels to fire wildly.

And that's bad, right? Right.

As several of the shots flew wild, most found the concrete walls, but one grazed the cheek of a man seated top tier (oh, oh) and another embedded itself into the calf muscle of that guy, right up front. That's going to hurt.

The bots did not stop. Kill-Va-Nader blowtorched At'em Smasher's 9mm, melting it into a blob of liquid metal. In return the hammer came down and demolished Kill-Va-Nader's all-seeing eye, that is to say, its control center, without which Smitty would not be able to send driving or weapons commands or receive system status reports. In effect, Kill-Va-Nader was rendered useless.

Emboldened by Kill-Va-Nader's stillness and in spite of the taser that was thrashing wildly about, At'em Smasher moved in for the kill. And kill it did. At'em Smasher, literally, smashed Kill-Va-Nader down into a pile of recycle before it took a victory stroll around the cage.

Morgan stepped through the now open cage gate and spoke to the crowd. "Oh! That was exciting and so unexpected! Let's hear it for At'em Smasher!" The crowd went wild, and the Di Lombaretti family gave a standing ovation, waving to the grandson, who was now in the cage standing next to his bot.

Morgan announced, "We'll take ten minutes to clean up a bit but stay seated, there's more to come."

The crowd settled down as At'em Smasher was driven out of the cage and poor Kill-Va-Nader was loaded onto a cart and hauled away. Soon enough, the event continued.

"Ladies and gentle henchpeople," Morgan was slowly walking around the cage talking directly to the crowd. "We're playing today for a grand prize, the extremely coveted Big Bullet." A smattering of applause. "I know, right?" she smiled sweetly. "This brings us to our second bout of the afternoon. Is everyone ready?" Yaa's and yes's. "Then please welcome back At'em Smasher and our next competitor, Psycho Bomb!"

Applause thundered throughout the parking garage as both crime bots wheeled in. At'em Smasher looking a bit beat up with duct tape strapped here and there and Psycho Bomb looking all shiny and ready. They squared off on either side of the cage, anxious and ready.

Morgan stepped to the cage gate and as it was closing, called out.

"Crime bots! Let the mayhem begin!"

At'em Smasher rushed forward waving its hammer and positioning itself to deliver a blow. Psycho Bomb inched into position, aimed its Psychotic Weasel laser eyes and let loose a beam that hit and severed one of At'em Smasher's spinning blades of death from a rear wheel. The hammer came down but only grazed a wheel guard, doing no damage.

Psycho Bomb reached out with a grabber hand and sank its shark teeth into At'em Smasher's jabbing knife, ripping it out by its electric cables. At'em Smasher was down both its butcher knives, one wheel's spinning blade of death, and the melted 9mm. This left the crime bot with only its blades of death on three wheels and its smasher hammer, which it was determined to use.

Psycho Bomb wheeled away slowly as if sizing At'em Smasher up. Finally, it turned but At'em Smasher rushed forward, its hammer hacking up and down at random. Psycho Bomb, in almost a calm manner, sighted its Gatling gun on the hammer and let go a *Tat-Tat-A-Tat* with surprising accuracy that made everyone jump. The action froze, both bots stared at each other, the audience hushed in wide-eyed, breath holding anticipation.

Then as if in slow motion, At'em Smasher's large and deadly hammer slid apart into two pieces, thunking down onto the cage floor with a jolt. It took three seconds for the audience to recover from its stunned silence but recover they did! The place went wild with excited chatter and everyone was smiling and laughing.

Di Lombaretti rushed into the cage to tug the beat up At'em Smasher out and Psycho Bomb did a slow drive around the cage before exiting to the staging area.

Morgan announced a twenty-minute break and folks moved to the refreshments and the betting windows.

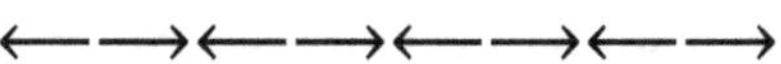

"I thought you'd like to see this," Morgan smiled as she addressed the crowd. "This is what it's all about." She waved an arm to direct everyone's attention to a cart that had been rolled into the cage and now stood center stage. It was clearly holding an object that had been draped with a canvas tarp.

Morgan took hold of a pleat of canvas and stood for a moment building anticipation before gently tugging the cloth off, letting it puddle on the floor around the cart.

"The Big Bullet!" Morgan called out.

It was awe-inspiring. The Big Bullet and its base easily stood three-foot tall, was twelve inches in diameter and shaped like a WWII M793 Pest Chaser. Robot pincher arms protruded from its sides and wild cables encircled it like ivy. It was blindingly shiny silver with sequined accents, and was engraved, "Death Slam. First Annual Psychotic Weasel Crime Bot Competition" with space for the winning bot's name. So endearing.

When Morgan was convinced that everyone had gotten an eye full of the fabulous and soon to be coveted award, she waved a couple PW henchpeople forward to wheel the Big Bullet out. She then leisurely strolled around the cage arena addressing the high rollers. "Today is a momentous day, as I know you will all agree. There's been nothing like this is the history of crime and it's all been made possible through the generosity of Psychotic Weasel LLC!" A big cheer went up. "Thank you, that was heartwarming," she smiled that sweet smile, then continued, "Enough aggrandizing, let's get down to what we've been waiting for: the fight for the grand prize, the Big Bullet!" The crowd went nuts with whoop whoops and yea's with a sporadic few stomping their feet to send thumping sounds up and around Parking Garage Level Four

"Please welcome back Psycho Bomb!" Morgan's voice rising, "and the final competitor," her voice calling out, "Raging Blender!" Everyone cheered loudly and appreciatively as the bots entered the arena and Morgan stepped out of the cage, slamming the gate tightly closed behind her. "Crime persons," she announced, "Let the mayhem begin!"

And just like that sparks flew and loud bangs filled the air as Raging Blender tossed three popper cannon balls in Psycho Bomb's direction.

None of them connected but bits of hot metal shrapnel rained down on one section of spectators. Ouch!

Psycho Bomb wheeled around and, with the agility of a ballerina, kept Raging Blender in front of its sights and setting its Gatling gun cross hairs on the Squid logo eye, let go…*Tat-A-Tat-Tat-Tat* grazing and cracking the logo enough to scratch the laser lens embedded in it.

Morgan glanced over at Smitty, Psycho Bomb's engineer/operator noting his calm as he worked his remote control with a steady focused eye. Then she looked at The Squid who was frantic in his actions to turn his bot and move it into an offensive position. Morgan watched as The Squid's attempts proved futile and became cautiously concerned as The Squid became more and more angry with each unsuccessful attempt to harm Psycho Bomb. She thought, *"Better keep an eye on him,"* and shared her concerns with three PW security henchpeople.

Meanwhile…

Psycho Bomb made a grab with one of its grabber hands for Raging Blender but missed so moved closer and grabbed at it again. Raging Blender lifted up and flipped upside down, aiming its battle blades and dropped down to chomp at Psycho Bomb's grabber hand but got a taste of the flamethrower instead. Raging Blender jerked upward and flipped right side up but too late, one of its popper cannons was toasted and one set of hover blades was burnt and melted.

The Squid recovered flight stability by compensating for the out of balance blades, but it was taking too much of his attention to maintain. He also found that neither of the large caliber guns were responding.

Psycho Bomb loosed another round from the Gatling gun taking out Raging Blender's main rotary wings which caused it to list sharply to the side and lose several feet of altitude, just enough so that Psycho Bomb was able to grab hold of the dangling tentacles and yank Raging Blender down out of the air.

The Squid screamed out, "NO!" and furiously set off a rapid succession of popper bombs to no avail. Psycho Bomb had Raging Blender in both shark tooth lined clamper hands, was cooking the outer casing with flamethrowers, and pounding it up and down on the arena floor. Thudding booms filled the air and only stopped when Raging Blender had been thoroughly incapacitated.

Someone in the crowd yelled out, "Raging Blender…more like Raging Blunder!" that was answered with uproarious laughter and jeers.

Psycho Bomb positioned its large lotus flower bud just above the prone body of Raging Blender and shot several loads of acid that immediately sent up clouds of toxic smoke as the acid ate through the drone's metal shell.

The Squid's show of anger caused several security henchpeople to position themselves just behind him and when he turned to glare at Smitty, saw the security men, swallowed down his outward anger and stood gazing into the cage at the awful remains of Raging Blender, his beloved Tentacle One.

All this went virtually unnoticed by everyone on Parking Garage Level Four because the place had gone absolutely insane with cheering and applause the second Morgan had declared, "Death Slam victory goes to Psycho Bomb!" Most everyone had jumped to their feet in their excitement.

Psycho Bomb had abandoned the rubble that had once been Raging Blender and took several victory laps around the fighting cage, waving its eight-foot-long grabber hand cable arms in slow lazy circles and puffing out flames from their palms while nodding the Gatling gun up and down. Smitty so wanted to fire the gun, but fortunately his good sense not to machine-gun the concrete ceiling prevailed.

And the crowd went wild.

Chapter Twenty-One

Circular Logic

The weeks following Death Slam were crazy! Argyle had to "procure" a cash counting machine and put Miss Q in charge of three additional staff to sort, count, and organize all the cash that began to pile up, pay the bills, and fund department budgets.

Feartha was happy that the event went over so well, conveniently ignoring the few audience injuries from stray bullets and hot sparks that would have occurred under any circumstances anyway, that she immediately started drawing up blueprints and making notes about Death Slam Two that included a total Parking Garage Level Four remodel.

Smitty was reported to have said, "This was a valuable learning curve," referring to the pulverization of Kill-Va-Nader, and he excitedly threw himself back into designing a fierce fighting bot even more determined to win next year, too.

Tanner and Jones completed the rebuild of DOOM and so impressed Morgan and Argyle that they ordered up another robot. "Maybe one with a few advancements?" Morgan had chided.

At the end of month two, post Death Slam, Argyle found he had very little managing to do. Seemed that operations hummed along quite smoothly.

His Squid stalker wall was current up to the final pictures of Squid standing in full Squid regalia at the fight cage manically working his drone controls. Argyle especially liked the pics of The Squid kneeling in the cage next to his mashed pile of drone, crying. It was the sweet, sweet icing on the Death Slam cake. The only thing bothering Argyle was that after the competition, The Squid went silent. That's probably not good.

The days passed in an easy rhythm, that is, until one mid-summer day about 2:32PM when alarms sounded from Argyle, Morgan, Davis, and Hansen's computer monitors, sending their adrenaline surging as they leapt up and started for the elevators. The alarm was coming from the roof of the Parking Garage. Someone was trespassing.

Argyle and Morgan were the first to burst out through the roof door, guns drawn, ready. What they saw was a man, stiffly standing in the middle of the roof looking a little dazed. Suddenly there was a flash of light, followed by another so bright that Argyle and Morgan had to pinch their eyes shut and shade their faces with upturned hands.

Davis and Hansen burst out onto the roof as the lights subsided and called out, "What is it?" and "Are you alright, boss?"

Argyle stood frozen staring at the apparitions before him, stammering, "Yeah, yeah, we're fine. Hold your positions." Then slowly, as recognition came back to him, Argyle said, "I can't believe it," then called out as he moved, hand raised in greeting, toward the three men standing there, "I can't believe it's you fellows! Wha…what are you doing here?"

Before they could answer, Argyle rushed on, "Morgan! This is Grotcom," pointing to the taller of the three, "Bintcom," pointing to the man next to him, "and Malcom," pointing to the pot-bellied man who was gazing up at the sky for no obvious reason. "They're travelers from the future!"

Morgan looked the three men over then glanced at Argyle as if he had lost his mind. "What did you say?" she asked dubiously.

"They're from the future. I met them about three years ago." Turning to the men who were now acclimated enough to speak. "Isn't that right?"

Grotcom stepped forward, "Yes, that's pretty close," and extending a hand toward Morgan, said, "My pleasure."

Morgan looked at his hand, up to his face and then over to Argyle. "I'm not sure whether to believe this or not. Help me out."

Argyle pitched into a fast ten-minute summary of how these guys (thumbing at Grotcom, Bintcom, and Malcom) had travelled back to this time ("Well, three years ago.") to stop The Thrasher from completing work on his time machine, but that Argyle didn't believe their story until he actually did see the time machine down on Sublevel Six and that after Thrasher had used said machine and had disappeared, Argyle, now believing what the guys had warned him about, lit up Sublevel Six with C4 explosives ("I mean the earthquake hit," he stressed!) and got the Lake of Fire out of there before he, Argyle, blew up with it.

~ Phew! ~

By now, the Psychotic Weasel henchpeople had holstered their guns and were listening to Argyle's story.

Grotcom interrupted with, "We've got another two minutes."

Argyle asked, "Until what?"

Bintcom was messing around with a little tech device, but looked up and said, "Until The Thrasher comes through."

Practically in unison, Argyle, Morgan, Davis, and Hansen said, "What?"

Bintcom looked at the small group with confusion and then speaking as clearly as he could, repeated, "Until The Thrasher comes through."

Argyle was momentarily stunned but as he recovered and forced his racing mind to slow down, he thought to ask, "So, how did you hook up with Thrasher?"

Too late.

A blinding flash of white/blue light accompanied by the sound of crackling static electricity charged the air and when the smoke cleared, there stood The Thrasher.

Argyle's jaw slacked open and all that he could compel his mind to say was, *"Unbelievable."*

The Thrasher stood his full 6'3" tall but appeared much more youthful. His face was smoother, less creased with deep lines and furrowed brows, although his eyes and mouth still appeared sharp with barely hidden anger. He had put on a few pounds, in a good way. He used to look starved and lanky but now looked a little buff. *("Has he been working out?"* Argyle mused.*)* Thrasher was not dressed in some version of a Halloween sequined nightmare but in jeans, an elegant boat necked sweater and a tailored two buttoned sport coat accented with a very long hand knitted scarf draped casually around his neck. His look was topped off, or bottomed out, if you prefer, by a pair of boat shoes that totally looked like they were covered in dazzling blue and gray fish scales.

Clearly the future had been good for The Thrasher.

"Argyle Stevens!" Thrasher called out. "Just the man I wanted to see." Then stood silently eyeing Argyle as he stammered through a greeting and introductions of his cohorts, only speaking when Argyle asked if he would like a tour of the lair and a cup of tea.

"A cup of tea would be nice," Thrasher flashed a creepy smile.

"Don't be too surprised," Argyle practically whispered, "but things have changed since you left. There are a lot of new faces since the turnover."

Thrasher wagged a hand and shrugged one shoulder as if to say, "whatever," and strode to the roof access door to leave, followed closely by Grotcom, Bintcom, and Malcom.

The others sorta meandered out next with Davis whispering to Hansen, "This is a whole tub of tuna."

Hansen nodded in agreement.

Morgan and Argyle hung back a step or two.

"So, what's the plan?" Morgan asked Argyle.

"I don't have one other than to find out why he's back. I'd like to know if he's going to stay."

"This is going to be chaos."

"Yeah, something he seems to thrive on."

Argyle had directed Davis and Hansen to return to the office pit to warn everyone that Thrasher was back and to stay low key. Then Argyle herded the little group of travelers down to Sublevel Four and into the Lizzie Borden room, his office, then he asked Miss Q to bring six cups of tea, maybe some cookies, too.

Once seated around the meeting table, Argyle managed to ask Thrasher a question. "How was the future?"

Thrasher had been acting distracted while trying to remain calm. He slowly turned his head and leveled a look at Argyle. "The future is fine." Staring.

Grotcom broke in, "When we," indicating his two friends and himself, "returned to the future, we found it rife with new technologies."

Malcom held up a small flat device, saying, "Look! I got a new device. It's an iPhone450M. It can do everything!"

Miss Q, pre-warned that Thrasher was back, brought a large pot of tea and cups, set the tray down and served. No one spoke except Morgan who thanked Miss Q as she was quietly letting herself out.

Malcom had helped himself to the cookies and sat making mouth noises as he chomped and slurped to his content.

Thrasher hadn't really taken his eyes off of Argyle and was clearly pleased that it was agitating Argyle to no end. He finally said, "So you're curious as to why I've suddenly appeared after three years. You would like to know exactly what it is that I want." Staring.

Argyle tried to look in control. He "calmly" took a sip of tea, gently put the cup down and answered, "Sure," in the best non-committal way he could.

"Well, I'll tell you." Thrasher put his palms down on the table and made to stand up, pushing his chair out behind him. He stood up to his full height and in a voice edged with barely controlled rage, said, "I'm here to smash Meglamon! I swore I would get him," his voice rising, "and I will!" Practically shouting, "I will smash him!"

The three travelers didn't seem shaken at all at Thrasher's pronouncement. In fact, they almost looked like they would break out in applause at his performance.

Morgan noted that little charade as she tightened her grip in the handgun in her pants pocket.

Argyle had pushed back from the table and looked like a cat ready to pounce.

Thrasher had paced the length of the room and now spun around to face the group. Glaring.

"Well," Argyle started, "Meglamon retired."

"WHAT!!" Thrasher's voice cut through the air like a knife.

"Retired."

Thrasher thrust both fists up into the air as if to curse the sky. The veins in his neck had bulged out and his face was contorted with hate and anger as he yelled out, *"NOOO!"*

Everyone was silent, watching.

Thrasher recovered enough to bring his breathing down before striding to the door and leaving without another word.

Argyle looked at Morgan and then to the three travelers. "Why didn't you tell him that Meglamon was retired? You must have known that being from the future and all," Argyle found that his tone had turned a bit snarky.

Grotcom spoke, "It's been his dream to smash Meglamon," he said in a nonchalant manner.

Bintcom added, "Based his whole career on it."

Malcom sighed, "Must be frustrating."

Grotcom said, "I'm surprised at the question. We didn't want to derail his commitment. It was endearing to see such passion."

"Yeah" said Malcom, "Who are we to do that?"

Argyle was experiencing extreme fluctuations in his emotions at this moment that vacillated wildly between frustration and anger, but choked it all down enough to ask, "Where do you think Thrasher's going?"

"Oh, hard to tell," offered Grotcom.

Argyle and Morgan had the lair searched from top to bottom but had not found The Thrasher. The last person to see him said that he had taken the elevator up to the Parking Garage Level One. Argyle had to conclude that Thrasher had left.

The three travelers were put into Davis' care, given a fast tour of the lair that was limited to the office pit and the shark tank, then taken out into town for a huge Italian dinner.

The next seven days were nerve racking for Argyle. He scanned news reports to catch even the slightest bit that might suggest if Thrasher was up to something.

There was nothing.

He sent out plain clothed henchpeople to canvas the town.

Nothing.

He had Alexey hack into police radio scanners to hear their calls and bulletins.

Again, nothing.

He grilled Grotcom, Bintcom, and Malcom to find out what they knew or what they suspected or what they could remember The Thrasher saying or referring to that may give a clue to his whereabouts.

Still nothing.

Argyle had to conclude that Thrasher had disappeared. And while this totally wigged Argyle out, he had to accept it. The thought that Thrasher could pop in and pop out was the worst.

Four days into The Thrasher's disappearing act, Argyle ran into Grotcom, Bintcom, and Malcom in the break room with Tanner. They had their heads together over a piece of technology that Malcom was showing off.

"It's got eighteen different modes of instinct loom. It covers the entire spectrum of estium," he was saying. "And that is out to the eighth."

Tanner was nodding, then asked, "Has turbo tenth temp been graduated to another level?"

Grotcom gave an animated answer, "You bet! It was all the rage ten years ago, I mean, many years from now, ten years ago for us. Sorry. Anyway, it took off! It's now dimensionally available in length! Very cool."

Argyle did not have a clue about what they were discussing but had a thought. "Mind if I join you?" he asked and being welcomed to do that, sat and listened quietly for about five more minutes, then took his opportunity.

"It must be very exciting to live in your time," he ventured.

"Not really," offered Grotcom. "Everything is the day-to-day same."

"This time is more interesting, full of ideas and action," Bintcom said. "A time of making history," he smiled

"Well," Argyle ventured. "How would you men like to stay here? In this time? And work for Psychotic Weasel?"

Tanner smiled and said, "What a great idea!"

The travelers were surprised at the suggestion and sorta stumbled over each other's words trying to find an answer. Grotcom held up his hands to halt the confused chatter and smiled at Argyle. "I think we're going to have to talk about that among ourselves. Can we meet later about it?"

"Over dinner?" offered Argyle.

"Yes!" Malcom cheerfully answered.

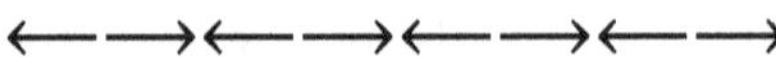

Dinner was an interesting exchange of questions and answers, what-if's, and contingencies, but no definitive answer to Argyle's query about the three men staying.

"We're still discussing," was all Grotcom would say.

On day six of The Thrasher's disappearing act, Morgan took it upon herself to "interview" the travelers. She tempted them to a meeting with promises of fascinating stories about the town and a platter of cookies and cinnamon buns.

After indulgently watching them consume cinnamon buns, do a lot of finger licking, and making mouth noises, Morgan began.

"What work do you do in your time?" she asked.

No one answered.

"Anyone?"

Grotcom wiped his mouth. "I'm a historian by education and I fill my time working in the National Public Archive."

Morgan nodded. "Bintcom?"

"Huh?"

"What is it that you do? In the future."

"Oh," he said, "I do a little of this and a little of that."

"Exactly what is 'this' and 'that'?" Morgan leveled a look at him.

Bintcom looked at Morgan looking at him and decided he had better answer with something more solid. "I'm a freelance writer, alt-hough in my time writing is no longer fashionable. I'm a freelance typer. I type."

Morgan said, "Alright," and looked to Malcom, who was ready.

"I'm a software/hardware engineer. I create software then design hardware to run the code." He sat back smiling very satisfied with himself.

"What is it that you have developed. Malcom?"

"Hmmm. The last copy patent I filed was for an inter-time travel turn signal. It works by processing your thoughts. So far, I've sold a few dozen units."

"Grotcom, do you have an area of specialization?" Morgan asked.

"Well," he started, "I have started writing a history on GPS advances in the twenty fourth century. Should be a best seller."

"So," Morgan said, "you," pointing at Grotcom, "are a historian, and you," pointing at Bintcom, "are a typer, and you," pointing at Malcom, "are a coder engineer. Do I have that correct?"

Bintcom spoke, "You might consider me more of a non-specialist in the field of bioengineering."

Morgan raised her eyebrows into a look of surprise, "That's a big difference from 'typing'."

"Yes," Bintcom added, "It's a hobby of mine."

"Oh! We're listing hobbies?" Grotcom asked rhetorically. "In that case, my off-work interest is in space chemical engineering. I have an avid interest in meteor mining equipment."

Morgan's mind added it up like this... *"Three engineers with four specialties between them. Space chemicals. Meteor mining. Bioengineering. Software/hardware development. We've hit the jackpot!"*

Morgan leaned over and picked up the desk phone and punched in a short series of numbers, then spoke, "Miss Q, is there any more chocolate cake?" The boys looked at her expectantly. "Anything else?" Morgan listened. "Would it be too much trouble to bring both of those to the Ted Bundy meeting room?" Morgan paused then smiled. "Thank you, Miss Q," and hung up. Turning to the boys, Morgan said, "I think I owe you a couple of good stories about our timeline and maybe I'll share a tidbit or two about Psychotic Weasel. Sit back and relax. There's chocolate cake *and* jelly donuts coming."

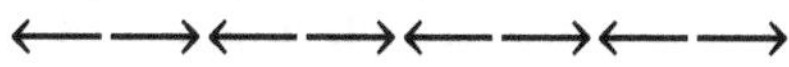

Day eight of The Thrasher's disappearing act, as it was now being referred to, Argyle was alone in his office running monthly budget numbers when without warning his office door flung open, causing him to jump at the suddenness of it.

Well, in strides The Thrasher looking stylish and confident with a slight twinge of barely disguised agitation. "Stevens," he said more as an identifying fact than a greeting. "We have to talk."

"Oh, oh," Argyle thought, *"Nothing good ever comes from 'We have to talk'."* He remembered the last time he heard those words…Argyle stood up and motioned for them to move to the meeting table. "Want a cup of coffee or anything?" he asked.

Thrasher didn't answer but did grab the chair at the head of the table and scarcely waited for Argyle to sit down before launching into a speech…

"I'm very disappointed in the current state of crime, very primitive comparatively speaking. There doesn't seem to be any creativity. Crime seems stalled."

Argyle made to offer some conversation, but Thrasher stopped him by raising a hand saying, "Don't bother." Then continued, "There's no imagination, everything has lost its luster for me. I don't think I can stand the snail's pace with which things move, here. I don't fit in any longer." Thrasher sat back in the chair, which did not make a jaw-tightening grinding noise as expected. Thrasher pointed to the springs and said, "See. Even the chairs are bland."

He got up and paced in a slow circle around the meeting table as he continued to explain. "I have weighed my options. Stay here and carry on in the slow, sloth-like pace of crime and change, stewing in my lost opportunity (voice raising) to smash Meglamon! (voice back in control) and living a life lost to…" Thrasher turned to face Argyle, shrugged his shoulders to express helplessness, and said, "Meh? Or return to my future where crime is inventive, original, and almost always fun?!"

Thrasher stopped talking and glared at Argyle who thought Thrasher *now* wanted him to say something but all he could come up with was, "Always go for the fun."

"Exactly!" shouted Thrasher, slapping a hand on the table for emphasis. "So, I have decided to return to my future, and I would like you to come with me. No, no, no," he said stopping Argyle from speaking, "Do not make any snap decisions. You have until noon on the day after tomorrow."

Thrasher strode to the door, whipped it open and turned to say to Argyle, "You have until then." And was gone.

Argyle was floored to say the least. The future? *"What do I know about the future?"* He returned to his desk and picked up the handset of his model 500 telephone and dialed. After two rings, "Morgan, do you have a few minutes? Will you come to my office, please?"

One hour later…

After weighing the pros and cons of Thrasher's offer and what that would truly mean for Argyle, including what would happen to his classic 1958 VDub (it would be properly stored on Parking Garage Level Two), it really came down to this: What was keeping him here?

He and Audrey had broken up months ago, his apartment rent had recently been increased by 20%, and he had done such a good job of managing PW LLC that he had managed his way into being an accountant of sorts. ("Boring," he admitted to Morgan.)

No capers. Not a lot of gun shooting. ("Outlining it like that makes it sound depressing.")

And while he knew nothing about the future or what he would do once he got there, it was an interesting prospect.

"I think I'm going to take Thrasher up on his offer."

This didn't really surprise Morgan. She had watched Argyle talk himself into it for forty-five minutes. "What's going to happen with Psychotic Weasel LLC?" she asked.

"Oh," Argyle thought for a whole two seconds, "It's yours," he declared. "If you want it, that is."

Morgan smiled and nodded and smiled some more. "Absolutely! It's a deal!"

They shook hands to seal their agreement with Argyle promising legal papers would be signed and delivered by end of day.

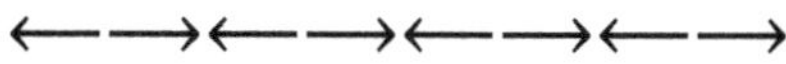

Argyle spent every waking hour between then and noon the day after tying up loose ends, packing his stuff into storage, and saying goodbye to Psychotic Weasel.

Many in the organization were bummed that Argyle was leaving while others wondered at the good sense of pitching yourself into the unknown future and with The Thrasher no less! But all were glad to continue under the leadership of Morgan Taylor.

So, here we are, noon on the day after tomorrow, that is to say, today, right now.

The group of people gathered on the Parking Garage roof were, Thrasher, who had popped in a minute ago, Argyle, backpack and suitcase at the ready, Morgan, and the three travelers: Grotcom, Bintcom, and Malcom.

Thrasher was speaking, "So, Stevens, it looks like you have decided to join me. Rightfully so."

"Sometimes you have to roll the dice," Argyle said in general, then turned to look at Thrasher, "This seems to be one of those times." And turning to face Morgan, he said, "Good luck."

Thrasher snapped at the travelers, "You ready?"

"Ahh, not quite yet," answered Grotcom.

Bintcom piped up, "Yeah, we've decided to stay here for awhile. To study history before it's even made!"

"How exciting is that, right?" Malcom smiled and nudged Bintcom's arm.

Grotcom added, "We want to live off the grid…but not too far off because we're overly excited about tech development and joining the Psychotic Weasel team."

Argyle was smiling and nodding "well done" at Morgan who was looking pretty pleased with herself.

Thrasher sharply said, "Stevens," and pointed to a place by his side, and Argyle moved himself and his things to that space.

Argyle raised a hand to Morgan, and she called out to him, "Look for me in the future!"

Then…

Epilogue

The move into the Lizzie Borden meeting room was easy enough. With the help of several henchpeople it went fast and smooth. And while Argyle's desk was a nice one, Morgan's crew of henchpeople surprised her with a gift of a beautiful solid oak antique executive desk that they had boosted from one of the old Victorian mansions up in the east foothills. Another caper crew gifted her a very fine ergonomic desk chair boosted from, of all places, a family run furniture store down on E Street. One of the guys had left a ten-dollar bill at the checkout as a good will gesture because he remembered seeing the store logo on a DOOM sponsorship sticker.

Morgan settled into her office space with ease. She had left Argyle's Squid stalker wall as a reminder that some situations still needed paying attention to. She added more lighting and a small kitchenette tucked into a sideboard but other than that, the room was the same and as Morgan thought, *"Perfect."*

Today is Monday. It's significant only in that it is the beginning of week three since The Thrasher and Argyle had left for the future.

Today, Morgan sat at her desk in the company of Davis, Smitty, and Watson. The informal meeting was just informational, nothing serious. Morgan was listening to Watson.

"The two tow trucks that we have are driving fine. I've set up a small repair shop up on Parking Garage Level Two adjacent to where we park the trucks and company vans so that periodic service can be done in-house." Watson pursed his lips and furrowed his brow in concentration then a thought came to him, "I'd like to put an item or two on the maintenance caper list, if I may."

Morgan asked, "What'cha got?"

"I'd like to list cans of motor oil, belts, spark plugs, and other items that need to be supplied regularly. I think truck maintenance will go smoother and faster. And more efficient."

"I like the way you're looking ahead, Watson," Morgan said, "Add your items to the list with a note about how often you need those supplies and how many henchpeople might be needed to make it happen. And good job."

Watson smiled at hearing this. *"Good job. Haven't heard that for a while. Nice,"* thought Watson.

She then turned to Smitty and asked, "You've been "in charge" of our three travelers for a couple of weeks now and I'd like to hear your opinion of their usefulness."

Smitty smiled and answered, "My opinion is that they're subject to rambling on and on about a wide array of off-topic subjects but if you can keep them focused, they do add to our technical knowledge base. They tend to talk about many "future" things that seem usual for them but are years ahead of us." Smitty paused to take a short breath and continued, "However, I believe that in time, based upon the information they can provide, we'll make huge strides in robotics and I'm very excited about helping Tanner and Jones expand their android repertoire."

Morgan replied, "This is good news and I'm very excited about the possibilities. You're doing a nice job wrangling our three travelers. I don't imagine it's as easy as getting them to eat a cookie, though!"

Laughter rippled across the group.

Just as the chuckles died down, Davis offered a comment, "Boss, everything is running smoothly, caper-wise. All henchpeople seem to be working to their potential and enjoying the systemized schedule you have put in place. The only grumbling I hear is about the lack of donuts in the break room."

"Well," Morgan said, "I'm pleased that the structured maintenance capers are moving along smoothly, which, I'm afraid, accounts for the lack of donuts, but how about this?" she ventured. "I'll institute Bagel Thursday."

Davis smiled and nodded.

"That may hold 'em for a while, don't you think?" Morgan smiled and waited for an answer.

Watson spoke up, "It'll hold me!" Watson thought *"As long as they aren't poppyseed bagels. I hate those!"*

The meeting ended on that happy note and as the men were getting up to leave, Morgan asked Davis to stay behind for another minute. "I'd like your opinion on something."

Davis repositioned himself closer to Morgan's desk and sat quietly waiting as she riffled through a small sheaf of papers getting herself organized. After putting a couple of pages into a sort of order, Morgan laid them out for Davis to see.

"Take a look at these and tell me what you think."

Davis leaned in and studied the papers from left to right. He took his time and thought a little bit about the pictures he was looking at.

Morgan gave him a few uninterrupted minutes then ventured to ask, "Which one do you like?"

Davis picked up the three pages that Morgan had laid out on her desk, looked at them all once again, and spoke. "I think they're all very fine drawings but this one," he handed Morgan one of the pages, "stands out from the others."

Morgan took the paper from him and looked at it. "Yes. It's the one I thought was just a slight hair better than the other two." She then laid the page flat on her desk so they could both look at it together.

"I think this is the one. I think I've got a logo." Morgan smiled with deep pleasure. "Meet the Elegant Jaguar."

Davis stood back, admiring the new corporate logo, and nodded his approval. Then he switched to another subject.

"Have you been following the news about The Squid? It seems he's been pretty active lately, threatening to outdo us in the caper department. What can we do about him?"

Morgan just smiled sweetly and said, "I will crush him." Then she reached for her tea, took a leisurely sip, and then continued reading the latest edition of CYBORG!

Misadventures in Crime
By N. K. Hart

A puzzle to sharpen your mind. *DO IT!*

ACROSS

1. Thrasher's Main Rival
3. Death -________
6. Best Designer, Ever
7. Beer Bust Special
9. PW
12. Won the Big Bullet
15. One Who Disappeared
17. Killer Robot

DOWN

2. First Henchwoman
4. Our Main Man
5. Knee Capped for No Good Reason
8. ________ Slam
10. Grot ___ , Bint ___ , Mal ___
11. Cephalopod
13. Best HR Person, Ever
14. Thrasher Has This
16. Everyone Has This

Misadventures in Crime

The answers. *STOP CHEATING!*

About the Author

N. K. Hart was born in upstate New York, moved to California as a grown child and lived in the San Francisco Bay Area. After an illustrious career in the tech field, NK studied horticulture, design, and began writing suspense thrillers, humor, and sci-fi stories as an expression of a very active imagination.

NK has been in love with stories and storytelling since early childhood. Forays into fiction have included The Innocence of Power, a modern-day suspense thriller, Up the Crime Ladder, a humorous look at the sometimes complicated lives of henchmen, Swimming Through Air, a collection of short stories and musings, The Future of Crime, because everyone wanted to know what happened to the henchmen, and Stories and Lies: The True Account of Tåsan Sulac, a marvelous sci-fi story destined to become a classic.

When not writing, NK creates high relief ceramic tiles and lives in Cottage Grove, Oregon, with a brilliant, sharp-minded little cat named Awesome.

Also by N. K. Hart

The Innocence of Power

A private detective has been hired to locate a missing girl. His investigations lead him to The Hartfield Connection LLC, owned by a sociopath and run by a power-hungry egotist. The further he looks, the more he finds that the corporation has dark secrets that neither the owner nor the top manager want known. The girl may have stumbled upon damaging proof that The Hartfield Connection is guilty of something big, something bad. What exactly is The Hartfield Connection hiding? Unaware that a covert government operation is also looking into The Hartfield Connection, the detective must fight to find the answer to this question and to locate the girl before time runs out.

Swimming Through Air

From ancient times, before calendars and clocks, to the far, far future, where science dares to remake humankind, N. K. Hart's imagination mixes with hope, resourcefulness, heartbreak, and humor. This volume contains a rare collection of holiday essays spanning several years and there's no denying that for N. K. Hart… imagination is everything.